10 - 2021

DATE DUE

PRINTED IN U.S.A.

Hayner PLD/Large Print
Overdues .10/day. Max fine cost of
item. Lost or damaged item: additional
$5 service charge.

ANIMAL

ANIMAL

ANIMAL

LISA TADDEO

THORNDIKE PRESS
A part of Gale, a Cengage Company

LIBRARY OF CONGRESS CIP DATA ON FILE.
CATALOGUING IN PUBLICATION FOR THIS BOOK
IS AVAILABLE FROM THE LIBRARY OF CONGRESS.

ISBN-13: 978-1-4328-9027-8 (hardcover alk. paper)

Published in 2021 by arrangement with Avid Reader Press, an Imprint of Simon & Schuster, Inc.

Printed in Mexico
Print Number: 01   Print Year: 2022

3862278

For my mother and my father

pale and soft and I couldn't stop looking at
them.

He was never Victor. He was always Vic.
He was my boss, and for a long time before
anything happened, I looked up to him. He
was very intelligent and clean and had a
warm face. He ate and drank voraciously
but there was a dignity to his excess. He

1

I drove myself out of New York City where
a man shot himself in front of me. He was a
gluttonous man and when his blood came
out it looked like the blood of a pig. That's
a cruel thing to think, I know. He did it in a
restaurant where I was having dinner with
another man, another *married* man. Do you
see how this is going? But I wasn't always
that way.

The restaurant was called Piadina. On the
exposed brick walls hung photographs of
old Italian women rolling gnocchi across
their giant floured fingers. I was eating a
bowl of tagliatelle Bolognese. The sauce was
thick and rust-colored and there was a
bright sprig of parsley at the top.

I was facing the door when Vic came in.
He was wearing a suit, which was usual. I'd
seen him only once in casual clothes, a
t-shirt and jeans, and it disturbed me very
much. I'm sure he could tell. His arms were

pale and soft and I couldn't stop looking at them.

He was never Victor. He was always Vic. He was my boss, and for a long time before anything happened, I looked up to him. He was very intelligent and clean and had a warm face. He ate and drank voraciously but there was a dignity to his excess. He was generous, scooping creamed spinach onto everyone else's plate before his own. He had a great vocabulary and a neat comb-over and an extensive collection of fine hats. He had two children, a girl and a boy; the boy was mentally challenged, and Vic some-what kept this from me and the other people beneath him. He had only a picture of the daughter on his desk.

Vic took me to hundreds of restaurants. We ate porterhouse at big clubby steak-houses with red banquettes and the waiters flirted with me. They either assumed he was my father or my older husband or they figured I was a mistress. We were, somehow, all of the above. His actual wife was at home in Red Bank. He said, I know you won't believe this because of what a slob I am, but my wife is actually very beautiful. In fact, she was not. Her hair was too short for her face and her skin was too white for the colors she liked to wear. She looked like a good mother. She liked to buy little salt dishes and Turkish towels, and in the beginning of our friendship, I would walk around the city and if a bamboo salt dish caught my eye I would snap a photo and text him, *Would your wife like?*

He said I had wonderful taste, but what does that mean?

It can feel very safe to be friends with an older man who admires you. Anywhere you are, if something goes wrong, you can make a phone call and the man will come. The man who comes should be your father, but I didn't have one at that time and you will never.

At a certain point I began to rely on Vic for everything. We worked at an advertising firm. He was creative director. I had virtually no experience when I started, but I had this talent, he said. He promoted me from a regular assistant to copywriter. At first I enjoyed all the praise and then I started to feel like I deserved everything I got, that he had nothing to do with it. It took a few years for that to happen. In the interim we started up a sexual relationship.

I can tell you a lot about sex with a man to whom you are not attracted. It becomes all about your own performance, your own body and how it looks on the outside, the way it moves above this man who, for you, is only a spectator.

While it was happening I wasn't aware of how it was affecting me. I didn't notice until several years later, when three showers a day were not enough.

The very first time was in Scotland. Our company had landed an account with Newcastle beer and Vic suggested I take the lead, go to all the meetings and get the ball rolling. It was a big account and the rest of the guys were jealous. I was new to the company and the work in general. They stopped flirting with me and began to act like I was an exotic dancer, jerking themselves off and judging me at the same time.

Newcastle put me up in this luxurious hotel just outside of Edinburgh. It was cold stone and big windows, and the front entrance was a circular gravel drive. I would look out my window to see the cars that came through, old antiques and bright black G-wagons and small silver Porsches. There was a tartan quilt on the bed and the phone was a mallard duck. The room was fourteen hundred dollars a night.

I'd been in Scotland for about a week when I began to feel blue. I was used to being alone but it's different in another country. The sun never came out but neither

10

did the rain. Plus I was very naive about the work and the Newcastle representatives could see that. I called Vic at the office. I didn't mean to, but I began to cry. I said that I missed my father. Of course I missed my mother, too. But in a very different way, and you'll come to understand why.

Vic was in Scotland the next evening. His last-minute flight had been exorbitant, upward of twelve thousand dollars, and he paid out of his own pocket because I was terrified that our colleagues would think I'd failed. He didn't come to any meetings. He just drew up some talking points. He got his own room down the hall. The first night we had dinner and drinks in the hotel lobby and each went to our separate rooms. But the second night he walked me back to mine.

Smart older men will have a way of crawling up your leg. It won't feel seedy at first and it might seem like it was your idea.

I was wearing a cream wool dress and my legs were bare. I never wore pantyhose or leggings of any kind, even in winter. I wore black Mary Jane heels.

Vic wore a suit. He was perennially dressed like the men in cigarette advertisements. I wasn't attracted to him but I was comforted by his cologne. We were laughing, walking down that green and gold hallway. A couple passed us and I remember the way the woman looked at me. I've gone around with that feeling for a long time.

In my room we opened two medium-size bottles of red wine from the minibar, plus three airplane bottles of Scotch that he drank all on his own.

Probably out of self-preservation, I can't remember exactly how it got started. I'm sure I had a lot to do with it, testing the reach of my sexual power. The extent of my prettiness. But what I remember starkly is the mirror on the wall opposite the windows where I'd listened for days to the sleek cars crunching the gravel. I got up to look in the mirror because he'd said the red wine was in the corner of my lips and I looked like a crackhead. Haha, I said. But that man could never have made me feel ugly.

He came up behind me in the mirror. His head was abnormally large next to mine. My long dark hair made an elegant contrast against the cream of the dress. He placed one hand on my shoulder and the other against my hair, near the ear, tipping my head to one side. I watched the look in his eye as he touched his thin lips to my neck. It sent a shiver down my spine, partly in repulsion, but there was also an involuntary

12

sexual response. He lifted the dress over my head. I stood in heels and a white lace bra and white underwear with little red bows at the sides. I was dressing for someone in those days and I liked to believe it was me. Once, in a little kitchen store in SoHo, I bought an apron with printed rabbits and chalets and little girls licking ice cream cones.

Thereafter came the trips to Sayulita, to Scottsdale for the nice spa. There were blue-tiled bathrooms and wonderful sushi. Table-side guacamole, belly dancers, valet everything.

Eventually I grew too disgusted, but for a long time I managed. There wasn't much physicality overall. You can get away with a lot of nothing if you play it right. Especially if the man is married, you can talk about morality and what your dead father would think. You can make the man feel trepidation to merely hold your hand and all the while you are in these warm places with palm trees and golf carts.

I didn't stop dating all those years. There were a few minor obsessions but no one truly serious. I told Vic about some of them. I said they were friends and I let him balance the suspicions in his head. But mostly I lied. I would say I was going out with

13

girlfriends and then sneak from the office and run toward a subway, looking back the whole time, terrified he'd followed me. Then I would meet some unkind boy and Vic would go home and patrol the Internet looking for signs of me on social media. He would write me around eleven, *Watcha up to kid.* He didn't use a question mark so it would look less inquisitive. You begin to understand human nature at a cellular level when an older man is obsessed with you.

The status quo was manageable. We were both getting what we needed, though I could have done without him. It turned out he could not do without me. He likened his relationship with me to Icarus. He was Icarus and I was the sun. Lines like these, which I wholly believed and still do, made me sick to my stomach. What kind of a girl wants to be a sun over a country she doesn't even want to visit.

Everything was fine for a number of years, until the man from Montana. I called him Big Sky and, in the beginning, so did Vic. I sent Vic to the depths of what a man can stand. I don't recommend you do it, and you should know what it does to a human being.

I think Vic came to shoot *me* that night, is what I think.

2

If someone asked me to describe myself in a single word, *depraved* is the one I would use. The depravation has been useful to me. Useful to what end, I couldn't say. But I have survived the worst. *Survivor* is the second word I'd use. A dark death thing happened to me when I was a child. I will tell you all about it, but first I want to tell what followed the evening that changed the course of my life. I'll do it this way so that you may withhold your sympathy. Or maybe you won't have any sympathy at all. That's fine with me. What's more important is dispelling several misconceptions — about women, mostly. I don't want you to continue the cycle of hate.

I've been called a whore. I've been judged not only by the things I've done unto others but, cruelly, by the things that have happened to me.

I envied the people who judged me. Those

who lived their lives in a neat, predictable manner. The right college, the right house, the right time to move to a bigger one. The prescribed number of children, which sometimes is two and other times is three. I would bet that most of those people had not been through one percent of what I had.

But what made me lose my mind was when those people called me a sociopath. Some even said it like it was a positive. I am someone who believes she knows which people should be dead and which should be alive. I am a lot of things. But I am not a sociopath.

When Vic shot a hole in himself, the blood leaked out like liquor. I hadn't seen blood like that since I was ten years old. It opened a portal. I saw the reflection of my past in that blood. I saw the past clearly, for the first time. The cops came to the restaurant looking horny. Everyone had been cleared out of the place. The man I'd been eating with asked me if I would be okay. He was putting his jacket on. He meant would I be okay alone tonight and for the rest of my life because I would never see him again. Once he'd asked me who my group was and I didn't know what he meant and now I did. The dead man on the floor was my group. I was part of a group that Dartmouth didn't recognize. After the cops left I walked home to my apartment. I thought I had no carbohydrates in the house, but I found a taco kit. The worst thing about eating too much is that you need more Klonopin than usual. I got just high enough to be decisive. I decided I was going to find her.

Vic was probably cold by then. I pictured his cold tentacles. When someone suffocates you with what they believe is love, even as you feel your air supply being cut off, you at least feel embraced. When Vic died, I was completely alone. I didn't have the energy to make someone else love me. I was inert. *Vuota.* A word my mother would have used. She always had the best words.

There was one person left. A woman I'd never met. This was terrifying because women had never loved me. I was not a woman whom other women love. She lived in Los Angeles, a city I didn't understand. Mauve stucco, criminals, and glitter.

I didn't think Alice — that was her name — would love me, but I hoped she would at least want to see me. I'd known her name for years. I was almost positive that she didn't know mine. For the first time in a long time I was going somewhere for a reason. I had no idea how it would go in California. I didn't know if I would fuck or

17

love or hurt someone. I knew I'd wait for a call. I knew I would be rabid. I had zero dollars but didn't rule out the prospect of a swimming pool. There were many paths my journey could take. I didn't think any of them would lead me to murder.

She'd been untraceable for years, no social media, no real estate transactions. Once in a while I would look for her. But I had too little information, on top of which I was scared to death.

Then one afternoon I went to a dentist because two of my teeth had been knocked out. A man had done it but not technically with violence. It was an expensive dentist but the man responsible for the loss of the teeth was paying for it.

I waited in reception for over an hour, flipping through one of those aspirational magazines for people who make over five million dollars a year. There she was, on the cover, with four other pretty women who were the best of fitness, Ashtanga, aikido, and so on, in Los Angeles.

I was so drawn to her looks that I read the article and saw her name, which I'd kept on a slip of paper for over a decade. I gasped, and air whistled through the hole between my teeth.

18

She was prettier than I ever could have imagined. Her breasts were absolutely perfect. An old boyfriend — not a boyfriend but one of those purveyors of multiple and uncertain mornings — once said that of an actress who'd bared her breasts for a scene. Her breasts, he said to me while eating cheap vanilla ice cream, are absolutely perfect. I am still impressed that I didn't kill him.

For years I'd dreamed of her. Oftentimes I dreamed of hurting her. The rest of the time it was something else, equally worrisome.

Within days of Vic's death, my apartment was cleaned out. I was an expert at leaving. I didn't know where I would live. I called about a few rentals near her place of work. But I was low on money and there weren't too many options in my budget. It got so bad that I called a place off of a rental site whose main photo was a bathroom with mold in the grout, a bottle of Selsun Blue in the stall shower, and nothing else.

I mapped out a quixotic, impractical route and drove my Dodge Stratus to California. It was a very ugly car but large, and I was able to fit many things inside. My mother's jewelry in a taupe tin. My best dresses, each sheathed in plastic and folded over the pas-

19

senger seat. There were my Derrida and photographs and menus from restaurants where I'd spent memorable evenings. Essential oils from a holy place in Florence. A shallot of marijuana, a pipe, ninety-six pills of varying shapes and shades of cream and blue. Very expensive copper yoga pants and mustard bralettes. Boxes of smoked Maldon and twenty squat cartons of pastina, which I'd heard they did not carry at the Ralphs or the Vons. I took the things that could come with only me, that could not be trusted to travel under anyone else's care. My favorite scarf, my panama hat. My Diane Arbus. My mother and my father.

They were both in plastic baggies. It was the safest way I could think for them to travel. The baggies were in an old cardboard clementine box on the floor of the passenger seat. My father used to call me Clementine, or he would sing the song, in any case. Maybe he did both. He had a goatee and when he kissed my forehead I felt like an angel.

There were eighty million cars on the Pacific Coast Highway. The sun on their hoods made it feel even hotter than it was. The beach looked dry in the distance, more shimmering surface than cool blue depth. Just before the turnoff into the canyon I noticed an outdoor market with furniture and decoration for sale, hollowed oaks made into tables, the heads of gods rendered in resin.

I pulled in because I wanted new vases for the ashes. I'd thrown out the old ones. Naturally it was awful for me, the idea of carrying their remains in baggies, but I was infinitely more shattered by the remnants in the vases that hadn't made it. I kept thinking that parts of them were gone forever. A toenail might have lingered in a vase. One third of a brow bone.

I got out of the Dodge and walked past hurricane candleholders. I drew a slash in the bushy dust of a gazing ball. I passed topaz seahorses, Mexican sugar skulls, aquamarine sea glass in rope nets.

I was approached by a round-faced boy wearing a hooded sweatshirt in all that heat.

— Miss, he said, how I can help? His happy smile made him seem ignorant to everything going on in the world.

—You can't, I said. I said it kindly, but by that point in my life I had a very low tolerance for unhelpful conversation.

The marketplace shared its parking lot with Malibu Feed Bin. Seed for birds, vats of grain for horses. There were lots of horses in the canyon. Women with long braids rode them over rocks. I picture you being one of these, taller than me, stately in all aspects.

There were vases inside the shed next to some hanging petunias and dusty roses. One vase was black with yellow blooms. A glass frog with orange eyes and feet hung from the lip, peering in. It was vulgar, something you'd find in an elderly person's house in Florida. I was attracted to it.

The young man at the cash register noticed me and then didn't take his eyes off of me. I was in a white nightgownish dress, thin as smoke. He was picking a pimple on his chin and staring at me. There are a hundred such small rapes a day.

I picked up the vase and walked around with it, pretending to appraise outdoor pillows and jade foo dogs. The acned clerk got a phone call. I could hear the other boy behind me, moving seahorses from one place to another. People rarely think you will steal something larger than your own head.

With the vase in the car, I felt like I had all the important pieces I needed. The movers were meeting me at the house with the balance. A truckload of pieces I'd sat upon. I began the climb up the canyon. Wilted dark greens rose from the sandy cracks between the rocks. There were hot bushes, maiden-hair ferns, false indigo, and bent grass. There were occasional splashes of color, but mostly it was brown and olive and untidy beyond expectation. The houses I could see from the road were 1970s-style structures built of campfire wood and smudged glass. They looked out over the rattlers and the tanned grass. The view in the canyon was important. The Realtor, Kathi, kept saying the word over and over. *View.* Eventually it stopped sounding like a word I knew.

She also talked about the coyotes and the rattlesnakes. But don't worry, she said. On the phone she sounded red-haired and pretty. Don't worry, Kevin likes to catch the rattlers and move them to a happier place, no problem.

Kevin was the former rap star who lived on the property. I wonder if he will mean anything to you. Relevance is fleeting. There was also a young man named River who lived in a yurt in the meadow. The landlord lives nearby, said the Realtor. In case there are any issues. You are going to love it there. It's fucking heaven.

I climbed the winding road until I saw the sign for Comanche Drive. I was filled with terror because already the street didn't look charming. It was treeless and the house was at the top of a steep gravel driveway. It was the highest point of Topanga Canyon, nearly piercing the clouds. Mostly it looked like someplace to make meth.

There was no formal parking area, so I pulled up beside a black Dodge Charger on a strip of land overlooking a steep drop. Up close, the property resembled the pictures the Realtor sent but not in the ways that counted. The Realtor sent the dream. She sent the view through the glass windows plus the pellet stove. She did not send the rusted bathtub outside the front door that was filled with browned succulents. Next to the bathtub planter there was a wrought-iron table with two chairs. The ginger sand was scattered with pebbles so neither the table nor the chairs stood evenly. The windows were moth-skinned. The house was dark orange adobe and shaped like an ocean liner. There was nothing attractive about its design, nothing symmetrical. Both outside and inside it was the kind of hot that kills the old. When I think of you being alone in heat like that — the way that I would come to be — I have to force myself to think of something else.

I'd been instructed to knock on Kevin's door. His place was a somewhat-attached structure beneath mine. I suppose it was a house with two apartments, but it didn't read that way. Kevin would give me the keys. His stage name was the White Space. The Realtor, Kathi, spoke of him the way that a certain type of white woman speaks of a Black man who's achieved fame.

Before knocking I took a walk around the property. Kathi was right. The view was theatrical. Every time we spoke I pictured her at an outdoor table in the sun, nibbling gravlax. I felt sure that if I got to know her, I would hate her.

Beneath the mountain you could see the ocean and on the other side of the canyon the slim rectangles of the city rising behind the trees. The skyline was underwhelming. I walked to the tallest point of the property. It was miles above the car-phoned traffic. There was a delicate mist that must have been the clouds. When I was ten, my aunt Gosia told me that was where my parents were. Up in the clouds. But are they together up there? I would ask, and she would get up to wash a dish, or shut a window.

There was a large firepit at the highest point. It looked medieval with its big rocks and charred wood. There was a giant store of firewood under a black tarp. A Michelob beer bottle filled with rainwater.

I noticed the canvas yurt in the valley a

few hundred feet below me. Down a grassy path in the other direction there was a small red saltbox. It looked like a glorified potting shed, something you bought at a home improvement store but larger and more elaborate. It was the only area with grass on the property, on account of the oaks. Everywhere else the ground was dry nut brown, but around that big potting shed it was moist and green. There were two flower boxes full of marigolds flanking a Dutch door. I worried the tiny home belonged to the landlord. I didn't want to be so close to him. But Kathi hadn't mentioned that sort of proximity. Not at all.

I peeled the dress away from my body and it clung back down with the gum of my sweat. I would come to learn there was no respite from taking a shower in the Canyon. It was a matter of moments before you turned a t-shirt translucent.

I knocked on Kevin's door. I heard some bluesy rap and after a few moments I knocked again, louder. He cracked it just a quarter of the way, then blocked the view with his frame. It smelled like tinctures inside.

— Miss Joan, peace and welcome to the neighborhood. He was very tall and good-looking and his eyes were friendly. He didn't

26

look at me. He looked through me like I was barely there.

I extended a hand and he stepped outside and closed the door behind him. I'd seen him onstage, crouching with a mike. Strobes and girls in Lycra short shorts. The man in front of me looked like he'd never spoken loudly or danced.

— How was the drive?

I said that it was good.

— Man, I love that drive. It's been too long. Planes trip me out.

He made wings of his long arms. By now my scalp had begun to sweat.

— Planes trip me out, too.

— You want your keys, I imagine? You need some help moving some things?

— I've got movers coming, thanks.

— All right, all right. I ain't got no lemonade to offer. I didn't bake no meringue pies. But I'll get something to you. This is gonna be nice. You'll like it here, Miss Joan. We like it here. We're like a small family. You met my man Leonard? My boy River?

— Nobody.

— Whoosh, he said. The lady swoops in — his palm dove down and sliced by my waist — under cover of night. I'mma get your keys, Miss Joan. Let you get settled. Let you get your house in order.

When he returned, he handed me two keys held together by a twist tie.

— Mailbox, he said, pointing to one. House, he said, pointing to the other. No, wait, other way around. He laughed delightedly. I'm all turned 'round today. Forgive me, Miss Joan. I recorded all night. I do that and then sleep all afternoon. This is five a.m. for me.

I took my keys and our hands touched and I shivered and I thought, oh for God's sake. I looked at him and he considered me; I could see him taking my measurements. Then he smiled. He was over it.

Along the drive I had been wanting to sleep with a real cowboy, someone without social media. Sex made me feel pretty. By the time I reached Texas the trip was almost over. The man I fucked was named John Ford. He wore a western shirt and placed my palm over his zipper in the lobby of the Thunderbird. The walls were aqua and there were cowhides on the floor. He said he'd once worked on a ranch. But it turned out to be a Boy Scout trip he remembered like it was yesterday. He was in liquor sales out of Chicago. He'd never heard of the film director who shared his name. Or Monument Valley, where the films were made, the soaring westerns I watched with my mother.

He belched twice, too loud to ignore, and ordered the flatbread pizza with balsamic onions. But his name was John Ford.

3

Inside the house it smelled of toothpicks. What is it about moving into a new place that makes you want to kill yourself? I imagine this isn't true for women with labeled boxes. Women who own flyswatters, who store their winter clothes for the summer. Me, I had my mother's eyelash curler. I had old yellow lotions from stores that no longer existed. My unpacked boxes would stay unpacked. Full of mementos, full of smells and especially the pungent odor of the mothballs my mother placed inside her handbags. As a child I thought they were balls of crystal.

The house was a giant sauna, three floors of all wood. It could have been beautiful. It was, in a way. But as with many run-down places that had potential, you needed to bring a skill to it. The ability to position certain rugs and lamps. You had to not mind dirt in places you couldn't get to. I imagined

Alice to be one of these people.

The first floor was made up of the kitchen and the living room and the only bathroom. In the living room the black pellet stove was filled with lilac crystals instead of wood. The side of the house that faced the mouth of the canyon was all windows. In the photographs the Realtor sent me, there was a towering ficus and assorted singed palms. But without the plants the sun was white-hot and despotic. It illuminated the dust in the sockets of the outlets.

There was no dishwasher and none of the cabinets lined up with one another. The insides of the drawers were sticky, as though honey had been mopped up with plain water. I wouldn't be able to cook long, lovely meals in there. Steaming bowls of mussels or crackling hens. It was a kitchen for turkey sandwiches. I once had a boy-friend from Ireland who would make these schoolboy sandwiches with old tomatoes and cheap turkey, slicked in gloss and full of nitrates. He would leave the turkey out on the counter after making the sandwiches, and in the morning it would still be there and then he would put it away.

I was reminded of that boyfriend in my new kitchen. The notion of making do. The first night we made love it was so hot in his

31

railroad apartment that he was sweating profusely above me. The sweat dripped off the paintbrush ends of his hair onto my face and chest.

The second floor was supposed to be a bedroom. You reached it via a spiral staircase. There was only enough room for the bed. There was a small pine closet. It looked like Colorado in the bedroom. There was an old western saddle slung over a beam. I could picture a different life, Rossignol skis lining the walls.

I climbed a short attic staircase to the third floor, which had been advertised as an office. There was makeshift shelving left over from a former tenant, a few old record sleeves dredged in sand and hair. It felt like walking into a steam room. By that time droplets were falling from my underarms and plinking the floor.

I sat down on my thin white dress. I could feel the splinters of the wood pricking the silk and knew that when I got up, the dress would be ruined. I'd worn it across the country, washed it once in Terre Haute and again in Marfa, in the sink of John Ford's hotel room. I'd pulled it on wet that morning and let it bake dry against my skin in the sun. It was my mother's dress. She'd kept it for so many years in mint condition.

A silverfish sprinkled across my kneecap and then someone banged on the door. I ran downstairs and opened the door to two broad men in black shirts and denim shorts. I always thought, If I had to fuck one man in the room, to save my life. If I had to be ground down. Which would it be?

With these two, I couldn't tell which was safer. The one with a neck tattoo looked like a man who lets a dog hump his leg until one day somebody sees, so he has to shoot the dog.

They asked me where I wanted certain things. When they saw the spiral staircase, the one with the neck tattoo grunted. For the first few minutes they made me feel alternately like a rich old lady and a baby-sitter. I didn't want to be either.

The second man, the one with a gold front tooth, looked from my eyes to my breasts so often that I thought he had a tic. I wasn't wearing a bra, so my nipples poked out, looking like whelks. I don't know why these thoughts came to me, but I pictured myself being bent and raped by the one with the gold tooth over the shallow sink. I reasoned that I might then feel comfortable asking him to build my IKEA furniture.

Halfway through the move I realized that the men were doing meth in my bathroom.

They were going in one after the other, every thirty minutes, and coming out like goblin versions of themselves. I wonder what to tell you about drugs. I took pills and I smoked marijuana and there were monthlong stretches here and there when I blew coke alone at night. I would snort it off of my mother's antique makeup mirror with a five-hundred-dollar bill of Monopoly money. Then I would stay up until three and four, buying dresses online. But mostly it was pills. I wasn't strong enough to get through life without being able to go to sleep on command. Maybe you won't need to take pills. I dream that you'll be so much stronger. One time on an island I swam in a green lagoon and saw through the clearness of the water the simple fact of my limbs. I watched the purple, red, and blue fish moving around my body and I paddled to keep myself afloat for a long time. Afterward, I lay down on the sand and concentrated on the sun warming my kneecaps and my shoulders. I can count moments like that on my hands. My dream is for you to have many such moments, so many that you notice only the times you slip into your own brain and recognize those instances for the traps that they are.

In the living room, while the men brought

in heavy things, groaning, angry about the weight of my life, I shook my father into the frog vase and placed it on top of the pellet stove. For the time being I left my mother in the baggie beside it.

I walked around the place looking for interesting things. But the refrigerator was the kind you couldn't put imposing bundles of romaine in. It wasn't for kale or stocking beets. At best, bags of peeled baby carrots. There was barely room in the pantry for all of my pastina and the cartons of College Inn broth. As a child I'd had a girlfriend whose parents were nineteenth-century poor. They had a pantry full of old food in boxes brought by ladies from the church. One night when I was over, the mother opened a package of macaroni and cheese to find milk-colored maggots slipping around, tinkling the dry elbows. The mother picked over the pasta, tossing the maggots in the sink, and turned on the hot water to melt them. Later my friend looked at me across the table with bright, wet eyes. The family said grace and I tucked my chin and pretended to close my eyes but kept them instead on my plate, watching for movement. My dear friend's hand in mine was small and warm. After that night we never played again. It was early enough in the relationship that it didn't feel, at the time, like a wound. But now I think about her all the time. I think about her every time I open a box of pasta.

— Where you want this? asked the one with the neck tattoo. The movers were holding my burgundy Ploum loveseat, an armless velour nest that Vic gave to me. He'd had me on it more than once. That was the point of many gifts.

I wanted it on the third floor, but the movers were sweating. The beads of sweat glistened on their foreheads like those maggots.

I shook my oily hair out of a ponytail and rubbed my shoulder.

—You're clearly very strong, but it's probably impossible to get that up to the third floor?

— Nothin's impossible, said the one with the gold tooth.

I smiled and thanked him. I fluttered my eyelids. It was something I actually did. Then I turned and moved sensually toward the kitchen. I don't think there's anything wrong with using sex. I know some people think that there is, but I don't understand why. I'd been coached by my aunt Gosia. Gosia wasn't my aunt by blood; she was my father's brother's second wife. She was

Austrian and garishly beautiful — blond pompadour, black Dolce & Gabbana suits, excessive filler. She trained me in the art of sexual combat. She told me that women must deploy all their strengths in order to prevail. People will call you names, she said. They are only hating themselves.

As they moved past me with the couch, I saw the lightened spot where I'd scrubbed Vic's semen off. At first it was revolting but lately it had become a faded badge.

— Yo, you know the White Space lives under you? said the neck tattoo.

I told him that I did.

— Fuckin sick, said the one with the gold tooth. What kind place is this? Some artist commune'n shit?

— I have no idea, I said. The men had become very ugly to me. I looked out the windows, wishing again I had moved some-place where it snowed, with big yellow Bobcats that roared down blizzardy Ketchum mornings. I loved headlights in snowstorms. But I had come to Los Angeles for a reason. I'd stayed in New York for too long when I should have tried to find Alice. New York is a lie, I will tell you. Each city is its own lie, but New York is a whopper. I don't expect you to listen about that. Every-one needs to learn it in their own time.

37

The men noticed I'd stopped playing. Men are never okay when you stop. I had the fear of angering a man. Of not being an amenable woman. I had the fear of being murdered. To assuage the guilt that I didn't follow up the flirtation by fucking them, I gave the movers each a tip of fifty dollars. I wondered if they had to buy their meth or if it was something to cook in an oxidized Airstream. I pictured them eating oyster crackers from the soup counters of gloomy grocery stores in the Valley.

There had been times in my life when I didn't think of a hundred dollars as anything. But when those fifties left my hand, my forehead grew hot. I felt the familiar fear. There was a month when I drove to a gas station every night and bought scratch-off tickets from the lottery vendor. I scratched them off under a bug lamp next to the air pressure machine. I used a dime because it had ridges. One spring evening I won fifty dollars and it made me feel like I could run for office.

I'd considered not tipping the movers, saying I had no cash on hand, that I would send something along in the mail. I thought, with some perverse relief, that if things got terrible anytime soon, if I couldn't find work, I might perform blow jobs on the burgundy Ploum. I could sit the pizza deliveryman down, and the propane guy, separate their giant knees, and let them depress my head like a flush valve.

4

I knew where to find Alice, but you should
never engage a stranger until you understand her world. Don't let anyone have an
advantage.

I drove to Froggy's, which was built on
the sharpest curve of Topanga Canyon
Boulevard. Kathi had told me it was where
the locals went. It was a bar and a music
venue and a fish market. It was decorated
like a Mexican restaurant under the sea.
They sold oysters on the half shell, steam-
ers in nets, tacos with carnitas, coconut-
crusted tilapia. I sat near the stage where
live music played on the weekends. I ordered
shrimp quesadillas to have a plate of food
in front of me. I drank a Bloody Mary. It
was the only thing stronger than wine that I
liked. Perhaps it was the way the thickness
of the tomato quieted the vodka, or perhaps
it was because my father had ordered them.
I used to eat the celery from his, the

pimiento-stuffed olives.

There was an old couple at a nearby table with their thirtysomething son who looked like he had cerebral palsy. His hair was trimmed into a crew cut and when he stood his limbs jangled like a puppet's. His father helped him to the bathroom. His mother, a pale and pretty woman in her fifties with glazed eyes, sat at the table when her men had gone and squeezed a lemon into a Coke. There was someone, I thought, who might understand me.

I watched a career waitress say to the bartender, You have to take my tables. I gotta go back there. I'm gonna be some time. Somethin didn't agree with me.

The waitress ran into the kitchen, her gray ponytail thwapping behind her. Now that I was looking in that direction, I saw the next wrong thing sitting at the bar with dirty-blond hair and light eyes the color of blue hydrangea. He looked back at me and smiled and then suddenly he was smiling more and walking over.

— Hey, he said, I saw you walking out to your car before, at the house. I would have come over, but I was.

He didn't finish his sentence. He was one of the sexiest men I'd met in person. He didn't have to do anything except not be cruel.

— Sorry. I'm River. I live in the yurt. You must be Joan.

— Must be, I said, biting my lip inside my brain.

— Mind if I sit?

He was twenty-two, I'd been told by Kathi, who also called him eye candy. He had pink cheeks and his bottom lip was thick and I thought I'd learned my lesson. He'd brought his mug of beer with him. His demeanor was gentle but indifferent, the gutting indifference of the young.

I said, I don't mind, even though he'd already begun to sit down. "Werewolves of London" was playing. Behind his head a great silver and blue marlin hung from the wall. He asked what had brought me to California, and I said, Acting. That was what I was telling everyone so they would leave me alone. I figured there was enough shame associated with trying to be an actress in one's late thirties that they wouldn't press me.

River liked Japanese folk tales. He sold solar panels to celebrities in the Canyon. The company was owned by a couple of bros in Santa Monica and they'd promised him a stake. He drove the work truck during the week and on the weekends he had his fixed-speed. If he went out with friends they'd pick him up. They'd drive all the way into the Canyon from West Hollywood or downtown LA or Culver and they'd head down to Bungalow and drink whiskey near the water. Last week he'd sold a bundle to Lisa Bonet. Her hair was all cornrows and she was in raw silks. She had hundreds of children around her and they kept goats and the children drank the milk of the goats. River tasted it and said it was the flavor of grass.

— How do you get home at night, from the bars in Hollywood? I asked him. Kathi had told me there were no real taxis that went from Hollywood up to the Canyon. Or if they did, they were hundreds of dollars.

— Usually I don't come back up here, he said. And of course I knew what that meant.

River was from Nebraska. He talked about hunting deer with his father and selling the meat to local purveyors.

— Where I'm from, he said, they sell deer meat at the gas stations. You can pay at the pump and someone will walk out a big bag of meat.

I pictured the bloody bag and the snow falling at a gas station on a country road.

43

He leaned back in his chair and rested one foot on the bottom rung of my seat. He was wearing very light jeans that I don't think were in style. You will always meet a new kind of man just when you thought you'd exhausted the supply.

"Werewolves of London" played again. Something must have been stuck in the system.

— Good thing I like this song, I said.

He laughed in a way that meant he'd never heard it. Sometimes I dreamed of being married to Warren Zevon, eating drugs with him at Joshua Tree and curry out of stained boxes in the rains of Shoreditch.

— Have you met Lenny? he asked.

— No.

— He's an odd duck. He lost his wife a few months ago. He's still pretty fucked up over it.

— How long do you think people should grieve?

— My father died eighteen months ago. That's why I moved out here.

— I'm sorry.

— He had a heart attack while he was shoveling snow. I came home and found him on the driveway. You could see the asphalt in some parts. He was almost done.

I shook my head in pity. I meant it. I felt

44

so much for him, but I was always feeling more than I should when it came to death. The bartender came and removed our dirty glasses. I was about to ask for another round when River said he should be going. He needed stamina to ride his bike up the two treacherous miles.

— I can give you a ride if you want.

He thought for a moment and said that would be great. For a third time, "Were-wolves of London" came on. I said I hoped it would go on forever and realized that made me sound ridiculous.

— So nobody told you how the bills work, he said.

I told him no. The word *bills* filled me with dread. I was deeply in debt across many different cards. I'd sold some of the things Vic had bought for me and that had paid for the trip across the country, the movers, two months of rent.

— How it works is you and Kevin and Leonard are on the same propane, water, etcetera. I'm totally off the grid, so every month I read my meter. My total kilowatt-hour usage hovers around twenty-one hundred. My last reading was twenty eighty-five. So over the last twenty-four days I used ninety-seven. My total solar-power production is nine hundred eighty-seven. That means I produced a hundred and thirty-seven kilowatt-hours over the last twenty-four days, and that was directly subtracted from the group bill. So I'm responsible for minus-forty kilowatt-hours. I owe zero dollars and ten dollars was subtracted from the bills. Does that make sense?

I just looked at him.

— I save you guys money. I produce energy.

— And the rest of us suck it, like cows.

He laughed.

— It's a good thing we like this song, he said.

I left two twenties and followed him into the warm, fragrant night. At the valet stand we waited behind a man in his sixties with a woman in her twenties. The woman wore a pink bandage dress and cheap shoes. The man had his palm on her rear. He moved his finger pads in concentric circles. He didn't tip the valet.

River looked from them to me and smiled. Few things are more aphrodisiacal than looking down on another couple.

In the car his knee touched mine. And his hand touched mine when I shifted in the parking lot. Something about his youthful spirit made me think of all the times before something terrible happens.

46

— There are a lot of wild places in the Canyon. Great hiking spots. I've been thinking about getting a dog. But the coyotes.

— And the snakes? I said.

His bike bumped around in the back. I drove slowly because the trunk was open. The first thing he did was open his window all the way and stick his elbow out.

— The snakes are not as bad as the coyotes. Listen, be careful around Leonard. Lenny. I mean, he's a great guy. But he's really needy.

— Okay, I said, thinking of the way the young feared need. I was concentrating on the curves, which frightened me. I felt like the side of my body was scraping against the faces of the rocks. I was still wearing the white dress but I'd added lime oil to my neck and wrists and a thin gold bracelet of my mother's.

River told me that Leonard's father had envisioned something of a commune back when. A McCarthy-era bunker. Had I seen the Japanese soaking tub behind Leonard's place? At one time there had been a fixed stream of tan ladies, porn stars and Satan worshippers and your general loose fun-loving types coming through the place. Their big bouncy breasts would float at the black surface of the tub.

47

He talked about the missile launch in North Korea. He talked about it the way young men spoke of threats, with political engagement and zero fear of radioactive death. River was deathless; I knew the mark of the deathless. They ate wasabi peas and used the same unlaundered towel for weeks.

— I practice stoicism, he told me.

In the driveway we stayed in the car for a few minutes. He was talking about Rotterdam. I thought it would be nice to have sex, mostly because I was thinking about the loss of his father, and that endeared him to me. The problem is it's very difficult to find someone who will feel your loss with you. The same people who cry at movies will not blink an eye if you relate a tragedy. They will say, I'm so sorry for your loss. Like you have lost a thousand dollars on a horse race. Like it's something replaceable. A pittance, in the grand scheme of things.

Sometimes he doesn't come out of his house for whole days, River had said of Leonard. But he watches from his window, so don't do anything you wouldn't want anyone to see. Like hanging laundry in a bikini or grilling topless.

I was imagining how many girls River had slept with. Probably he saw women naked

48

several times a week. I liked the way he said *topless* like it was nothing. I've tried to explain that to other women — the feeling of liking men who don't look for sex actively. Most men are crabs, crawling around with their pincers out.

I looked to the side and did the thing I always did when I moved into new, cramped quarters. I imagined a bassinet beside the bed. How crazy and stupid it would look. How terrible the staircase would be for going up and down with an infant. How dangerous everything was and how exhausting it would be to safeguard a ratty home. The bassinet was always wicker and white, something old-world that tottered when you walked into the room. I myself had never been in a bassinet. I'd slept between my parents for longer than was reasonable. They used to pass Marlboro Reds across my tiny body. I remembered the long reach of my mother's slender arm across me and over to my small but muscly father. He would tip the ashes off. The ashtray was always on his side. Mimi, my mother called him when the cigarette was waiting over my head. Yes, Cici, my father said back.

I wanted to tell Alice those details before the end of that life as I knew it. I dreamed that night that she was the Antichrist, that

49

she would be cruel and try to hurt me. Part of me wanted to hurt *her.* Sometimes I went around wanting to hurt everyone.

I woke in sweat at three in the morning. It was not the heat that woke me but a bright devil noise — a tone somewhere between the cry of a baby and the bray of a small dog. It felt so near that I didn't want to turn on the light. Afraid there would be a tuft of silver fur on the bed.

I looked and saw only one coyote out of my bedroom window, but there were more out of sight. The one I saw stood on the tallest mound of land, about five hundred feet from me. It was slighter than I expected. I looked at it and it looked at me and then the sound abruptly stopped. It was a peaceful moment. It was windless and none of the landscape moved, as though it were a painting. Then the animal cast its head back, opened its jaws, and emitted a howl like stones cracking in fire. It was joined in chorus by the invisible others.

I ran around the house shutting all the windows. Down the grassy path I saw a light come on in Leonard's shed-home. I tore my dress off in the agony of heat and noticed, for the first time, an air-conditioning unit mounted on the wall between the first and second floors. The Realtor had said there wasn't one. Probably the unit wasn't working but I dragged my dining room table toward the door. I hoisted a chair on top of the table and climbed up. Standing on my toes like that, I could switch the thing on. Twice I nearly fell. Then I got it, hit the switch, and it turned on with a gratifying rumble. I smelled paint chips but soon felt the cool air. I was so happy that I began to cry.

From the daisy recipe tin next to the toaster I extracted two 10-miligram tablets of Ambien. I bit one in half. One and a half was my magic number for most pills. It was more than necessary without being too much.

In my dreams I was seldom as alone as I was in life. I wore baseball caps and had a child with me, almost always a girl. My breasts ached in my dreams as though they were heavy with milk. The girl was too old to nurse but I always had the feeling of pulling her into bed with me, against my chest. The bed was by the porthole of a window in some Greek or Italian seaside town. The child was in a white dress and always in danger. Other times we ate, happily, at a fast-food restaurant until suddenly a car was behind us and I understood it was someone coming to take her away from me. When I woke there was the mean little pain of missing someone's laughter. There was also relief. I had no one for whom to care. No one to fear losing.

That first morning in the Canyon I woke to pounding on the door. It sounded as though it had gone on for a long time before I'd become aware. One time Vic woke me with knocking like that. He said he'd thought I was dead. I hadn't returned his calls for a few days. He was ashamed when I opened the door, but also he'd been angry. Later, after I'd sent him away and looked in the mirror, I realized why. There was mascara under my eyes. My mouth looked raw. I hadn't done anything with anyone the night before, but he wouldn't have believed me. Partly he liked to think I did.

BANG BANG BANG BANG. Then a pause and then four more.

From an opened suitcase on the floor I pulled on an itchy sweater that fell to my knees. I opened the door to find an old man.

He'd been angry but then he blinked. He looked down at my long legs.

— Joan, he said.

I nodded and squinted. When I woke too early on Ambien there was always the quivering terror — who did I fuck last night,

52

what did I eat.

— I'm Leonard.

— Nice to meet you.

— Sorry, I seem to have woken you.

— Is everything all right?

— Well, he said, stepping into the house without invitation. He led with a cane. He wore old-man sneakers, a beige pair of New Balances. He indicated the air conditioner with his cane. That unit, he said, is not to be used. It's very dangerous. It's got asbestos. It causes cancer. It's unsafe and the filter hasn't been changed. It's not approved by the city.

— Oh, I said. So why is it here?

— I need to have it taken down. Didn't you see in the lease the line about the air conditioner.

— I thought all leases were standard.

— Well, yes, it's a standard lease, but all leases have provisions.

He said this like I was a dumb thing.

— One about the AC, he continued. Another about pets. Female pets must be spayed.

— On account of the coyotes, I said. Kathi the Realtor had explained this in depth. She'd said anything in heat would be torn to shreds by the coyotes. She'd instructed me on how to dispose of my tampons. To

53

triple-bag them in dog waste sacks.

Leonard nodded. I lifted the chair on top of the table.

— What are you doing? Leonard asked nervously as I climbed. Don't do that, he said, I'll have Kevin come turn it off.

— Kevin is probably sleeping. He records through the night. I said this as I balanced on the shaking hardback. I wasn't wearing any underwear and I felt the old man's eyes between my thighs like a flare.

When I got down, he was winded, as though he'd been the one climbing on chairs. What a cheap little bastard, I thought. We pooled our bills. That was the reason he didn't want me to use the air conditioner. And I couldn't offer to pay extra. There were multiple periods in my life when I'd bought something in every store I walked into. I'd bought furniture on a whim, big Edison bulbs for antique iron lamps. I'd bought museum wine stoppers even though I had never not drunk a whole bottle the same night it was opened. But this was not one of those times. I had to turn off old air conditioners. I had to suffer the grotesqueries of crushed old men.

— There, I said. All better.

— I'm sorry to have woken you.

He had nice soft hair and a patrician face,

but beyond that he was just another man who could smell it on me, the loss of a father.

— I'm late for an audition so I needed to be up, I said.

He was still nodding as I shut the door in his face.

5

Alice's face in that magazine confirmed everything I'd always feared. She was more beautiful. At a rest stop on the way in Alamogordo I overheard a four-year-old child tell her mother that her friend's mother was *beautifuller.* The little girl's mother smiled and said, Yes, Vanna's mom is really pretty. No, the little girl said, she's *beautiful.*

After my brutal little landlord left, I got dressed. I used the same rose-colored balm on my cheeks and my mouth. I tried to look attractive but I knew before meeting her in person that she was, and would always be, beautifuller.

The notion of seeing her in person was nearly too much. I wanted to put it off indefinitely. But I couldn't. It had become, by that point, irreversible. Seeing Alice would be the key not to my survival but to yours. Sometimes you are little more than a crimped apparition, like the heat that rises off the macadam in front of your car. By the time I'd been two days in the Canyon, you had come to exist. I couldn't see your form, but I could feel you slipping from me. I could feel someone, something, pulling me away from you. Pulling me into a white room as I screamed for you. *Give her back to me!*

I would have burned the whole world down to get you back. But what if I could not?

Los Angeles was both more remarkable and less beautiful than I expected. Cayennes and narrow streets and skinny women and the air of posh mystery. The grand homes of Beverly Hills were gruesome up close; the paint was chipping and everything felt empty, as though once-famous actors were dying inside.

But the canyon was different. It was orange and rocky, and the greens, the ragweed and the beach burr and the saltbush, were not plush but dry and brown or a singed yellow. In between the rocks sprouted sedge and mule fat. In the pictures I'd seen there had been up-close images of Indian paintbrush, the shocking canary of a beach evening primrose and the carpets of

California poppy, like the Technicolor land of Oz. But now I saw it for what it was. The golden yarrow rattled with snakes.

A few weeks earlier it would have been just fine. I'd always taken comfort in knowing that as long as I could scrape together the money for gasoline, I could drive. I could visit the Grand Canyon. I could sleep in the Argo Tunnel and rise in the morning before the tour groups came through. But I couldn't leave Los Angeles. It was the last place and I knew it. And here I was in the queerest part of it. I had to get a place minutes from where she worked. Just as when I was a child and I wanted a tennis skirt and tennis sneakers before ever once striking a tennis ball. As an adult I was no different. I needed to feel that I owned real estate before I used a bathroom.

There was no nucleus, no central village, of Topanga Canyon. Just clusters of shops a mile or more apart.

The old hardware store was otherworldly. It was not California-precious but neither was it a holdover from the fifties. It smelled of chalk inside. I loved the smell of hardware stores nearly as much as I loved the smell of chlorine.

I stopped at the thrift store scratchy with tutus and sequined dresses and polyester palazzo pants and vintage greeting cards and postcards that once upon a time were cherished.

Dear Mom,
The weather is beautiful, even in winter. School is going well. They sell 24-karat gold in the shops for a good price and I'm enclosing a necklace for Susan for Christmas. Please give it to Susan, Mom. Tell Dad I saw a Ferrari 312 here, just coasting the streets of downtown Padua. Cherry red, with a tan leather interior. Love to all.

Jack

Not too long ago everyone wrote in script. My father wrote in script. I used to think he had the most beautiful handwriting in the world. But everyone from his era did.

I drove up and down streets where you couldn't see around the curves. People seemed to drive blind, on instinct. Every so often there was an impressive Spanish-tiled house, grazing horses. There were art installations and peace signs made of hubcaps. There were bamboo fences and no clouds in the sky. When I got hungry, I stopped at a place called La Choza, next to a dry cleaner. I was in the same white dress. It smelled of sweat but I hadn't come across anyone who would notice.

A Mexican woman behind a counter waited with a wide tin spoon. There were instructions for how to order written on a piece of cardboard. PICK ONE: CHICKEN ADOBO, STEAK, CHAR VEG.

I wanted half chicken and half charred vegetables. I didn't want any rice.

— You only pick one, said the woman.

— Can I have half of each, and you can charge me for the chicken, which is the more expensive one.

— No, you pick one. The woman wore a honeycomb hairnet that starred her dark head.

— But I want half of each, and you — the store — will be making money off this order. Because the chicken is more expensive and I am having less of it. Do you understand?

The woman shook her head.

— Why? I asked. Can you explain to me why?

The woman set the spoon down and wiped her plastic gloves on her apron, stained with yellow and brown juices. She picked up the spoon and aggressively scraped it under a section of rice.

— I don't want rice, I said.

The woman walked away then, into the kitchen. I was still hungry.

Back in my car I drove and listened to Marianne Faithfull and Joni Mitchell. I will make a list for you of all the songs that meant something to me.

I parked at the health food café next to her studio, which happened to be world-famous. Rod Rails Power Yoga. Rod Rails was one of the phony stars of the yoga community. Shirtless and long-haired with a crooked erection like the bone of a porter-house, I would come to hear. In one picture holding a malnourished child in Nepal, the next with his arm around the spiky shoulders of an older actress. He led two times a month but mainly traveled to high holy grounds and franchises. Most of the classes were taught by girls like Alice. Hot girls who had never smoked a cigarette.

I walked up to the door. My legs trembled and I felt like a nobody. On top of that, I hadn't planned what I would say.

There was a schedule on the door. I looked for her name. The day was a Tuesday. She wasn't teaching until Friday. I was so relieved that everything inside of me quieted immediately. I would come back on Friday, I told myself. But I didn't have to come back at all. I could find a nice used-car

61

dealer, let him buy us a split-level in Baldwin Park and refuse to fuck in any position but doggy-style.

The other thing I always wanted to put off was getting a job. After running out of the money that came from selling my parents' home, I'd held a lot of different jobs. Often I didn't have a job at all. I would sell something a man gave me, and the profit might last several months.

Next door, I walked through the beaded curtain of the health café. Fat flies buzzed inside. The café sold kombucha, rope baskets, chapbooks of poems by local writers, chocolate bars made with Oregon peppermint. A sign that said HELP WANTED looked like it never came down. There was a bright pink La Marzocco machine. A young girl in a cowboy hat with two long braids stood behind the counter. An unlaminated name tag pinned to her chest said NATALIA. She was young enough to have been my daughter had I gotten pregnant at seventeen.

— May I have the frittata, I said.

— The spinach or the kale?

— Spinach.

— It comes with corn fritters.

— I don't want them.

— I can wrap them up and you can take

them home.

— You want to take them home? I said.

I ordered an Americano to see the girl use the bright pink machine. She was pretty, the kind of simple, inarguable pretty that I had never been. I was sexually attractive. Sometimes other women didn't see it.

— May I also have a job application?

— Sorry?

I tapped the HELP WANTED sign with a dusty fingernail. The girl leaned across the counter, craning her head to see it. Her breasts were big and jammed together. She wore a rose quartz Buddha on a leather string around her neck.

— Oh, huh.

— Do they not need help?

— Yeah. I'm actually leaving for school.

— Great.

— How many do you need?

— Just the one.

— You want the frittata to stay or to go?

— I'll stay.

I walked outside with the application and the coffee to the partially covered patio with bright butterfly chairs and old sewing tables and round wood tables, each with a bottle of Cholula on top. I felt a terrible premonition; I've had these throughout my life and few people have believed me because I'm always relating them after the fact. I don't trust myself enough to say something when I have the feeling. So this time, like every time, I quieted my mind the best I could. I concentrated on the paper in front of me. I hadn't filled out this type of application since I was in my teens. It asked if I was available to work weekends, holidays, how many hours I desired to work per week. It asked what subjects I studied in school. Yes, yes, many, I wrote, and art history.

Before Vic I had, for a time, kicked men in the testicles with high heels. One man gave me a painting I turned around and sold for twenty-five thousand dollars. Another gave me a vintage silver print of Diane Arbus's *A Widow in Her Bedroom.* I treasured that photograph. Sometimes I felt it was the finest thing about me.

Suddenly there was an extreme noise on the road. I have to tell you that terrible things always happen around me. I was marked at ten. People don't want to know that many bad things can happen to one person or around one person. A bad thing happens and coworkers circle your cubicle, their grating palms on your shoulders. Another bad thing happens and you're no longer someone upon whom they could try out their munificence. You're a squashed pack of Merits on the highway.

The girl, Natalia, came out with my frittata on a plate. A Chevy Tahoe had headonned a yellow Beetle. The Beetle, which looked like a human being, was compacted, its face smashed. There was the braking of other cars and a single horn sounded but otherwise a snowy peace settled across the Canyon. I looked at the girl and the girl looked back at me.

It took the man a long time to come out of the Tahoe, and when he did, he was covered in frosty dust. He staggered toward the Beetle. It was a seventies model with the handlebar on the hood and the headlights like a ladybug's eyes. Medium-dark gray smoke poured out.

It felt as though the driver of the Tahoe walked for hours but he never made it to the other car before the ambulance did. It was possible the ambulance came the quickest an ambulance had ever come. The driver of the Beetle, a woman, gave the impression of burned toast. She was laid out on a stretcher. The urgency they saved for the other passenger. I turned my head when an entire infant seat was lifted out by the broad-shouldered men. I could see the baby, who was not crying. I could taste the metal and the tears of the father in

65

the morning.

Beside me the girl's mouth hung open but otherwise she didn't shield her eyes or make a noise. She'd likely never seen death. She stood there with that white plate. She'd been taught to put a wedge of tomato on the rim. I wanted to shove her nose in a slick of blood. But I couldn't. I had to let the girl go home, sit on her mother's couch, and tell her boyfriend she'd seen a woman and her newborn die on the road today. The boyfriend would ask about the types of cars involved.

Back at the house I found my landlord sitting at the table outside my door. He had a pitcher and two crystal glasses.

— Joan, he said. This table is for all of us. I moved it to be closer to your door where there's some shade, but if you don't want it here, I can move it back. If you don't like company.

It was hot and still. I hadn't cried about the car crash and I thought that if I went into the house alone I would lose it. I would take a pill and sit on one of my boxes. I felt I could have stopped it somehow. I knew for a fact I could have saved my father and my mother. I liked to think that one of the reasons I'd lived through my own nightmare

was so that one day I might prevent someone else from suffering. But the infant died.
The mother died. I watched. I finished filling out the job application.

— How'd your audition go? he said. He
poured me a glass. Dreamily he said, Lenore's lemonade.

— My audition, I said quietly. Likely I
didn't get it.

— You're a certain age. Do you mind my
asking?

— About thirty years younger than you, I
said, and he smiled. The older the man, the
more my specialty. I knew that when I met
God one day it would go well.

The lemonade was vodka-forward. There
were bits of mint floating at the surface. I
thought of the radio in the car, of what the
mother and the child had been listening to.
I imagined it to be Peter, Paul and Mary
and that the song would live in the air there
forever. Sounds didn't die.

He told me to call him Lenny and asked
me what everyone wants to know. Where
did you come from, what do you do for
money, why are you alone. I gave him a list
of odd jobs. Babysitting, floral arrangement.
The time I'd made up dead people.

Underneath our bodies the ground rum-
bled and I looked up at the sky. An earth-

quake was one of my most vivid fantasies. But it was only Kevin waking up, turning the silver dial on some large box.

Leonard's knee began to tremble. He had the face of an old movie actor, a Paul Newman. It was an interesting face and I liked him better than I had earlier that morning with his cane and metal breath. He looked fresh. He wore a white sweatshirt and gray pants. Gone were the old-man sneakers. In their place a good pair of loafers. Still, his ankles looked like they had been dug up.

— Are you through unpacking?

There were boxes I would never unpack. Six large ones. They contained things like the square packets of hotel shower caps my mother saved. And, from the first time my mother cut my hair, a loose braid of black.

— Yes, I said. Do you live in the potting shed?

He smiled and nodded at me, like, *I know the kind of woman you are.*

— It's not a potting shed. It's one of these tiny homes. I don't need a lot of space. I used to live here, in your place.

—Why'd you move?

— I didn't need all the space, he repeated.

I could tell I'd gone too far. I wished I didn't care.

— Have you always wanted to be an actress?

— No. I didn't want to compete with all the other pretty girls when I was young. So I waited. I figured I'd be more interesting now. I was biding my time.

— Kathi told me you came all the way out here alone.

— I drove.

— She drove, he said, rubbing the rim of his glass. He looked at me in the familiar way.

I finished my drink and stood. He placed two fingers on my wrist and poured me another glass, saying, A bird cannot fly on one wing, my friend. You can flap one wing, but you can't fly on it.

I sat back down. Lenny had a controlling air. At some point he had been in charge of things — family money, legacy, oil futures, a wife, a mistress — and old men like him never stopped flexing their alleged power. Sometimes, when he was being gallant, he reminded me of my father, but so did anyone. For a very long time I had written the word *Daddy* in the steam of shower doors. This was when I lived in places with glass doors. At the apartment in Jersey City I had written it on so many different spots that, when the sun came through the cloudy

69

window, you could see the letters in many directions, like a crossword.

— My wife died, he said, a little under a year ago.

— I'm sorry.

He nodded. He seemed to believe I should feel the pain alongside him.

— Her name was Lenore. Lenny and Lenore. Do you want to know how we met?

— Of course, I said. And I did. Everybody always wanted to know how everybody else met. It seemed possible the key to life was contained on street corners in springtime when a man retrieved a woman's scarf from the sidewalk.

— It was on *Love Connection.* The television program.

— Wow.

— It was the first season they were on the air. She wore a purple skirt suit with little white kitten heels.

— Was she beautiful?

— Beyond beautiful. That something extra. Chuck Woolery asked her if she had any fetishes. She said yes, she had two. The first was that shirts and socks have to match. She didn't like it if a man wore a white shirt and then black socks. She thought it was sloppy. At this point, Chuck Woolery looked down and he was wearing a white shirt with

70

black socks. Lenore laughed. I don't think anybody in the world will ever have a laugh as wonderful. Tough, said Chuck, if you wear argyles. She didn't laugh that time. She knew how to suspend a man. It's a rare talent. I was jealous of Chuck from the start. I was always worried, in the beginning, that Lenore was going to love someone better.

— What was her second fetish?

— The second fetish was cowboy boots. She said she didn't like them. They disgusted her. They made her think of backwoods things, Jimmy Dean sausage.

— It sounds, I said, like she didn't understand the meaning of the word *fetish*.

Lenny blinked.

— She was young. She was hardly twenty-four. I was in my late thirties, probably your age right now.

— Did you sleep together on the date? I always wondered that about *Love Connection.*

— People did the same things then that they do now.

— So you fucked right away.

Kevin, showered and dressed all in black, came outside at the hottest point of the day. He said hello to both of us on his way to his car. I felt like a whore.

6

The Friday that Alice was working, I dressed in Lycra pants and a tank top. I applied mascara and blew out my hair. I drove to the studio. I was sweating so much that warm rivulets ran down my arms.

There was no evidence of the crash. It was wiped from the Canyon. The air was crisp because it was early and the sun was imposing like in a Hollywood western. In New York the sun was a pellet. We get over a death as though it happened only in a movie.

Looking in the rearview mirror, I absorbed the oil from my cheeks and nose with a powdered rose-scented blotting paper. I stared at my face, hating it, for so long that I became embarrassed for myself, as though others were watching me hate myself, and judging me for it. Then I got out and walked languidly to the door, an entirely different person from the one I'd been in the car.

When I opened the door a brass bell tinkled. Like everything else in Los Angeles, it was nothing like what I expected. I expected white glossy walls and orchids the color of dawn. Instead there were dusty snake plants and mammillaria in terra-cotta pots. The green paint was peeling off the walls and the place smelled like summer camp. Waiting in line to register, I watched sweaty thin women exit with towels around their necks and rolled-up mats on cords over their shoulders. I thought of the way men talked about women who'd lost their beauty. I knew what they meant because it was happening to me. There was a fading in the eyes and an overall parch, like an old orange. But I believed it was less a physical change than a by-product of seeing their husbands become moony over a babysitter, as though the babysitter had solved the unsolvable equation or brokered world peace instead of merely braiding the child's hair without the child crying.

I paid for a single class, twenty-six dollars out of a wad of cash that felt like last breaths. I wrote down my age and it looked back at me. Through the glass door I saw her. At first I saw only the back of her head and I was struck at once. Sometimes you can be struck by the back of someone. You won't have to wonder if that person is as striking from the front. When she turned, I gasped. She had the kind of look that you saw very rarely, even in a place full of beautiful girls. She was so unequivocally flawless that I wanted to hit her.

My aunt Gosia was the one who told me about her, or left me information about her, in any case. When Gosia and my mother became close, I was disgusted. She was an interloper, a second wife, and I was jealous. Apparently they talked on the phone often, three times a week or more, when I was at school. I couldn't believe I didn't know. I was intimately involved with every part of my mother's routine, to her increasing irritation. *I can't even change my bloody pad without you in the room.*

After my parents died, I went to stay with Gosia. But living with her was not like living with a caretaker or a mother. It was like living with a casual woman friend. We shopped for clothes, she told me I had sex appeal, even at ten years old, and she showed me how to use it. She let me grow up alone. I went to school and I came back to the house and I ate her beet soup with its funny mushroom dumplings, but if I didn't want to eat it, I didn't have to. Most summers I spent in Italy with my mother's

74

cousins. There was a laxity, I didn't have to come home if I didn't want to. But Gosia gave me love whenever I needed it. If I wanted to be missed, she missed me. If I didn't, she let me be. I won't be able to give you that.

She also gave me all my parents' money that I wasn't supposed to receive until I turned twenty-one. Gosia didn't believe that I should be controlled by the government or by her and my uncle. I blew a lot of the money on clothes, on shoes, on hotels with televisions in the bathroom, on caviar and foie gras and steak tartare and oysters.

After high school, which was a blur of bad grades, stupid bangs, and cigarettes, I moved into Manhattan. Gosia didn't push me to go to college. My first apartment was on Rivington. The kitchen was a short strip of Formica with a butter-yellow fridge and a rusted white stove, but I was proud of it. I hung my mother's precious Venetian dish towels from the steel rod of the oven door. Gosia came in and we would go to Barneys and have tea and poached salmon. She would give me a few hundred dollars every month, even though I was still living off of my inheritance. She bought me expensive shoes. She was the first one to do that. Manolos and Louboutins. One pair of petal-pink Chanel mules that I wear only when the weather is gorgeous.

Gosia told me as much as she knew, but she could not have prepared me for the reality of Alice.

Alice had a long, almost mannish nose, but it was offset by the largeness of her blue eyes and the thickness of her lips. It was a trick. Her big nose made you feel like you had to keep looking at her to determine what was so stunning. Her hair was thick and long and the color of Coca-Cola. She wore a bralette and a pair of Lycra pants. Her body was cartoonishly perfect. She had an hourglass waist and her hips were dramatically wide. I could picture someone gripping them from behind. She was twenty-seven.

Alice began the class with sun salutations. Unlike other instructors, she didn't rhapsodize about energy or gratitude. She barely spoke but when she did the husk of her voice was hypnotizing.

The class made use of small arm weights and leg weights, five-pound sacks to Velcro around the ankles. The music was curated and varied — steampunk, blues, grindcore, Indian ghazel.

I tried hard to look elegant in the poses. During crow I was cognizant of the sinkhole between my breasts. I watched the men, inserted myself inside their heads and saw the ways they might bend the young instructor. It was erotic and eviscerating.

During corpse pose she played Cibo Matto's "White Pepper Ice Cream." She padded around the room to all the lying bodies, squatted by their heads, and flattened the flesh between their shoulders and chests. When she did this to me, my eyes involuntarily slipped open and we looked at each other. I saw the reflection of her blue eyes in mine. I almost passed out. I got up soon after and left the class before namaste.

The encounter left me feeling like I was sixty. I wanted to call Vic. I wanted to call Gosia. I needed someone I already knew to stabilize me. I had nothing left but Alice.

Afterward I drove to Rodeo Drive because my mother loved it there. She was impossible to please or excite, but there were places she worshipped as though they were cast in gold, and Los Angeles was one of them. She'd seen so many noir films as a young woman — *Double Indemnity, Sunset Boulevard* — and Los Angeles was the rich velvety heart of them.

I counted palm trees and did not miss New York. I couldn't divorce what had happened in New York from the rest of New York, from the Broome Street Bar with its copper cups and sexy bartender, from Spring Lounge the night I fell for the sexiest man in the world. From midnight on Broadway, way downtown where Manhattan looked like Rome, large and stone and anodyne. All of the city, now, was slicked in his big bright blood.

We'd visited Rodeo when I was nine and my parents bought me a dress for $425 that required a slip. It was black with tiny white flowers and a Peter Pan collar. My mother was angry about the dress but she herself had gotten a pair of ruby earrings and it was only fair, said my father. Her birthstone is not even ruby, I spat, speaking to my father but looking at my mother. It's *garnet*. When I see you in my dreams you are wearing all the dresses I ever wanted.

I took the Pacific Coast Highway to Sunset. If someone told me this was hell, I wouldn't have been surprised; the palm trees might have risen from beneath the mantle of the earth. But if this was hell then it was nice, the feeling of having crossed over. I recalled one of the final descents with John Ford, how I felt like a canal that this small balding man was passing through. I'd turned around to see his scummy eyes fluttering like a slot machine as he came.

Are you a prostitute? a man once asked me. I was eating alone at the bar of a fine restaurant. I had a mouth full of burger. The burger was terrible, it tasted oxidized. I was using my sweater like a blanket over my bare legs. You look like a Sylvie, he said. Is your name Sylvie?

I'd loved only one man. *Love* was not the right word. He didn't love me. To this day, I still couldn't face that. He would have loved Alice.

I was eating dinner with that man, the one I loved, when Vic walked in and shot himself. He shot himself in the nose. I tell you the nose because details are important. The splatter of blood on the wall was the shape of a maple leaf. What remained of his face was a suggestion. I saw a fetus once when I worked in the hospital, its image in an ultrasound, and the baby had no nose. The mother, a heavy Brazilian woman, reacted to the news as it was translated for her by a young nurse. She nodded serenely. *Como Deus quer,* she said.

As God wishes.

The sunlight was white in Beverly Hills, whereas in Topanga it was orange and gaseous. I was learning that Los Angeles is made up of distinct countries that are merely minutes apart. Not even countries but ecosystems. The homeless beg differently from town to town.

I walked into Lanvin. I was still wearing the same white dress. It made me feel young. I wore also a canvas cross-body bag. On my feet were old dirty sandals. Women can tell another woman's worth by her shoes and bag. You can wear a tarp across your body, but the shoes and bag have to pass. I was conscious of this when I was greeted by a heavily made-up young blonde.

There was a time when I wanted to have a lot of money. I wanted the best of everything because I'd come to realize that expensive things were truly made better, lasted longer, and helped you live longer. Expensive cleaning products did not cause cancer. Chanel nail color lasted at least four days longer than the kind they used in regular salons.

All of that was still true but now I thought of life differently. What I wanted most in that moment — in what I felt might be the last year of my life — was to be poor, with a child. To go through the drive-through at a fast-food restaurant and order two items from the secret menu plus a Coca-Cola to share. Sit in the Dodge, both of us in the front seats, pretending to eat delicately, like we were at a queen's tea party instead of in the parking lot of a fast-food restaurant. The yellow splash of light from the sign would illuminate the crud in the cupholders. In the morning we would eat milk and biscuits, the kind you can get for free in the breakfast rooms of travel lodges.

In the store I tried on a beautiful pair of emerald suede sling-backs. The salesgirl had nothing better to do so she watched me. My feet were dusty. I lifted my dress to see how the shoes made my calves look.

I paraded around in the green heels. I was trying to feel normal, or not even normal but at the very least like the girl I was before I met Vic. Of course I knew I was half dead already by the time I met Vic — a great many segments of myself I pictured to look like the *baba au rhum* my mother used to love, little yeasty cakes saturated in rum. My lungs, for example. When at night I couldn't breathe I imagined my lungs were soaked in sweet liqueur.

By the time I got to California it was even worse. I was embarrassed that I'd ever thought I could be a mother. The desire to be beautiful had been replaced by the lowly fear of looking ugly. But seeing Alice had done something I hadn't expected. Her beauty made me remember my own.

My phone rang and I picked it up because

81

it was a familiar-looking number and I thought it might be my aunt even though she was dead.

It was a woman with whom I'd never spoken but about whom I knew a lot.

— Is this Joan, she said.

— Who is this?

— My name is Mary. I'm Vic's — I was Vic's wife.

The first time Vic and I had sex was in Scotland, but sex has little to do with any first time. For some it might mean the hand on the knee. The clearing of sticky hair from someone's forehead.

The whole team was in Jekyll Island for a conference. I'd already begun to take ocean-front rooms for granted. The first morning I skipped the group breakfast and went alone to the breakfast room called Jasmine Porch, where I ordered sweet tea and grits and red-eye gravy with a side of country ham. I sat in that spacious dining room looking at all these people who hadn't lived a lot. They were mostly older than me but I could tell this was their first time drinking from a glass with an iced orchid inside.

I was tan and young and careless. The waiter filled my large coffee cup from a polished silver pot. I saw a woman in her early thirties enter the restaurant, using two canes to walk. Her husband and their child walked ahead of her, following a hostess to a table, and an older woman, her mother probably, was holding the younger woman's elbow. I had this urge to send over something, French toast for the table. After all, the firm was paying for our meals. I called the waiter, but before I could ask him, Vic materialized.

I wish I could include a picture of him. I don't have any. He was more of a feeling sometimes. His nice but too-big suits. So much suit material, like a factory.

— Hey, kid, he said, looming.
— Oh, hey.
— Rolling solo?
— I wasn't feeling a group situation.
— Me neither. Mind if I intrude?

I had with me a *Departures* and wanted badly to be alone. I knew the precise color I wanted my coffee and how to have an orgasm in under thirty seconds. I needed everybody in the world — including waiters — less than they needed me.

— Sure, I said.
— Sure you mind, or?

He was terribly afraid of me. He was the most gorgeous listener in the whole world.

— Of course I don't mind.

83

How had he found me? How did he always seem to find me? One time, inexplicably, he found me on the second floor of a deli with buffet islands of old but glistening orange chicken.

He sat down and I forgot about sending over the French toast to the handicapped woman. I didn't remember until later that night in Vic's grand hotel room with the ocean just below us. I'd never stayed in such places with my parents.

It was me and this other girl who worked at the copy desk and who'd brought a complaint of unwanted sexual aggression to HR, and this young man, a sort of lackey of Vic's, but then everyone was. Vic had a bottle of Johnnie Walker Blue and we were drinking it on the balcony from rocks glasses with pebbled bottoms. Vic's room was a suite so he had a couch out there and we'd dragged two chairs from the bedroom. It started out with the two of us girls on the couch, but at some point the pairings got rearranged and Vic was on the couch with me. I'd had two glasses of Scotch on top of the three glasses of red wine at dinner. I don't know if I laid my head down. My guess is that he, by measured increments, lowered it down: Aw, poor, tired baby. I remember only the airplane runway of his lap, the navy miles. The ocean shushing. The other two watching me lie across him. Nothing happened, but merely the position of my head on his lap, it was somewhat a rape. That he had hunted me so quietly, that I had allowed my neck to get caught in the teeth of something stupid. I closed my eyes so that it was happening only for the others and not to me and that was when I remembered about the handicapped woman. And I felt sad about not sending the French toast with vanilla bourbon cream and whatever lavender flowers came on the side. Then a moment later I thought, She doesn't need you, idiot. She has a mother and a child. You have nothing.

That was the first time with Vic. He caressed my hair. My earlobe, which thereafter felt whorish and diseased.

Anyway, that's what Vic's wife — Mary — that's what she asked me.

— How did it start? she said.

I told her to hold the line. That it might be a while.

I walked out of Lanvin in the heels I was wearing. It's easiest to steal when you don't know you're stealing. The heavily made-up blonde had been watching me the whole time but she was violently texting when I walked out. They were display shoes, so they didn't make a peep when they walked me out of there.

Suddenly I was in the sunshine in these bright, beautiful Lanvin sling-backs. Their strings were like thin snakes around my ankles. Tourists were ordering cupcakes from a cupcake ATM. They were Italian and laughing. The shoes took me to Spago. I was seated in the courtyard. It was windless out there, I was early for lunch, and everybody seemed to enjoy my presence, the busboys especially. I ordered the Maine lobster salad and a glass of Dr. Loosen. I unmuted the phone.

— I'm sorry, I said. Can you repeat the question?

— I want to know how it started.

I didn't say anything for a long time and held the phone to my ear and my hand to the mouthpiece as the waiter poured me a glass. He smiled at me conspiratorially, like here we were being bacchanalian and the person on the other end of that line was probably folding laundry.

— Do you understand the question?

— Yes, perfectly, I said. I think it's what I'd want to know, too. It started on his lap.

She made a noise of disgust that doubled as reproach. Like I was stupid to lay my head on a married man's lap.

86

— You know my husband is dead, of course. But do you know my young son got into an accident a month ago, and he's dead now, too? You didn't know that, did you? You *cunt.*

I had, up until now, taken many measures not to think of the children.

Because it was a cold dish that only needed assembling and because I was the first customer of the afternoon, my lobster salad was delivered quickly. Bright wedges of avocado. The haricots verts were glossy and dark, the bacon was crisp and auburn, and the lobster was so fresh it looked raw.

— I didn't. How — ?

— He drowned.

Now Mary began to make these little noises on the other end, like a guinea pig. Vic had met her in high school. He told me he'd never cheated on his wife with anyone other than me. It might have been a lie but I didn't think so. He'd probably slept with five or six women before her; high school girls in the sixties, I pictured no condoms and the girls just going home and angling a faucet to exhume it out of them. Maybe there was an abortion or two. I bet I was the first woman he did not come inside, and anything new, for a man, can be an erotic discovery.

I started crying. I knew something of the world in which Mary was now living. The heart pills he'd no longer need. Things in the refrigerator are the worst because you cannot save them indefinitely. What if the dead person comes back and wants his coffee yogurt.

But the child. I couldn't imagine. Or I could imagine. Before I even found you, I imagined losing you. It felt like someone was serving my heart to me on a plate and forcing me to carve out pulsing segments and eat them without condiments.

— Why are you crying?

— I'm sorry, I said. I shouldn't be crying. I didn't ask for him that way. I'm so sorry about your boy.

— You're a lying cunt!

She would never understand. If I'd said, Go home to your wife, you pig, he would have wanted me even more and her even less. You can't say these things to any woman, let alone a grieving one.

— I'm sorry, I said more quietly.

— I'm calling, she said, for another thing. My daughter, Eleanor — in case he never told you their names — I don't know where she is. She hates you. She said she wants to kill you. And I'm thinking. If she's coming for you. If she comes for you, will you give me the dignity of telling me?

I nodded into the phone.

— Do you hear me, you cunt!

—Yes, I said. I thought of the word *dignity* and wanted to kill myself.

7

On the way home I took two milligrams of Klonopin. It worked enough for me to forget a little about the child. But it would come back in terrible notions — anime eyes blinking inside of a child-size coffin.

When I walked into my place, I found my landlord sitting on my couch. I had no one to turn to, aghast.

— Darling! he said, standing. I'm so sorry, I feel so awful. I've been here, pacing, wanting to off myself.

— Leonard?

— Yes, my darling. Is it over? Did you do it?

— Do what?

— You didn't do it and that's all right. That's fine, darling. We will get through. We will manage. Come, sit by me, my life. Let's eat a nice dinner and see a funny movie.

He had a drink in one hand and a book in the other. William Carlos Williams, *Spring and All.* His hair was rumpled. There were green stains on his collared white shirt.

— Lenny, I think you're confused.

— Yes, and I've confused you. I'm a terrible man, Lenore, and I don't deserve our life. Come close to me, my body. My woman in blue.

I worked for a few months at a supermarket in Utah, sealing chicken breasts in plastic. My boss was a man in a cowboy hat and a bolo tie. He always had his hands in his pockets. He went crazy one day and shot his wife in the neck. Of course, these things don't happen *one day.* It was likely brewing for months, but how could I have noticed, sealing chickens and not looking at the clock for chunks of time so that I might be pleasantly surprised at how much of it had passed. But when the police came and they started asking questions, I recalled how my boss had several times called me Shelley: Shelley, we need more breasts on the cooler, and transfer yesterday's into the discount section. I never corrected him. I hadn't seen the point at the time.

— Lenny.

— Love?

— Leonard, I said. I'm not Lenore. I think you're having an episode.

I said this calmly. I watched his mind

91

return to his body. As reality crept in, his color faded. His face drooped and he appeared a decade older.

He looked around the room, realizing it was his old house and that he didn't live there anymore.

— Oh God.

— It's all right. Why don't you sit back down, I'll get you a glass of water.

— Jesus. I'm embarrassed. I'm so embarrassed.

— Don't be.

— Grief does strange things to you.

— I can only imagine.

— It's awful. One day someone is screaming at you for how you're driving. The next day you're free.

I brought him warm tap water in a dusty glass.

— On top of the grief, he said, there are also the drugs I did in my youth.

— What sorts?

— LSD. Mescaline. Peyote. And on. They make me lose my mind for a stretch. Here and there.

I thought of the groceries I'd bought on the way home, the milk warming out there in the heat. This second child's death had twisted my intestines. Going to grocery stores was one of the best ways I knew to

92

calm myself. The clean, cool aisles. Everything was brightly lit at any time of day.

— Do you mind, Lenny, I have to get my groceries from the car. I'll be right back.

— Let me get them. Let me be a gentleman so I don't feel like an embarrassment.

— No. Stay.

It was almost four and I decided to cook him dinner. I had many fresh vegetables and they wouldn't all fit in the fridge.

In the beginning I cooked for Vic all the time in my apartment. You shouldn't do that. If you cook for a man, and you cook very well, as I did, they will think you belong to them. The truth was I was always practicing for a man I might actually love. Big Sky, for example. With every crisp quail I roasted for Vic I was perfecting my technique for Big Sky. There would be long oak tables set for Thanksgiving in his deluxe lodge in the mountains. There would be twigs and pinecones strewn about, no tablecloths, and fresh sparkling water with twists of lime.

Lenny sat on one of my modern barstools, which were out of place in that rustic hovel. He watched me mince garlic. My mother minced garlic very quickly, so fast I would always check that all her fingers were still there when she was done. I took my time. Unlike her, I didn't have a child at my knee and a husband on his way home.

But this time I minced sloppily. I nearly sliced my finger. My mind was on that phone call. I hadn't thought about the people Vic left behind, not enough, anyway, until I heard her voice. When you've suffered as much as I have, you begin to see everything in perspective. You know exactly the ways in which people will move on and you know that they will laugh again. It makes their present suffering seem prosaic.

— What are you making?

— I'm sautéing broccoli with garlic, red pepper flakes, and bread crumbs.

— Sounds spicy.

— Are you one of these old men who can't tolerate spice?

— You have some cruelty in you.

Let me tell you: men love cruelty. It reminds them of every time their fathers or mothers didn't think they were good enough. Cruelty looks better on a woman than the perfect dress.

— How about gluten? Salt? How's your heart?

He knocked his chest.

— Strong, he said. A few things I have are still strong.

I knew he meant between his legs. I wanted him to know that there was nobody left in the world who would fuck him.

We opened a bottle of wine. Garlic skipped in the pan. When I tossed the thick stalks of the leek, Lenny said, You can tell the worth of a woman by how much food she wastes. There were moments like that when I wanted to strangle him. And then he would compliment me, tell me my hair was like onyx, or reach with an old arm to fill my glass.

I asked about Lenore because it soothed me to hear people talk about love like it was real. I want you to know about Lenore, about the women who men make you feel are better than you. I want you to know about everything I may not be able to teach you.

Lenny was happy to oblige. They'd known each other only a month before he asked her to marry him, and the wedding was two weeks later. He went on about their honeymoon in Anguilla. Snorkeling and creamy pineapple drinks. A friend of his got them upgraded to a suite in one of the finest hotels. Two bedrooms, two giant marble bathrooms. Lenore said she would be able to maintain her girlish mystery with the second bathroom for at least ten more days. They made love on both beds; the poor maid, he said with a grin, like it turned him on that the housekeeper had to make two dirty beds. There was a Jacuzzi on the balcony, stone and round. Just beneath their room, palm trees and white muslin umbrellas ringed a giant blue pool. There were buckets full of sparkling wine and bikinis in bright colors and more women than men, in sunglasses and straw hats, reading tall glossy magazines, and nobody as far as the eye could see in distress, nobody who had just come from a hospital or knew they might have to go back. He said he looked at all the women in their bathing suits, some in thong bottoms with their nice rears exposed, and not one of them, he said, held a candle to Lenore. And just beyond all of that luxury they were blessed with the Caribbean ocean, teal and endless, rolling gently against the bone shore.

— Did you ever have second thoughts? I asked. Since you hadn't known her very long?

— Let me tell you something, he said, looking into my eyes like an asshole. If a man takes longer than two, three months to ask you to marry him, he doesn't love you. He won't ever love you. Do you have a man in your life?

— Until recently I did.

— Did he provide for you, financially

96

speaking?

I thought about that for a moment. Vic had indeed provided for me. He promoted me several times. He bought me plane tickets and couches and computers, fine wines and a substantial wine cooler in which to store them.

— In a way I didn't need.

— So he provided for you?

I nodded.

— Did you leave him in New York? Did he leave you?

— I suppose, in a way, we left each other.

— There's no such thing.

Old men are so sure of everything. He was forking broccoli into his mouth. I tried to determine whether he had dentures. Or he could have had caps. He came from a wealthy family. Now he was worried about air conditioners but that is how all old people end. More surely than we fly toward death, we go to parsimony.

— He killed himself, I said.

8

When I was ten I drank grappa in Grosseto. Down the hill from my parents and the cousins, in a field that had nothing to do with farms or horses but was full of haystacks. It was late September. The horizon was a stand of cypress, some scattered clouds, and a dry field. The remnants of an old olive grove.

I met a boy named Massi, short for Massimiliano. Max, I would tell my friends back home. He was much older, fourteen. His red hair was too thick but everything else was consciously set there by God for a small American girl to love. He was the last boy to make me feel worthy, to put me on a pedestal the way Lenny had for Lenore. Of course, that sense of worth coincided with the fact that I had not yet been to hell.

We were at a villa party given by posh distant relatives of my mother's. The day lasted forever. A string quartet played "Hallelujah" on the tall, crunchy grass. There were figs in that grass, heavy as hearts.

I'd seen the boy playing soccer, noticed his strong, tan legs and skillful footwork. What does a girl love at ten? What will you love? I loved the air around this boy. It was mixed with the strong cigarettes of the men and the flowery perfume of the ladies and the lemons in the trees.

I stared at the boy as I sat beside my father. I felt babied by my father's hand on my shoulder as he spoke to a circle of men, smoking and drinking, most of them paunchy. I'd eaten so much of the shrimp cocktail being passed around that one of the men appraised me in what I'm fairly sure was a sexual manner. He said to my father, The girl likes expensive things. She will have to marry a man with money. My father smiled. No, he said in his decent Italian, she will make it on her own. I'd thought of that often since then, my father's belief in me. My mother thought I would need to marry someone with money, maybe she thought that because of her own life. Either way, the boy, Massi, was from a wealthy family. I was thinking of pleasing my mother. On top of that or because of that, I wanted to kiss him more than I'd wanted anything outside of my mother's love.

Massi looked at me several times. Italian boys are good at eye contact. I looked older than ten in an off-the-shoulder dress, with my long dark hair and the coral lipstick from my mother's purse. I'd wanted to fall in love since kindergarten. I'd always had crushes, had liked boys since Jeremy Bronn with the calloused thumbs. Four years earlier, in the lingerie section of a department store, I'd picked a sapphire teddy off the rack, with trickling garters and a net bodice. I begged my mother for it, and my mother, because she was either innocent to the request or uniquely understanding of it, let me have the silky bedroom thing. In the privacy of the house I wore it, baggy and bright, over my colt legs and flat chest.

I watched my mother get drunk. She was laughing uncharacteristically loudly with some of the musicians. Most of the time she stood beside a stone-faced beautiful woman with an ivory cigarette holder. I felt a hatred rise up in me that day, one that had always lurked. My mother locked me out of her bedroom many nights of our life and I cried and begged at the door, pushing my finger pads against the cheap pine, and where was my father? I couldn't think, it had been so long ago, but I remembered the bitterness I felt, and it came back around now, seeing my mother laughing with new people in a somewhat wanton way. Wearing a necklace of bones around her neck. Ah. My mother's bone necklace.

So that was when the boy, when Massimiliano, came around with his rich red hair and his confident saunter and his attempts at speaking my language — Wud going for a walk with me? — I took off with him. My father was distracted and he would always think I was his little girl — sexlessly beautiful — so we walked out of the sightline of the guests, down into the cool shade of a cypress grove. Massi picked up some figs and placed them in my hands. He'd hidden away a half bottle of grappa from one of the tables. It seemed the worst thing in the world if he were a cousin, but I didn't ask, I only thought it, and my cheeks glowed like the stove burners we had in the Pocono house, the glass kind without iron that got hot and red behind your back.

You wait for me, he said, and left and came back with two juice glasses. He took the figs from my hands and put them in the cups and filled them with two inches of grappa. You say cheers? he said, and we sipped our grappa and I almost choked but first love like that inures you.

That was the year before the year my

parents died and if only I had known. But I did know. I knew for the whole sunny day; when at night we went back to the fig and it was swollen with one of the strongest liquors, I knew. When the boy kissed me — the tongue and the lips, more sensual than I'd imagined — I was drunk in a way that was more mature than any drunk I would ever be in the future and I knew that this was the first and last perfect day of my life. I wanted to tell Alice about that day. I wanted to rub her face in the cow-trampled grass. I wanted her to know everything that she had taken from me.

9

The next day I was hired at the health food store. Nothing had ever come so easily. A man called. His name was Jim and I would never meet him. He burped on the other end of the line. The phone call was supposed to be an interview but it seemed I was hired before we even spoke.

— We need someone every day. Can you work the whole day those days?

I was frying an egg on my yellow range. Every time I accepted a job I felt terrorized, like I was about to be sent to jail. For most, it's the opposite. The money is freeing, so they see the hours of work as a way out. I've had a strange relationship with money, as I've told you. I've been gifted things that are worth an entire year of steaming milk at a coffee shop.

— Yes, I said. When I flipped the egg, the yolk ran. I was so heartbroken that I stopped listening until Jim said the hourly rate. It was less than half a yoga class at the studio. In the news that week a lawmaker said that destitute Americans who complain about the price of health care should forgo buying the new phone they want and use the money on insurance instead.

— Sound good?

Out the window I saw River. He was loading heavy-looking panels into the back of his work truck. On the side it said SOLAR FORWARD. A sun was pushing a lawn mower. He wore a bandana and a white t-shirt. I watched his arms crank in the sunlight.

— Yes, I said. When should I start?

— Tomorrow.

— Perfect.

I figured I could always quit right away. Really I had just wanted to get off the phone. The previous night Leonard hadn't left until I yawned three times, the final time very aggressively. I'd washed all the dishes. I'd banged around so many pans, but he either didn't take the hint or didn't want to. After he left I'd taken two pills and tried not to think of Vic's boy.

I went outside. I walked by River while he was in the back of his truck, and I opened my car. Nothing made sense to grab. I picked up a pack of gum from the hairy console.

— Hey, he said. He was so awake. I smiled and shielded my eyes from the light and hated myself for waking up late almost every day of my life.

— So weird, I had a dream about you.

— Oh?

— Yeah. You were this wolf lady. Ha. Not in a bad way. Because of that song, I guess. You tore through the house looking for blankets, which is nuts because of how hot it's been.

The kid in New York, Jack, had been just like this. Young boys make you feel wanted but also like they could take you or leave you. Jack had long balls that hung like Dalí's clocks. He was unembarrassed about them. He would come to my apartment from the place he shared in Hoboken with two other boys. He would say my apartment was in violation of a fun code. It had not had enough fun for weeks. When I missed him, I wrote, all in lowercase, something about something I had to show him.

Are you trying to lure me into your city fort? he replied.

i don't know, am i? it's just that the city fort is buckling under the weight of its lack-of-fun-code violation. it needs to be violated . . .

Vic knew about Jack. He was the one who gave him the name *the kid*. He used to call

105

me that until I started seeing someone so young. Are you going to get ravaged by the kid this weekend? Vic would ask. I told Vic about Jack's long coral balls. He would ask if I served the kid cookies and milk after we fucked. If he sensed my anger he would say, Just joshing, kid. A woman like you will always be a girl. He's the luckiest dope in the world until you're through with him.

River was even more attractive than Jack had been. I laughed off his dream even though it had the power to make me feel gamy. I told him to have a good day at work and I walked back to my door in a way that would make him look at my backside. I was wearing small gray pajama shorts. The pills hit and my head went wavy.

Just inside the door, I pressed medium-hard with two fingers up between my thighs. I could have come like that, right then. I wanted to and then call Vic, say there was a new kid on the block. I felt sick to my stomach.

I didn't know how to dress for my first day of work at the health café. I'd always wished I didn't care so much. I have my mother's clothes to give you and a few of my favorite pieces. You can throw it all away but I found it's nice to have fabric. It stores memory in an accessible way.

I parked in the small lot. My Dodge looked old and sad next to two impudent convertibles. I walked by the studio but did not look inside. It was daunting to know she was in there. I imagined her sitting on the bench made of a single tree, my mother and my father flanking her. They would be talking about me as though I wouldn't understand something. Picturing the three of them together was one of the most sordid things I had ever done.

When I walked in, Natalia was rinsing mugs in the immense silver sink.

— How are you? I said, looking into her big Bambi eyes.

— Uh, good, she said, and asked if I wanted a coffee, which was nice. It seemed we were going to pretend the accident we'd witnessed together had never happened. I could tell she was nervous to be training someone nearly two decades older than she was.

I half-listened about everything except the coffee machine and the cash register. Both things had so many parts and I was nervous to make a mistake. Natalia was not a good teacher. She spoke too quietly and too quickly and hurried over the important things. To help her relax, I asked where she

107

was from. She was so stupid.

— Salinas, she said. My dad works on a farm. It was the most she volunteered. She asked absolutely nothing of me.

She came very close to me while demonstrating a knob under the La Marzocco. She smelled like drugstore vanilla perfume. When she texted on her phone, her pretty pink nails stabbed the screen adroitly. I flipped through the manual for the coffee machine. I read the ingredients on the chocolate bars.

Around noon the bell over the door jingled and a man walked in. He was in his fifties and wrecked and seedy and handsome.

— How are you doing, Natalia? he said.

— Good, thanks, she said.

He looked at me. How are you? he said. He said it like he didn't need a response, but it was enough for me. I nodded and smiled.

I ferried the dry mugs from the rack onto the shelf. He ordered a green soup from Natalia. The cook, a shrewd Mexican woman named Rita, made it once every three days and it lived in a vat. It was a puree of asparagus, kale, and onions, and full of butter. The whole canyon was crazy for it. He went to sit outside.

I'd been struck by him and suddenly realized why. He reminded me of Big Sky, of what Big Sky would look like a decade from now. Alice would make me see these things, my penchant for a certain flavor of man, a certain type of imbecilic self-destruction.

— Is he a regular? I asked Natalia.

— Dean. Yeah. He used to be famous.

— What's his last name?

— Um, I don't know. But he was Doctor Johnson? The lead singer of them.

When his soup was ready, I told Natalia I'd take it out to him. I didn't know much about Doctor Johnson. I knew the song "Jessica's Father" and that they sang Shel Silverstein poems.

He was leaning back in his chair, his jeaned legs spread. His loafers were expensive and his brows reddish, as though he'd tried to dye them from gray. I could tell he'd had eyelid surgery and I can't explain why I was attracted to old, young-acting men. I also liked big noses, dishonest expressions. Men who couldn't be bothered but were friendly. Ego. Former high school quarterbacks. Cheaters.

— Goddess soup, I said, setting the earthenware bowl down in front of him.

— Thank you. You're new?

— I am.

— New to the Canyon as well?

— Yes.

— How do you like it so far?

— Oh, I don't know.

—That was a stupid question. I hate when people ask me stupid questions like that.

He smiled. I could see clear through to his young self. I saw older men the way they still saw themselves. That was why they liked me so much; I was a solar panel, absorbing and refracting and reenergizing.

— It can get strange up here, he said, but it's the best air in Los Angeles. He had an accent like just about every man I've liked.

Big Sky, of course, had an accent. He'd grown up down south. His voice was heroic. Accents are also a lie.

I met him in a nice bar on Wall Street, beneath street level, with hanging lamplights and red leather banquettes. This was during Vic. Almost always in my life there had been one man I desired who was giving me nothing at the same time that there was another who didn't move me but from whom I was taking very much.

Big Sky wore a cashmere jacket. Underneath it a fishing vest. The second I saw him I thought, Here is the greatest man in all of Manhattan. We made eye contact from thirty feet away. He had blue eyes, too, a deeper blue, even, than my father's. I began

110

to sweat as he walked toward me. Instant dampness under my arms. I had a plate of oysters in front of me and a glass of Gewürztraminer. He was on his way to the bathroom. He purposefully paused near my seat and the bartender introduced us. We said hello and right away we both knew what was between us.

On his way back from the bathroom he asked me about my oysters. Like an asshole, I talked about why I preferred West Coast to East. After politely but ludicrously asking if he could try one, he slurped it off its rocky beach like he knew how much I already wanted him.

He was there with a friend, a blondish man who was married and lived in the suburbs. The chasm between them was considerable. The friend was a regular guy with a regular tie. He took the train into work and his wife didn't have to worry.

I wondered if Big Sky's wife had to worry. I saw a picture of her when he showed me one of his young son. Long brown hair, in shape, uninteresting legs. She'd held a good job in the city, something creative, before quitting it for the kid. She was from a city and from a family that made Big Sky proud. She ran every morning around the park.

Big Sky pointed at his friend with a gorgeous thumb.

— He still gives up shit for Lent, isn't that tragic?

I laughed too loud.

The bar, intended for after-work cocktails, began to clear at nine p.m. The bartender opened the door and I felt the cool spring air. I got cold. I was wearing a sleeveless dress. A man I knew from the bar came by with his coat, a thick patchwork pelt, and draped it across my shoulders. It was heavy and it laid across my slight frame in a tyrannical manner. It wasn't a nice gesture. It was like he'd rolled his balls out and stretched the sticky dough against me. Men were always putting their coats around my shoulders. They mark their territory that way. It's better to freeze to death.

Big Sky had been in the bathroom or making a phone call and I'd thought of nothing but him, but also I had tolerated other people's conversation because the first day you meet someone like that you still have your self-decency, you still can have an interest in life beyond every tendril of their hair.

He came back and said, What's this, and he took the pelt off of me and replaced it with his cashmere jacket; he laid it across my shoulders and one of his fingers brushed my flesh and he said, That's better, isn't it?

The friend left because he had to catch a train. We talked for an hour more. He worked in finance. He spoke candidly of what was going on, the collapse of Wall Street.

He looked me in the eye over his bitter-smelling beer and said that he and all the men down there were a sad bunch of losers.

— We don't create shit, he whispered at my mouth. We trade paper. It's all worthless.

It was the same type of thing Tim had said, but Big Sky made even more money. His dishonor was grander, sexier.

When men tell you they are pieces of shit, when they tell you they are scumbags, they do it because they subconsciously know that you are hooked. It hooks you more. They push you away to pull you in and the most terrible thing is they don't even do it on purpose.

I told him I needed an accountant, that I was in the midst of my own collapse. He smiled and said he had the best one. He said he himself would give me sound investment advice. He said his accountant was the type who should go to jail but never would.

— Write or call me, he said. I'll make an intro.

Then he said he should go, too. He wrote down his full name and number and email on an order slip.

I went home that night feeling beautiful.

A couple of days later I wrote to him. My note was all business and he wrote back, *How about a drink next wed?*

He wasn't much for punctuation, which I liked because it showed confidence and carelessness. *Sure,* I said, *same place?*

He wrote, *How about spring lounge?*

It was north about twenty blocks from the people he worked with and the place I lived.

I walked the whole way there. It was a bright day in early spring. I wore a leather halter top and jeans and riding boots. I'd pulled my hair into two loose pigtails. Some hypochondriacal thoughts were passing through. Cancer, mostly. A black-and-blue on the inside of my arm that I thought could be the first sign of blood cancer. A sharp headache meant it had now spread to my brain. I soothed myself with the thought that if I were dying it would all be over soon, including not being able to have this man who was the only man for whom I had ever felt this strongly, even after just one meeting.

114

I thought about turning back. But I looked good and a part of me knew I needed this, that you can't turn away from feelings like this even if they're wrong. I called my aunt, who told me to go inside. That, for God's sake, it was the most beautiful day.

So I did. And right away I saw him. Spring Lounge had these old picture windows with fly wings in the seams, and the Easter-time sun was shining on his face. All the anxiety left me at once. He looked imaginary, wearing the same fishing vest and a pair of cargo pants. I would come to know and love it as his uniform. He'd ordered us two beers and held a corner table.

— I hope you don't mind, he said, I took the liberty of ordering you a Stella.

I said hello and thanked him and said I had to run to the bathroom, where I looked in the mirror and screamed at my reflection. John Fogerty drowned me out. I was in love.

We had a couple of beers and everyone in there was less excited than we were. We glowed together. I was proud of a lot of things about myself. The way I always knew how to make a dish taste better with salt or turmeric or Parmesan or lemon zest or cardamom. How I could make another person feel comfortable or feel smaller. How

115

I was rarely drunk or out of my own control. I was even proud of my pain. It made me enigmatic and aware. But I had never felt better about myself than I did in that moment, with the sunlight coming through those filthy pretty windows, sitting next to that man.

— This secret accountant of yours sounds like he will be unbelievably helpful. I've gotten myself into a number of untenable situations.

— Listen, he said, leaning his chest across the table. Truth is, I'm not just trying to help you. Look, I was excited to come here. Looked forward to it all damn week.

I blushed and then we did what people in illicit situations do. We pretended something untoward hadn't been said but enjoyed all around ourselves the warmth of it.

I tried several times to pay for a beer of his. As a thank-you, I said. But he kept saying, No, that's not how it works. Gentlemen pay.

— I'm a certain type of woman.

— Okay, buy me a drink somewhere else, certain type of woman. This place is getting beat.

We walked to Tom & Jerry's, a bar that had the same bearded bartender for years. On the walk he smoked a one-hitter. He

116

smoked good pot. I thought it was sexy. We walked by a church in SoHo and he told me about its engravings. He knew the histories of places. He knew good bars. He was of an indeterminate wealth, somewhere in between a two-bedroom in Chelsea and a classic six on the Upper West Side. I said something funny and he laughed and then he stopped us on a block of Manhattan that I would, in the desolate future, walk over and over, trying to reconstruct the essence of that first night. I would stand in the very spot he'd stopped us.

— This is so weird. Seriously. It's like the best first date I've ever had. Only I'm married.

I was so happy. I was too happy. I should have played it cool. I'd have given anything to go back and play it cool. At Tom & Jerry's we sat side by side at the bar. We drank gin and tonics. He complimented my hair and my intelligence. Our thighs were touching, my jeans against his loose khakis. I felt the heat of his leg through the material. I had never wanted someone more.

— I have never wanted someone more, he said. I have a wife and a baby at home. I have to get out of here.

He paid and we left and outside it had started to rain, turning the streets darker.

That little stretch of Elizabeth Street would become hallowed. Within months it would feel like the love of my life was buried under the cigarette packs and the fallen magnolia blossoms. He hailed a cab. One flew past.

— We didn't want that one anyway, he said, laughing.

A second came and stopped and Big Sky opened the door for me. As I was getting in, he took hold of my shoulder.

— Hey, he said. Jesus.

His face looked like a wolf's. He had a long nose and clever blue eyes. He didn't look like a liar. His self-centeredness was sexy.

— May I kiss you on the mouth? he said.

The cabdriver's impatience was palpable but nobody else mattered.

— Yes.

He came forward. My heart was a rock knocking in my chest. The kiss was open-mouthed but tongueless and lasted no longer than three seconds. It was more sex, that kiss, than any sex I had ever had. Maybe it wasn't love, but I don't know what to call how I felt inside that moment.

Do you see how it's a cycle? I was standing there with the lead singer of a seventies folk band. I was attracted to this faded man because he looked like Big Sky, because I craved men who had big happy lives of which I would never be a part. The experience of Big Sky gored me. In a way, Big Sky was responsible for Vic's death. One man like that can be responsible for every big and small thing in a woman's life. A woman he isn't married to whom he doesn't think very much about at all. But it's not the man's fault. The man is nothing. It's what you think you are missing inside of yourself. I promise that you are missing nothing.

I didn't know if I could bear to see Alice again. I like to think I was lying in wait, sharpening a knife, but really I was only postponing the last thing I had left to fear. I considered writing her a letter.

Dear Alice,
I have had a lifetime of suffering. From what I know, you have not. I have something to tell you, and you have something to tell me. I am all alone. I thought about killing myself but I wanted to meet you first. I am depraved. I hope you like me.

On the way home from the café I passed River walking with a dog. They were on the crest of the lookout just before Comanche.

The sun and the greens framed them.

The dog was a mutt, gray and brown with a beard like a schnauzer and robust as a shepherd. River came to my open window and said, This is Kurt.

He told me Kurt was a stray he'd found on the stairs hike at Murphy Ranch Trail. Men and their dogs. They will bring them everywhere and never forsake them. Unlike their women, children. Dogs want nothing of a man except all the things a man wants to give.

He had no leash for the dog, yet the animal waited pleasantly beside him while we spoke. There's something admirable about a man who can keep a stray dog at his heels. It made me want to have sex with him.

Every single thing I did was to make that young man want to fuck me. Who are these people who have platonic conversations? They are adults.

I rubbed my chin against my shoulder, exposing half of my neck. I couldn't tell if that had turned him on, so I did twenty more things. Envying another woman made me ugly with need.

I had to leave first — you must always be the first to go — so I said goodbye and drove away like a person who drives unsafely. I passed the house with the aluminum gate all the way around. Palm trees rose from behind the metal and bougainvillea strangled itself against it. You couldn't see anything in the distance. Much of the Canyon was that way. Behind a wall of trees and fencing there might be a glorious house with good cars in the driveway, horses in the distance, and crops; or there might be a commune like ours, sandy adobe structures, the occult. That house, Lenny had told me, was the site of a former swinger's haven called Sandstone. Communal bathrooms and sleeping areas, hot tubs, naked women rinsing their legs in natural springs. You would go for a daytime interview, and if you were deemed suitable, you could come back that night for a trial evening. If you were trim and attractive, you might be invited to become a member. Lenny talked about it like he'd only heard tales and never visited. But he spoke in great detail of tan women with cornrows jumping on cowhide trampolines as the sun fell behind the red mountains.

Just then, as I passed the rusting gate, I had the premonition that I was going to become a killer.

10

One of the reasons I worked in the hospital downtown was to desensitize myself. I would still wake screaming in the night, feeling around my bed for their bodies. So I watched as emergency room doctors spoke to one another casually, arms swinging imaginary golf clubs while all around them short and long lives were ending. I went to work in a hospital so that I might learn the drill. That death was common and not so bad.

It didn't work. One September afternoon a woman came to find her pigtailed child intubated. The child had pursued a butterfly across the street, away from the teachers at the playground. She'd been hit by a bus. The mother could not understand. But a bus is so big, she kept saying. The nurses didn't get it, but I did. She meant, how could a bus only *hit* her daughter's twig body? *Merely* hit. I begged the nurses to undo the child's hair and they snarled at me like I was an idiot. But I knew that when the mother saw the pigtails, she wouldn't be able to make any rational decisions.

What worked better for desensitization was kicking Tim.

Tim worked at AIG and this was during the collapse of Wall Street. So many more terrible things will come to pass after the collapse that I wonder how big a deal it will seem to you. But back then it was a dark time for dark people. The men who'd been pulling in millions a year were suddenly broke or scared. I met him in a restaurant. I was always eating alone those days before Vic.

Tim was with another man like him and they were seated beside me at the bar where, a few months later, I would meet Big Sky.

I'd heard them order a 1966 bottle of French first growth, at fourteen hundred dollars. The other man had seventeen stents in his heart. He ordered the steak and ate the fries off Tim's plate. Elvis was playing from the sound system. The bartender poured the wine into a goosenecked carafe. It was a little darker than old blood.

They offered me a taste. I said no, no, no and they insisted. The bartender got me a glass and watched Tim to see when he should quit the pour. Think of how terrible that feels, to not even want the wine and then be metered out some amount. To be sized up. Was I worth a $100 taste, or a $250 taste?

— How do you like it? Tim asked me. He was balding and wore a shirt with a contrast collar. He had large teeth and the kinds of eyes that looked like they were in the middle of a sex act no matter what he was doing.

— It's no Yellow Tail, I said.

They didn't know to laugh right away. Eventually Tim did because I gave him one of my gazes.

I stayed for another glass. The bartender wiped down the bar, and the smell of rib eye faded out the door.

Back then the blue-collar men who worked at Ford would think of Wall Street and their veins would bulge. They thought of bars like that one, labels of wine that worked out to $350 a goblet. It's not that I was sympathetic to men like Tim — there was no pitiable plight of the Wall Streeter — but the other end of it was oversimplified. The hatred was misplaced and men like Tim, if anything, wanted you to hate them. If you told them they were not evil, they would say that yes they were. Men don't necessarily want to be the bad guys, but they don't want to be the ordinary ones, either.

— Down here, Tim said to me, gesturing around the bar, at the bottles of men and the glasses of women, you know at the end of every day whether we had a good day or a bad day. You can tell the market by the mood of this bar. We work hard and we play hard and at night we're either celebrating or we're drowning our sorrows. It's not healthy. It's like a boxer after a round; good or bad, it makes you dysfunctional.

I suppose I liked his honesty. He was somewhat guileless and somewhat a gentleman. Vic would end up being similar. All these paltry stand-ins for my father.

When I went to pay my check that night my card was declined. This had never happened to me or, I should say, this was just the beginning of those sorts of things happening.

— I've got her, Tim said to the bartender. He had a platinum card between his knuckles like a blade.

It wasn't inexpensive, my bill. I'd ordered the foie gras and the steak tartare, plus a few glasses of wine. Eating like that was the only way I knew to console myself.

He took my phone number and I took his and the next day I was about to write to him to say that I would send a check to his work address. But he wrote to me first. He asked me if I knew any women, any girls, for a friend of his who liked to be kicked.

Another message followed right away.

I'm the friend, it said, with a little winking face.

I looked around my room. It was an attractive and clean apartment that I had recently moved into and feared losing. It was barely furnished because I'd lost the job at the hospital downtown. I hadn't lost it. The contract had run out. The previous week I'd canceled my cable service and returned two dresses I'd already worn to Bergdorf. They accepted anything in those days, with the tags gone, with the smell of cigarettes. It wasn't without a price, of course. The women would gather the garment into their arms, sniff it, and look back at you like you were trash.

I think I have a friend who might be interested, I wrote back.

One minute later I wrote, *I'm the friend.*

Kicking Tim was healthier than all those steak dinners with Vic.

— Like just straight with the toe?

I was standing in his hotel room at the Soho Grand. The room was very small but tasteful and dark. He was up against a wall in his nice work shirt and tasteful boxers. Black, thin socks rose up the calves of his pale legs. I wore a pin-striped skirt suit with a high slit and a pair of heels he'd just bought me in the Meatpacking District. I was upset because I'd let him pick them out. Peep-toed black patent-leather sling-backs. Stupid.

He nodded quickly because to give instruction would have gone against the spirit of the thing.

Primly I brought my leg back, then smashed his testicles against the minibar behind him that held the Scotch decanter and rocks glasses. The room twinkled with the sound. He groaned but did not cover himself. Nor did he smile or look like he was in sexual congress with his pain.

That first night, with the Talking Heads in the background, I kicked him six times. Afterward he spooned me in bed. I felt him small and hard against my skirt suit. He moved in little increments, up and down instead of back and forth. He kept his palm flat against the side of my waist, the palm paralyzed like a stroke victim's. We sat for an early dinner at the restaurant inside the hotel. I ate an octopus appetizer and he had the endive salad. The leaves were glossed demurely in oil and lemon. We both drank water, then he went back to Connecticut and I went home to my studio, one thousand dollars in hand.

We never know how much worse it will be. That's the greatest gift we have in life. As a child you'll scrape your knee and the first time will sting terribly. It will shine like mica as it starts to heal. For maybe a week you'll look at it and think, God, that hurt. But then you will lose a child out of you. Maybe you should stop listening to me. Sometimes I think you won't endure life without what I've learned, and other times I believe the exact opposite. But mostly what I think is that you won't love me.

11

On my third day at the health café I worked alone. Natalia was gone. She and her braids and cowboy hat had gone home to Salinas for the summer.

The rumpled folksinger came in at noon. He ordered the green soup and waited inside with me. I hadn't given a sign that I knew who he was. I knew eventually he would bring it up now that Natalia was gone.

— When Doctor Johnson was a thing — do you know any of our songs, "Jessica's Father" —

— Yes, I do. I'm a fan.

— Are you?

— No.

He was leaning on my counter and looking up at the ceiling between us. He wore expensive casual pants and leather sandals and wasn't offended.

— When we were a thing, we did a show

129

at the Theatricum Botanicum down the way. We stayed with a couple of friends on Tuna Canyon and they brought us to lunch at this café. A beautiful young woman was slinging beans and rice. There was leche in the icebox and Pepsi-Cola. That's it. Now look.

My phone vibrated on the counter. *Vic's Wife,* said the caller ID. The warming timer dinged on Dean's soup. Some of the soup bowls were thick and brown. Others were shallow, light pink, and very thin. We weren't supposed to let the customers bring the latter outside themselves.

— I can follow you to the table, I said. I was holding the hot bowl of soup and my phone vibrated again.

— Do you want to get that?

— No, thanks.

— It's Vic's wife, he said, smiling. She seems anxious to get in touch.

— Could be a follow-up to "Jessica's Father," I said, and he laughed but not enough.

There was an old woman at a table in the shade. She wore glasses and had fuzzy ringlets of strawberry hair. I'd sold her a rooibos hours ago and she was only halfway through with it. She wasn't sweating. She'd told me she kept flamingos in a garden of flamingos, and if I ever wanted to visit I

130

needn't call ahead.

Dean Johnson sat down and jerked his thumb in the direction of the lady.

— If you're ever lost, the old ladies are how you know where you've landed. In Beverly Hills the biddies look like whippets. Here in the Canyon they're shriveled hippies with bright red hair.

I placed his soup bowl before him. He looked at my neck as I did. I liked it when good-looking men checked out the less obvious parts of my body.

When I got back to the counter there was a text message from Vic's wife.

CALL ME CUNT

Alice came in while I was on a phone app that took a picture of an item and automatically affixed a description and a title, and then you named your price. Somewhere, within fifteen miles, someone who wanted your Package of Two Krazy Glue messaged you that they would come and pick it up.

I was going around the café taking pictures of the bukedo and raffia baskets. I was setting the price at ten dollars more than their list. The plan was to meet interested parties after work and pocket the profit. I'd pinned my location as Beverly Hills and used for my profile picture a shot of myself in

Sayulita. Hair in braids, white bikini, sitting on the sand in lotus pose.

When she walked in I tripped on a basket and nearly fell. I wasn't prepared for her to be the one to come to me. I keep talking about her beauty and I don't want you to think it matters as much as it does. It only mattered too much to me.

I could smell her sweat. It reminded me of my father's. I said hello and she said it back.

Her eyebrows were bushy. Her hair looked sandy and sweaty. I was not one of those heterosexual women who said they were attracted to other women. Who were these women? I could see in their faces; they were trying to impress whoever was listening — men — with their fluidity. I understood the inclination, of course. But with Alice what I felt was very pure and shocking to me. When I looked at Alice, I didn't want her. What I wanted was to eat her, swallow her, and become her. I wanted to reach down between my legs and feel her cunt there.

Nervously I asked her what she would like to eat, and brightly she said, The green soup, please! Her manner was unhurried and self-assured. I'd never lived in the same place long enough to be meaningfully conversant with the grocery clerk.

I felt embarrassed, like she could see inside me — my roiling thoughts, my loneliness, my suffering, and most humiliatingly, my petty jealousy.

She walked to the fridge, selected a Tecate, and brought it to the counter. She tucked the beer under one bare arm and reached around to the back pocket of her leggings. She handed me a crumpled ten-dollar bill and looked at my face with intent. She moved in so close that I could smell her apple shampoo. I had the instinct to move away but I suppressed it. Or she suppressed it for me. I don't know how it happened, but our two heads hovered above the counter like magnets.

— Can I ask you a question? she said finally. I could feel the mist of her breath on my lips. I nodded. I felt expired. She sighed deeply and smiled as though she'd won the first interaction. In fact, she had.

Do you shave your face? she said.

I despised the requisite stunned look on my face. I said no and she smiled.

— I ask because your cheeks and chin are incredibly smooth. Apparently women everywhere are shaving their faces. They say the reason men look younger than women is because they shave every day. They remove the top epidermal layer so the skin is always regenerating.

Alice touched her face.

— I grew fur this year, she said.

— Well, I said, we're animals. I tried to sound dispassionate, but I felt exploded. I wanted to bolt. I'd spent a lifetime not caring what women thought of me. But that was merely the lie I told myself to tell others. The truth was that I was afraid of women.

When I brought her soup outside, she engaged me further, nodding to the seat across from her and saying, Did you want to sit down? as though I were the one engaging her and not the other way around. She wore small pink rose earrings that I recognized from somewhere.

The patio abutted the face of a small mountain. The rocks near our cheeks gave the feeling of enclosure, privacy, and claustrophobia. It was my lunch hour and it was all right that I'd put a sign on the door that said BE BACK SOON in seventies-style script. It was allowed, but this was the first time I'd done it in the several days I'd been working. I drank a Tecate as well. I had never enjoyed a beer so much.

I told her I was new to the Canyon and she could tell there was a reason I'd left New York but, like all self-assured people,

134

she didn't ask. She was startlingly forthcoming right away, which made her an alluring and warm conversationalist. At the same time she seemed difficult to please and too young to be so smart.

A well-built man with blond hair walked by the café.

— Hard eight, she said.

— What?

— There are so few attractive men up here. There are maybe two.

The man turned to look at us. She looked back at him. I think she could have broken up any marriage.

— Yes, I've noticed, and I've only been here a few days.

— We aren't supposed to like men these days, she said to me, still looking at the man.

— The wrong ones, anyway.

She nodded, turning back to face me, leaving the man standing there as though she'd never seen him to begin with. But, she said, the right ones are boring.

— The right ones don't lie. They don't forget to call.

— Who wants a man you can trust?

There was a pause. Then we smiled and laughed. There's nothing more sensual than a woman who makes you work to make her smile.

— Is it not better here? I asked.

— You mean men? Better than New York? It depends on what you want.

— I don't know if I want anything anymore. I'm just curious.

In those first few moments I felt a volcanic connection to Alice unlike anything in my past. It was stronger than any link I'd had with a man, with my parents, with Gosia, even.

— What kinds of men do you like? she asked.

— Too many.

— We shouldn't be talking about men. What if they see us? We should be talking about careers and emotional fulfillment.

— Let's talk about careers, I said, gesturing around the silly café. The shining crystals. She laughed again but it felt like luck, like I was playing a game of pinball with a broken flipper bat and the flaw was working in my favor.

— The last man I was with was a sailor, she said.

— A sailor.

— No, you know, one of these guys whose father has a boat. He had a regular job, whatever than means in Los Angeles. And then on the weekends he sailed around.

— Oh. A *sailor*.

136

— Precisely. He said that most of the time he was imagining me getting fucked by somebody else. That he was watching.

— I think I like that, too, I said, remembering the way I nearly came at the thought of River and a young girl having sex in a car.

— Most women like it, Alice said. I think they like it more than men do. They just don't want to access that part of their brain.

She walked out to the lot and came back with a pack of American Spirits and a book of matches from an osteria in Rome. She slid the pack across the table and I shook my head. I couldn't believe she smoked. I wondered if she was making a show of it because she was proud of the matches. A little cartoon boy in overalls with apple cheeks, eating grapes on the hood of a powder-blue Fiat. Then I realized that was something only I would have done, and I spent the next few moments so involved with hating myself that Alice thought I was bored. We told each other our names and there was no starlight. Hearing my name didn't ding her.

— Are you looking to date? she asked. Because you won't be able to do it up here. You'll have to go to Santa Monica. Or Hollywood, if you don't mind lice.

I told her I wasn't looking for anyone and she said we are always looking for someone and I hated her and I asked about her type.

— I don't know the types I like. I have to go through all of them before I can settle on the one I know I need to be with. I'm nearly through with the American WASP.

— You're done with sailors.

— Yes. Sailors. Check.

— I want a cowboy, I said.

— Cowboys don't exist. How about a logger? A stone-cold-sober logger. Charlie — the sailor — his profile was very well written. That's what got me. When we were in bed and he was asking me to tell him how much I loved his cock, I got to wondering. I found out later a friend of his from New York wrote it. I told Charlie his profile headline should have said, *Neptune, God of the Sea, Seeking Yoga Barbie to Have Conversational Sex With.*

— You learned a new art.

— I should include it in my profile. As a skill. Alice held out her palm like a placard and said, I can also do this.

We talked about certain bars to show each other we spoke the same language. We talked about plantains and books and elections and melatonin and shaving our faces but eventually we returned to the topic of

138

men. Boys. We were young girls talking about boys. I'd always been afraid that thinking about men meant I wasn't a strong woman. But Alice was strong and she liked to address the picayune strategies involved in replying to a message. She endeavored, for example, to always use at least one word less than the other person did in a previous text. She said women were considered strong these days only if they didn't talk about things they loved that didn't love them, if they didn't get hurt or allow themselves to be occasionally humiliated at their own hands when, really, strength was being unashamed to want what you want.

— Your turn, she said. What was your last relationship?

— I don't know which to tell you.

— Two at once?

I nodded.

— Tell them both but start with the one that you actually wanted to fuck.

I wanted to say, How did you know? But you can't compliment a new person too much at the start of a relationship. It will affect the balance of power.

She smiled and seductively took a drag of her cigarette. I told her about Big Sky. Our first meeting. I told her how he ended the evening by asking whether he could kiss me on the mouth. That's erotic, she said. What an erotic way to put it. I told her how that weekend I died the death of the single woman obsessed with the married man. I imagined that he and his wife were at farmers' markets picking out misshapen eggplants and herbs for pasta sauce. I walked and walked and walked. I tried to "find" him. On Friday I emailed him. He responded wanly, shortly. I felt like I'd not only exaggerated the emotions of our evening together but wholly invented them. I ate nothing but broccoli sprouts and broccoli florets rolled up in flaxseed wraps. My stomach felt taut and I thought, But what for, now. The weekend turned out to be beautiful. Everywhere I went, mothers bought juicy oranges and great stalks of leek and fathers pushed tiny butts on swings in the sunshine. Nobody was smoking cigarettes. All that weekend every ten minutes I tapped my code into my phone and opened my email to find nothing. I wasn't sure what I was expecting.

— Perhaps, Alice said, you were expecting *Sorry I was short on Friday, my wife was holding our baby in my face so I couldn't write you a long note. I missed you very much.*

—Yes, I said, that must be exactly what I was expecting. Nothing came. I started waiting thirty minutes in between check-ins to increase the likelihood of a reply. I imagined even my phone was through with me. It hungered for a more self-assured owner. Monday came. The air turned cooler and I felt calmer.

— Let me guess, Alice said.

I nodded.

— It's measurable by science, she said. A man will know the very moment you have stopped obsessing. The instant.

— An email popped up, I continued. His name. *Come by Harry's for a drink later?* I felt dizzy and at first not even grateful. My throat was dried out. How could I have felt so strongly so quickly? One of my friends turned every one-night stand into the love of her life. But not me. I had never met a man like this one. I love you, I said to my phone. Holy shit, I love you.

Alice was pitched forward in her seat. It felt good that someone understood the passion, that it was possible to feel strongly about a man after only one and a half meetings.

— I didn't reply to him for three hours. I showered and blew out my hair and applied an eye mask. Finally, at five, I wrote, *Sure. I'll come by. Great,* he wrote right away. *I'm walking down there now.*

— Good for you for waiting so long. But isn't it terrible? This is how we applaud ourselves. I bet you wanted to hit him and fuck him at the same time. What did you wear?

— A long-sleeved floral dress that came to the middle of my thighs and cowboy boots. I looked like a farmer's slutty daughter.

She smiled and shook her head.

— Please, I said. I know.

— Sorry. Continue.

— He was already seated, two martinis deep, with the same blond friend. Martini Monday, someone said, and glasses clinked. He looked at me.

— You look like you're going to cry.

— The bartender said, Well, hello, missy, and Big Sky smiled. His friend left after a hello and a few last sips. I'm always impressed that men know when to leave.

— Do you think they discussed it beforehand?

— I don't think so, no.

— God, this is sexy.

— Then we were alone. We looked at each other for several seconds. I saw him look at my legs and relished the feeling of power. And then he said, I thought of you all weekend.

— God bless him.

142

— He'd been at his family's home in the Catskills. In the basement he'd slipped a movie in the player, one he'd told me to watch, and he thought of me. He was building a fire, he said, and he thought of me. He was chopping down firewood and he thought of me. And you, he said, are such a BITCH. And he jabbed me lightly in the chest, right between my breasts, but politely. Because I didn't email him back right away.

— What a cocksucker!

— And there I was, I said, thinking of the long weekend I'd spent, the tap-tap-taps into my phone. How I'd done thirty walking lunges back and forth across my apartment floor, thinking that by the thirtieth one, he'd have responded to me. He reached for a greasy jar of bar cherries and said, I should be giving you one of these at a time. Instead here I am, passing you the whole goddamn jar at once.

— Was he drunk?

— Yes, but not like an asshole.

She said she understood exactly what I meant and what type of man he was. I went inside and brought out two more beers. I would have to replenish the register later. It was an hour of work I'd be paying back to the place, but I didn't care. When I returned, she was leaning back in her chair.

Her pose — shut but sun-searching eyes, long golden neck — belonged on a yacht.

— Thank you, she said, taking the beer. Please, get back to the story. Bated breath over here.

— We kissed, I said, right there in the bar he went to all the time. The bartender was down at the other end. I leaned in to him, put my hands on his thighs lightly. He left a hundred-dollar bill on a forty-dollar check. I hated myself for being impressed. We walked outside and he threw me up against a brick wall and I swung my legs around his waist and we kissed some more. On the way back to my place, a car honked as we crossed Broadway. We laughed at the car as it flew by, knowing whoever was in it was less excited to be alive. We were holding hands and I felt high. I thought, I'll always remember how beautiful a moment this is. I will always be grateful for this.

— And are you?

I smiled and shook my head. I wanted to cry, remembering.

— He sounds like a fucker. I love fuckers, too. Tell me the rest. I need another cigarette.

— In my apartment we went down on each other. We were all over each other. We kissed like animals. We knocked into my

144

stupid liquor shelf and it wobbled and in particular I noticed the Rémy Martin on the shelf. It had belonged to my parents and I never touched it or let anyone else touch it. But in the near future, I would let him drink it. We didn't fuck, he only went down on me, and I faked an orgasm because I was in love. Afterward, we were practicing a few yoga positions together, downward dog into crow jumping back into chaturanga, when his cell phone rang. His breathing was heavy but he clipped it somehow: Hey, honey. Yeah, no, don't sweat it. I'm gonna bring home a pizza. Yeah, coming right now. Okay, love you. He smiled as though nothing had happened. It wasn't that he was cruel but that he was tipsy and the moment didn't call for being strange or for acknowledgment. I followed his lead. We laughed some more about some things and he said, Well. And I said, Bye. And he said, Easy, girl. I'm going.

— The wife, Alice said, like it was a vital video game character we'd forgotten to include in our game of capture the banker.

— What about her? I asked, trying to be neutral, wondering whether she was on the wives' side or the other side.

— She's at home, throwing out dead coffee filters from the morning. She's too exhausted to cook and she doesn't think for a moment her husband is in a crow pose at some slut's apartment.

— You're judging me, I said.

— Of course I'm not. Morality is uninteresting. I'm intrigued by the idiocy of trust. I'll never trust a man I love. In fact, if I trust him, it will mean I don't love him enough. And a man should never trust me. Please, go on. I'm rapt. I keep interrupting because I'm rapt as fuck.

— Ten minutes later my heart was still beating hard and my rug was still a quarter up the wall and an email came through from his name. *Sweet dreams.*

— Fucker! They all should die.

— I was so *happy.* Because he'd left his Mets cap on my couch and his headphones. I went to bed without a pill and left my shades open and looked out at the moon. I was so happy.

— It's strange to think that there is some nice boy somewhere who wants to read us Pushkin and play records and not even fuck for a month.

She drank the rest of her beer down and threw her cigarette in the can. She rose and I counted her inches. She must have been five feet eight. Her mother was tall. Mine was not.

146

— I come in here a few times a week for lunch after class, she said. Will you be here tomorrow? I'd love to hear the rest.

I tried to seem flippant when I said that I was there every day. I watched her get into her car. It was a light green Prius. It felt so good to talk to her. I saw her arm out the window with a cigarette as she pulled onto the boulevard. The purple bougainvillea along the fences was washed blond by the sunlight. Happiness had come easily to her. She was a person who never had to make a haunting choice. Everything was laid out for her. She only fucked men with perceptibly clean dicks.

One of the best things about childhood is the lack of choices. Your parents make choices for you that you must inhabit. Even better is your lack of awareness. You have no conception of all the wrong choices that might have maimed you. Take the road to the left and you won't get run over by the car that will kill you if you take the road to the right.

The last time I was ignorant to the notion of choice was in the Poconos. It was 1989 and I was nearly eleven. I remember every single day before the day my life ended. I remember all the hot dogs and every sunset. We had a red cedar A-frame on an undeveloped lot. The Saw Creek Estates. The word *estate.* These ugly little summer and ski homes, linoleum and wall-to-wall oatmeal carpeting.

We never hung around the house anyway. We went to the Fernwood, the local hotel, to meet up with friends of my parents. There was a roller rink attached to the inn. My crisp, electrified memories of roller-skating make me want to kill myself. The sharp cuts on the rink floor. The smells of the pizza and the wood. I was so impressed by the teenage girls who worked there. Their rainbow socks and crimped hair. What they did after the rink closed.

For dinner we'd go to a steakhouse called the Big A. There was a huge iron bull over the door, and THE BIG A in red neon blinked like a beacon. That was where I grew my love for American taverns. Shoestring fries. Men drinking beer from thick mugs. Waitresses with bumpy faces. We never waited for a table yet the place was always packed.

Occasionally we went to a white-tablecloth place called Villa Volpe, which was cavernous like a catering hall. Waiters in bowties and more than five fish entrées on the menu. My parents took me now and then because I liked the idea of fancy things. I think about it all the time. How the fancy place of my youth could seem cheap to me now. Broke as I am.

There was a place right off I-90 that sold pierogies. My mother and I would share an order of six. I thought that we alone in the world knew about them. I didn't realize they were an ethnic food or that there might be variations. The little rings of scallion on top were thrilling. We ate in the sunlight by the window, sitting on stools and looking out at the passing cars. We dipped the pierogies into a plastic ramekin of sour cream. One time one of the pierogies was still frozen in the middle. I felt betrayed. We wouldn't have asked the kitchen to heat it up. I guess we tossed it in the garbage.

There was a flea market with funnel cakes, hubcaps, guns, go-carts, Mormons selling soap, candles, men in sleeveless shirts selling generators, patchwork quilts, old dolls with yarn hair, counterfeit Ninja Turtles, tin owls, pelts, hot grills with burgers, and Ziploc bags of homemade potato chips for fifty cents. We would always get the funnel cake. We would look around for the perfect amount of time and I would go home with a quartz crystal or a Civil War pin.

Occasionally on the fairgrounds there was a car show. I say *occasionally*, though I'm sure, like all things, it had a date and time.

But my parents seemed to happen up on things. They didn't plan. They were always on time for everything we needed to be on time for, but when it came to weekend events, especially in the Poconos, we would just get up and drive in the sun and if there was a car show then my dad would stop. He loved cars. He would talk to the owners about the transmission and he would peer inside the windows, blocking the sun from his eyes and getting close but never touching the vehicle. He understood the price of spotlessness. At home I wasn't allowed to touch the walls. Whenever I was angry at my parents, I would make a furious face and covertly press my palms against our cream walls, leaving prints that might not be discovered for years but would surely cause pain when they were.

But my favorite thing about the Poconos was the pool. There were two pools. One near our house, which abutted a lake with ducks and paddleboats. There was a logroll in the pool. Maybe it was only there once, but I remember vividly the feeling of not staying on for longer than a second. A terrible feeling that fades overnight so that by the next morning you feel good about your chances.

Then there was the other pool, in the

ritzier section of the Estates. This was called the Top of the World Pool. It was high up in the mountains and surrounded by trees and there was a bar and women who dropped their bathing-suit strings off their shoulders.

Inside the facility there were tennis courts, that pretty indoor green, the soft thudding of balls and the echoed grunts of men.

We went to the Top of the World sparingly. It was the more adult recreation center and my parents weren't so much day drinkers. I always felt they were keeping luxury from me and even from themselves.

The smell of the pool up there was deeper. The chlorine was richer. I know many kids love the smell of chlorine, though I wonder if they love it as much as I did. I suppose I'm laying a foundation for you. Another chlorine lover, loose in the world.

12

Vic's wife called again that night. I was in my kitchen. At night my damned house was tolerable. The glow from the lantern lamp over the sink was amber and comforting. I heard River throwing a ball for his dog outside. When I didn't pick up the call, Mary wrote, *Is my daughter there? Tell me, you slut.*

I looked for the daughter's Facebook page. I started with Vic's wife, who had not posted anything since four hours before her husband's death.

A friend of hers had recently tacked a Kahlil Gibran quote about death to Mary's page. I clicked on the friend's profile and read her most recent post.

I get up every morning and leave my 3 children to drive over an hour to work. I work some weekends. I give up that time with family and friends because I know that my work and the work of my organization make a difference. I can't travel to conflict zones but I can spend every day supporting lobbyists in DC to help prevent war and kids being separated from their moms (I would die if that happened) and overall make this a safer world for all. I believe with all my heart that intl peace matters to Americans and hope that Congress agrees.

You cannot be one of these, who says or writes these things, who needs others to think something about them.

I clicked around in Mary's profile to find a picture of Eleanor, the daughter, who was seventeen. Strawberry hair. Vic's wide, flat cheeks. She looked kind and smart, as Vic was. She didn't seem to have a boyfriend. She had thick calves and played softball.

If she were indeed coming for me, it made perfect sense. I severed her life with a snip-snip of my inconsiderate fingers. Most people don't worry about threats like those. Little girls don't kill people. They're just silly little girls. But almost no one understands a little girl. We begin hard as marbles.

I pictured this little girl in a small, clean car, crossing Texas with a ball gag and a knife. Just then, as I was lost in that thought, the door handle jiggled and I jumped.

It was only Leonard. He strode through, speaking as though he'd been speaking for a long time.

— Leonard! I shouted. Part of me wondered if it wasn't a ruse, if he wasn't fully cognizant.

— Oh, he said, seeing me at last.

— Jesus.

— Oh, dear. How sorry I am.

He touched the top of his forehead. It shone with perspiration. I looked at his hands. Many hands reminded me of my father's. In particular there was a gas station attendant down the street from the house where I grew up. The day I got my license, I drove past my old house. It had been sold to a family of six. As I approached the tall oak with the haphazard patch of tulips circling its trunk, I found them all outside. The dad was playing catch with one of the girls. The mother was drinking iced tea and smiling at her herd. Afterward I went to the gas station. The attendant remembered me, or rather, he remembered my father's car. He didn't ask me where my father was. He was Pakistani and quiet and warm and, when I looked in the side-view mirror, his hands on the gas pump were my father's hands. I'd have known them anywhere. I tipped the man more than he would make that week. He'd loved my father in the silent way that men love other men they see infrequently.

— Lenny, I said more gently, it's okay.

— It's Parkinson's *and* Alzheimer's.

— What?

— That I've got. Please don't tell the others. He pointed idly out my window, then gestured downstairs, toward Kevin's quarters.

— Oh. I won't.

— Even the doctor was stunned. He's an old Jew, too. He said, You must have done quite a lot wrong in your time. Ha!

— When did you find out?

— I've known.

In the distance we heard the coyotes howling. Their voices were bright and bony. At night in the canyon everything stilled. There was either a terrible wind or there was no movement at all.

Leonard looked around my house. He looked at the envelopes on my tables as though they were bits of lingerie. Most were overdue bills.

— You're a mysterious woman, Joan.

— You're a nosy old man.

— I may be. But I'm a rich nosy old man. Why don't you be nice to me, and you never know who remembers who in their will.

— You never know, I said, gripping the counter. I wanted money so badly. When I had money, I could drive away from myself.

He checked the time on a watch I'd never noticed, then jingled it at me.

— You see this, old girl?

— What?

— This timepiece is the only one of its kind. Patek Philippe 1939 Platinum. My father was a cunt. I figured he was going to bury himself with this watch. But he left it for me. The only thing he ever did. I don't think it was love, anyhow. This watch, old girl, is worth a lot of money.

— It doesn't look it.

He laughed at me.

— Don't laugh at me, Leonard.

— I'm sorry, dear. Precious things are not always comely.

He turned toward the door, then back to me.

— Joan. Would you come back to my house with me? I am overdue for my pill. Long overdue, in fact.

I didn't want to go, but I went. I'd done the same thing with every other man I'd known. I went with them in case it got bad and I needed to be saved. I don't mean saved by a man. I mean saved by money, by someone doing something dirty for me. The dirty part was how I couldn't accept someone's help without subjugating myself in some sinister, sexual way.

I followed Lenny outside and down the grassy path. There was a breeze for a change. The wealthy people had all the breezes, in the Hills, in the Palisades. Lenny had money, so I wondered why he lived in a garden shed at the top of this rusted canyon. Whenever I had money, I lived beautifully. I was good at living in the present, in believing that tomorrow would be taken care of. Gosia always told me that. Money will always come back, she said. It goes and it comes back more than anything.

Lenny unlocked his door. That he kept it locked was interesting.

— Here we are, he said. I followed his little body inside. The smell hit me. That elderly smell of bone dust on medium-pile carpets. Of coffee and orange juice dumped into the same sink together. Whenever I smelled old people, I felt cheated out of not having parents. At the same time I was grateful. While the death of my parents when I was so young had brought me a world of devastation, I would at least be spared seeing them come undignified. My mother would always be beautiful, my father would always be strong. His big hands, pumping gas in the side-view mirror of the car.

The place was all pine, even the ceiling, and overstuffed with furniture and Persian rugs from the larger house I now occupied, which did indeed make it feel cozy. But the cozy feeling lent itself to some suggestion of dread. Perhaps because it reminded me of the Poconos. It was cozy there, too. Cozy like the first few minutes of a horror movie.

Lenny had a twelve-inch television on a gloomy TV stand and the bedroom was behind an accordion partition. There was a pipe and packets of vanilla-flavored tobacco. Every wall was covered in shelves for all of his books. I pictured River building the place, his arms and neck beading sweat in the canyon sun.

— Please, sit, he said, indicating a corduroy recliner.

— It's very quiet on this side of the rock. Do you hear the coyotes at night?

— I only hear what I want to, he said, victoriously tapping a hearing aid.

When he scratched his head the watch fell down to the middle of his skinny arm. Now that I knew it had worth, I couldn't take my eyes off it. He caught me looking. My face grew hot and I looked away, focusing my

158

eyes on his china cabinet. I saw he had a set of Laboratorio Paravicini plates. My mother had only one, a dinner plate, that she cherished. Had I broken it, I wonder if she'd have hit me. She never hit me. I would have been okay with being hit.

— Paravicini, I said.

He nodded, impressed, which enraged me.

— We had them, growing up, I said, thinking of the lone plate at the top of our credenza, the way it shone. It never had a lick of food on it. I sold it at the house sale, along with nearly everything.

— Your family is from Italy.

— My mother was, yes. I was born there.

— Your mother is passed? he asked, without enough kindness.

I nodded. There was a spider unspooling from a web above Lenny's head. I didn't say anything, even when the spider was nearly on his nose.

— And your father?

— As well.

— I'm sorry. Recently?

— No.

— You were young?

— Quite.

— Dear God, child. What happened?

— An accident.

— Motor vehicle?

— No. In the home.

— A fire?

— Leonard, where is your chamomile collection? I'm sure you have one. I could make you some tea if you would shut the fuck up.

I was teasing and he smiled. Now that I knew he had a disease, I'd softened to him, but just a bit.

— I got the drug. L-dopa. How do you like that name? It sounds like a female drug lord. He also gave me Razadyne to slow down the dementia. Which sounds like a character in one of those senseless science fiction books that Lenore liked.

— Lenore read science fiction? I asked. I rose to make the tea. There was a fine bone-china teapot on the stove, which was meticulously clean, the burners lined with foil.

— Yes, Lenny snapped. Lenore was a great reader. A *varied* reader. Do you think a man like me could have been with someone who didn't read?

— How do you feel with the drugs?

— It'll take several weeks before they're metabolized into my system, before we'll see results. He walked to the couch and sat down. He looked like he needed to be re-hydrated, like a dried sorrel. I might pump some oily water into him and suddenly he would be able to jump on trampolines again.

— You're fond of that dress, aren't you?

I brought Lenny his tea. He blew across its brown surface.

The white mug shook in his hand. He had a collection of those as well. I would never have a collection of anything. I had only one coffee cup. It said MY SAFE WORD IS WINE in loopy print. Vic had bought it for me on a family vacation to Napa Valley. He also brought back several bottles from his favorite vineyards. Everywhere he went, something reminded him of me. I drank the most expensive bottle — a silky grenache — one Monday while I was preparing to see Big Sky. I was delirious that evening with fear and excitement. I was so turned on that sitting on a bicycle seat would have made me come.

— Leonard, I said, to endear him to me.

— Yes?

— May I ask you a question? Why did you never have children?

— Why didn't *you*? he replied.

Something cracked inside my skull.

— It's not too late for me, I said.

— It's not too late for me, either, he said.

I looked at him and smiled like he was irrelevant and half dead.

— We wanted to, Leonard said finally.

Lenore wasn't barren. But she was. Challenged.

— How do you know it wasn't you?

I noticed that he was shaking all over, so I
picked up the throw from his couch and
draped it around his shoulders.

— Goddamn Parkinson's, he said. Of all
fucking things, Parkinson's. I'd have been
fine with cancer. The all-over kind.

— I didn't mean to be coarse, I said.

— Of course you did, dear. It's all right. I
know it isn't easy for you. The past is all
over your face.

He rose and the throw fell from his shoulders. I picked it up as he crossed the short
room. He turned to see if I was looking, but
I pretended to have my eyes on the blanket
as I folded it. I watched him quickly open a
small black door in the wall and even more
quickly toggle a combination lock. Then I
heard a click, a jingle, and the little door
shut. He turned back to me nervously.

— I have a taste in my mouth, he said. He
walked back to the couch. I noticed what I
had already guessed would be true — the
watch was gone from his wrist.

— A bad one?

— Like. Copper.

— Decomposition? I asked sweetly.

— I wish I didn't like cruel women.

162

— Perhaps you'd like a mint.

— It's no use. I'm sorry you lost your parents too young.

— Thank you, Lenny.

— I like it better when you call me Leonard. But that's another sad, old story.

— Lenny, I said, thank you.

13

I dreamed, that night, of the Poconos. I didn't dream; that's not accurate. I closed my eyes and played the reels that couldn't exist in daytime.

My parents and I were out to dinner with a couple and their adolescent son, the Ciccones. We dined with this family often when we were in the Poconos — they had a home near ours, larger though tacky, with shiny black furniture and gold accents — but there was one night I remembered in particular.

The boy's name was Joseph Jr. and he was about my age though there was nothing romantic or even friendly between us. He was the type to sling cats down stairwells. Whenever I've wondered what rapists were like as children, I think of Joseph Jr., his black fleck eyes across a table from me.

Joseph's mother, Evelyn, was plump, with very dark, big hair. Her husband, Joseph

Sr., was an oral surgeon. He, too, had inky hair, plus a long, swollen chin and a sexuality that has always stayed with me. We begin to form our opinions of sex very young, and for me, Joseph Sr. maintains a looming post.

I suppose it was on account of my mother, Pia, who had an inner tube of extra skin around her waist from her cesarean section but otherwise dripped with sex. Her breasts, I've mentioned before, were audaciously large and white.

We were sitting down at a Shaker-style table between the bar and the fireplace. A broomstick hung from the brick wall beside the fireplace alongside family pictures of the owners. Over the mantel was that reproduction of the bull. It had frightened me until just that summer.

My parents didn't drink much. My mother generally had a light beer with dinner and my father drank red wine but never more than a glass or two. Sometimes he had a Bloody Mary with a plate of raw clams. Joe and Evelyn, on the other hand, drank vodka cocktails. I remember Evelyn's big fingers sliding pimiento-stuffed olives off of toothpicks. They both had rumbling laughs. All four adults smoked cigarettes and the men would light the women's, whichever woman was closest.

This night I was seated next to my mother, and Joseph Sr. was on her other side. My father sat across from me, with Evelyn beside him and Joe Jr. beside her. I was always beside my mother. It was imperative that I could smell her and taste her food at will.

She was wearing a salmon-colored sundress with a belt of tiny tin leaves. A natural brunette, she dyed her hair blond and curled it twice a week so it was golden and spiraled. She wore these huge red-rimmed eyeglasses and a pretty shade of coral lipstick. All of her lipsticks were drugstore brands and all their tips were ground down to flattish mounds. She took out her soft pack of Marlboro Reds, and Joseph Sr. got ready with the lighter.

— Mariapia, he said, to get her attention. This was the name spelled on the gold necklace she wore. She'd been Pia in Italy, but after coming to the States she'd begun to go by Maria. It was easier for Americans to understand. After a while she started missing her real name, but because too many people at that point knew her as Maria, she couldn't simply and quickly change it back. My father got her a *Mariapia* necklace to ease the transition. Joseph Sr., who would have met her as Maria, was poking fun, flirtatiously.

My mother laughed. Even her laugh had a heavy accent. She turned away from me and toward Joseph Sr. with the cigarette between her lips. His Zippo had a pinup girl on it. Long brown hair with bangs and a pink bikini. My youth was marked by such images — seeing them on playing cards or drawn crudely on bathroom stalls. It's possible I was just poised to notice them.

My father was telling the story of a friend of his, an Indian doctor named Madan. His wife, Barbara, who suspected him of having an affair, had placed a tape recorder in his big black Mercedes. My father was speaking in the conspiratorial and hushed tone he used when he was telling a story around me that wasn't suitable for children.

It still hurts me to even think of my father's face. He was short and he had a big nose and he was partially balding even then, in his early forties. But he was incredibly magnetic. He was always having a good time, always laughing, but he was also responsible. He could fix anything on a car or in a house. And because he was a doctor, he could save your life. In terms of his being a father, I know I am biased, but I can't imagine a man loving his daughter more than he loved me. Whenever I walked into the ocean — even just a few feet in — every time I turned around, I could count on him to be propped up on his elbows, watching. He had a smile on his face but really he was just waiting to save me.

— So? said Evelyn. Did she catch him?

My father took a noisy drag of his cigarette. Joe Jr. was singeing pieces of dinner roll over the flame of a votive candle. I saw my mother listening to something Joseph Sr. was whispering. My father saw this, too. But the smile never left his face. I sidled closer to my mother. She'd put on her silky navy blazer with the pussy bow. I loved the feeling of her warm flesh through dainty material. She smelled like smoke and L'air du Temps. I pressed close to her to let her know I was there.

— Oh, she got him, my father said with a crooked smile on his face. She really got him.

For years afterward I would try to make sense of that. How had Madan's wife gotten him? What did she pick up on the tape recorder? Was it the noises of sex? How did she know the other woman would be in the car with her husband? For a very long time, whenever I saw a Mercedes, I would imagine black panties stuffed into glove compartments and silver tape recorders slipped

168

under passenger seats, their tiny red lights blinking.

The waitress brought a bruschetta appetizer to the table, plus a plate of too-thick mozzarella sticks for Joe Jr. and me. I didn't like food meant for children. I always wanted to eat whatever my mother was eating; this included kidneys in mustard sauce, which she'd ordered a few times in Little Italy. The kidneys smelled like urine, tangy and old, but there was something about the way my mother held her fork, the way she enjoyed food, not voraciously, like my father, but picky and graceful.

I watched her select a piece of the bruschetta, drizzled with condensed balsamic vinegar. She had very white teeth and opened her mouth wide so as not to disturb her lipstick. I watched Joseph Sr. watch her. There were always at least two cigarettes lit at any moment, even when everybody was eating. It made those dinners last a long time. Unlike me, Joe Jr. ignored the adults and entertained himself. He had a mini pinball game and another little game box wherein the objective was to get miniature marbles into certain holes. He didn't share any of his toys, but I didn't care. I had both my parents to look after. That whole year had been tricky; I could tell there was

169

something I didn't know, and I felt I couldn't miss a moment of observation.

What followed, I didn't fully grasp at the time; like most of childhood, some darkness is downloaded, but you can't decode it until later — after losing your virginity, for example. My father's beeper went off. He left to call his answering service back. For short, it was *service.* So that any time I picked up the phone at home and it was for my father, I'd yell, Daddy, service!

The waitress came around to take our dinner order. My mother ordered the prime rib for my father. He cherished all kinds of meat except chicken. He liked his steaks bloody and once I saw him scoop some raw meat loaf filling into his mouth from a big glass bowl in the refrigerator.

I waited to hear my mother's order, a pollo alla Valdostana, which I'd tried once and didn't like. Then I ordered the surf and turf off the regular adult menu. Evelyn looked at my mother.

— Kid has expensive taste.

Joseph Sr. was looking at my mother like she was a prime rib. I have always wondered why men don't do a better job of turning off their eyes.

My father came back to the table. The color was gone from his face. I'd never seen

170

him without a smile or an expression of anger at my failure to listen to my mother. I had never seen anything in between. There was a mist of sweat on his forehead.

— Mimi, my mother said, what is it?

My father shook his head.

— I have to go, he said.

My mother stood and went to him. I heard him, I heard what he said. As usual, everybody underestimated how tuned in I was.

— My mother was raped, he said.

— What!

My mother, with her accent, had a way of saying that word. It sounded like *waht!* It had an exclamation mark even when she didn't mean for one.

I saw that Joseph Sr. heard him, too. My parents often spoke Italian to each other, specifically when they didn't want someone else to hear them, and I did wonder why my father hadn't communicated the news in Italian. Perhaps the word in Italian, *stupro,* sickened him too much. The Italian word was more carnal, more visual. *Rape,* by contrast, sounded like something you might eventually lock away in an aluminum drawer.

I listened as they spoke for another minute. The details were filmy. I merged them

171

with my own experience of my grandparents' house to create the scene. My grandparents lived in a part of East Orange that used to be a nice neighborhood but now had weeds growing in the cracks of the street. In the middle of the afternoon my grandmother let a man into the house, a man she thought was a technician of some sort, and he raped her on the floral couch where their Doberman regularly pissed. He left with her wallet, her wedding ring, and her gold crucifix. My grandmother was seventy-two years old at the time. She wasn't slim and she wore gaudy makeup on her fleshy face. Peach lipstick that settled into the wrinkles of her lips, powdery blue eyeshadow on the withered lids of her eyes. Their whole house smelled like urine. The rapist struck her once, hard, on the face. The Doberman and the German shepherd were outside, in the fenced yard. I wondered about the cats. They had five cats in that house. She had a bruise under one eye. She'd cleaned herself up before the police came. She'd inquired with the police as to whether there was a way they could keep it from her husband. My grandfather was a cold, small, stern, racist man. In retrospect I believe he was evil. He called Black men *coloreds* in polite company and worse in his own home. My grandmother's legs were big; her calves were like columns. She wore nude pantyhose, even in the summer, which made the skin on her legs look the color of uncooked chicken breasts, an unsettling pinkish white.

My father would be driving the two hours to New Jersey alone. He told my mother he would be back by morning. He came toward the table, kissed me on the forehead. He left his American Express on the table; my mother didn't carry any cards of her own. He didn't say goodbye to Joseph Sr. and Evelyn. I'd never seen him care less for other people.

After he left, Joseph Sr. asked my mother what had happened. Evelyn leaned forward like her type does, lovers of gossip.

My mother sketched the story quietly, saying the word *rape* even quieter, trying to make sense of it herself.

Joseph Sr. let out something like a laugh. A disbelieving guffaw.

—Who in the hell would want to rape an old bag!

Evelyn smiled despite herself and said, Hush, Joe!

My mother somewhat nodded, sharing the energy of the table's disbelief. I felt she should have taken me home, walked away from these monsters. But she didn't. She took out another cigarette. She gazed at the fireplace. Joseph Sr. lit her cigarette. Joseph Jr. selected from his rucksack a different palm-size game.

The waitress brought the big charcoal tray of our food. There was some talk about my father's prime rib, and my mother told Joe and Evelyn they could have it wrapped and take it back to their house. Evelyn wondered if they should send it back to the kitchen; it was too rare for her taste. I looked up at the big bull over the mantel, his horns and teeth that, until recently, had the power to make me wet my pants. I stared at him and wished he were as real as I used to think he was. I prayed for him to animate suddenly and rip the rest of his body through the wall and gore Joseph Sr., make a rhubarb pie out of his wide dentist chest.

— Eat your food, my mother said to me. That was all she said to me for the rest of the meal.

I still remember the cheap hash marks on my slab of filet mignon and the lobster tail beside it. I knocked over the metal dish of clarified butter, but nobody saw, and I knew I couldn't ask for another.

14

All the next day I hoped that Alice would come. I stared at the fridge where I'd lined up the Tecates. I felt like a teenage girl with a crush.

When the bell jingled, I almost dropped a cup I was washing. But it wasn't her. It was River with Kurt the dog at his side. Meeting Alice had muted my desire for him.

— Whoa, he said. You work here?

— It appears so.

— What happened to Natalia?

— She went into politics.

He smiled and looked at me like I was crazy. Jack had been better at understanding sarcasm. But River was better-looking.

— Is it okay that Kurt's in here?

— Of course. How's he doing?

— Terrific. Aren't you, boy?

The dog sat and lowered his scruffy chin. He was at once regal and a little silly but, above all, loyal and smart. I felt that if I had

175

been the one to rescue that animal, he'd be peeing in the cracks of my uneven planks and whining by the door.

— What can I get you boys?

— An iced genmaicha for me. Maybe a bowl of water for Kurt?

— Sure.

I filled one of the expensive soup bowls with water. My mother thought it was disgusting to use human bowls for dogs. After taking showers, my parents dried the stall with the towels they had used on themselves. The steel drain was always sparkling.

— I'm taking Kurt for his first dunk in the ocean.

— How do you know it's his first?

— Oh. I don't.

I felt bad so I walked around the counter and knelt to the dog's eye level. I wore a frilly light green apron. I gazed in the dog's eyes and then stood up quickly before the animal rejected me by looking away.

— It will be his first time, I said.

River laughed. One time I wrote to Jack, *Last night was the best it's ever been (for me, with you).* Of course, I bookended it with several jokes. I addressed him as *Fisheye.* He wrote back, *Hey handsome!* He replied to my jokes with jokes, he told me about an

176

interview he'd had with some start-up firm and asked for my advice. He included some song lyrics and ignored what I wrote about our sex.

I made River's tea and handed it over to him. I took his money, a few crinkled dollar bills, and gave him change. He didn't put any of the change into the tip jar. Each time Dean came in, he slipped all of his singles into it. Both actions — the tipping and the not tipping — made me feel like I had lesions.

— Thanks, River said. He brought the bowl of water back. The dog had splashed a good amount on the floor and I would have to wipe it up with one of the dirty bar mops.

It was just about closing time and I had given up on Alice coming in. Out of frustration I denigrated a woman on Letgo about the price of a basket. She wanted to give me five dollars less than what I was asking but was willing to drive nearly forty minutes to meet me. *Stop haggling,* I wrote to her. *You're embarrassing yourself.*

Then I wrote to Vic's wife, Mary:

Hey . . . tried you back a number of times. Calls not going thru?

She wrote back immediately:

I didn't get any calls! Call me now!

I waited a few minutes and wrote:

177

Okay, as soon as I get off of work.
When?? she asked.

I thought of all the nights when Mary must have sat at home, feeling something wasn't right, that her husband was not where he said he was. I never noticed him step away from me to call or write to her. Once, just once, he didn't take me up on an offer for dinner. I'd emailed him from across the office. I wrote the name of the restaurant where I wanted to go to in the subject line and a question mark in the body. I could see into his office from my desk. He had a large one with big windows. I saw his face fall. I watched him type a response. His pain was like a graveyard I could stroll about and mark up as I saw fit.

Can't do dinner, kid. Can't tell you how sorry I am. Could do a quick drink before? Any drink, any bar in the city.

I let him take me to Bemelmans in the Carlyle with the drawings of Madeline and little girls in hats with ribbons in Paris and balloons, ice-skating elephants, picnicking rabbits, and little boys and their gray dogs. Nobody had ever read *Madeline* to me as a child. My mother used to tell me the story of Cinderella. In her version there was a cop in lieu of the prince. Cinderella and the Cop. She told it in both English and Italian.

I have her on tape. I haven't yet been able to listen because I worry that her accent will sound stronger, all these years later, than it did in my head. That she would sound like someone I never knew.

At the bar I drank a gimlet and so did Vic. By that point I'd been avoiding him quite a bit. The season of Jack had begun. Young-boy bars and beer and waking up next to a strong body with soft skin. I was waiting to hear from Jack all the time, so I rarely made dinner plans with Vic. But that night Jack was going to Queens to see a friend and I knew he wouldn't be back until late. He would eat cheesesteak sushi in Astoria and possibly he'd want to fuck when he got back but most likely he would pass out on his friend's couch or make out with some girl his own age. He would fall asleep in a pair of breasts. We were not exclusive. Or rather, I was exclusive with him.

I was upset that Vic couldn't have dinner and take my mind off of the boy but it helped me to see how sorry he was that he couldn't. I was cruel that night. I said, What a real shame, we haven't spent any time with each other in ages. I thought we could watch a movie and be cozy with popcorn.

— Kid, he said. You don't know how bad I wish I could.

— Did you know, I asked, pointing to the murals around us, that the author of the *Madeline* books exchanged these murals for a year and a half of accommodations at the Carlyle for himself and his family?

— No, I didn't, he said. They must have been a happy family to live in such close quarters and not go crazy.

He knew how to hurt me when he dared. He stayed for a second round, which I could see he would regret. He paid for our drinks and got up. There were fine beads of sweat in the creases of his forehead.

— Tell the car to take Ninth to the tunnel, I yelled after him. You can't be late to your wife's birthday!

Now I looked at her text message. The stillness of a message, even though you know the person on the other end is trembling, staring at her phone. The desperation of the poor, poor woman! I couldn't believe it, actually, that Vic had left her with the pain of knowing her husband killed himself over another woman. Left her to care for a child with challenges. Some people had suffered so much that it seemed they could handle anything. I was not unfeeling. I had been through my own gauntlet. I knew someone like Mary would survive. Most women do.

The lady from Letgo wrote back, *Your a fuckin pyscho cunt!*

I wrote back, *You spelled you're and psycho wrong.* I deleted that and wrote, *WHATEVER CHEAPO.*

Then the bell rang and Alice walked in. She wore a long gray sleeveless cotton dress. Her hair was pulled back into a wet ponytail. Her eyes didn't need makeup.

— Is it closing time? Can we have some beer on the patio?

— Sure.

—You don't have somewhere to be?

Her grin was acerbic, vaguely judgmental. She took out a ten-dollar bill.

— I didn't pay for our second round yesterday, this one's on me. I hate people who pretend to forget to pay.

Within moments we were in the middle of our conversation from the previous afternoon. Then she said something that made me feel we were speaking on a heightened plane. They were similar to the experience of psychedelic drugs, those first conversations with Alice.

— There's something about your story — Big Sky — all of it, I feel like there's a purpose. Do you know? Like we are getting somewhere. Of course I sound crazy. This is colder than yesterday. It's fucking beautiful.

Of course the beer was colder. I'd turned the dial down on the beer fridge for her. It was so cold it glowed. I pictured her mother's lips with my father's lips.

— You're going to hate the women here, she said to me.

— Aren't they the same as in New York?

— I think they're worse. They're opossums. This one woman, Lara, I'm giving her private lessons in her Japanese garden in Santa Monica at six in the morning. She wants to have these talks with me. Her child is with the nanny staring out the window. Hands and face pressed to glass. Lara wants to talk about nothing, about how her hairstylist gives her preferential access, more so than celebrities. She wants me to be jealous of her. One time her husband came out to the garden and saw me and then she switched our time to nine a.m.

Alice had a light accent, maybe affected, but the artifice would have made her sexier to me. She pulled a cigarette from a new soft pack. I thought to light it for her. But I didn't want to be the man between the two of us. I took a sip of beer and the flavor was suddenly bad. I felt an inch-thick lake of saliva coat my throat. My head buzzed. I willed myself back into the moment.

— Where did you grow up? I asked her.

182

— Are you asking because of my accent? Continental? Does it sound affected? Sometimes I think I'm affecting it. I totally am. I'll try to be more genuine because I like you.

She explained that she'd been born in New Jersey but had spent much of her childhood in Italy. I told her I was from there, too. We "discovered" we both had Italian mothers.

— What brought your family to Italy? I asked, trying to neutralize the acid rising in my throat.

— We went back there when I was a toddler. Then we returned to the States for high school. Italy was not as my mother remembered it.

— And your father?

— Out of the picture, she said, fluttering her hand like half of a bird, squinting, and taking a drag. You have to tell me the rest of the story, she said. We are getting somewhere.

My dress felt too tight. She was right, we were getting somewhere. As I told her each part, from the end backward, we were getting to the beginning. We were getting to the reason why I was there. Some people say they do work inside their own brain. They learn that jealousy is a childish emotion. They teach themselves such things. But I could do no work inside my own brain. The interior of my brain was a snake pit. I couldn't survive in there alone.

— I'm not the important one.

— Yes, you are! Alice said. I won't say I feel like I've known you forever because that's the kind of thing that woman Lara would say. Over bee pollen shots. She has celiac disease, so the housekeeper has to be very careful.

— Maybe one day the housekeeper won't be careful enough.

She reached over, laughing, and placed both of her palms on my shoulders. Her forehead went into my chest. I thought, grotesquely, of my father having a type.

— Everybody is full of shit, she said. I called my mother *Maman* from the age of ten until the age of sixteen.

— What happened at sixteen?

— She died, Alice said, still laughing.

— I'm sorry.

— She was only in the hospital for two weeks, getting gray. She was an amazing woman. A perfect mother. I really think I'd think that even if she weren't my *maman*.

I asked her to tell me about Rod Rails. She said that he was one of these gurus who left his penis inside of a woman to calm her.

That he would never thrust.

— How did you get the job?

— You mean why did I take the job? she asked, as though of course, if a man were hiring, she would get the job. I want to open my own place someday. Not in LA. Back in Italy, maybe. A small oak studio amid the olive groves and the cypresses. And this is the best. Rod, for all of his tantric nonsense, is the best at combining business and the spirit of yoga. He may not believe in it, but I believe in what he claims to believe in. And that's all I need.

— You're very smart for your age.

— You say that like you're so much older. What are you, thirty?

— I'm nearly thirty-seven.

— Well, you don't look thirty-six, but even so, thirty-six is nothing.

— Thirty-six may be nothing, but thirty-seven is the end.

— Are you almost done here?

— Closing time was a half hour ago.

— Were you waiting for me? she asked, nearly lasciviously.

— No, I stuttered.

— It's okay. I was waiting to see you, too.

Already she had the power to coax rage from me one moment and make me feel lucky and loved the next.

— Let's go to the beach, she said.

We got into her Prius. A cherry air freshener dangled from the smudged rearview mirror. It smelled like the 1980s and everything that was the color red.

On the way down we stopped at my house because I said I had a pack of cigarettes lying around. She didn't seem surprised by the absurdity of the compound. While I went upstairs to my stupid lofted bedroom, I heard her moving around downstairs.

— I shouldn't smoke, she said. It aggravates my throat.

I found the pack of American Spirits. I'd taken them from my rapist's hotel room.

— What's wrong with your throat?

— I pulled something back in my bulimic days. Took months to heal properly. I wouldn't have stopped otherwise.

— You were bulimic? I said.

— Give me a break, Alice said, fanning herself with her palm and looking all around. Jesus Christ, it's so hot in here. Jesus! You know there's an AC unit up there?

— I can't use it. It's in the lease.

— What?

— It's in the lease that I can't use it. He can hear it from his house.

I pointed Lenny's shed out to Alice through the kitchen window.

— I'm turning it on, she said. She dragged one of my unpacked boxes to the wall, climbed it, and switched the unit on. An oily sweat glistened between her breasts. Why don't you buy some window units?

The notion of the accordion, of stuffing the gaps, it was so large-seeming a problem that it made me want to curl into a fetal position.

— I hate window units, I said.

— Window air conditioners make me feel cozy.

— They make me feel poor.

— In Maremma, Alice said, most everywhere in Italy, as I'm sure you know, air-conditioning isn't necessary at night. The breeze is enough. There is nearly always a breeze. And it's really only at night that you need to feel cool.

Alice had told me earlier that the house they moved to in Italy was across the road from a dairy farm and on the same dirt road as a rifle range. She would look out the window to see the brown cows on the dusty knolls, finding swatches of grass and munching in their homely way, and then she would hear a gunshot; both she and the cows would flinch, each in her own fashion. Violently bucolic, she called it. I wondered how many times she'd said that to a man who admired her.

— Is that why your mother went back to Italy? I asked. The night breeze?

— You want to know the truth? It makes me sick to say it.

I nodded. I felt the cold of the air conditioner against my face and weirdly missed the oppressive heat. In the Poconos we had a miserable old toaster that darkened one side of the bread while barely warming the other and so you would have to flip the bread and babysit the process. When, that final summer, we bought a new toaster from the Two Guys in Harrison, the settings were precisely calibrated, the toast came out perfectly every time, and it made me irrationally sad.

— My mother left America, Alice said, following the death of her lover.

— Lover, I said.

— A married one. Perhaps the same sort of situation as yours. Everything reminded her of him. It was too painful. She couldn't be in the same country where he died. She told me some of the story when I was younger, and then when she was dying, she told me the man was my father.

— Oh. How did he die?

— Cancer, she said. Throat.

Right then I wanted to tell her the truth

188

of how it actually happened, in part because I hated her for not knowing. For having had the childhood that had been ripped from me.

We took Tuna Canyon to the beach. It was a one-way road through the Canyon, from the village down the mountain to the base, ending bluntly at the Pacific Coast Highway. People raced their cars from the summit to the beach, Alice told me. Jimmy Dean died on that road. In his perfect little car. She opened all four windows and the sunroof to give the impression of a convertible. Her caramel hair whipped against her face. There were no guardrails on the road and Alice took the twists fearlessly. Through the gaps in the sycamores you could see the extent of the canyon, the mop of jade like the canopy of a rainforest.

When we arrived at the bottom, it was like everything else I'd seen in Los Angeles — you came out of something gorgeous and untamed into something lurid, the unlovely row of houses on the ocean side of the Pacific Coast Highway. The gas stations and the garden centers with overpriced terra-cotta pots.

She pulled into the parking lot of a restaurant with nets and buoys. She said we were going to get some clams and beer and bring them to the beach. There was a red neon sign that said REEL INN. The air smelled of crabs as we got out and the sun hit me in that evocative way it does after you have a beer on an empty stomach. Inside there were colored lights strung from the ceiling, plastic red gingham tablecloths across long tables, an ordering booth for clam rolls, raw clams and oysters, thick steaks of Chilean sea bass on paper plates. There was a patio with heat lamps and pebbles on the ground and picnic tables and petunias in galvanized Corona buckets.

I stood behind her in line and stared at her pornographic legs. Strong calves and soft thighs. I imagined cutting into parts of her with a fork and knife.

She ordered two dozen clams without asking if I ate clams or whether I wanted something different. And a bucket of beers, she said to the boy behind the counter, who knew her. No charge, he said. She smiled and slipped a twenty into a tip jar.

I was afraid in that way you can only be afraid in an early friendship with a woman. I was afraid of being too careful. I was afraid of being too old, of not understanding music. She carried the clams they'd packaged in a to-go container and I carried the bucket of beer. We crossed the median. Cars zoomed past and my heart thumped between my breasts. The times you are most willing to die are, ironically, the times you are having the most fun.

— There's a fine for drinking in Malibu, she said, but I don't know, I've never been caught.

The beach was remarkable because of how close it was to the highway and because I was with Alice, who took off her sandals and led me to the shoreline. She was a Pisces, like you. She sat down on the sand and set the box of clams before us.

— Here, she said, they don't need salt but lemon, all right?

She indelicately squeezed lemon across them all. I hated clams. They tasted like blood and metal. My father loved them. I'd watched him eat hundreds.

— Oh, God, she said, sucking one down, that's all I need in life. Clams, beer. The occasional fuck. Twice a month, someone nice. Hey? I really weirdly want to know all about you.

— It gets darker.

— Tell me the rest of Big Sky. We are getting to something. I can feel it. Please don't call me crazy, I'm not sucking up or being a metaphysical twat, I can just feel this.

191

A V of birds flew by overhead. There weren't too many people on the beach, just some wetsuits in the distance. The water was dark. Suddenly I missed him so much that I felt I was about to get swallowed by the blackness all over again.

I told her that he was more than a man for me. He was a jetliner to a world I so terrifically wanted to be a part of. As a girl I was enthralled with the American restaurants my family never went to. Places with teak banquettes and warm lighting. One place in particular, a vegetarian American café, I dragged my parents into, and the waitress, who had a thick blond braid down her back, served us a loaf of warm pumpernickel bread on a scratched walnut cutting board with a knife and soft butter in a steel ramekin. Ivy plants dripped from the ceiling. At home, it was melting slices of prosciutto and wedges of Parmesan wrapped in cloth beside a grater. Big Sky was a passport to being American.

— Everybody wants to be Italian, Alice said, and there you are, trying to slough off your own particular beauty.

— Where in Italy did you and your mother return to?

— Porto Ercole. Have you heard of it? It's in Maremma. We had a wonderful little cottage near the water. I don't know why we left.

— You never asked her?

— Please, she said, I'm boring. Continue with your story. It's like a warped fairy tale.

I smiled and told her how Big Sky grew up in the mountains and rivers, fly-fishing in Wisconsin and Montana and riding horses and herding cattle. He was a man you could put in a seersucker suit for Easter, but he also chopped wood and understood how meat was processed.

I told her how he emailed me the very next morning after our sloppy session in my bed. *I left my gear, can I pick it up later?*

The font looked different to me from the *Sweet dreams* message of the previous night. I could feel the chill. I thought of all the boys I had jerked off because I didn't want to risk disease by putting my mouth on some twiggy, contagious penis. With Big Sky I finally understood why other women risked themselves. I wanted to walk around with him inside of me.

— Fuck, Alice said. I have never felt that way. In the moment, sure, but not after the man left. Does that mean I haven't been in love?

— I think it means that *I* haven't been in love.

She smiled.

— I wrote back, *Sure.* He said he'd come by after work. So I spent an entire day getting ready for him. The whole day. Every little thing, including putting a flower in a rocks glass in the bathroom. At five thirty my doorman — don't misunderstand, it was a shitty building, it was one of those accidental grandfathered-in doorman situations — called up and announced Big Sky's first name and I began to shake. Do you want to know what I was wearing?

— Oh, God, she said.

— A long-sleeved navy Henley, very fitted and tight around my waist. It ended just above my hip bone. Then my white lace panties and that was it. Bare legs down to a pair of high-heeled Manolo Blahnik Mary Janes.

— Jesus Christ.

— The colors were off, the navy shirt and the black shoes and the white underwear.

— I was going to say.

— It was humiliating. I was a disaster.

— But he didn't care.

— No, in fact, I am fairly sure he did. It was one of those moves you think is a good idea in your head. But if you slept on it, you'd say, Whore! Dumb whore.

— Had you consulted with any friends?

— I had nobody, I said, but I thought of Vic. I hadn't told him about Big Sky until Big Sky began to drip away from me.

I told her how I heard his knock and the blood from my heart leaked down my legs and I walked to the door with his headset and cap in my hand, and the sound of my heels clacking immediately wrecked my confidence. The sound of my heels was the sound of loneliness. I considered running into my bedroom, pulling on a pair of pants or sexy shorts, but at the very least removing the heels for fuck's sake. But I opened the door as planned. He saw me half-naked, took me in. He looked shocked but not in the way I had hoped. I suppose I was hoping for him to be a cartoon of the regular man. Horny, tongue-wagging. Or to look at me the way Vic would have if I'd ever opened the door for him like that. Vic would have looked at me like I was an angel.

— This Vic, Alice said.

I didn't want to tell her about Vic but she had to hear about him. I wanted a woman to finally see me. At the same time, I worried she would be disgusted, the way Big Sky was when he saw Vic and realized he was my group.

I explained how the outfit, the ludicrous idea, was based upon the previous evening.

A couple of martinis, darkness. But I hadn't lived an emotional life in between the night before and that moment. I was stuck in last night, whereas he had gone home to his family then to work in the morning and now, in the innocent light of half past five, I looked like the reason he married his wife and not a girl like me. Imagine the mother of his children, presiding over a roast in the big nice oven, and then me there with my bare legs and my old heels. Here, I said to him, shaking, nervously handing him his headphones and his Mets cap. I thought of my father loving the Yankees. I thought of what my father would think if he could see me now.

— Okay, Alice said, so let's stop for a moment. Because this is important, right? I mean, let's really stop and get inside this man's head. So he comes to the door of a woman he ate out last night who wasn't his wife. Now it's the next day and he's sober. He showered last night and once again this morning. He ate pizza with his wife in their apartment off the park. He felt like he could erase it. Now if he can just get back the very expensive headphones his wife bought him last Christmas, it will be like he never stepped foot in a strange animal's apartment. He spent a weekend thinking of you

but then last night he put his mouth between your legs and he felt wrong and sad.
Last week he only kissed you, and it felt innocent and full of promise. But last night
was too quick and sour. He wondered how
many men you did that sort of thing with.
You had no compunction about his wife and
for God's sake his infant. Because of course
you are the temptress and he is the tempted.
And now here you are, opening the door
with no pants on. In high heels. His dick is
like hey whatever what's up, but otherwise
he feels like you're nuts. Already he felt
strange and awkward coming here, but now
he is downright appalled.

— Fuck, I said, are you trying to kill me?

— Do you still love him?

— No.

— You do. Well, you can't. Maybe that's
why you're telling me this.

It turned colder and the water blew the
salt air against our bare skin. Alice was one
of those people who didn't feel cold. The
littlest thing can make you feel another
woman is better than you.

— This is important, she said. Please don't
stop.

— The next part is terrible.

— Go.

— I said, Here. And I handed him his gear

197

and he looked down at it and I began to close the door.

— Like you were just, what, dusting the cabinets in panties and heels?

— Yes, I said, groaning. I'm ashamed.

— No. You are all of us. You are the parts of us that no one wants to admit to. Go on.

— He said *hey* because he had to say *hey*.

— Otherwise he'd be a monster!

— And I said, Did you want to come inside? Can you imagine? Like you said, it's daytime, everyone's sober. He looked confused. But he came inside.

— Probably, you think, he wanted to end it then? Just get his gear and take off?

— I never thought of it like that. My aunt once told me that if you have feelings for someone, feelings that are very strong, they can't exist in one direction alone. That the other person feels them, too. But you're probably right.

— You don't believe I am.

— I don't, so what?

— So nothing. Go on.

— I offered him a beer. I was the devil, I guess. We sat on my couch and —

— What?

— I can't.

— Joan, she said, then paused. That's interesting. I've never said your name. I've

198

never said the name *Joan* out loud. Or I must have. Joan of Arc. Etcetera. It's silky. Joan, please, you must go on. This is how we learn from one another.

— I asked him if he wanted a massage. I never liked a man that much before. I didn't understand what was happening. I was flooded with emotion. I took off his shirt and he lay on his stomach on my couch.

— Couches are less barbaric than beds. There is something half-assed about cheating on a couch.

— And I gave him an excellent massage. I imagined exactly what would feel good and did it.

— I just was thinking, when you're with someone you're tired of, you give them a massage to get things over with. You expend the least amount of energy. But the first time with someone new, you massage a back like you're before a committee, competing with every woman you've ever felt threatened by.

—Yes, I said, that's exactly what I was doing. And his back was stippled with freckles and scars. It wasn't a pretty back, but I loved it anyway. It was pale. Eventually he lifted himself up and sat down. He pulled me close and I straddled his waist and wrapped my bare legs around it, heels still on. I must have looked like a prostitute. We kissed for thirty minutes, maybe more. My legs wrapped around his waist and no other touching, just kissing. He took my shirt off. When he couldn't take it anymore, he leaned up and began to jerk himself off and he came on my chest.

— Romantic.

— I'm saying it out loud, now, so you are my witness. What I thought was sweet, what I looked upon later as a gesture of, I don't know, kindness, affection, *love?* was how he got up to get one of my paper towels and wiped his semen from between my breasts.

— Fucking hell.

— Then I spilled a beer in anxiety on my rug and I got so paranoid about the smell of beer lingering that I sprayed it with carpet cleaner right away.

— In front of him?

I nodded.

— What a marvelous complexity, though! So you didn't come at all?

— No.

— He just jerked himself off and you cleaned up some beer.

— Jesus, I said. You're making me see the rot on a moment I thought was golden.

— That's the point! Now, is coming im-

portant to you, as important as it should
be?

— No, I don't think so, I said, realizing
I'd never explored the question.

— That's funny. It's all I care about.

— Really?

— It's all I think about the whole time.
And when I have one, I'm like, Goodbye!
So people need to get there with me. Or
they will be having corpse sex.

She tilted her head to one side and stuck
her tongue out and I laughed.

— I'm too busy thinking, I said.

— About?

— How I look. How he's feeling.

— So you fake orgasms?

I nodded.

— To what end?

— I don't know.

— You want to please him, to let him know
he has pleased you?

— I suppose.

— I find that men have a better time when
they think they are terrible in bed. It inspires
them to read magazines and find a new nub
to tweak. They come back and back until
they feel they've figured it out.

I was upset that she was more sexually
conversant than me. She was younger and
better at fucking. She would have eaten Big

201

Sky alive. I shuddered to imagine them together.

— Are you cold? she asked, rubbing the tops of my arms with her palms.

— Not a lot, I said, trying to hide how loved I felt.

— Please, she said, continue, I'm sorry.

— I'm starting to feel silly.

— No, we need to get to where this is going. So you didn't come and he did and he watched you clean the rug and pretended it wasn't weird.

— Yeah, and it was tax season and he asked whether I'd received all my forms yet. Then he just stopped and looked at me and said, Who *are* you? His eyes, I have to explain his eyes. He was like a wolf. Fuck and I loved him. And I didn't know what he meant. I said, What? And he said, Like, who do you hang out with? And Jesus, I thought he meant — I thought he was trying to inhale me, the way I wanted to inhale him, you know? I thought he was trying to get to know me.

— Oh, you poor thing.

— And I began to name friends of mine, like first names. Like an idiot. Because I didn't understand what he really meant. Which was: What circle are you in? Will my wife find out? Do you hang out with weird bouncers from New Jersey, because you just acted like a girl who does. Then he gave me tax advice and I thought how lucky his wife was — her name was fucking Parker — I thought how lucky she was to have this beautiful, smart, sexy man who does her taxes, who makes a lot of money. Who fishes and hunts. I felt so empty and shitty and stupid. I put on a pair of sweatpants. He left with his gear.

— But that wasn't the end.

— No, but every time was the end.

I felt like I was going to cry. I didn't want her to see. I looked ugly when I cried.

— Perhaps we need an interlude. I think you should tell me about Vic.

— You're right, I said, because Vic is part of the actual end. But I'm tired of my fucking voice.

— I'm not, she said, taking my hand.

I didn't think another woman had ever taken my hand in that way. We sat there on the cooling sand and I began to tell her about Vic. I told her about Scotland, our naked bodies on the bed. She didn't look at me like I was disgusting, and for the first time, I didn't feel that I was.

15

When I got back to the house that evening I felt alive. All my life I'd avoided women. They complicated my time. I'd learned how to do everything alone, how to use men for what I needed, and whenever another woman was around, there would invariably be jealousy, or I was bound to act differently, to be less sexual and exacting.

But with Alice it was the opposite. I felt the need to turn myself up more. She made me feel the way that Gosia had — valid.

Vic had questioned Gosia's role in my life once, when he was feeling me slip away. He knew I told Gosia everything. He asked whether I was sure she was the best influence on me. I slapped him across the face. His stubbly cheek jiggled and he apologized right away.

The truth is, who knows, she might have been a bad influence. She taught me that men will use you unless you use them first,

204

that sometimes men must be punished because women are in important pain from the moment they are born until the moment they die. But you could also say that my mother taught me that, and you could of course say that it was my beloved father who fucked the whole thing up. Gosia did the most for me and did the least to hurt me of anyone in my life.

I remember vividly the first night she brought me to a bar. I was fifteen. She didn't drink much, a glass of Grüner here and there. I ordered a Bloody Mary. The bartender, a kind-looking man in his fifties, didn't question it.

Gosia unclipped her hair, which was in a chignon. I loved that word. She shook her head and I watched her platinum hair fall around her shoulders. I was not the only one. I clocked three men staring at her neck. She looked at me and smiled. She knew they were looking at her.

There were many such evenings. She never told my uncle where we were going. She never even told him when we were going to the mall.

Always ask questions. Never answer them.

Have more secrets than the person you are with.

She spoke in epithets. She never implicitly

said it, but she was teaching me how not to end up like my mother.

She taught me well. I could turn it on at any time. I had a man I would never fuck move the contents of one apartment to another, all on his own.

Gosia couldn't erase what I'd seen as a child. She knew that she could not. But she tried very hard. I became a sort of Franken-stein's monster. I could make a man like Vic cut another man's throat for me, but I could not get the twenty-four-year-old to call me the morning after we fucked. Even with Vic, though, I wasn't using him to nefarious ends. I was just afraid to be alone. I was looking for fathers in every train car.

That afternoon Lenny wasn't sitting at our outside table, which annoyed me because I'd asked Alice to wait while I ordered him a paper boat of fried calamari. She asked me about him and I told her some stories and she alternately laughed and shook her head. My life amused her.

She dropped me off and we didn't inquire about what the other was doing. It was that early time in a friendship when you respect boundaries and evenings are off limits.

I walked with the squid to Lenny's tiny home and knocked. Because the last time we'd spoken he'd been alert and very much himself I wasn't expecting him to be in the middle of an episode, but he was.

I heard him through the door say, Lenore, is that you?

I was depraved. I stole from stores. I used men, but I always gave something of myself in return. But plain and mean deceit? Never. Until that moment.

— Yes, I said. It's me, darling.

Leonard opened the little door to his home.

— My life! he said, pulling me into his body and kissing me on the mouth. I inhaled the smell of his age. He was wearing linen pants and a cotton t-shirt.

— Tell me the news of the world! he said, smoothing my hair back with the palm of his hand and gazing into my eyes so intently I thought for sure he would snap out of it. But he didn't. We sat together on the couch.

— It's vicious out there, darling. I'm happy to be back. Shall I fix us a cup of tea?

— What's that in your hand?

— Fried squid. I brought it from Malibu.

— What were you doing in Malibu? he asked, looking haunted.

— I was down there with a girlfriend of mine.

— I see. Lenore, let me ask you — I worry you are still upset by the thing that happened?

The way he spoke to Lenore was saintly, unreal. With me, he was his crude, erudite self; with Lenore, he was a gentleman. One of my greatest furies was the way men treated me like I would not merely endure their filth but endorse it.

— Oh, what thing? Do you mean the other night when you went into my ass?

— What?

— The other night, darling, when we tried what you've been wanting to try.

— Oh. Was that at Sandstone? The mickey I took . . . I can't remember so much.

— Yes. We were in the red bedroom. After the pool.

— I can't —

— It's all right if you don't remember, my love. It hurt a little, but. Overall I'd say I enjoyed it.

— Did you?

— I enjoy everything with you.

— That's good to hear, he said, patting my wrist like the elderly man that he was. I squeezed the wedge of lemon across the paper boat and handed him a leggy clump. An expression of pure gratitude came over his face. He took the whole boat from me.

208

He made humming noises, overchewing each piece and swallowing with occasional difficulty. It's a particular heartbreak to watch an old man eat something he's enjoyed all his life. His brows moved like inchworms and he didn't look up at me again until after he'd finished.

I walked into his kitchen for a piece of paper towel. He bought the cheap, rough kind. I wet a corner of it in the small sink and brought it back to the couch. I took the empty boat from him and dabbed his mouth with the moist paper towel.

— Lenore, you're so good to me.

— And you to me, my love.

Lenny had an eight-bottle wooden wine rack next to the television; I selected the most expensive-looking one and poked around for glasses. He once told me he had all the good china in storage, save the Laboratorio plates. Storage for what, I wanted to ask him. He had no children, nobody to whom to pass along his china. I found two short glasses made by Oneida with seventy-nine-cent stickers from some dollar store in the Valley.

I brought our glasses to the couch. I moved slowly, wary of shocking him back into the present.

— We are in a low, dishonest decade, he said.

— Isn't that true of every decade?

— No, not all of them. In any case that's Auden, not me. But it's truer now than it was then.

— Do you agree with that, darling?

— Somewhat, Lenore. Somewhat I do. September first, 1939, and November eighth of this year. They are mirrors if you look in the right light. Do you know what else Auden said? He said we all have Hitler in us.

— Hmm. I believe all men have a rapist in them, just dying to get out.

— Excuse me?

— Nothing, my love. You seem tense. Is something troubling you?

— Your feelings for me, Lenore.

He took my arms in his bony hands. His pupils were hazy, like those of a fish on ice at a discount grocer's.

— After I lie down, love, after I take a rest, I wondered if we might lie with each other?

I could feel his penis wanting to rise. He was not wearing the watch. I would come to learn that he wore it only when he had those few hours of definitive clarity after taking his drugs. But one day he would make a mistake. I would be patient.

— I would like nothing more, darling. I'll go and take a shower, get the sand off my feet. I like to be clean as a whistle when we — when we lie with each other.

It was easy for me to say the things that Leonard wanted to hear. I have always and unequivocally known what a man needed from me. With Big Sky I trembled in fear at saying the wrong thing. I tried to keep every message short. I rewrote lines to make them sound nonchalant. I spent morbid hours on one sentence.

With Vic I knew very well what to say but often said the exact opposite. In the very beginning of our relationship, the second or the third time I let him fuck me, he lay beside me after, staring with those wet little eyes of his. We were in a hotel room in Zihuatanejo. The rooms were all open air, white curtains billowing, the blue sea. Lanterns and rattan and ripe mangoes in a bowl. You're going to throw me out one day, he said, caressing the side of my arm. The breeze was gorgeous. I was in the prime of my life in that orange and blue place. The coconut grove down the road.

Oh, no, I said. Not one day. I'm going to do it very, very gradually.

I waited until Lenny fell asleep. When he

began to snore, I walked to the safe in the wall. I tried fifteen or so combinations, looking over at him every few seconds. I reminded myself that there was no rush. I turned it back to where it had been and used the hem of my dress to rub off my fingerprints. I looked inside of his little closet. I found his old man robe, his old man record collection, and a photo album. I tucked the latter under my arm and I also took the pipe from his coffee table and a packet of tobacco back to my place. I sat at the outdoor table and drank a greyhound with fresh grapefruit juice and puffed on the pipe. If I'd had a child, I thought, I never would have been able to fresh-squeeze a grapefruit, to rim the glass with salt.

I lit the bowl of the pipe and looked through the album. It was almost exclusively full of pinup-type shots of Lenore. There was something sordid about them, even by my standards. Lenore sitting on the toilet with a scrunch of toilet paper in one hand. Lenore, naked in a bathtub with no water. Lenore drinking a martini in the nude on a velvet settee. Her hair up in her classic Lenore chignon. None of it was pornographic, exactly, but there was something aggressive about the pictures. Lenore had an embarrassed smile in every shot. Her relationship to the photographer, Lenny, was clear. He was the bullish director, telling her how to sit and how to hold her body and she was smiling like a woman who didn't want a man to be angry at her.

Around five Kevin came out, wearing black jeans and a black t-shirt. He was handsome and warm, but there was something distant about him. He would speak to you on one level, but his train of thought seemed to exist on another. I kept wondering if he would start wanting me, and the not knowing gave me an enormous amount of pleasure. Being with Alice made me feel confident that sooner or later he would.

— Miss Joan, he said, coming close enough that I could smell him, eucalyptus. Haven't seen you around too much.

— We keep different hours, I said.

— How true, how true. What's up with Lenny.

— He's kind for being a bastard, I said.

— I like that, Miss Joan. You got verve.

— Coming from someone with verve, I said, that means a lot.

— Nice of you to be checking on him. Why do you think you do that?

— I don't know.

— He still in there? Little nappy for the old man? Nonnyboots, my mother used to

213

say. Get into your nonnyboots, son.

— I like that.

— Yeah, I always dug it, too. Tonight is his regular poker game. It's the only night he looks good to me. He gets together with a bunch of old friends in Hollywood. Long black car comes to pick him up. One of these days, Kev, he says to me, it's gonna be a hearse.

— Sometimes I feel bad for him, I said, and other times I don't.

— You know, I think that's just about everybody.

I was always going around wondering where everyone got their self-assurance. Kevin's mother sounded like she loved him in a pure way. She didn't make him take care of her. It made me want him. His mother's love for him turned me on. I worried that with every man I met, either I was going to want him or he was going to want me. It had never truly been both at once.

— Just keep your wits about you regarding Lenny.

— River said the same thing. What do you mean?

— Nothing, really. He's harmless, of course, but he isn't innocent.

— What does that mean? I asked.

— Oh, I don't really mean anything. You

live in the Canyon long enough, you hear rumors and such, and anyway, you don't move up here unless you have something to hide.

He looked at his watch.

— My lady is waiting, he said. You have yourself a fine night, Miss Joan. Young man River went to Froggy's, 'case you're hankering for something to do. It's half-priced caipirinhas. All night long.

He winked and ran to his Charger. The music was all the way up as he sped down the drive, trailing baked dust in his wake.

I couldn't hear the coyotes but I could sense them. The rustle of the breeze might have been their tails thwapping against the saltbush and the milkweed. It was easy to pin my fear on the animals and the darkness of our queer compound. I wished I were in a place where I wouldn't be afraid to be alone, to turn in early with a book and a cup of chamomile. But even when I'd lived in such places, in the Jersey City apartment building, for example, surrounded by city lights and the noises of families, even then I had been afraid to be home early, to be sober and unaccompanied as dusk approached.

Very quickly I dressed in a black jumpsuit and my new, stolen heels and drove down the winding road to Froggy's.

I saw River right away, sitting at the bar, alone in an unalone way. We spoke candidly for a while. I was very attracted to him. I felt safe because I wanted to fuck him more than he wanted to fuck me.

He told me the story of how in grade school he'd been walking home one day with his best friend, Eric. They took the same route as always and it was a bright spring afternoon. Cherry blossoms, baseball season. Eric was wearing a blue sweatshirt his cousin sent him from Hawaii. It said ALOHA HAWAII on the front in rainbow letters and there was a rendering of all the islands.

A white pickup truck drove past, slowed, and came to a stop. A man got out. He had long gray hair, a silvery goatee, jean shorts, and paint on his bare knees. He was flustered and nervous and asked if one of the boys could help, his little girl had fallen into a well on Shroudsbury Road at the old pump house. He was on his way to get help, but he didn't want to leave her there alone.

— He was looking at me the whole time, River said. And I didn't say anything. I guess I believed him, but I don't know, I didn't say anything. But Eric said, Sure. Eric hopped right into the cab. The old man

216

told me to run along home and call the fire department, tell them to go to the pump house. But he kept looking at me as he backed away. Then he got into his car and they sped away. Eric waved at me out of the window.

That was the last time River saw Eric alive. The next day they found the old truck a few counties over. It was a florist's van. It had been stolen from a funeral home during a wake. They found Eric's body in a ditch, naked, a few days later.

— Jesus, I said to him. We were very close to each other in that moment and I looked into his eyes. I suppose, like anyone, I've never lost the hope for perfect love to come out of nowhere. River was not brilliant but he was physically perfect and kind and a life with him would be like a Grateful Dead t-shirt.

— I knew, River said, that the man wanted me. I knew I was the one he really wanted. And I've been living with that for all of these years.

Despicably, that story was like foreplay for me. I needed to have him; just as I needed to see all the sides of a new town, I needed to feel wanted by a good-looking man. To feel good, to feel as pretty as Alice, to feel potent enough to be near her.

By the time we left, the whole bar knew we were going to fuck. We parked in the driveway of our compound and were about to get out of my car when a long black car drove up. Down! I hissed. And we both shrank beneath the windows.

— It's probably just Lenny, River whispered.

— Yeah, I said.

— Why are we hiding? he asked.

— I don't know, I said. I stayed down there until the car took Lenny away.

River led me down the rough terrain from our driveway to his yurt, holding my hand as my heels scraped the rocks. I knew they were getting ruined but I didn't care; I hadn't paid for them. I followed him into his yurt and recalled all the times I'd been fucked in creepy places. It was a circus pavilion. Thin balsa beams held the structure up. The beams were in diamond shapes, an accordion; then they straightened and met at the top like the spokes of an umbrella. There was a pellet stove in the center like the one in my home. On the floor were many mismatched carpets. There were Aztec pillows and bright burlap blankets covering arabesque floor couches. His bed was in the back and center, the focal point. Right above it a skylight, a hexagon of navy sky.

He undressed me the way young boys undress a woman. Tentatively they undo one button or tug a corner of the shirt off your shoulder, then they lean back, smile, and wait for you to do the rest. If you never moved, neither would they.

I slipped the jumpsuit off and left my heels on. I wasn't wearing a bra, so I stood there in just my black thong and those delicious green shoes.

— Do you know what happens, he asked me, when you pour hot aluminum into ant-hills?

I laughed and said I had no idea what happened when you did that.

— It travels into all the passageways and hardens there, and then you dig it up, and you have this castle, this aluminum castle, with all these doors and intricate hallways. It's amazing. It's insane.

— What about the ants, I said.

— Yeah, he replied solemnly.

We began fucking standing up. His body hard and warm. Touching his rear made me self-conscious. After several perfect minutes he laid me down atop his shitty mattress and plunged in and out so rhythmically that it seemed choreographed to go with the Penguin Café Orchestra tinkling from his laptop speaker.

219

He rolled us over so that I was on top, and I performed the required spectacle. I held my hair above my neck, making triangles of my arms. I swiveled my hips and did not mash myself the way I have done with some men when I just wanted to get myself off. I did everything that I figured he would want. I sucked my stomach in, though I was mostly bones and tendons. I even turned around, reverse cowgirl. I felt the oldest then, the most ridiculous. I decided reverse cowgirl had its expiration at thirty-seven, at least with a new and younger man.

Oh man, he said a few times, but otherwise he wasn't a grunter. He held my hips firmly but tenderly. Nothing about him was gruesome or untoward. You'd be surprised at how few men you can say that about. Vic held me more gently and timidly than anyone, but it was insidious. His fingers like a Venus flytrap, closing in imperceptibly, wary of offending its prey.

I wasn't able to relax that night, but there's nothing better than fucking a beautiful man who is also kind and elusive. I faked an orgasm forty minutes in. I liked that he brought his mouth between my legs after we'd already started fucking. I liked the messiness. I looked up through the skylight at the wolf-gray stars and cried out like I was calling up to someone in the galaxy. I looked down to see the proud look on his shining face. The dog, Kurt, lay near the door, his chin resting on his paws, watching sex the way that dogs do, like they are confused as to why you're making more of it than it is.

In the morning I woke before he did. I didn't know how anyone could sleep past dawn in a yurt. The sun made me feel like a slut. River lay there, lightly snoring and handsome in a way that I found offensive.

I rose and gathered my jumpsuit and my heels. He woke up and looked at me and didn't offer water.

The previous night, after he'd come, he almost immediately began talking of his life plans. I was dismayed when the hemp curtains parted to reveal his boyish ambition. He was the same as Jack. They wanted you to think they didn't need technology and meanwhile they were furiously mining bitcoin.

I'd looked up Jack around that time. He wasn't the Internet entrepreneur he'd planned to be; in fact, his online presence was slight and bland, with one exception. Photographs of him were featured on the blog of a young woman named Kylie who was studying in Ireland for a master's program in something esoteric and unexciting. Jack had gone to visit her in a small town in County Clare where she lived with a bunch of other skinny girls in jean jackets. During Jack's visit they milked goats and burned peat moss. They went on hikes to well-known cliffs. They drank beer or wine in every shot. There were several still lifes of bouquets. *Jack buys me flowers any time he sees them,* the accompanying caption read. *And if they aren't available for purchase, he makes his own bouquets.*

At the top of the blog was the customary Kerouac quote, though I was sure a girl like Kylie knew no mad ones. I was a mad one who had held her new love's scrotum in my palms and kneaded it like dough.

Women have the upper hand. It's taken me half a lifetime to realize it. We don't actually care about the man who is bringing flowers to another woman. River was a stand-in for Jack. All present men are stand-ins for former men. And all men are stand-ins for our fathers. And even our fathers mean less than our own self-preservation. May you not go around the world looking to fill what you fear you lack with the flesh of another human being. That's part of what this story is for.

On a practical level, both young men, Jack and River, were proxies for Massi, my first kiss, at ten, following the figs soaked in grappa. When I saw boys in the streets with their low-slung backpacks, I thought of the girls they liked, the girls who got to be eleven and twelve and thirteen, with unicorn stickers and slap bracelets. I did not get to be any of those ages. I was ten and then I was thirty, and then I was thirty-seven.

That's the best reason I can give for why I lingered near the door until River called out to me.

— Hey, he said. A muscular arm reached from the bed and made the shape of a hug. Come back, he said. You can't leave without cuddling.

We fucked again, short but intense. We were on our sides and every thrust was deep and thoughtful. Kurt was circling near the door. His scruffy ears twitched at the sounds of squirrels and birds outside. Midfuck, River told the dog they'd be going soon. He asked me if I wanted to accompany them on their morning hike. *Did you want to come,* were the words he used.

I said no and River told me to stay for a bit, under the covers. They left without me. I walked around the yurt. On the "walls" were pictures of his father, many of them, stuck to the wood beams. There was a tray of crystals and rocks, each of them labeled. Fancy jasper, stone of relaxation. Golden sheen obsidian, stone of personal power. Titanium aura quartz, stone of high energy. There was a collection of homemade walking canes. There was a pair of panties on the floor next to the stove. Brown silk. I picked them up and smelled them.

I was in pain for the rest of that day. My abdomen was turning in on itself. I thought that it was because I'd had sex. Even if you don't believe in God, you can chalk it up to biology; your body will occasionally be confused if a penis pokes in and out and doesn't ejaculate inside of you. You didn't fulfill your biological purpose, nor did you have a sincere orgasm.

I took the jumpsuit off — how stupid clothes are after you've gotten drunk and fucked in them — and lay on the cowhide couch I'd owned for many years, the one on which I'd given Big Sky that first massage. My thighs and the backs of my arms stuck to the leather. I was afraid to turn the air conditioner on because the noise might summon Lenny. I didn't want to see anyone, especially him. I thought an orgasm might unclench my abdomen so I flipped onto my stomach. I rode one of the wide leather pillows and thought of River fucking someone even younger than he was. I thought of Jack and River double-teaming some small blonde wearing an anklet. Finally, right at the edge, I pictured Alice's huge naked chest squashed against a Corian kitchen counter and Big Sky plowing her from behind, an expression of ecstasy on his face that he'd never had with me. I came easily, explosively, but the pain did not subside.

16

At the end of the dinner that day my grandmother was raped, Joe and Evelyn dropped
us off at our little red A-frame. At the
restaurant they'd ordered dessert, a Baked
Alaska. My mother smoked and watched
them eat it, two herons drawing their big
lips over the creamy forkfuls. Joe Jr. and I
each got a scoop of rainbow sherbet in a
little silver bowl.

— Bye, Maria, keep us posted! Evelyn
called from the car. Meanwhile Joe Sr.
walked us to the door. He held my mother's
elbow. She was a little unsteady in her noisy
wooden heels. He insisted on coming inside
to make sure the place was secure.

— No need, Joe, my mother said. She was
always appropriating English idioms with
her accent. It made me hate her a little.

Joe made a show of poking around, going
upstairs into our bedrooms.

I need to describe the house. Right as you

walked in, there was the galley kitchen, a little rectangle of Formica and a four-burner white stove. My parents were very clean people and yet the Pocono house of my memory is covered in a film of grease. There were those plastic salt-and-pepper shakers — a brown top to indicate pepper and taupe for salt — and every time I touched them I felt the need to wash my hands.

Alongside the kitchen and extending to the back of the house was the combination dining room and living area. This was covered in wall-to-wall beige carpet, thick and cheap. Our dining room table had candlesticks and a plastic tablecloth that my mother wiped down nightly with a sponge.

My mother was always cleaning, using her long nails to scrape hard crusts off of cabinets, spraying Windex at cloudy windows and moving her arms industriously to battle the streaks. Yet the house, for me, seemed categorically contaminated. Clearly I had some sort of a premonition.

At the rear were the stairs to the second floor; these, too, were carpeted. The stairwell was very narrow. As a toddler I'd once tumbled from the top to the landing. I can still remember the curved pain in my neck when I thudded at the bottom with my feet in the air. I was afraid I'd broken myself.

But I was more afraid of my mother getting angry.

The second floor was railroad-style, a long, slender hallway with three bedrooms and one bathroom. My parents' — the master — was at the end of the hallway with the bathroom directly opposite. I slept in the bedroom closest to theirs, although most nights I slipped into bed beside my mother. The third bedroom, the one closest to the stairs, had two creepy twin beds with very tight sheets and knit blankets and light pink pillows with eyelet fringes. Sometimes I dreamed of two little girls in there, vicious ones who would pinch me in my sleep.

The bathroom was small with white and black subway tiles and a cheap shower curtain circling a claw-foot tub. In the mirrored medicine cabinet my mother kept a backup of her Valium, blue pills with V-shaped cutouts in the middle that I used to think were hearts. I've saved those, along with many of her other pills. The expiration dates are about twenty-five years old, but I've found they still work if you triple the dose.

Joe Sr. came downstairs. I was always having strange thoughts; I remember wondering if he'd stuffed a pair of my mother's panties into his jacket pocket. She wore full-bottom underwear, often sheer, in dark colors like purple and mahogany. I inherited some of my mother's allure, but it passed through a filter. She was old-fashioned sexy, pinup sexy. I have been hotel-room sexy, succubus sexy, too skinny to be remembered.

— All clear, he said.

— Thanks, Joe.

— If you feel nervous, anything at all, you give me a call, any time of night.

My mother nodded. She'd kicked off her shoes and was rubbing her ankle with the red-painted toes of the opposite foot.

After he left, the girlish smile left my mother's face.

— It's time for a bath, she said to me.

— Can we have cocoa?

— No cocoa. It's bedtime. It's been a long day.

— Is Grandma going to be okay?

— Yes.

My mother moved into the small kitchen, putting dishes away. She was angry and I didn't understand why. I thought she should be worried, nervous. I'd expected we would cuddle and comfort each other.

— Why didn't we go with Daddy? I asked, knowing it was the wrong question.

— I don't know why. Go to bed.

— Mommy, please, I'll have nightmares.

She shook her head at me. She said something in Italian about nightmares being unavoidable. I don't want you to think she was cruel. But she didn't hold anything back. She didn't treat me like I was ten years old. My father loved me so much more. I always thought that. But the tragedy of my life is proof that he did not.

— I always have nightmares if you're angry at me. Daddy would tell you to read me a story and make it better.

— Why isn't your father here and do it, then?

— Because. Grandma.

— Go to bed!

— Don't you love me, Mommy?

My mother turned to face me. I wasn't going to get the answer I wanted. I remember the feeling inside my heart. It was shocking how cold she could be. As a child in rural Italy, she'd been very sick and her parents had put her in a sanatorium, hours away from the family home, where she was quarantined in a sick ward with other children, coughing blood and not getting outside. Nurses with masks treated her brusquely, washed her in ice water to curtail the infection. They left bowls of farina with lumps for her to eat. They didn't care if she didn't eat. For nearly a year she was in that hospital and her mother came to visit her only once. It was a long trip and they were very poor and my mother said she didn't blame her. She accepted it without reservation. In their bedroom in New Jersey my mother had a shrine for the woman who left her in the sanatorium. She told me I didn't understand how hard life could be. That I was lucky.

Silently she taught me that we are all monsters, we are all capable of monstrosity. Unforgettably and unforgivably, she taught me several days later that there is always a reason behind the monstrosity. So all my life I have never had to wonder, How did that thing happen? With a mother killing her toddler, with a girl texting her boyfriend into committing suicide, with a child blowing the priest. Other people wonder *why*. I know exactly why.

— There are no stories or cocoa this late, my mother said instead of answering my question.

— But Daddy lets me when I'm scared. Daddy said —

— Your father is going to ruin you! she snapped.

I have long puzzled over that response. Somehow, because of how much warmer my father was on the whole, I think I metabolized it to mean that men can ruin you in wonderful ways, like lurid, bright white jawbreakers with beautiful rainbow specks.

17

I woke in the morning to two text messages. The first had come in the middle of the night, from Vic's wife, very long and all in capital letters. She must have been drunk or on pills. I thought of her dead husband and especially of her boy, how it was exponentially easier to go on if you decided to go mad.

JOANNN. COME IN JOAN. WHERE ARE U? ARE U WITH A NEW HUSBAND? ARE YOU GOING TO TEAR ANOTHER FAMILY TO SHREDS? MY DAUGHTER HATES ME AND SHE HATES HER FATHER. SHE THINKS ITS MY FAULT THAT A WHORE WAS ABLE TO STEAL HER FATHER FROM ME. WHAT DO U THINK JOANNN ? DO U AGREE? ARE U A WOMAN OF GOD? DO U PRAY TO A HIGHER POWER? WE USED TO GO TO CHURCH EVERY SUNDAY AND AFTER TO THE ROSE GARDEN AND HE PICKED ME ROSES AND WE PUT THEM IN

A VASE AT HOME AND THEY LIVED UNTIL THE NEXT SUNDAY. I WAS ONE OF THE LUCKY GIRLS. HE WAS THE LOVE OF MY LIFE. I WONDER IF HE GOT U ROSES. I HAVE ALL THE BILLS HERE THE CREDIT CARD I WASNT SUPPOSD TO KNOW ABOUT. ALL THESE FANCY DINNERS! U ARE A LUCKY GIRL TO. HE NVR GOT ME CAVIAR.

I read it a few times. I'd begun to tremble, though I didn't realize it until I saw the phone shaking in my hand.

The other message was from Alice.

Your day off right? Come by for a comped class at 10? Then ill take you to the farmers market on trancas for banana blossoms.

Five minutes before the class, I checked my face in my rearview mirror. Why do some straight women need to be beautiful in front of other women? If men were wiped from the planet, how long would that need linger? At what point would we just focus on becoming strong?

Inside the studio Alice was seated in lotus pose. Her hair was all the way down. She winked at me as I unrolled one of the rental mats near the window. She led us in sun salutations to Dylan's "Mozambique." I wondered whether any of these tight-faced

234

women were thinking anything other than how beautiful Alice was. How stable yet dainty her wrists looked on the mat and how demure her rear was, high up in the air, in downward dog. There is so much power in the way we obsess. If we could only harness it. If we would only redirect it.

I watched Alice's body move and willed my bones to lengthen like hers. When I shot my legs behind my hips into chaturanga, I felt as light as I had ever felt.

At the end Alice readjusted me in corpse pose. She smelled like pears. I was the first to get up and quietly roll up my mat. I didn't look at her as I left the space. I waited outside on one of the benches. The front-desk girl came outside to ask me whether I had paid for the class, whether I would like to purchase a membership. I told her the class was comped. I felt like a wrinkled thief.

When Alice came outside, she regarded me with a queer smile on her face. I worried that maybe I'd acted needy in the studio. It was impossible for me to know the right way to be around a woman.

We drove too fast in the left lane of the Pacific Coast Highway with the windows down. We passed several empty garden centers, we passed the stone pillars of the Getty. That stretch of Malibu felt void of animals. The wind was too hot, the cars were too fast. Only crabs thrived.

Alice played music loud and didn't always answer a question right away. A lot of her actions felt cruel to me. Eventually I stopped asking questions. I held my arm out the window and tried to exist as a needless thing. I felt around her much the way I'd felt around Big Sky — that I should be as seductive as possible but take up the least amount of space.

We pulled into the Trancas Country Market. It was a cluster of shops, a café, a bank, and a few boutiques. All the storefronts were made of wood planks. It felt more like Montana than it did the dry throat of Malibu. Alice parked between a bright yellow Karmann Ghia and a powder-blue BMW. There were G-wagons and Land Rovers and weathered Volvos and Porsches and Priuses. Every car in Los Angeles felt like it was the perfect car.

The farmers' market took up a strip of roadway behind the shops. Individual white tents shaded twin rows of long tables. Some tables were full of flowers in vases, and others had tight clusters of young broccoli florets and healthy-looking artichokes. Some had shallow tubs of ice with plastic containers of *taramosalata* and whipped feta. There was a fishmonger and there was a meat man and there were gray-haired ladies selling soap.

Many of the patrons looked like us, women in yoga clothes with good hair. There was a woman a few years older than I was, with her daughter. I was always picking these women out of crowds — my age, give or take a few years, with a young girl. The child wore her blond hair in cornrows and had gangly legs. The mother pushed her own hair into a messy bun — something that beautiful women do on autopilot. My mother did things like that but not with her hair; more so with cutting onions, eating persimmon. This mother looked rested and scheduled. I watched her buy black garlic and let the hippie farmer keep the three dollars in change.

There was a group of young men in neon Ray-Bans wearing backpacks. They were hikers coming down from one of the nearby trails for a glass of aloe vera. They looked at us. Next to Alice, in similar clothes, I wondered if I became a part of their fantasy or if they pushed me out of the picture altogether. I would have preferred the latter. To be a part of the dream of Alice would have made me feel like the scrapings from a pan. By that point in my life I knew that my obsession with beauty had everything to do with my father. When you are young and you see your father choose something, the thing that he chooses will be the thing that you want to be. I'm thrilled you will not have this problem.

So far the two men who'd loved me were dead. Big Sky was alive and well, with his young son and his Southern belle wife, on the Upper West Side and in Montana. For some reason I always pictured them on their big decks eating peaches, sweet yellow wedges with vibrant red-orange skin.

I'd been in the apartment overlooking the park only once. His wife and son had been at the lodge in Montana. Back then they went sporadically, but I'd recently found out they had moved most of their life there.

He was flying to meet them at the lodge the following day. With Big Sky, my hatred of weekends intensified. Only people who live their lives very routinely, who have never known abject grief, can love Saturdays and Sundays. For me there was a rickety lonesomeness to them. It always seemed everybody had escaped somewhere I hadn't been invited to. Blue pools and cocktails circulating on round trays. Or black lakes and tire swings. I bet that's true for most mistresses. But it's laughable to call myself a mistress, with either Vic or Big Sky, or with Tim, for that matter. I wish I had been something so quaint and definable as a mistress.

That Thursday night on Big Sky's deck I looked out at the city beneath me. I was wearing a white dress with wooden buttons down the center. It was one of the most expensive dresses I owned, though it didn't look it. He brought out two glasses of rosé and we peered over the stone balustrade. I felt the heat of being next to him. I wanted to make myself wider, I wanted to spread my legs as far out in either direction as they could go and take everything he could possibly shoot inside me. I asked him if he was excited to get to Montana and he said, Oh, yes, I can't wait.

I don't know what I expected. But I didn't expect that. I was savoring every second with him and he was merely passing the time before he could be in the mountain air with his family. We fucked on one of the striped deck loungers under the silvery Manhattan starlight. He didn't wear a condom; he always pulled out and came across my chest. That was our thing.

Even though I wanted to stay over I knew that I couldn't so I took a cab home just after midnight. It was my choice to be hurt in these ways.

Talking to Alice about Big Sky made my feelings for him both more painful and more manageable. I had only told her the first part of Vic, what you might call the honeymoon period, though I cringe to think of it in those terms. She was giving me exactly what I had always wanted. She was making me feel seen and heard.

— Are there any herbs you absolutely hate? she said to me when we were before a table of them. Tall fronds of dill and glistening bunches of cilantro and parsley and basil, arranged like tiny trees inside of mason jars.

— In general?

— These are things we should get over with now. Otherwise you become close and then one day you discover the other person doesn't like dill. And you're forced to hate them forever.

— Dill is a deal breaker?

— No. Cilantro. I can't stand people who don't like cilantro. They're closed-minded.

— I could do without oregano, I said.

— Everyone can do without oregano. That's fine.

— There isn't any herb I hate. I think chives and chervil are beautiful.

She turned to me and smiled. I'd gotten the answer right.

— Do you cook? she asked.

I nodded. I worried that she was more skilled in classic techniques, like poaching fish. She was likely a neater chopper; I could never take the time to dice an onion into comely cubes.

— Is it too soon, Alice said, for us to cook together?

— Maybe, I said. We both laughed. There is no better invitation in the world than women laughing. The boys in the bright Ray-Bans stopped in their tracks and un-abashedly stared at us. There were four and not one was better-looking than another. None of their eyes were kind. I wondered how many women between them they'd got-ten pregnant. Sometimes I can't get down a city block without seeing the quiet abor-tions in the air above everyone's head.

They were frozen in that airless atmo-sphere of men waiting to aggress. The way they stared — lips parted in a lively leer, gleaming eyes — often forced the woman to say something first, often out of fear.

I was wondering if Alice noticed them, or if she was even more used to being hit on than I, when suddenly she spoke.

— Do you recognize us from somewhere?

The apparent leader — the tallest, wear-ing a highlighter-pink sleeveless tank with highlighter-yellow Ray-Bans — pushed the glasses up on his sandy head.

— We were wondering if you girls might know where the vegetarian masala dosas are?

— Masala dosas are traditionally vegetarian, so you don't need to qualify, said Alice.

— Actually, some have meat, the captain said, smiling.

— Actually, some have meat, Alice mimicked, her lips pursed.

As a group, they looked wounded. It was funny how men could look that way. For years they could violently finger and push just the tip in, all the while saying, Just the tip, just for a second, not like a question but like a mantra. They could thoughtlessly fuck you from behind, their hips on hydraulics. They could be tired, sick, sad, rageful over having the flu, yet their hips would be completely fine, moving back and forth like a car part. Men were dependable fuckers. But suddenly they could look sad like that. After all, they were only trying to make conversation.

— The Indian culture is more meatless than any other, Alice said, but you boys look like you could use some. Meat.

She said the word *meat* very softly. But not sensually. I watched the rape in them shrivel up.

— Maybe it's not too soon, I said, staring at the boys, to cook together.

Alice's house, close to the Venice canals, was nothing like what I expected. I expected to be jealous. Teak and windows, clean lines. Not rich but well planned. Single flowers in old Italian lotion bottles.

I'd followed her in my car, and when we pulled up, I had that sinking feeling I get when something is the opposite of beautiful. I used to feel that with my parents when we'd pull up to hotels they'd booked, or the first time I saw the Poconos house.

Alice's house was not clean and holistic. It was an exhausted bordello. From the outside it was a tiny cape with blue aluminum siding. There was a shabby porch with two stained armchairs and an old steel planter. The area beneath the porch was covered with broken white lattice. There was a strip of dead grass between the edge of the porch and the start of the sidewalk. From the outside it looked the home of a couple who'd met in college, settled into this spot after a bender, and never left.

The front door opened directly onto a depressing kitchen. Yellowed wallpaper. Cheap white cabinets with pine trim. Beige linoleum floor peeling up at the corners. Coil stove. A dirty white Mr. Coffee. Then there were the inexplicable touches. Dried lavender hanging from the ceiling, Jem dolls and Barbie dolls with dyed blue and pink hair posing from the tops of the cabinets.

Alice, unembarrassed, gave me the grand tour. The living room had a black leather couch and a nineteen-inch Magnavox sitting on a stack of books. Many Persian rugs that looked expensive, some of them beginning on the floor and finishing a few feet up the wall. Ruby and emerald settees, pink and mahogany pillows on the floor, lanterns filled with battery-operated candles. It was both operatic and small, overstuffed and empty.

The bedroom made the least sense. A patchwork quilt. Glossy black cabinets. Lots of unwatered plants, the smell of myrrh. Posters of heavy-metal bands with curled-up edges. A framed picture of a naked man, his crotch obscured by a python. A pink neon sign over the bed, in wild font, said, LOVE ME. I could only think of the stains of many sex acts.

Alice waited for me to turn around after seeing the bedroom. Her arms were folded and she was smiling.

— What do you think? she said.

— It's kind of insane.

— It's a reminder not to get comfortable.

— It's like this on purpose?

— It's like this because it's like this. Some of it is laissez-faire sloppiness, laziness, what have you. Mostly it's cheap, whatever I had on hand, garage sale things. Some of it's from an escort's place on the boardwalk. She gave me her pillows.

Because my expression didn't change, she squinted and cocked her head until I looked directly into her eyes.

— Don't forget, she said, I'm younger than you.

In no time, the ugly home transformed before my eyes, the way the ugly homes of beautiful women are wont to do. Alice cranked open the window in the kitchen and the California breeze blew in. She set a bushel of basil in a vase filled with water, and a bunch of cilantro went into an empty creamer carton. She took out all the fruit and vegetables we'd bought, arranging them in bowls and tall carafes until the kitchen came alive. Dusty orange watermelon radish, prim pearl onions, grassy spring onions, vine tomatoes, and limes. Sandy spinach, mustard greens, and arugula. Green papaya and avocado, and the banana blossom looking like a panicked bird in its own white bowl. She placed the hunk of ruby tuna we'd bought from the fishmonger on a white cutting board and then rubbed the bluefish with salt and oil and left it in its brown waxed paper. She washed her hands with Mrs. Meyer's lemon soap and played calypso from her laptop.

She was going to make a salad and ceviche and she asked me to tell her about Vic as she worked. She asked me what he looked like. I described him as best I could but said that he was more of a feeling than anyone I had ever known. I told her about his hats and his suits, how large they were, that he'd never worked out in his life beyond the weights he lifted in high school. And though he wasn't overweight, he was definitely ashamed of his figure, and so he wore these big suits.

She asked me again if it was crazy of her to think that we were getting somewhere. I told her no, it wasn't crazy. I could have said more then. I could have told her everything, and I wanted to. But she was right that Vic would lead into the rest.

I'd already told her about Scotland and Cumberland Island and Mexico. The sunny days. The times when I'd still felt like a girl, when I could still pretend that I hadn't flushed myself down a drain. Now it was time to tell her when the rot set in.

In as much detail as I could remember, I described the company trip to Palm Springs. The scaly heat of the desert. Vic was always arranging events so he'd have an excuse to be with me for a long weekend. It's funny to think how many corporate dollars are spent so that one man can fuck one woman.

We stayed at a ten-bedroom guesthouse that had natural-rock hot tubs with unobstructed views of the mountains in the distance. I'd never been attracted to any of our colleagues, but there was one man, Paul, who had just come from Virginia, from some old tobacco family, and he hunted and fished and wore Minnetonkas and swore very graciously, the words *goddamned* and *witch's tit.*

Paul was something of a precursor to Big Sky. He was an amuse-bouche. I sat next to him at the first dinner. It was held at a decent chain with a huge kitchen and a gas-burning fireplace that stretched horizontally across the room. We sat in long strips of two and Vic was diagonal from me. Poor Vic folded the napkin in his lap very meticulously, but for some reason I always had the feeling it was tucked into his shirt, beneath his neck. I listened to Paul with my chin in the cradle of my palm. I laughed a lot. I did that with most men at first. I'd done it with Vic. I told Alice how I was sure I'd gotten this from my mother. Paul talked about hunting like an asshole. But he was also self-effacing and had a nice head of chestnut hair so that overall it was charming, and had I been a little healthier, I might have tried to date him. But I didn't. I flirted in a way that a man from a good Southern family couldn't quite comprehend. It made Vic angry. I could feel his wrath across the table. His skin was red. He drank glass after glass of wine. Then he switched to Scotch and flicked his eyeballs to the back of his brain.

But he didn't erupt. What he did instead is what all men do when they feel like another man has touched something they think they own — they try to reclaim you. That night he came into my room. There were no locks on the doors and I had the room on the top floor between Vic and some woman named Crystal whose eyes ping-ponged from side to side when she talked and everybody made fun of her all weekend long and so did I.

Around midnight there were still some men playing poker in the kitchen, but most of us had gone into our rooms. I heard my door open. I couldn't believe it. I thought to pretend I was dead asleep. I heard him walk very quietly to the side of my bed and kneel down until his face was next to mine. I opened my eyes. Hey, he said. My stomach turned. His eyes were small. His skin was dry and he looked like someone who'd let himself go for many years and now, he'd found a reason to live and he wanted to drink purified water and join a gym. He smelled like Scotch and cologne. He kissed my forehead and then my eyelids.

— Jesus Christ, Alice said. Please tell me you did not let him fuck you.

— No. I said I was feeling sick from the wine. He got into bed and held me. In his boxers and t-shirt. He didn't let go all night.

— Bloodsucking pig.

— In the morning we overslept. I remember the room was very cool, someone had cranked the air-conditioning, and the shades were down and we slept past eight thirty. Nine was the time we were all being picked up by a limo to be brought to the breakfast spot for a team-building exercise. Someone knocked on my door. I bolted up in bed. Vic did not. He snored peacefully. Just a second! I said. The voice outside said, Joan, are you okay? The limo's here. It was Paul's voice and I could tell he hadn't heard me and meanwhile Vic stirred and said, like a hungover boor, What?

— Oh my God.

— And the door began to open and I ran up and pushed back against Paul and I told him that I was running late and I would be right behind them in a taxi. And he seemed to peer around me and Vic was making waking-up noises and I was sweating, I was so afraid. Then Paul left and it was just the two of us in the house and so we both arrived late to the team-building exercise. I insisted in going in a taxi by myself, but Vic popped in about five minutes after me, freshly showered, looking jovial.

— He wanted everyone to think he had fucked you.

— Paul barely said another word to me for the rest of the weekend. Every one of them avoided me. I was garbage.

— You said you ruined this man's life. And all I've heard so far is how he pissed all over yours.

I told her she didn't know the whole story. By now she had diced the spring onions, tomatoes, and avocados, and cut the tuna into textbook cubes. She'd minced the serrano peppers and cilantro. She used a wooden spoon to gently fold it all with lime juice and a few teaspoons of sugar. We were drinking Sancerre out of short cups, filling

250

each other up frequently. It was just before two on a Monday afternoon.

— We'll eat the ceviche now, and then I'll make the salad outside while you grill the bluefish. Does that sound okay?

I nodded. I wished she would do or say something that wasn't perfect so that I wouldn't have to kill her.

— Now tell me how you hurt this man, because I have to tell you, Joan, I think you've got it wrong.

I told her about the week I met Big Sky. It was the same week that I had a big project due at work, and what she had to understand was that this was the first time in my life I had a job that wasn't odd. For Christ's sake I'd made up dead people, and poorly, because I didn't have any training. At the advertising firm I'd been promoted from a secretarial position to an associate very quickly. I was telling the world to buy beer and cars and to shop at big department stores. I was involved in a conversation, I was involved in the making of money. It had become somewhat lost on me that the reason I was in this vaunted position was because a married man had become infatuated with me.

And Vic was happy to provide for my progression. He prided himself on his connections, his ability to vault people, but with me, of course, he also wanted to prove indispensable. He promoted me again. I met Big Sky a day or so later.

— You have to understand, I said to Alice, the situation with Vic had begun to fester. Palm Springs had happened a few months before, and I was done. I was disgusted. And he could tell.

— Did you tell Vic about him?

— I couldn't bear not to. I had nobody else to tell.

— Not one girlfriend?

— Nobody.

— You've never had girlfriends? Alice asked.

— Not really. My aunt.

— You haven't seen a point with women?

— I wouldn't say that.

— Even though, all around you, men were fucking you right in the ass.

— That's not entirely true, I said, feeling myself flush.

— Joan. This is why you met me. Don't you think so? Everything happens for a reason. Even the scary things.

We had moved outside to her terrible yard with its yellow-green grass and its Char-Broil kettle grill. It felt like we were in Alabama instead of Southern California, and she was mocking me with her continental accent and her absolute beauty, and I wanted to dislike her very much. But I also felt she was on my side. It was hard to experience the feeling, let alone explain its effect. I wanted her to hold me. My whole life I'd been waiting for a woman to hold me.

We drank our wine and grilled the fish and the sun lowered and some more breeze came. I felt a little nauseous and Alice decided it was time to eat. She set the table and served the salad. It was a wonderful salad, with the banana blossoms julienned and the vibrant pinwheels of watermelon radish, the arugula coated with olive oil and bright lemon and a dusting of pecorino across the top. It was odd to eat something so fresh on stained armchairs in that unkempt yard with a gorgeous woman. A lot about Alice was a contradiction, but that was true of most beautiful women. There was one poet, one author, they knew backward and forward, which lent them some intractable intellect. Once I knew a beautiful girl from the Midwest who had read everything Barry Hannah had ever written and that was it. That was all she knew. The more obscure the writer, the more suicidal, the better.

— I told Vic about Big Sky after the first weekend when I didn't hear from him at all. I was so desperate I just wanted to tell somebody who cared for me. I wanted Vic to tell me I would hear from him again.

— Oh, Alice said. That's always it, isn't it. Will he call me again? Just tell me I'll hear from him again, even if it's only so he can say, This is over.

Alice took a bite. She ate like a European — small, neat forkfuls. A piece of fish with a strip of arugula or radish. Mixing things.

— You grilled the fish perfectly, she said.

I thanked her and she nodded impatiently while chewing, reminding me of my mother, and gestured with her hand for me to go on.

— I told him, and I was breathing heavily, and I was scared. He could tell. We were out to lunch. It was a Monday at this Bavarian bar far from our office and I was drinking Belgian ale though I hate Belgian ale, and he was staring at me with his beady eyes. I kept looking at my phone to see if Big Sky had written and I could just sail out of there, leave Vic forever, the whole disease of it. And this is where it gets awful. Just sickening.

— Yes, tell me.

— Vic told me to write to him. He told

me to give him a directive. He told me to write and say, *Was just thinking of you. I'm making martinis at five. Stop by when you knock off for the day.*

— That's somewhat good advice, Alice said.

— It was scary, he had this look on his face like he was accessing a haunted part of himself. Then he sat there with me and we waited. I said, I cannot believe I just wrote that. And Vic said, You had to, it's fine, he'll come. And I said, Jesus, that is so unlike me. And Vic smirked, and I remember this verbatim, he said, He'll be rock-hard the second he opens that email, kid.

Alice doubled over in disgust. I'd thought I would feel shame recounting that, but instead I felt relief. So I continued.

— By now he had this very strange look on his face, this very strange mask. His eyes glittered, he wasn't sad but enraged, even —

— Turned on.

— Yes. And he said, So tell me about him. And I said, Huh? And he just repeated himself. Tell me about him. Blankly. Straightforward. As though he were just any man and I were just any girl. He said, Is it nice? And I kept saying, What? And he just kept saying those same words, Tell me about him. What's it like? Is it nice? And finally I said, What? The sex? And he said, Yeah. I said, Aren't you bored with this? And he said, Nope. I remember that, specifically. *Nope.* I said, I told you everything. Which of course wasn't completely true, but I told him so much. I had certainly told him more than a woman has ever told a man who loves her about another man she's been fucking. And Vic said, Is he a total stud? And I said, Yeah, in a sort of strange way. He's unthreateningly assertive. Now, this, of course, was the thing that most drew me to Big Sky, but Vic, like every man, didn't care about that. He sailed over that. He said, Big? Just that, like that. Big? I said, Yes, because I wanted to torture him a little, because how dare he talk to me that way.

— That's the right thing you should have felt.

— But I was cruel.

— We'll see.

— And he said, Huge? So I said, Not huge, but big. And he said, Nice. Heavy cummer? And I looked at the tables around us. I was always looking at the tables around us, everywhere we went. I was always feeling depraved and hideous. I said, Who *are* you? Are you a porn writer? I didn't understand where this was coming from. And he could see that I was angry and confused, so he said, Aw, come on, kid.

— He was trying to get off.

— But I was never that way. I'd done so many questionable things in my life, but I was prudish in these respects. You know?

— I can see that about you. You're a little girl in many ways.

— I told Vic the best part was kissing, and the way he held me while we did, and the way we moved against each other. And he laid down a fifty-dollar bill and said, Awesome. Have a great afternoon, kid. Let me know what he says. I've gotta get back to the office. I know you don't like to walk back with me anymore, your morals and such. So I'll leave you to it.

And I said, I can feel it, he's not gonna respond, and I'm going to feel like an asshole. And Vic said, He'll come, trust me. And if he doesn't, like I said, it's not because he doesn't want to. I thanked him for being a good friend, in a very strange way. And he said, Okay, catch you in a bit. He'll come. Just wish I was the one getting that note. And, seriously, of course. Look, I love you. I really do. Sometimes I think you don't get that.

— And then, Alice said, he went to jerk off in the office bathroom.

— But you don't understand, I said, there

was something more. There was love there. He loved me.

— That's not love. That's abuse.

— He finished my project for me. I had that big project, I couldn't think, I couldn't concentrate on it because of Big Sky, who, as you know, did show up that night, and after he left, I was wounded all over again, and Vic did it for me that week. He'd been there, he'd listened about all the other boys, all the other men. I didn't tell you everything.

— So you'd been telling him about other men you were with.

— Yes, a doorman, for example, that I slipped my room number to in San Francisco.

— That's hot, Alice said.

The way a woman could make you feel sensual was utterly different than a way a man could. Especially a beautiful woman. I looked at her big nose, at her big white teeth. Her ferocious eyebrows and her nude fat lips. It was a mystery where the striking beauty came from. It came from everything at once, and although it was hard to put my finger on, I didn't for a moment doubt it. Unlike my own, which I'd been doubting in mirrors my whole life.

— And the young kid, Jack, I said.

— So he suffered, listening about all these men.

I nodded, feeling for the first time that I'd been unfairly blaming myself.

— But he didn't have to, you understand.

— We worked together. Should he have fired me?

— No! He should have sucked it up, that he was married with a family and that a young woman who lost her own family might be looking for something that replicated that. And that just because you wanted connection, someone to make you feel protected, that didn't mean you wanted someone to chain you up. To emotionally jail you. Joan, this man took advantage of a sad young woman. Joan?

— But the truth is I kept going back to him and back to him. Every time I was hurt by some little thing, every time I needed help with my work. Every time some fucking little boy hurt me. I felt loved by him. I needed that so badly. But this time it was different. The way I felt for Big Sky, Vic could tell I was blown away. Vic saw it and it killed him. Plus, Big Sky was a man, he wasn't some kid. He had more money than Vic. He was powerful.

— But these games he was playing! Asking you about the size of another man's dick? After we returned to Italy, I worked as a waitress at this café on La Dogana beach in Maremma. Every day this bald man with one of those cartoon guts came in. Every day he ordered the linguine con vongole. They made it the best there. And every day this man, Carlo, would ask for extra parsley, but he wanted me to sprinkle it on top right there in front of him. Some days he was my only lunch table. He didn't act untoward with me, unless you can count him wanting the parsley sprinkled tableside, and the way he would watch my hands. I used to apply clear polish every other day because I was conscious of Carlo watching my fingers. Joan, do you understand? There are rapes, and then there are the rapes we allow to happen, the ones we shower and get ready for. But that doesn't mean the man does nothing.

— It's a finer line than that, I said. I wasn't innocent. Don't forget, I'd slept with Vic, I'd even tried to get off. I could never come with him. But I tried. I exhausted myself trying. I told him I cared for him. More than once.

— And then one day you didn't and he wouldn't lay off of you. He stuck around. You didn't force him to. Not only did he stick around, he suctioned himself on like a fucking octopus!

— But I lied to him. And all he wanted was the truth. He didn't want half-truths. And I would lie. I could have just said, I love this man, this married man. Now fuck off, please.

— And it should be your responsibility to talk to someone that way? You don't think he knew you didn't love him? Didn't want him around?

— But it would have been honest. In the beginning I would see him everywhere, as though he were a man I loved. Probably he felt real love from me. Of course, I was confusing it with a fatherly love I'd been looking for. But to change suddenly. To start to talk to him about other men. I didn't believe him that he wanted to hear these things. But he also didn't want me to lie. I was confused, but still I was never doing right by him. I sent him into a pit of despair. And at home he had this wife and this son with problems.

— Oh, fuck his problems! You lied because if you told the truth, he'd make you feel terrible. In his own little ways. And you are saying that *you* changed suddenly? What about the ways he must have changed? Going from a man who reminded you of your father to a man who made you feel like a

261

slut, like a bad, bad girl. He scared you, the way men scare women, into submission. He could have fired you, and you needed the job! You're still under the spell of him. And Big Sky. You need to come out from there. Where is Vic now? Where is this blood-sucker?

— That's the part.

Alice poured us both some more wine and raised her eyebrows in curiosity. At the very least, I didn't feel boring.

— A little over a month ago, just before I came here, Big Sky got in touch with me after a very long time. I was so happy. I cried for a day. I went to a Turkish bath. I buttered every inch of my skin. I had everything plucked, tinted. We met for din-ner at this Italian restaurant in the Village. I can't tell you how delirious I was. I didn't tell Vic, I didn't tell anyone. In fact, Vic asked me if I'd heard from Big Sky lately. He acted like it had just popped into his mind. Of course, I realized later he'd been reading my email, he knew my security question, having to do with my mother's maiden name, because he had all my em-ployment information. And my email was always saying that my password had to be changed. So I knew he was reading my email. At home with his wife, sitting there and clicking away like a teenage sociopath. So he must have known. He must have followed me. I had a hunch that he waited outside my apartment. Once I saw him and he played it off, said he'd been in the area and was going to ring me up. Other times I felt his energy. I would turn around quickly in the street, expecting to find him there. I started to wait longer and longer to reply to his messages. One time he texted and then, when I didn't reply for over an hour, he called me. I shoved my phone in my bag and roamed the streets. I finally wrote back: *You don't have to follow up a text with a call. It's obsessive. I'll reply when I see it. What's up?* And he wrote, *I was calling because I saw you. I saw you on the street.* I wrote back, *Why didn't you call my name?* But I was frightened. The streets of Manhattan are the most naked places. If there's someone you want to see, that person lights up, they glow. *I know you don't want to be seen with me at certain times, in certain spots. I was respecting your boundaries.* God, how I hated myself. That I allowed people like him to feel they owned pieces of me.

— Joan, Jesus. It keeps getting worse.

— This night in question, I wore a very pretty green wool dress, long-sleeved, wifely, you could say. I felt aware of everything.

When I saw Big Sky at the table, I was happy but I was also ready. After all that time I felt strong. He told me I looked beautiful. I could see in his eyes, he had that fear about him, when a man hasn't seen you in a long time and worries he no longer has his thumb over you. That was the look he had, and I savored it. We ordered fried zucchini blossoms and a bottle of expensive wine. His hair was long and I loved it but I didn't say anything. I was clever and restrained. He spoke vaguely of some problems in his marriage. By the time our entrées arrived, I felt like he was feeling all the things for me I'd always wanted him to feel. God, I felt so *happy*. And then Vic walked in. I saw him come in, I saw him the whole time, and I knew I wasn't seeing things. I told you how he hated that I lied to him, that he once said that was the worst part. And there I was with the man whose existence in my life had almost killed him. And Vic thought it had been put to bed and likely he thought there was still a chance for me and him. That one day I'd grow older and Vic would be there for me. And sometimes I thought that, too, that eventually I'd be too tired, too wrinkled. A woman like me can't exist past a certain age. And Vic must have dreamed about that day. He'd get us a condo in Sayulita with white stucco and a little Jacuzzi on the balcony and he'd buy me high-cut bikinis and we'd eat plantains and just live out our days. But I think seeing me there with Big Sky, seeing me wearing a wonderful dress, looking more beautiful than I'd ever looked with him, I think it was a concentration of every raw hurt he'd ever felt at my hands. I could see his face melt from the inside.

And he pulled out a gun. I was barely shocked to see it because I could feel it, I'd been feeling it for years. I didn't close my eyes. I felt I should die, anyway, it would make sense. I thought of the imminent freedom. A woman at another table screamed and Big Sky turned to look behind himself. But then something switched again in Vic's eyes and I thought he would point it at Big Sky and in that moment I felt I didn't care about anything, about anyone. I figured how natural it was for my life to go this way the first night I felt happiness. The screams around us were muted. Everyone was frozen, waiters with two bowls of pasta on each arm. And then Vic turned the gun on himself and it went off and his face blew through itself onto the wall behind him.

— Oh, Jesus Christ!

—That's the reason I left New York, I said.

265

I wanted to tell her that it was to see her. I wanted to know what only she could tell me. The thing I didn't expect was that telling her about me would force me to look at myself, at the way I craved the love of men who would never love me. At the way I could not abide women who needed me. At the way I destroyed some while allowing others to destroy me. I felt sick with myself and, at the same time, unburdened. I thought I'd been honest with myself. But I hadn't. I'd been telling myself ghost stories my whole life.

Alice rose and hugged me. All afternoon we'd been performing the little acts that women must perform when they come together after high school. The extreme politeness of gesture. The focus on being both feminine and its opposite. And with this embrace it was no different. We were trying to exude kindness without being overly effusive. I wished she would never let go.

— There's more, I said. She let go of me and sat back down. I told her about Vic's wife, Mary, and his daughter, Eleanor, who was apparently on her way to find me. I showed her the text messages, the latest one, its crazed length, its capital letters.

— No, Joan, Alice said in a tone of what I

believe was genuine anger. No, she said. This is enough of this.

I laughed, trying to make light of the absurdity.

— From beyond the grave, he finds me.

— Is this crazy girl thinking she's going to kill you? This is insane.

— Maybe she has a point.

— Oh, no. She doesn't. Her father is — was — a bloodsucker, and that's that. She needs to learn from that and move along.

— I don't know. I think maybe she's justified. You think she wants to kill me?

— Clearly she comes from a line of sociopaths. You haven't spoken to the mother since that text?

— No.

— Nothing will come of it. It's so stupid. Shall I pick you up tomorrow? We can go to Cold Spring Tavern, flirt with Harley men, and get food poisoning. You need to put this ridiculousness out of your head.

I used the bathroom as she began clearing the plates. I tried to help but she refused. I hated when people didn't refuse, when they gave you something to do. Julienne these carrots.

The bathroom was tiny and there was mold in almost every line of caulk. There was a Tasmanian Devil mud flap, the kind you see on an eighteen-wheeler, on the floor of the tub. I pressed a piece of toilet paper to my forehead and nose to blot the oil.

— Sorry for the heavy afternoon, I said before I left. She ruffled my hair. I kept my hand pressed to the same spot on my scalp the whole way home.

18

Back in the Canyon I showered off the wine. A breeze blew in the scent of honeysuckle. When it wasn't unbearably hot in Topanga, the mountain air was reviving and the color of the falling night was extravagant with tangerines and purples.

It felt wonderful, leaving her house. Every time I left a man's house after a long afternoon, or if he had been the one to leave mine, the evening was tainted. I would wander the blocks of Manhattan, stopping in certain bars and eating raw meat — carpaccio or tartare. Martini Mondays with Big Sky were devil dark. On Martini Mondays he would come at five and leave before seven. My chest would be cool with perspiration. Glasses of pilsner in the sink. I'd leave my apartment just after he did, like it was on fire. I couldn't bear to be in it after night fell. He would eat takeout on the Upper West Side, sating the hunger that came from beer on an empty stomach and fervent fucking on my leather couch. His wife had these incredible teeth and I would picture her jaw opening for a triangle of steaming pizza. Laughter and the baby and Coca-Cola. Meanwhile I would sit on a stool in a dim bar and make the tartare last for an hour.

In hindsight, it was obvious. Talking to Alice made me realize the thing that I would end up doing was inevitable. Every single man in my life staked the path to murder. I'm not supposed to feel this, but I do: I don't think the act was vile. I think it was necessary. You can decide that for yourself. I will never lie to you. You are the only person to whom I will never lie.

Before going to bed, I stepped outside to get some air, to walk around the mounds of dry earth. I was happy. I should have known I didn't deserve it.

I saw Lenny in an unlikely place, walking toward Kevin's house, down the ravine with the bluestem scratching at his old ankles. I figured he was having an episode and I called out to him.

More rapidly than I would have thought possible, Lenny made his way up the hill.

— I'm terrifically happy to see you, Joan.

— Are you?

270

— I'm having the clearest of days, the clearest I've had in a very long time. I suppose I'm trying to coax the clarity into hanging around by offering a sacrifice unto the universe. The drugs I have to take turn the funhouse mirror of my mind's eye into a pane of glass, and it's sublime. But even better, even more sublime, is this: right before the dosages are due, I'm able to make out a different scene in the funhouse mirror. It's only available to me once every several days, nothing to do with providence but, rather, something in the timing of the drug interactions, the wearing off of one joined with the peaking of another; it would take me, I venture, longer than I have left to live to figure the timing enough to replicate it. But in that sliver of time, I can see even clearer than twenty-twenty. I can see the whole past with flawless vision. Better than hindsight, because it's as though I am reliving it. I can see things like a god. The clarity is so perfect that it transcends the pain. I imagine this is what dying is like.

— Would you like to come inside?

— I would love that, he said.

I made us tea and we sat at my kitchen table. Lenny slurped his tea and clasped his hands and breathed in deeply.

— There are things, he said, all the accumulated bits of a lifetime, they come back to you suddenly, when you have clarity, some peace because something you dread is no longer there. You know the way you listen to the cleaning ladies of a hotel, the network of them, talking loudly to one another, and to the maintenance man? They are all cousins, related, all of them roasting pigs on the weekend, buying kegs of beer with their crumpled dollar bills. They're loud and raucous around each other, but then, when they knock on your door, they are suddenly quiet. Housekeeping, they say, in a certain tone.

I nodded hatefully. For one month I had been a housekeeper in a hotel, not a fine hotel but a decent one with both an indoor pool and an outdoor pool. I took naps or read books in the unused affair rooms. They smelled of paint and funerals. I was so young then. I didn't mind the married men looking at me in my black uniform, the starched hem falling at my knees.

— Oh, Joan! I can't explain it well enough, I fear. The reasons for everything come to me in those moments of hyper-clarity. I can understand the lives of those housekeepers. I never thought of them enough. But somewhere I ingested their souls. I wouldn't be human if I hadn't. Perhaps a better way to tell it is the smell of grass. You know, of course, the smell of cut grass. But when was the last time you truly smelled it? I believe the smell of grass exists more as a trope after the age of twelve. Between twelve and thirty, I'd venture you never smell it. Then suddenly you are thirty, forty, and you think, Ah, cut grass!

I was bored. He was an old racist who thought he was progressive. But I wanted what he had. I wondered if he would leave it to me. His money. His plates. His watch. Even if he would, I couldn't wait that long. The easiest thing would be to take it when he was out of his gourd and I was Lenore. But he would know it was me when he came out of it. I was sure of it. In any case, that was the last night I would feel sorry for the old man. After that evening, I would want to kill him.

— And that's the thing I want to tell you, Joan. That's the thing that became clear to me early this morning. One of the visions. I am, in fact, worse than damaged.

He began to tremble.

— I've told you, he said, about Sandstone?

— Yes, the swinger mansion.

— Just down the road. Now it's nothing, all boarded up, but then it was something.

— I thought you didn't go.

273

— I did. We did.

— You and Lenore.

— You must understand, and few people your age can, but those days it was — Everything was changing. We didn't know. We thought we were being swept in a wave to a new world. In a way it didn't feel like there was a choice. The first time we went, it was after a soiree at the Getty. A couple we were talking to, the husband was an important producer and his wife was this gorgeous thing. I'll never forget it, she wore a silver dress, just two strips of material going down either side of her chest, meeting at the waist, so there was just bare skin all down through here — Leonard elevatored his hand in the air an inch away from my breastbone — they told us they were going to an after-event at Sandstone. They invited us along. We'd heard of it, of course. I was intrigued, I'm a man, but Lenore was, too. She was curious about all life. She wasn't afraid of anything. We took our champagne flutes along and followed their car. The first thing that happened when we pulled into the drive was we watched the other couple emerge from their car completely nude. We sat there for a minute, turned our headlights off. Lenore looked at me and rubbed my shoulder. Come on, Len, she said. We're bound in all the right ways. Then she kissed me deeply, lifted her white sundress over her body — very much like the one you never seem to take off — and she opened the car door and walked to meet the other couple. They both put an arm around her, the man's touched her rear. Something happened inside of me. I wanted to kill her. I wanted to kill all three of them. More accurately, I wanted to fuck the other woman until I came and then pull it out and jam it down Lenore's throat until she gagged.

I had to hold the vomit back with my palm. At that point I didn't even know the half of it.

— Joan, he said, I'm sorry. The skin may crease but the blood is the same. I was always a jealous man. Protective, I used to say. Ha! Protective of my own ego is more like it.

— But you went inside, I said.

— I did. Women in braids with their small, tight bodies. Men fawning over them. In the living room where the largest clump was gathered a bearded man played a guitar and around him couples kissed, all naked, in each other's laps, stroking each other's legs. Every part of me wanted to jump into it, to just fuck and suck and become wet with those women, and with Lenore, but the idea of something being done to Lenore by someone else, I couldn't manage the rage. Until that night I don't think Lenore knew that part of me. I'd hid it all along. But that night there was no more denying it. She'd thought we could enter together, as a couple, into this new land. The idea was that if you truly loved each other, if your love was deep and your heart was pure, that you would want your partner to experience the bliss of other bodies, you would respect the animal tendencies, you could fuck and let fuck and call it making love and yet after making love was over, you would go home with your wife and eat ice cream and wash yourselves and go to bed.

— What happened?

— Nothing much happened that night. We observed. The couple we'd followed there, they'd been leading us around. At one point, the woman tugged on Lenore's hand, she tried to bring her into an embrace, tried to coax her back to her husband. Like Lenore was a fresh catch she was bringing her master. She winked at me, like she would be my prize if I let Lenore go. I wanted to kill her for it. I wanted to fuck her first. I had my underwear on. I was one of the only ones in that room of snakes.

— Briefs?

— Yes, there were no boxers.

— Why did you keep them on?

— I hope you're not insinuating something. I never wanted for in that department. All the same, I felt discarded. I felt the whole room could sense my jealousy. Lenore stayed tucked in to me. She politely turned down all the looks. She squeezed my hand, we walked back to our car, put our clothes on, and drove home. We didn't speak of it for some time. But something had been lit inside me. A profound rage. Lenore and I had been trying to have children. We'd been married by then for four years and trying almost all that time. Each month that she bled she would try to hide her sadness from me. That same week we first went to Sandstone coincided with Lenore seeing a fertility doctor who told her everything in her system looked fine. He wanted me to go in and get checked, my count. I refused. She didn't nag me, she wasn't one of those. She was one of the last fine women. A European sensibility.

Leonard was tearing up. His grief was a lie. I knew when grief was a lie. It was one of my superpowers. Even though his voice had become odious to me, I was curious. Curiosity is something that has always driven me. I am depraved and curious.

— I went back, he said, groaning.

— Well of course you did.

— There was a night, Lenore lit candles all over the house, the one you're in now. She walked the rafters at the top and set red votives down. Pillar candles on the floor. The whole room was glowing like a church. We made love on the bed, it was the best lovemaking of our relationship. It felt like the best lovemaking in the history of the world. That was the night, she ordained it, that was the night she was going to conceive our child.

I shuddered to think of the heat in the house and the candles on top of it and this poor wife of his, spreading her legs for this insolent asshole. Once again I'd trusted a man. Once again I'd felt sympathy for a man who was not good.

— I don't know what kind of woman you are, Joan. Some women are not built for babies. I don't think that's bad. Biology is enigmatic but deliberate, it selects some for procreation and others it marks for a different path. Women like you are necessary to let off the steam. To depressurize the cabin.

— Women like me are good for men to fuck when they're not ready for babymaking with good Midwestern girls like Lenore.

— That's not how I meant it.

— Fuck you.

— I deserve that, old girl.

— So you and Lenore, the mother of all mothers, fucked in a temple of love. And lit all the magic candles to usher the insemination along. And then?

— And then nothing. Her cycle came. It was a terrible day. You know about the coyotes and the cycles?

I nodded and Lenny did, too, solemnly.

— The coyotes circled the house. They howled before she even started to bleed. They could smell the blood traveling down her tubes. I heard her upstairs, the whimper. My blessed bride. A good man would have gone and comforted her. But I only felt rage. Rage at myself, but also at her — like a real damned dog, I was angry at my bride for showing me the extent of my futility. Then further down it went, the boiling anger, down my hips and into my shaft. I wonder if you know how rage can stiffen the shaft. It's like a war cry. I left the house, engorged. I drove up the canyon to Sandstone. I didn't check in at the main house but sneaked to the yard at the back where the trampoline was. There was a tall American Indian girl laughing and jumping up and down, her tits like turkey wattles, shaking. Two men were watching, and two other women, a couple of pale whore blondes. All of them naked and slim as snakes. Nothing looked human to me. I was the stiffest I'd ever been. I climbed the trampoline and tackled the American Indian girl like a wolf. I stripped down and knelt her on all fours and got behind her like an animal. Look at me, I'm built like a rich man, not like a beast, but that day I was a beast, and none of them stopped me. After all, they'd built that place to act like animals and here was a man dispensing with the formality. I was full of rage because I was being denied the one right of all humans. The one reason we are on this earth. To procreate. So I fucked the American Indian girl with my rage and then the two blondes as the two men looked on. They stroked their cocks and watched me take what I was owed.

I shook my head in revulsion. I thought I'd expended all my disgust on hearing from men about what they were owed.

— You are shocked, Joan. I'm an old man now. The evils we have done would be pointless if they didn't get passed down so that others might not make the same mistake. Wouldn't you say, Joan? I know you have secrets, too. Nobody comes to the canyon unless they do.

I bit my lip. I tried to keep my hands in

my lap, away from his throat.

— My point was that Lenore was only for children. She wanted only to be a wife and a mother. But a mother first. A mother always. Joan, that isn't you, I don't know you too well, but I hope you'll allow me that. I love a woman like you. A part of me always wished to have that, a woman I could do battle with. Perhaps it would have suited me better. Perhaps my story would have turned out differently.

— I don't care how your story would have turned out, Lenny. You wanted to gag a woman with your cock.

— That's not the bad part, I'm afraid. I'm still getting there. You see, I want to come clean!

I pushed him to the door and then outside the threshold.

— Please, Joan, I'm an old man. I don't expect you to feel sorry, I only —

— I only feel sorry for your wife, Lenny. This stupid woman who wanted a child that you were too empty to give her.

I spat, and watched a bubble of my saliva land on the bridge of his nose. I don't know where the impulse came from, but it made me feel more powerful than I had ever felt before. I slammed the door in his face.

Then I walked up the spiral staircase and

took off my white dress to go to sleep. When you've been raped in a dress, you might think you want to burn it but I didn't.

In the morning there was a knock on my door. Alice was early. I hadn't pulled myself together as much as I'd wanted to. I checked my face in the hallway mirror. I smoothed down my hair and opened the door. I'd completely forgotten about the little girl.

She had Vic's face. That was the most remarkable thing — his face staring back at me, his probing eyebrows, the shining balls of his pale cheeks. The way she held herself in my doorway was all her father. An uneven confidence.

Then I realized we'd met before. She'd come to visit her father in the first few months of my employment. I was enjoying the early days of being the boss's pet. I remember she came around to my desk, smiling at me dreamily. She'd probably been ten or so and I'd been twenty-seven. She introduced herself and didn't say much more, just smiled and hung around my desk until her father called her away. He must have told her I was a star or something, a real go-getter in the advertising world. He must have said something so that she'd take note of me because he wanted to show me off to everyone in his orbit, even his own child. Women always talk about how men are so compartmentalized, how they can fuck some cosmetics manager all week, then go home and play Scrabble with their kids and scratch their wife's back. But Vic had just one compartment and it was only for me. His love for his children was real and large, no doubt, but his mania for me was tantamount.

— Eleanor, I said.

— You used to be hot, she said, adjusting the wire-rimmed glasses on her face.

I blinked. She wore frayed jean shorts and a pair of white sneakers and a pullover sweatshirt that said ESPRIT in large rainbow letters across the front.

— Thanks, I said.

— Do you know why I'm here? she said. It sounded foreboding because of how nice and childlike her face was. But for the same reason it also sounded ridiculous.

— I think so, I said. Her hands were trembling inside her pullover, which she was using like a muffler.

— Do you want to invite me inside?

— Wouldn't that be stupid of me?

— I'll do it right here, I don't care.

I could see she thought she meant it. She was soaked through with pain and rage. I'd been there before, I understood exactly. But how could I be afraid of this little girl, of my child self, standing there on the threshold?

I told her to come inside. I opened the door wide and walked backward. Eleanor advanced slowly, pulling a gun from the front pocket of her pullover. It was marvelous in its smallness and blackness and made her seem like an adult.

She kept the gun pointed at me. Gradually her hands stopped trembling. She looked up at the high ceilings of my oven of a house.

— Not what you pictured? I asked.

She shook her head.

— Not like the movies, I said.

— Fuck you, she said. Fuck you! Sit down!

I sat down at the kitchen table and she advanced until she was four feet away. I assumed that was the distance at which she was confident about hitting her target.

— I can see your nipples, she said softly.

I looked down at them. All talk of nipples made me think of my mother. In her big round eyeglasses with her layered blond hair and her white seventies breasts. She was the buxom beautiful of movie stars. Her nipples were enormous. You could see them through wool sweaters.

— Do you want to hear a story? she asked. The gun was pointed at my head. I told her that of course I did.

— You probably already know, she began, how we go as a family to Anguilla every year.

I nodded. Vic had spun it to me as his wife's trip, the highlight of her cold season, their Easter jaunt to Anguilla.

— Last year, she continued, Dad told us at the last minute he couldn't go. He said he had to work and it couldn't be remote. He had to be in the office. Such a fucking load, and we knew it. My mom was really upset. I think she knew about you or at least had an idea about you. She swept it under the rug, I guess. But Anguilla was really important to her. It was like the only time she had my dad in front of her every day for ten days. It was heaven for my mom. We'd get a nanny, too, this girl from the island, and she'd watch Robbie for most of the time so my mom could pretend she was this free woman with her husband, you know? Every night is date night on Anguilla, she said. She drank a lot, which she never did at home, and she was just so happy. Dad was happy, too, I mean especially in the beginning when I was a little kid, before Robbie was born, he and I would go snorkeling and shell picking and we built sandcastles and collected sand crabs. After Robbie, it was hard. My dad sort of detached from things, not from me so much but from my mom and Robbie. They were like this set of broken dolls or something. I think he thought that if he detached from them, he could live a normal life.

She looked like she was about to start crying. I asked if she wanted to sit down. She moved slowly and sat across from me. The table was long enough that she could keep the gun resting on it and pointed at my neck without worrying about my reaching and trying to grab for it. She talked as though we were friends and she needed to unload. Like she was me and I was Alice.

— Two days before the trip, he said he couldn't go. Literally two days. My mom was devastated. She had all their stuff packed in one suitcase. She'd been walking four miles every day to lose her "pooch" and she'd bought all these outfits. She said they should just postpone it and he said no, no. We would lose all our money, the flights, the house we rented. He was really smart, I'm sure you know, calculated like that. He told her after it was too late to do anything about it. He said, The kids deserve it, you deserve it. You've got to go. I didn't get it then. She knew what was going on and it was killing her, that he was sending her away so he could be with you, uninterrupted or whatever.

I thought back to the previous April. Big Sky had gone on a camping trip with friends to Chile. It was probably the second darkest time of my life after what had happened in the Poconos. In my apartment I looked at the couch where we had fucked and everything else he had touched or commented upon. I felt empty and scared because even though deep down I knew it was almost over, I didn't want to believe it and anyway nothing is sure. I didn't feel like drinking wine.

It was the early evening, five or so. I saw on social media the pictures his friends had posted. He was not online in any way and so I had to dig to find them. His group of friends, thirty-six to forty, wealthy and sure of their next forty years. There is no more powerful group in the world than men in that age range with money, with tasteful wives and pretty children. Family homes in Bridgehampton and Nantucket. Brunches.

I couldn't help thinking about the women who would let their attractive and wealthy husbands take group trips to Chile and Argentina where the men would get together with a group of girls in their twenties, building fires and drinking maté and climbing mountains with all the right gear. There was a blond girl in one photograph wearing rainbow leg warmers and holding a sausage on a stick to the fire, leaning toward the fire on slender haunches, and there was Big Sky beside her, looking at her. The picture came alive in my brain. I could see them close to each other the whole trip, walking in a pair up rocky terrain. I could see him helping her across a slim river, experiencing that brand of breathtaking crush that developed over time back in middle school. I could see day seven of the trip. I imagined it was cold and warm at once; they were together at the fire, everyone else asleep, sharing a thermos of whiskey, laughing quietly. He would bring her a thick serape blanket and wrap it around her shoulders the way he had done for me in the bar that night with his jacket.

That was the ridiculous moment when I arranged myself on the same side as his wife, like here the two of us were in homely New York City, waiting at home for him. I felt absurd.

I texted him, *How goes it, Montana?*

And a full day later, he wrote, *Hella fantastic chile is tops.*

The air went out of me. It was the end. I called Vic. I told him I was feeling suicidal and would he like to take me to dinner?

And now here this girl was because of what Vic had done to his wife, because of what Big Sky had done to me, because of what my father had done to my mother. The pattern must end with you.

— Do you remember April? she asked me.

— Yes, I said. The weather was beautiful.

— Were you with my father?

— We went to dinner every night.

— And he stayed overnight with you?

— No, I said. Which was true, because by then our sexual relationship was completely over. He would just sit across from me, watching me eat, listening to me talk.

— Why not?

— Because I didn't want to. I was in love with another man.

— Another married man?

I nodded.

— How did you become such a fucking whore?

— It's a long story.

— I don't want to hear your long story. I want to tell you about Anguilla. My mother tried to kill herself.

— What?

— That's funny that he didn't tell you. That's really fucking funny to me.

— He didn't tell me.

— That's probably the sickest part of it. My fucking mom tried to kill herself because she knew he was fucking you, or whatever, not even fucking you, but paying for your whore dinner. Actually, I think that's the part that really got to my mom. All the dinners. She spent like two weeks after his funeral just going over all the credit card statements and looking up the restaurants online and checking out what you both ordered. Looking at the dishes on Yelp.

I felt tears coming to my eyes. Not for Vic's wife but for my mother.

— Oh, are you feeling something for us? Wow. Cool. So let me give you the full picture. We ate dinner at Picante, our favorite Mexican place. It was really fucking weird to be there without my dad. And Robbie, who was three years old and would always have been three years old, you know he had Down's, right, Robbie was acting out. He threw a fork at the waitress. The fork hit her in the face and she started bleeding. And that was the last straw for my mom. We're there with the crab guacamole appetizer that was my dad's favorite and Robbie throws a fork at the waitress and Mom was just staring at this family at the next table, this young family with two little kids, a boy and a girl like us, but this boy was normal and the mom and dad looked happy and they were both in shape. Even though my dad wasn't, like, the most good-looking man, my mom always treated him like he was a movie star. Anyway, Mom didn't even apologize to the waitress. She left a bunch of bills on the table and walked out and I picked up Robbie and we followed her. None of us had eaten. Robbie was crying and hitting himself and Mom just kept moving. We took a taxi back to our bungalow. Later that night I found her in the bathroom, passed out on the floor. The grimy-ass bathroom that wasn't even nice because my dad had been renting a cheaper house the past few years. Probably to save up for buying you dinners and following you around Mexico.

— Jesus Christ, I said. I remembered the night she was talking about. Vic and I were having late drinks at a tiki bar in SoHo that dressed their drinks with pink orchids and green shards of shiso.

His phone vibrated in his pocket and he took it out. When he answered the phone in public, he always covered his mouth. I believe this was somewhat out of decorum, but likely he also did it for privacy. Vic kept so many secrets from all of us.

He rose and walked out the door of the

bar. He was gone for ten minutes or so. In that time I sipped my drink morosely and checked all the relevant outlets of social media for new information on Big Sky's vacation. His wife had posted on Facebook, *He's home!* with a kissing emoji, plus one of champagne and a bubble bath. Would they fuck tonight? I wondered. I had no idea how often they did. He never talked about her. Just as Vic rarely talked about his wife. The wives of cheaters lived in private rooms with white lotions in thick jars and soft lighting.

When Vic came back inside, he was not visibly shaken. But he was changed. I didn't think too much of it. Often after a few drinks he would begin to sulk in my presence. He spent so much energy during the day trying to convince me that he only wanted the best for me — even if the best thing for me was not him — that at night his goodwill would run dry and the whiskey he drank would turn him into a goblin.

And when he came back in from outside, he simply looked like he was in one of his brooding states. When he sat, his elbows dug forlornly into his navy knees.

— Were you with him that night? Eleanor said.

I stuttered and she cocked the gun. I couldn't believe it. She repeated the question angrily.

— Yes, I said. We had drinks and he walked me home.

— Do you remember him taking a phone call?

I nodded.

— I called to tell him Mom tried to kill herself. I called from the hospital in Anguilla that looked like a run-down motel and nobody wore gloves and Robbie was screaming so loud, Momma's dead, Momma's dead, and beating himself and slamming his head against a wall over and over and I was so scared, and I want to know, did my father take the phone call before or after he walked you home?

She was crying and her face was mottled, white and red. I thought about what to say. I almost always lied. Did that make me a bad person? I don't know the answer.

— Answer the question, she said, her hands trembling with the gun. If you lie to me, I'll fucking kill you so slow, man!

— He walked me home, I whispered, after he found out your mom tried to kill herself.

19

My father returned to the Poconos the following afternoon. In my memory it was the sunniest day. They asked me if I would like to get dropped off at the pool. Later I would realize it was because they needed to talk, but in the moment I remember thinking they were going to have sex. Sex defined their relationship, at least in my mind.

I couldn't believe they were willing to drop me off without supervision. I was excited by the prospect but more so wounded. My mother had exiled me from her bed the previous night. And now this. That was when it dawned on me, the unsettling feeling that my parents' lives did not revolve around me. I'd grown up thinking I was the center of their world. Even when my mother yelled at me or locked me out of her bedroom, it was because I had the power to infuriate her. It was because she loved me. It could be argued that my learning it when I did, at the age of ten, was perfect timing. Old enough to have experienced cozy solipsism for many years, young enough to change the way I walked through the world. To be cautious.

I went to my room and put on my black two-piece with the Technicolor butterflies. I applied coconut-flavored lip gloss and clopped out in my wood and leather Candies with kitten heels. I said, I want to go to the Top of the World.

My father acquiesced and took me to the rich pool. Rich! To think of it now. Perhaps it was the drab tiki bar that attracted me. All my life I have been charmed by the trappings of the South Seas. I've looked for establishments with lighted puffer fish in tanks, with towering fake palms, rock walls, and outriggers dripping down from the painted ceilings. And it started with that tiki bar at the Top of the World.

In the car my father was not himself. And yet my father was always my father in a way that my mother was not always my mother. There were hours, entire days, that my mother was an individual apart from me. I think it's mostly because of this — and not the devastation that would happen very early the next morning — that I thought I would always love my father more.

— You're not going to leave the pool area, you understand?

— Yes, Daddy. What if I want a snack?

— I'm giving you five dollars. You can buy a snack and eat it in the pool area.

What he didn't know was that there was no traditional snack bar at the rich pool, only a vending machine indoors, up two flights of sapphire stairs. It wasn't part of the pool area. Only the tiki bar was in the pool area. I was always making sure to follow rules, but I knew how to bend them. They were so strict, and my mother was so observant, but there were hours, like I said, when her eyes were closed to me, and these were the hours I figured out how to lighten my arm hair and have an orgasm.

— Daddy, I'm sorry about Grandma.

He kept his eyes on the tree-lined roads ahead. He nodded and swallowed.

— She's going to be fine, he said. My father accepted succor from no one. I can't imagine what it was like for a man like him to know his elderly mother was raped. To what extent the reel of that scene would play in his mind.

— Is she . . . scraped up?

— Not too bad.

— Does it look like she fell down some stairs?

He looked at me. He had no conception of what I knew. Fathers never know that about their daughters. Partly it's because they don't want to know, but really it's because they cannot know. It's psychologically dangerous to see inside your daughter's brain. And I knew so much more than most girls my age because of the way I listened.

— Tonight do you want to go to dinner at Villa Volpe?

— Yes!

— Maybe just the two of us? We'll give Mommy a break, let her take it easy at home.

My shoulders fell far down beneath my neck. I nodded. I longed for something that was in the past, only I didn't know it yet. Vic once said to me, Families are silly. The whole concept is silly. He said that because he didn't want his family. But he would have wanted one with me. Me and him at the supermarket, pushing around a pudgy Vic Jr. in a cart, buying grape tomatoes.

We pulled into the parking lot. I was saddened by the glass of sunlight on the macadam, by the fake smile on my father's goateed mouth. He would have died for me, but because he was a man, he didn't know how he was hurting me by doing the things he thought had nothing to do with his daughter.

— I'll pick you up at four thirty. Right here. The car will be right here, but I want you to wait inside the gate, do you understand?

—Yes.

— No disobeying.

— No disobeying, I repeated. He kissed my forehead.

I brought the book I was reading. All the books I read were hand-me-downs from my parents. My mother's V. C. Andrews, my father's Dean Koontz. In this case it was Stephen King's *The Stand.* I liked how massive it was, that it would last me a month.

I chose a chaise longue near the tiki bar. I removed my terry jumper and laid myself down like my mother, legs bent and knees pinched together. I read my book and concentrated on the way I looked reading it. I was only ten years old and yet I remember having that thought that day. Only a few years earlier I'd been a pure child. Reveling in the space between the Christmas tree and the corner of the wall where the colored lights blinked for me alone and it looked like heaven. Or wearing a princess dress to go to Maggie's Pub, this seamy place with a green plaid carpet and high-top tables. We'd go when my mother was in the mood for chicken wings. She loved the cheap parts of an animal, all varieties of offal, but wings were the easiest parts to come by, and we'd go for nickel-wing nights and I'd play on the crummy carpet beneath our table; they would talk and I would play with my dolls down there. Their voices, their love, above my head. Below, all the independence I needed. I didn't yet know my mother was a hypochondriac or that she could be crueler on occasion than she already was. I didn't yet know my father's secret, or maybe he didn't have it yet. There is nothing in the world better than the past.

That day at the rich pool, as I moved my body like an older girl, I noticed a man at the bar, perhaps because he noticed me. He had a mustache and wore a white linen shirt and khaki swim trunks. He was in his mid-forties, the age of my parents. He was sitting sidesaddle on the stool so that he could take inventory of the landscape. He was sipping something tall, reddish, and tropical. His bare knees made something thump inside of me. The way he held his drink. I could see up the hollow of his shorts, a miraculous darkness. I imagined my parents a few miles away, rustling in a hot, damp bed. I imagined my grandmother in Orange, pinioned against her brown couch with the

Doberman piss.

I made a fire between the insides of my knees. I thought of the word *fucking*. I wrote it inside my skull in Lite-Brite.

The man was close enough to talk to me from the bar. He waited until the bartender made drinks from his gun at the other end. I heard the man clearly over the splashing water and the summertime songs on the speaker.

He engaged me, to begin with, about Stephen King. He said he admired a young woman reading such a big book. That he called me a young woman was both tantalizing and repulsive. He told me his name was Wilt and that he was from Boise, Idaho. He was getting his parents' place ready to sell. They had just died, his dad of emphysema and his mom of suicide by cancer shortly thereafter. He laughed and I laughed, too, as though I knew what he meant.

— Joan, he said. I've never met a woman under the age of forty with the name Joan. Isn't that funny?

I didn't smile or nod. I'd learned that from my mother. Men go wild for a woman who is quiet like a cat. A woman who doesn't always approve.

— Joan likes mystery and horror and long walks on the beach.

— I don't like the beach, I said.

— She doesn't like the beach because it's very sandy. The sand is insidious. The sand makes her skin crawl.

—Well, I like the beach in Italy.

— Ah. Joan makes an exception for the Mediterranean. The sand there is more like pebbles. Less insidious. She enjoys fruit cups on the blue and white hotel towels.

I smiled. In the water a girl about my age was tossing a penny and diving for it. She was pale and wore goggles.

I knew what *rape* meant but only vaguely. I knew it meant sex against one's will, but sex to me was what I saw on HBO. Soft-core hydraulics. Fit bodies moving against each other. Very involved French kissing. So that when I pictured my grandmother being raped, she was one of those HBO women, only older, and her rapist was one of those men, only rougher. I pictured my grand-mother openmouthed kissing during her rape. Accepting a tongue into her mouth but with a look of dismay on her wrinkled, rouged face.

— Are you here with anybody, Joan?

— My daughter is playing in the pool right there, I said, pointing at the diving girl.

Now it was the man's turn to laugh.

— Joan of Snark, he said. When you're

ready to move on from Stephen King, I think you should like Henry Miller. Have you heard of him?

I didn't say anything.

— No? What a shame. What do they teach in those schools nowadays? Compound interest and fractions and pi. Let me tell you, Joan, you will never need to know pi in your life. School is only good for making other people believe you're smart. School doesn't make you smart.

— What makes you smart?

— Reading Henry Miller, for one. D. H. Lawrence a close second. Nabokov ahead of Miller, come to think of it. Have you heard of *Lolita*?

— No.

— Heavens! But I suppose you can name all six continents.

— There's seven.

— Aha.

The bartender returned to the man — Wilt's — corner of the bar and asked if he would like a refill. Wilt said yes and asked for a cup of water as well. I liked the way he spoke to the bartender. He was genteel like my father but a little more authoritative. He was even a little rude.

When the bartender disappeared again, Wilt poured the water out at his feet and

302

filled the plastic cup with some of his drink and then, in one deft movement, placed it on the ground beside my chair.

— Some geographers would say there are six, he said, not missing a beat, if you combine Europe and Asia, to make Eurasia.

I picked up the drink and sipped it. It was sweet and tart at once. I looked across the lounge deck at the mostly female bathers. Holding books or magazines and wearing big sunglasses. Taking the sun, my mother called it, with her accent. It sounded spoiled, the way she said it. But she took the sun, too. She undid the strings of her bathing suit so she wouldn't get tan lines. She'd drink water from a tumbler and the SPF cream from her lips would melt onto the rim of the glass. Why did I always want to be around my mother? She didn't make me feel terribly loved. She didn't give herself up for me, the way many mothers did for their children. At the same time, besides taking the sun and eating chicken wings, she also wasn't living for herself.

— In Idaho, Wilt said, we don't traffic much in municipal pools, or association pools. We don't have any tiki bars.

— I've never been to Idaho, I said. Which was such a stupid thing to say because I'd never really been anywhere. My parents didn't travel much beyond the Poconos and Italy. That went for everything else, too. We ate Chinese on Sunday nights. Otherwise we had steak or pasta. For lunch nearly every day my mother made pastina.

— Idaho is the most beautiful state. I don't say that because I live there. Pennsylvania, he said, well. I'm from here. In Pennsylvania they grow a lot of bad apples.

— Are you a bad apple? I asked. I don't believe the words came out of my mouth in a sultry tone, but some lines can't be anything but sexual.

He laughed and winked.

— New Mexico, he said, is number two. The second most beautiful state in the union.

— Our next vacation is going to be to the American West, I said, echoing my father.

— You and your little girl?

— Yes, I said. Me and Lulu.

— Lulu, what a nice name. How old is Lulu?

— Hmm, seven, I said. She'll be eight next week.

— Well, happy birthday, Lulu. What does she want for her birthday?

— Damned if I know.

He laughed heartily at that. I spoke like the characters in the adult books I was reading. He swished his drink around in his cup. I drank the rest of what he'd given me. I'd had only one hard-boiled egg that morning because I'd been nervous about when my father would come home. Now I felt the liquid, cool, in the floor of my belly. My head felt like there were star-shaped bubbles inside of it, lifting my skull up from my neck.

— Joan, I need to get out of this heat now, Wilt said rather abruptly. I'm going up to my room for some shade.

I nodded, heartbroken. My hair felt too short and dry. My book seemed like the biggest waste of time and I never wanted to swim like a child again.

— Catch you around sometime.

He rose and I saw how tall he was. I wondered if my mother would find him attractive. His legs were very dark with curls of hair. He wore fine leather shoes, the kind you wouldn't wear to a swimming pool. I watched him walk up the steps to the clubhouse.

I looked back at the bar and saw a black leather wallet on the bamboo bar. The bartender noticed it at the same time.

— I know him, I told the bartender, I'll catch up.

The bartender nodded carelessly. I grabbed the wallet off the bar and ran after him, barefoot, in my two-piece. He'd already made it to the upper-level parking lot by the time I got there.

— Wilt, I said breathlessly.

He was opening the door to a big black car when he turned to look at me. He smiled wide and his teeth were very white in a way that was frightening. I was holding the wallet out and hopping from one foot to the other because of the burning macadam.

— Jesus! he said. Get in for a second, will you?

I slid into the passenger side and he got into the driver's side and started the car and lowered all the windows and blasted the air-conditioning. The front seat was one long black leather bench. It smelled so foreign in the car, like snakeskin and old people.

— Joan of Snark, thank you. What a chivalrous thing to do. You know how rare it is to find a chivalrous woman in the world?

What's funny is how I remember almost everything up until that point. After that my memories are little blots. Driving through the Top of the World community, the light blue sky interrupted by trees. I don't remember talking. In the home of his dead parents, I do remember an old-fashioned wet bar. It was the coldest place I'd ever been. All the furniture, polar to the touch. We drank brown liquor in thick glasses with giant ice cubes. There were low leather couches the color of the cordials in my parents' liquor cabinet.

I don't think I chose not to be afraid but maybe I did. Maybe his hands did not frighten me because they were the only warm things in the place. I know that he helped form my body into the certain position he wanted, which was on all fours, on the mustard carpet next to a gold-edged glass coffee table. But I knew from HBO movies how to hold myself. Also because of HBO, I'd already been having orgasms for over a year. Watching steamy scenes and riding a balled-up comforter in the early morning while my mother made breakfast. As long as I could hear the spatula against a pan and the fridge opening and closing, I moved heartily toward a sensation I could barely comprehend.

I don't know if the decor of the house comes from my memory or from the movies I saw. Maybe it's both. I don't remember if he ever went inside of me but I do remember feeling pain. Sometimes I could see very clearly the way he licked every part of me above the knees and below the belly button, like a mother animal bathing its young with a wide tongue. He never took my bikini bottoms off, just uncovered the fabric section by section, looking for unlicked strips of flesh. I stayed very still. There was no music, no sound at all, except the sound of his tongue.

I was back at the Top of the World Pool by four. I went into the deep end, sinking myself down to the uneven aqua floor and sitting there for as long as I could hold my breath, which was a very long time.

By the time my father arrived at 4:29 I was inside the gate, exactly where he told me to wait, holding two books and drying my wet hair in the yellow mountain sun. The man had left the number for the landline of his parents' house on the first page of *Tropic of Cancer*.

20

Eleanor stood and stretched her arms, extending the barrel of the gun at me.

— You have no idea how you fucked up my life! she screamed, and the walls of windows rattled in the hot house. You know my fucking baby brother is dead! Do you?

— Yes. Your mother told me.

— Did she tell you she's pretty much the reason!

She cocked the gun.

— Please, I said, and I didn't know where the next thing I said came from; it came from beyond me, from the seat of my stomach. Please, I lied, I'm pregnant.

— You're what?

— I'm pregnant. I found out last week.

— What the fuck!

The gun began to shake so much in her hand that it dipped toward the floor. I pictured it falling, going off, and opening a cherry hole in my belly. One of those accidental deaths, the specialty of toddlers in Walmarts.

I imagined Alice at my funeral. Big Sky, too. Then I imagined him seeing her. She would be in a black tuxedo. She would lay a red rose on my gleaming coffin and he would get an erection.

— Is it my father's!

— Yes.

— Are you fucking sure!

— Yes.

She found the wall with her hand and slumped down against it until she reached the floor. She cried and the gun shook in her hands. I was not one to comfort other women. I never embraced them or ran after them when they cried.

— Eleanor —

— Fuck you, don't talk to me!

— Okay, I said. I wanted to get up and clean some dishes. But I knew she wanted what everybody wanted — for me to remain in the same place forever. My rigidity reminded me of the way I used to still my body when I'd finally reached my mother's bed, afraid to make any moves that would wake her so that she might tell me to go back to my own room.

The girl was trembling. I saw the ant-colored hairs piercing through her white skin. I'd stolen from her. I was a very care-less thief who didn't even want her plunder. I'd been stealing my whole life. I'd walked out of bookstores with armloads of books, carried whole lobsters thwapping about in their sturdy white bags out of supermarkets. I'd stolen truffle honey, truffle salt, two-thousand-dollar dresses, twenty-dollar dresses, bras and underwear and shoes, headphones and batteries and flatware and Sharpie markers. I'd never in my life bought a container of Advil. And I'd stolen this child's father and then dumped him off. By proxy, I'd stolen her little brother.

I thought to move toward Eleanor, to kick her hard in the face and take the gun and call the cops. But she kept her eyes on me even through the tears. Anyhow, I didn't trust myself to do those things.

Her face was so remarkably his, it was as if he were right there. We sat for what seemed like a half hour and I had the time to recall the things Vic told me he'd done for her. Out of the blue he would write to me, *I'm going to be busy a little later, kid, if you don't hear from me, I have to fix Elea-nor's car. Eleanor has a deadly banana al-lergy so I'm going out to stock up on about ten thousand more EpiPens.* Or in conversa-tion he would say, I'm buying Eleanor a

311

pony for Christmas. Many of the things he said he was doing for her I knew he was telling me so I'd see what a devoted father he was. That he had the money to buy a horse, the skill to fix a carburetor.

One night after I said I wanted ruby-red slippers like Dorothy's, my father stayed up very late to glue red glitter onto a pair of ballerina shoes. In the morning the shoes were at the foot of my bed, twinkling like fire. They were very hard with glue and when I put them on they scratched my skin. I was enthralled with the love behind the effort, the sweat on his brow. I loved him even then as though he were already gone.

— I remember that day I met you, Eleanor said. At the office.

— I remember, too.

— You ate half of a grapefruit, cut into sections, with a spoon. I started doing that, too. Basically I wanted my father to see me eating grapefruit like that.

I nodded. I didn't remember eating grapefruit in the office.

— When my mother was pregnant with Robbie, she found out from the doctor that he had a one-in-three chance of having trisomy twenty-one. And she didn't tell my dad. Because she knew, or she thought, he would have made her get an abortion. When

Robbie was born, that's when he found out. When he saw his face as he came out of my mom's stomach. That was the moment Dad left us, that was the moment we lost him. It wasn't you. You're nothing.

— Eleanor, I said, I'm sorry.

— Don't tell me you're sorry. You're a piece of shit.

She transferred her weight from one foot to the other. She wiped her nose with the side of her arm.

— If you're telling the truth, then you're carrying my baby brother. His second chance.

It was hard to believe Vic had a child who could believe a thing like that. Eleanor had been brought up by a religious mother and a devout grandmother. Vic hadn't been much for religion, though he took his wife to church every week. He christened his children. But the notion that Eleanor thought an unborn child might be her brother reincarnated was a bridge too far. On top of that, I wondered how she could be so sure that my fake pregnancy was a boy.

— And I'll let you live until you give birth to him.

It was a ludicrous, medieval thing to say. I didn't know how to respond. I wanted to laugh. I wanted her whole family out of my life.

— Please, Eleanor —

— Don't say my name. I will cut your face. You don't need your face to give birth. And if you're lying, I'm going to kill you. I'm going to cut out your eyes!

Her eyes were so little. I was tired of being a sponge. I wanted to kill her for saying something so silly.

— Where's the nearest supermarket? she said, as though she were asking for directions.

One time with Big Sky there was a scare. We never used condoms. He always pulled out. He was good at it. There are men who don't know when they are about to come, and those men shouldn't be allowed to fuck. But Big Sky was careful and aware. This one time he was about to come at the same time that I was. And I didn't want him to pull out and ruin mine. I was on top and I squeezed my knees into the sides of his waist and crushed myself onto his pelvis with all my weight. I could feel him bucking to get me off, but I kept my eyes closed and pinned myself down. It was like the time I rode a mechanical bull in Nashville. I just concentrated on becoming one with the thing beneath me. At last I went limp and he shoved me off. What the fuck, he said, are you fucking crazy?

And I thought, Am I? No, I decided, I was not. In fact, I believe that was the only time in lovemaking that I truly acted for myself.

He was in agony for the weeks that followed. I could tell that Sundays were the worst. Probably he and his wife and son would come back from a stroll around Central Park, eat a nice summer dinner on that impressive stone patio and, after putting the child to bed, the wife would retire to their bedroom with the book that everybody was reading and he would tarry downstairs, drink a Boddingtons. He would text me around eleven, just a question mark.

Once I waited until the following morning and typed only the letter *N.* And then, realizing he might think I meant *Negative,* I wrote another message to follow the first: *Nyet.*

We had the talk one weekday afternoon at Salumeria Rosi. I ordered prosciutto and bufala and, to fuck with him, I also ordered a pot of pickles. He said, Listen, if it's. If you are. I'll take care of everything, obviously.

To make sure I didn't misunderstand, he said, I mean financially, the procedure. I'll come with you, too, of course. If you need me.

I nodded. I loved that restaurant, the silken slices of prosciutto and the pillowy discs of mozzarella, but I didn't have an appetite. I thought that if I swallowed the pickles, I'd throw them right back up. Then he really would have shit his pants.

My period finally came on a Sunday and even then I didn't tell him I'd gotten it until Wednesday. When you're in love with a married man, the truth is that you are in hate with a married man, and you have to take succor where you can find it.

The supermarket I chose was the Ralphs in Pacific Palisades. I liked it because it was easy to park there.

In the car Eleanor kept her gun pointed at my face the whole time. She told me she didn't care about going to jail, that she would shoot me anywhere. I didn't believe her. The gun was likely not loaded. Or maybe it was. It's not that I didn't care if I died. It's that I knew I would survive.

I parked my Dodge next to a motorcycle. She pressed the gun against my back going into the market. Once we got inside she put it in her pocket. She followed me down the women's health aisle. There was a teen and there was a woman in her forties. The teen was looking at Monistat, the older woman was reading the back of a lubricant box. I took an EPT off the shelf because it was the brand I always bought.

In the single-stall bathroom I knew there was a small chance I might die. There was nothing I could do. I said, Everyone will hear. And she said, I have nothing.

I held up my mother's white dress and peed over the cream strip. I had always been fanatical about peeing for a very long time on the strip. But that time I did it quickly. Then I shook it off and rested it on the edge of the grimy sink. In the past I would leave the strip in the bathroom for a long time. There's nothing more horrendous than coming back too soon.

I didn't think about the possibility that the strip would be positive. I obviously hadn't fucked Big Sky the night Vic killed himself. I hadn't slept with Vic in ages and I hadn't slept with anyone else.

Until Marfa. Which I didn't consider sex. Because the thing is, one could call it rape. It was half a rape, or three quarters of one. Like Alice said, there are rapes for which we shower, put on our nice shoes. The man, John Ford, had one of the ugliest faces I'd ever seen. Large brownish teeth, horny gray

317

eyes, zero lips. There was a sign outside the
hotel: WE'RE OPEN WHEN WE'RE OPEN. I
sat in the lobby bar eating ceviche with too-
thick rings of jalapeños and drinking Bloody
Marys. The cubes of tuna on my plate were
dark and warm and stringy. He sat down
next to me and asked the bartender for a
grasshopper. Even from not very close his
breath smelled like metal.

A song I liked played in the lobby and he
smiled as I moved my body to it. Later,
when we were in his motel room, he would
play the same song. He acted like I should
be impressed. I found it ridiculous.

I tried to leave twice. I couldn't say how
he got me to stay the first time — maybe it
was the idea that it would be a free night of
sleep — but the second time he gripped my
arm. The hold didn't really hurt. I could
have freed myself in that first moment. He
turned me so I was facing away from him
and lifted up just the back of my dress. He
swiped my underwear to one side and
pulled my right leg away from my left. He
did it very crudely, laughing, so that it was
like a mock of rough handling. His penis
was indefensibly small. When he slid himself
inside of me, I couldn't believe it wasn't a
finger. It felt like a little length of chalk.
Yeah, he said over and over, going in and

318

out, pincer-gripping my arm. I squirmed and said, Please stop. But I didn't say it loud enough. I didn't try to push him off because I was worried he would become more violent. Grossly, I was feeling bad about the size of his penis. I didn't want him to know how absurd it felt and yet I hated him with every cell in my body. That was when the seed of what I would end up doing was planted. Of course, it was planted when I was ten years old, but I hadn't been paying attention to how tall it was growing all my life.

Finally I kicked a leg back at him, like a horse, and tried to free my arms. But he exercised a remarkable strength, pinning both my arms against the wall. It lasted less than a minute. He thought he pulled out in time but I guess he didn't. In the morning I washed my dress in his sink and left before he woke. I sped away in my car and the first minute on the road a bird flew into my windshield and remained there — orange, red, and blue — until hours later, when I stopped for gas. The horrified attendant scraped it off while I bought lottery tickets.

So I suppose Marfa was the thing that did it. In the wheelchair-accessible bathroom of the Ralphs the test took a minute or so. Eleanor stared at it and I stared at the ceiling. I was waiting for the sound of the gun. I knew what one sounded like now. Then there was an intake of breath and the small noise of a dumb young kid. I looked down. I saw the plus sign, rendered in cornflower.

21

She put the wet pregnancy stick in the pocket of her shorts. She had no idea what to do. I suggested we go back to my house.

In the car she sat with the back of her head against the window and the gun pointed at my face. I scraped the doors of the Dodge against the branches of the dead trees that flanked the road back up the canyon. She flinched like it was an affront.

I imagined a little cream bubble swimming in my blood. I imagined calling him up. Is this John Ford? Do you remember me from Marfa? I'm the woman that you held against a wall. I am fairly confident you didn't fuck anyone else on that trip, and I for certain did not. The reason I'm calling is that I'm pregnant with your child. Shall we raise it together? Are you in Virginia? Shall I come to you or would you like to come here? I forgot what you do for a living but there are lots of industries in Los

Angeles.

— Slow down! Eleanor yelled. I hadn't been going over twenty-five miles an hour.

At the top I saw that Kevin's car was not there, but Alice's Prius was. I'd forgotten she was coming.

Alice wasn't inside her car. She could have been walking around the place, down in the ravines. I didn't know what I would do when she found us.

— Whose car is that? Eleanor asked.

— My friend.

— You knew she was coming?

— I forgot. The events of this morning. I hope you might forgive me for forgetting.

I saw Alice at the door of River's yurt. Then I saw River in the doorway. His arm was raised, his hand against the top frame of the door, right over her head. The nearness was unsettling.

— Get in the house, Eleanor hissed, before they see us.

— She's going to come and knock on my door because my car is here. What do you want me to do?

— Tell her I'm your friend!

I felt Eleanor put the gun in her pocket. I called down to Alice. It was strange to say her name. Her head snapped up. She was startled. She ran up the ravine. I wasn't

imagining the guilt. Its concentration was
like a skunk smell in the air. River, nonplussed, waved and went back inside.

— Hey, she said. She was out of breath.
She wore a red dress that could twirl. She
was breathless and extra pretty.

I smiled, trying to act normal.

— I was asking if he knew where you were.
You know what's crazy is that I know River.
From my yoga class.

— Small canyon, I said.

Alice turned toward Eleanor.

— Hi, she said, I'm Alice.

— This is my friend Eleanor, I said. I
bought my car from her. She was the first
person in LA who asked me how I was.

Was Alice smart enough to know that
Eleanor was Vic's daughter? I hadn't told
her the girl's name.

— Nice to meet you, Eleanor. Joan and I
were just about to go on a mini road trip.

I was pregnant and standing before a
young woman who wanted to kill me and
yet all I could think about was Alice inside
River's doorframe. The way his arm was
arched over her head.

Eleanor seemed on the verge of tears.
God, how she looked like her father, espe-
cially when her expression was one of pain.
Vic was either jovial or in pain, but toward

the end it was almost always pain, and then rage. Eleanor was infinitely more attractive than her father, but the night he killed himself he looked better than he ever had.

When Vic shot himself, all the servers stopped in their places like they were playing a game of freeze tag. His large body slid down the wall. A few droplets of blood got on our table, landing specifically in the folds of the bufala mozzarella that Big Sky and I were sharing. It looked like a bit of berry compote. Every time we ate together, the food was perfect, the drinks were perfect. I had so much to give. His wife had scarves, so what.

And that night it had been so long since we'd seen each other. I could tell he had missed me. More accurately he had completely forgotten about me and now, seeing me again, he was confused and captivated. I was distant. My dress was not revealing at all. In the past I'd always dressed too seductively. But now I understood what a man like him wanted.

I took a bite of bufala just before Vic came in, and Big Sky watched me eat it like I was a curiosity. He watched me with his face in his palm, shaking his head.

— Who *are* you? he asked in that roping-steer accent.

It was the same question he'd asked me at the very beginning of us. But this time it had a positive connotation. I didn't smile. The cheese felt like chilled silk in my mouth. I was the loveliest I had ever looked. That was the moment I felt something good might happen to me.

And that was the same moment Vic walked in. Oftentimes I would see him in the streets, either the real him, trailing me, or the wraith of him I saw in every man with a combover in a nice suit. For several months I'd been worried he would kill me. My building had a small but well-appointed gym with Woodways and the latest ellipticals. They all faced the giant bay window where you could look out at the glassy buildings shimmering in the sun. My back would be to the door, so I'd find myself turning around all the time. Each time I heard someone enter the room, I'd whip my head around to see if it was Vic.

Now here he was. The gun appeared like a magician's trick. The more I think of it, the more certain I am that it was for me. But he couldn't kill me and stay alive. He could not, in every sense, live without me.

He said nothing. His eyes were wet, he smelled good and wore a pin-striped suit I'd never seen before. He looked at me in a way I'll never forget.

Then he turned the gun to the side of his head, blinked, and pulled the trigger. Pink brain and sharp bits of skull went flying. Big Sky did not jump back. He held his arm in front of me like a gentleman. He tried to cover my eyes, but I wanted to look. I wanted to look at the next man who had come along to ruin my life. I wanted to see him bleed.

— I don't think Joan is going anymore, Eleanor said to Alice.

22

The night my father left us in the Poconos, my mother slept with her arms folded in an X across her chest, her hands gripping the opposite shoulders. She was protecting herself from everything, it seemed, including the blind-vole need of her only child.

I was angry with her, but God how I loved her. My need and hate were twins in my nervous belly. I stood in the doorway of her bedroom and watched her back and the digital clock that read 11:47 in electric red. It felt like the latest and most terrifying hour. Maybe she knew I was in there. Little by little I inched toward the bed. I can still recall the way I did it. There could be nothing worse in the world than being rejected by her, than her telling me I couldn't sleep beside her.

It took perhaps three minutes for me to reach the bed. During that time I concentrated on the ridges of stucco in the ceiling.

I gasped when I spotted a spiderweb in one corner. I was shocked my mother had missed it. She didn't miss anything. She was the most diligent cleaner. The most observant woman in the world.

I spent another few minutes working up the courage to lift the cover and press one knee on the mattress. Even though I laid my weight down one teaspoon at a time, there was no way to do this perfectly. All of a sudden, she whipped around. I jumped back and nearly wet myself.

— What are you doing here? she said. I felt like something large and ungainly. My mother had the power to make me feel the opposite of a little girl.

I said, Mommy, please. I'm certain that I begged. I always begged with her. I felt safe enough to beg. I knew she would always be my mother. It wasn't like the feeling I've had with some men, with ones like Big Sky where I thought any sign of need on my part would send him running in the other direction. But I've since realized that such fears stemmed from nights like that one, begging my mother, crying until I was heaving. But she stood her ground. I could not sleep with her that night. She wanted to be alone. And I needed to learn how to sleep by myself. Those were the reasons she gave. I couldn't argue with the latter, but the former burned a hole in me. When I close my eyes, I can call up the exact pitch of her voice. The way her accent formed the word *alone.*

Alunn.

I was forced to slink back into my room, closest to the stairway. I lay on top of the covers because I still harbored the hope that she would come for me, scoop me into her smooth mother arms and carry me to her bed where we would cuddle and she would kiss my tears away. I would rear my butt back until it was tucked into the curve of her hips and thighs. She would hold me tighter than she ever had before.

I lay on top of the covers for hours like that. I imagined my grandmother's rape. I imagined the man ripping her nude pantyhose off. I could hear her scream very clearly in my head.

By that time I was already obsessed with sex. It would only get worse. But by that evening in the Poconos I was preoccupied with it. Only recently have I been able to trace it back to a fuzzy memory from when I was five or six. I was sleeping in my parents' bed, as I always did at that age. I had seen a movie about werewolves and was convinced they were going to come for me in my sleep. Every few months my mother tried something. New bedsheets, even a new bed. But nothing could get me into my own room. This one night they tried very hard. They began to prep me at dinner. Over pastina, naturally. My mother made it sound like I would be disappointing her very much if I didn't at least try. And so I did. I tried for an hour and when I finally fell asleep I dreamed of a plush gray carpet in a room with a mirror, and I was looking in the mirror when suddenly the mirror cracked in half and I saw a stripe of black blood across the carpet. I heard the howl of a wolf. I woke in terror and ran into their room. My mother held me and I fell asleep easily. Hours later I woke again, this time to movement. It was a king-size bed and sometimes I would wake up not knowing where my mother was, and if she was in the bathroom, I would wait restlessly until she returned. This time she was not to my right, but she *was* on the bed. She was on my father's side and he was moving on top of her. I turned slowly back to the other side of the bed and saw her bra and underwear and nightgown on the floor. I suppose I lay there until it was over and I fell back asleep, but I can't remember. I blacked that part out. Though it definitely happened — my parents fucked in bed beside me.

330

That night in the Poconos my mother didn't care if I slept or not. My grandmother had been raped and my father had gone home to be with her, perhaps to hunt the rapist in the streets of Orange, New Jersey. Yet there was something else my mother suspected my father of doing that was the reason he didn't take us with him. Now that I know most of the story, everything makes sense.

All of that aside, I still don't understand why my mother wanted to be alone in her bed that night, why my body beside her would be anything but helpful. To this day it's the same chemical burn in my heart that I cannot cool.

23

The two women sat quietly at my kitchen table. I asked if anyone wanted an iced tea. I wondered if Alice could tell I was trembling or whether she'd noticed the way the girl was keeping her hands inside the pockets of her pullover. Eleanor, meanwhile, was projecting the same fearful rage that I'd witnessed so many times on her father's face. He would be angry at me for lying about something, some nascent love affair, but he couldn't show it. So he had to conceal it through clenched teeth. There was also the fear that I'd see through him, recognize his rage, and leave in disgust.

Alice said that she would love a glass. At the beach that magnificent day, I'd told her I didn't think anything could grow inside of me. She touched my belly and said she was sure I was wrong. I said I didn't want anything to ever grow inside me.

— I had a miscarriage once, she told me.

I didn't even know I was pregnant. I'd skipped two periods, but I was an idiot. My boyfriend was French. We were fifteen at a hiking camp in the Dolomites. I told him, I think I'm having a miscarriage. He didn't know what to do. So he fell asleep. He didn't sleep on a sleeping bag, or with a cover, and in the morning when it was over and I'd returned from washing myself in a creek, he told me he'd slept uncomfortably all night. That was his gift to me. His night of discomfort.

— Something came out of you?

—You don't have to look at it. I remember how badly I wanted my mother. Do you miss yours?

— No, I lied. I only wish my aunt were still around.

— Your aunt raised you? How did your parents die, Joan?

— Gosia, yes, she raised me. Or she let me raise myself.

— Tell me about her, Alice said. And happily I described Gosia to her, her smells and clothes and furs. Her large black Mercedes and how, every time she spoke to me from her car phone, I would hear the seatbelt chime and I would say, Gosia, put on your seatbelt, and she would say in her heavy accent, Shut up! Tell me, how you are feeling?

I explained to Alice how it had been calming that Gosia wasn't my mother, that I didn't have to care for her in that way. That I didn't have to know everything about her. There was no backstory through which I had to sift. Her own history only served as a lesson for me. She mined it when she had to give me advice.

I thought of Gosia then in my kitchen, what she would tell me to do. What mental strategy she would instruct me to employ. She always thought that anyone who hurt me should be punished severely. She wanted me to destroy Vic's life, tell his wife. I told her that he had children and Gosia said, I don't care about this man's children. *You* are child. Look what he is doing to *you*.

I'd seen pictures of Eleanor. I never wanted another child to hurt the way that I had. The truth is that even then, in my kitchen, I felt sorry for her. I didn't feel fear. The only fear I felt was that I would lose Alice. Already I had the premonition that Eleanor's presence would push Alice away.

Eleanor was what my mother would have called a poor soul. She'd suffered so much. I couldn't decide which parent had been crueler to her. I thought of her little brother in the tub. The last moments of a child's life. I pictured him looking at his mother, the only thing in the world he knew to trust, looking at her wild eyes as she made that decision. It was easier for Eleanor to blame me than to blame her parents.

I took the glass pitcher from the refrigerator. The fragrant mint leaves floated at the top. I selected three wineglasses by the stem and handled all of them with the skills I'd learned as a waitress at an all-glass restaurant on the marina in Jersey City. That terrible winter I slept with two clients, one of whom — the married one, though I didn't know that at the time — asked if he could fuck me in the ass the very first night he came to my apartment. We had been fucking for barely five minutes when he asked. The next night he came into the restaurant, this time with his wife. I lifted the rubber bar mat and poured the evening's spillovers into his Long Island iced tea. Then I stirred it with a knife that had just deboned a raw chicken.

Now I set the glasses on the table and filled Alice's cup first. As I did so, I saw out of the corner of my eye a blur of activity in Eleanor's lap. I thought she was going to shoot Alice. I thought of the time her father had me on all fours, going in and out of me, his hands lightly gripping my waist. Not making any noises because he was too happy, too scared it would all end if he made an unpalatable move. I thought of his warm breath in my ear and the glee in his eyes. I thought of what he had done to his daughter and his wife.

— Eleanor, I said. I said it so calmly and sweetly that it shocked her, that she let the gun drop in her lap.

Alice realized what had been about to happen, what might, in fact, still happen. She screamed and then she began to cry. I had never seen someone look so beautiful while they cried. But it made her seem immature. It was such a stupid thing. To be afraid of a little girl with a gun that she didn't know how to use.

Then Alice pitched forward and projectile-vomited onto the girl's face. The stink was immediate and terrible. Eleanor stood and screamed and the gun dropped to the floor. The vomit — the color and texture of oatmeal — was in the girl's eyes, coating her eyelashes; it covered her entire nose and mouth, and as she was screaming, the vomit was seeping into her mouth. She tried to wipe the vomit from her eyes and crouched down, blindly grabbing for the gun on the floor. I picked it up like it was nothing and walked into the kitchen. I placed the gun behind the toaster and ran warm water and soaked a rag and came back and knelt beside the girl.

I noticed then a gold locket around her neck. I didn't have to open it to know it contained a picture of her little brother, crudely cut into a circle.

— Oh, Eleanor, I said into her ear. Oh, you poor, poor thing.

24

Eleanor showered the vomit off. When she came out of the bathroom, she looked like the age that I was when I died. The gun hadn't been loaded after all. I didn't know what to do with it, so I put it inside my potbellied stove. I laid it across the crystals. When it became clear the girl was no longer a threat, Alice, in shock, went home. It hurt me that she did but I acted like it didn't.

That night the girl and I spoke until the early morning. The guilt I felt was enormous. I did what I had to do. I told her the grand calamity of my childhood. As with her father before her, it bound her to me in a way that erased any hostility. There was no way to hear my story and still hate me. And like her father before her, she was going to keep me company. Alice, I knew, might abandon me at any point, but this girl would never.

Over the next few weeks she stayed with

me. She never left. It happened slowly. Every day I hoped it would end. She slept downstairs on the couch. My parents hadn't allowed sleepovers. They didn't think there was any reason for them. For someone to come into our home and in the morning go into our refrigerator for orange juice. They thought it was unseemly. I began to feel the same way and the feeling only deepened over the years.

Eleanor and I talked every night, late into the night. Sometimes I liked it but mostly I felt like I couldn't breathe. It went on like that for so long that I lost track. Alice called or wrote every few days and I told her the girl was still here. I could tell that she was appalled.

Thankfully I had a job. I could drop her off in Santa Monica or Zuma Beach and leave her there for the day. But the moment I clocked out, she expected me to collect her. I was in an emotional jail.

Still, I owed it to this child not to turn her away. Turning her away would have been the same thing the world had done to me. I needed to be her Gosia. But I couldn't face the notion that I might have to care for her indefinitely. I knew I would sooner kill her. Because sometimes it's better to kill someone than to leave them.

One day, behind her back, I called in sick to work. Eleanor, as though she knew, told me she didn't want to go anywhere. She was too depressed and wanted to stay in the house. I was terrified that she would hitch-hike to the café and find that I wasn't there. But I had to take the risk because I felt I would otherwise lose Alice. I hated Alice for not wanting to be near the girl. That she thought of me differently now, as one half of a strange couple.

Two hours later I was in Alice's car, the air-conditioning blasting wetly. We drove down Abbot Kinney looking for parking. She was taking me to a yoga class that she said would make everything better. Her hair was pulled up into a high, dark bun. She wore no makeup and I wanted to kill her. But first I wanted to put her in a cage, fatten her up, feed her hormones and pig cheeks and Fanta. Knock her teeth out and shave her eyebrows. I wanted her to die ugly.

She told me she'd missed me, but she didn't apologize or explain why she hadn't been in touch.

Every so often she would look at me, at my belly, and say, I cannot believe you're fucking pregnant.

I was terrified that she would leave me. She asked me to tell her everything that had been going on and I explained how I couldn't do anything just yet, how I had to let her stay. I didn't say how much I'd begun to feel for the girl, how she was a mirror of me. I couldn't yet tell Alice about what had happened in my tenth year. She might, at this too early stage, leave me for good.

Abbot Kinney made me feel old. The girls on the sidewalk in their cowboy hats and the boys in their baseball caps and the skateboards and the surfboards on top of Volkswagens. If you were poor in Venice, you had to be beautiful, and if you were old, you had to be rich.

Alice slipped her dusty Prius between two G-wagons. She was an excellent parker.

She said she needed a coffee and led me up a ramp and through an alley to a line of people waiting outside a building that looked like a greenhouse garage. It had very high ceilings and bicycles on the walls and women with asymmetrical hair, men in red plaid shirts pouring hot water into Chemexes. We ordered our coffees and waited too long for them. So many men looked at Alice as we waited in line.

— Where is the little freak now?

— At home — the house. I tell her I'm going to work even when I'm not and then I drop her off for excursions. Trancas

341

Canyon, Encino, etcetera.

— She lets you leave the house?

I laughed.

— Joan. Why are you doing this?

— I feel bad for her.

— Just as you did for her father.

— No. This is different.

— She's probably in love with you.

— Please, I said. But I was grateful she considered me someone who could be loved.

— Let's go, she said. This class will reset your head. It might knock some sense into you. You might go home and tell the little barnacle to fuck off.

The studio smelled of raw onions. The walls were lime green and the mats were threadbare rubber, even worse than the ones at the famous studio. Some yogis seem to believe that the cheaper the yoga accoutrements, the better the practice, but this was different.

At the head of the room a rangy instructor pulled his Christly hair into a topknot. His lips were buttered with balm, his neck snaked with tendons.

Alice and I took two places next to each other. Aside from the instructor there was only one man, skinny, in long black shorts and a white tee. He adjusted his towel at the top corner of his mat. I felt sorry for him but didn't know why. Soon others trickled in. The instructor dimmed the lights and it felt like evening.

— Dear friends, the instructor said, his voice quiet and meditative but resounding all the same, I invite you to come into your bodies. Please take *vajrasana,* kneeling pose, and ease yourself into the forty-seven corners of your frames. Melt your bones out to the recesses of your skin, but at the same time stay within the boundaries of your flesh. Good. Very good. Take a deep breath in, now a deep breath out. *Ahhhhhh.* Excellent. Please go ahead and thank yourselves for coming into class tonight. For giving yourself this gift. We have a very whetted understanding of time in this room, don't we, and we appreciate that this hour is precious. This is a *special* class. We are a *special* group. And because we are unique in yoga, I thought we deserved a unique flow. Our very own, this night.

He slipped his eyes closed and pressed his hands in prayer. The room was still. I looked at Alice, but her eyes were closed, too.

— When I was a boy, the instructor said, we used to hold these undercover séances. We'd turn off all the lights and repeat the

names of our dead grandmas. Grandma
Sue? Grandma Beth?

A small collective laugh filled the room.

— You there, Grandma Jo? To our great
relief, we never heard back from our dead
grammies. The last séance we ever held, one
of us was trying to reach a dead parent. Our
friend Bobby, his dad was a truck driver
who died when his eighteen-wheeler flipped
off a mountain pass in Idaho. Holy moly,
how we all hoped he wouldn't come to us.
Even Bobby. We couldn't fathom how far
his dad had fallen, and we were terrified by
the notion. If he spoke to us from beyond,
we'd have probably pissed our dungarees.
Looking back now, I realize that the purpose
of those little séances was not to talk to
these dead relatives but, rather, to scare
ourselves "to death." Because wasn't that
the scariest thought in the universe? Death?

In the darkness I saw the room nod. There
were soft squeaking noises in the walls that
I was sure were mice.

— Now, my friends, we have a unique gift
in the world. All of us on this earth have a
life sentence, we are walking around with
an expiration date under our cap, but most
of the people you see out there, bouncing
around without a care in the world, they
don't know *when*. They might live to a

hundred and ten. The way they act, it's like coffins are for vampires, am I right? Well. For those of us in the room, the sentence is a tad bit sooner than that, isn't it? And as I'm sure many of you have come to feel, there's a marvelous freedom in that. We are not scared of death, not in the same way, because from this point forward, we *begin* at death. Are you with me?

Again the room nodded. A Poland Spring bottle crinkled. I heard the sound of water slipping down a throat. I used to hate the noise my father made when he smacked his thirsty lips to make moisture. He was a diabetic and sometimes his mouth ran dry.

— So this evening, I'd like us to begin in *savasana*, corpse pose. May we, in yoga, as in life, begin at death and travel onward from there. Now bring yourselves to lie down, release the legs, and push out through the heels. Soften the root of the tongue, the wings of the nose, and the taut flesh of the forehead. Let the eyes fall to the back of the head, then turn them downward to gaze at the heart. Release your heavy brain to the back of the skull.

Once the room was lying down, Alice's hand found mine in the relative darkness, grasped it, and the instructor began to whisper.

— You are not your disease, dear friends, HIV/AIDS does not define you. HIV/AIDS are merely letters. You are not your body. Your body is a rental, as K. Pattabhi Jois famously, *exquisitely* said, and soon it will be time to return your lease. You won't be penalized for the dents and the overage of miles. Instead, you will be given a brand-new car, more beautiful than you could have ever imagined, and this one, my dear friends, will have the ability to *fly*.

After the class was over, we walked outside and stood in the sun. The line where Alice's jaw met her neck was so beautiful as to be licentious.

— What the fuck? I said.

— When you're depressed or in grave trouble, she said, people think you should be near children, amusement. They invite you to dinner, they prop you up and shine their happy light in your face. It's bullshit. The opposite is true. You should seek out the dying.

I felt there was something evil about that, something evil in her. I asked her if she'd gone to HIV yoga before and she said of course, many times. She said she went to desperate places whenever she was feeling unfortunate. She liked to do her taxes on the quiet patio of the Beverly Hills Cancer Center, with its flushed jacaranda and its sterile herringbone bricks.

Now I worried she was cruel and careless enough to leave me even after she knew who we were to each other. I wanted to stitch our bodies together.

At a crowded restaurant we ordered pâté on baguette and arugula with Treviso from a girl with interstellar bangs. There was porridge on the menu and something called a risky biscuit. The font on the menu was old diner style. The slices of bread were tremendous, ash-powdered, hard on the outside, cloud-soft within. We sat out on the patio, arid with brown vines and piles of firewood.

— How far along are you? she asked.

— I have no idea.

— Are you going to keep it?

— I don't know, I said, even though I knew I would.

She put her hand on my arm. Moments like those, I couldn't imagine she wouldn't love me.

— Why don't you go to the police? Tell them this child is a runaway. Have them send it back to its mother.

— I can't go to the police.

— Such an outlaw, Joan. Are you wanted in New York City? Are you the one who killed Vic?

— I just don't trust the police.

Alice nodded and didn't ask me to clarify, but the police officer appeared to me then. There were two who came that night; one of them dealt with the bodies and the other dealt with me. He was in his early thirties with the pale bloated face of a young boy that merely expands out at the sides as he ages. It took me a while to realize that he thought I'd done it. He wasn't intelligent. Even an hour later, when the trajectory of events became clear, he remained cold. He treated me as so many men in the future would.

— So tell your landlord, she said, laughing. I'm sure it's another coda in the lease.

— She's a little girl, I said as I touched my stomach.

— You have your own child to protect. Are you a warrior, I want to know? Or are you some husk that men — and now this girl — have had their way with?

After the words left her mouth, there was no trace of them on her face. I realized that no matter how much I'd told her, she didn't understand my life. Of course, I hadn't told her the end. Big Sky, in one of his pontificating moods, said it took fifty years for a death to be completely forgotten, but sometimes it took only two weeks. Some people, he said, were stronger than others.

I realized in that very instant that I would never see Big Sky again. I would never see his face again. Feel his warm and reticent touch. Of all the rapes I'd sustained, this was the worst degradation — the way a man who thinks nothing of you can loom larger than your life, and another life inside of you. That was the most awful thing. That, like my mother before me, I felt that my child was a burden.

25

Lenny met Eleanor one 103-degree afternoon. She was curled up on the couch when he knocked. I felt I was opening the door to a shameful secret.

I introduced her as a friend who was staying with me. She was quiet and looked homely in a pair of inexpensive pajamas.

— For how long? he asked. I knew Lenny wanted to continue to unburden himself. I missed the jail of Lenny. How easily I could dip in and out of it. On top of that, my plan to pinch the watch was stalled.

— I don't know. A bit.

— There's a provision in the lease, no long-term guests.

I knew that he was upset because he would not feel free to come and see me as often as he wished. Eleanor was not beautiful. If Alice had been staying with me, he would have been fine with it. He would have been more than fine. He would have been excited.

— She's not. She's staying for a few days.

I was thrilled there was now an hourglass on her stay.

— In any case, Lenny said, trying to regain ground, I was coming to inform you that I have not received your August rent.

— It's August twelfth. I have a fifteen-day leniency.

— Well, yes, but. I'm informing you.

— Thank you.

Belligerently he turned and walked away.

— I can't leave, Eleanor said when the door closed behind him.

— At some point —

— I want to stay, she said, until the baby is born.

— You will be a part of its — his — life. I promise you that.

— But.

— Forever.

Then I sickened myself.

— He's your brother, I said.

She began to cry. She said she had nowhere else to go. She didn't want to go home. There was no home left. She asked me, through her tears, what her father had been like with me. Had he always been happy. I told her he talked about her all the time.

— In what way?

— He was very proud of you. When you learned how to drive, for example. How you parallel-parked so well.

She looked at me in that way all children do when hearing specific stories about how their parents felt about them. I'd had that look with Gosia many times.

— But what about how he was with you? Was he always happy to be with you?

— Yes, I suppose. But he was also sad.

— Because you didn't love him back.

Eleanor was sitting on the couch with her legs bent to one side. The pajamas were tight around her thighs and chest. She'd come to Los Angeles with fourteen hundred dollars, which in that city was barely enough for several dinners. At least it was barely enough for dinner the way that I ate dinner. The way that I racked up debt to cool my fever.

I'd taken her to a giant discount clothing store in the Valley. We shopped beside a mother with stringy blond hair and twig legs in ripped jean shorts. Her child, a toddler with glorious green eyes, walked placidly beside her as the woman ranted into a flip phone, alternately cursing and crying. Eleanor and I were both greatly affected. We looked at each other and I knew we felt the same way. We wanted to pick the child up and bundle her in our arms and whisk her away. We could not abide selfish parents.

I bought Eleanor a pack of white briefs and several pairs of shorts and t-shirts, a yellow sundress that I'd seen her admiring. I bought her pajamas as well, but she wore mine nearly every night.

— He took it out on us because you didn't love him back.

— How did he do that?

— There were just nights he'd come home and he was depressed. He'd say something went wrong at work, or when our grandpa — his dad — died, he said he was depressed about that for a really long time. Then he just started drinking a lot. Most nights he'd come home after Robbie was put to bed. A couple of times I heard my mom ask him to go in and kiss him good night. And Dad would say he did. But I knew he didn't.

Vic never told me about his father's death.

— I really don't know how to tell you how sorry I am.

— Sometimes I hate you so much. Other times I think it's not your fault. Like that stuff my dad wanted — you, whatever — he wouldn't have done what he did if it wasn't for how miserable he was at home. He was unhappy. I guess he always was, when I think back. He never loved my mom. I mean, he cared for her, like you care for anyone you live with or anyone who loves you. But he didn't *love* love her. And after Robbie . . .

I took her hand in mine. I didn't want to but felt I needed to.

— Before Robbie, he came to my softball games. Every single one. He wore a dumb PROUD DAD hat or whatever. We played catch every day after school. We made meatball sandwiches at night, after Mom went to bed. I knew he wasn't totally happy, but he was happy with *me*.

I walked to my little tin and brought out three one-milligram Xanax pills. I swallowed two dry and offered her the third. Perhaps it was irresponsible of me but I didn't see any reason for someone in her kind of pain not to take pills.

She took it from me. She had never done any kind of drug, had never smoked a cigarette. She told me she was a virgin, that she thought she would wait until marriage. And now she didn't want anything. In one day, she told me, she'd gone from wanting a love story for herself to not believing in love at all.

— What about God? I asked.

— What about Him?

— Do you still believe in God?

— Of course, she said. Don't you?

— No. I don't.

— That's weird to me. That's kind of totally nuts.

— Why?

— Because how else are you going to see your parents again?

26

I'd been writing to Alice for two weeks and she would write back sometimes an entire day later. Her replies would be friendly but distant. They were the sorts of replies I'd gotten from Big Sky toward the end.

It made me remember the way all my female friendships had exasperated me. I realized that was how Alice now felt about me. It was hard to believe. In the past, if a woman didn't immediately hate me, then she would eventually develop an unsavory need for me.

There was Carly from college, whom I reconnected with during a dark spell, in between lovers. On my way back across the country, I stopped to see her and we spent a week pretending we were better friends than we'd been in school. We ate pressed sushi and read the same biography of Jackie Onassis on Butterfly Beach. She wanted me to sleep in her bed, but I took the couch every night, peppery with sand.

She had a crush on the bartender at the sushi place. That was what made him attractive to me. He was good-looking but not tall and not clean. She introduced me to him at a party. When she went to tap the keg, I let him bring me to a filthy couch with a bedsheet over it where we kissed. I wasn't even a little drunk. I felt someone poking my arm and looked up to see it was Carly, rage and disbelief on her face. She downed her drink. The cranberry froth clung to the fine hairs on her upper lip. I'm going home, she said, waiting for me to follow.

I'm not finished with you yet, the young man whispered into my ear, gravelly, like a junkie. I was disgusted and humiliated. With the last spittle of my inheritance, I got a bungalow at the Four Seasons in Santa Barbara. I drove us there in my rented car, leaving Carly to cab home. We didn't fuck, I was too afraid he might carry disease. I half-heartedly blew him and let him finish on my chest. I remember the color was a terrible greenish hue.

In the morning I called my friend. I didn't apologize but asked her to come to the pool. She was over in a flash.

It was one of those pools that impresses

people. Olympic and clean with coral grounds and white umbrellas and the private beach just below. I found it depressing and wished it were half the size. We ordered mimosas and shared a club sandwich. But eventually Carly couldn't take it. She wanted more from me and tried to pick at my insides to get it. She didn't know anything about my history — nobody did besides Gosia and, later, Vic — but anyhow turned to me with a piece of sandwich in her mouth and said, Are you the way that you are because of your mom or your dad?

I stood up. I was twenty-six and wearing a red bikini, my body was at its peak, the best it would ever look. Without another word I walked back to my room, my rear swinging, polo-shirted pool boys watching, packed up my car, and left town. I slurped some Belon oysters at a harbor bar on the way out because I'd already spent so much in one weekend that it didn't seem to matter.

I never spoke to Carly again. I often wonder how she thought of that day. How long she hung by the pool after I'd left, expecting me to return. She'd become marvelously invested in me within mere days. Had it been me, had I been the one who was left, I'd have lain on the chaise through dusk. I'd have sucked the day down to its bone.

But now I was the jealous friend. I couldn't even go back and look at our messages because my need was so shameful to me. The most recent one —

I am eating cilantro and thinking of you.

She didn't reply for hours and then asked me if I'd ever been to the Santa Monica Pier and I said that I hadn't. By bringing me to that place — thick with the tourists, their lips stained in Slurpee, their rotten children running wild — I knew it meant she was going to leave me for good. I didn't know exactly why, but I was sure of it all the same.

We ate chili dogs and drank lime rickeys and headed for the Ferris wheel. She led me up the steel stairs of the ride, treating me like I was a dog and my arm was the leash. She was much taller than I, and even though she was slender, her bones took up a lot of space. Her hips were like my mother's. I can't be sure because it's been so long, but my memory is that my mother's hips were very wide. I pictured Alice on my father's arm, not as his daughter but as his lover.

I reveled in that feeling of her holding my arm. I hadn't loved a woman's touch that much since my mother. I worried that when

Alice left me, I would go looking for her forever.

Once I followed Big Sky. I waited outside of his office building on Wall Street for an hour until he finally emerged, laughing, with a well-dressed woman. Was he fucking her? No, probably not. But from afar it appeared they had that flirtation, the one we'd had at the magical start. I followed them to the nicest lunch spot in the area. I watched from the window as they ate. Frisée. Bald black olives. They each drank a glass of red.

Vic had followed me like that, probably more times than I could even imagine. In his too-large suits, his teeth gritted behind his thin lips.

Alice and I sat across from each other inside one of the cups of the wheel. The steel clanked with a risky noise as the wheel began to turn.

— I miss you, Alice said, but it didn't sound genuine.

— Eleanor is going to leave soon.

— Good.

I wanted to know why it bothered her so much, why I wasn't enough on my own, even with this barnacle on my back. Hadn't we hit it off perfectly? Didn't she realize our bond was deeper than a new friendship?

— She's much younger-looking than I expected, and built like a circus strongman.

— She's a little girl, I said.

— Joan, you don't need to take care of her. Tell her you're going on a trip. Tell her you're going to see your parents.

— She knows I don't have any, I said, thinking how strange it was that Eleanor knew my secret and Alice did not.

— Well, for God's sake. You two sit up talking all night? You don't think this is a bit fucked?

— Her father just killed himself, I said. Her mother is shattered. She had a brother with Down's.

— You didn't tell me that, she said.

— I thought I did, what does it matter?

— It matters a lot. That's a big thing.

— Why?

— What do you mean, *why*? Did Vic agree to have a child with Down, I wonder?

— I don't think he did.

— She kept it from him?

— She knew there was a one-in-three chance or something, and yes, she kept that from him.

— Let me ask you something. Can you imagine what it was like for the child, growing up as the only child her father could love? I have a second cousin with Down syndrome. In Maremma. It's better there.

Roman Catholics are more about the heart and less about the way something should look. I'm not religious, you know, but if both parents are the type to love whatever form something takes, then fine. Then you take the kid to the market and you don't give a flying fuck who looks at him three times. But if you are a man like your Vic, who is upwardly mobile, who is more intelligent than the family he came from, than his wife who he married too soon, who got a taste of a woman like you, can you imagine the rage you'd feel? And now his daughter there — she knows that you were the reason her father stopped trying to get it up for his family. He met you and became even more withdrawn. Jesus Christ, it's more than just her father cheated and now she wants to kill the slut who fucked her dad. It's she wants to kill the slut who made her family seem like a pile of garbage. It's not your fault, Joan, but this is worse than I thought. I can't believe you didn't tell me about the boy. That girl will never leave you.

I told her it was worse than that. I told her the boy was dead and about the way it happened. Alice looked at me like I was the one who'd killed the child.

— Almost all of them, Joan. Someone else's men.

— Fuck you.

— It's weird.

— You don't get me.

— You're a fucking trope. There's nothing more to get.

I felt my cheeks sinking, my mouth parting. She could barely look at me because she knew how much she was hurting me.

She said she should be getting home and I tried to say I would take a taxi but I wanted to be right beside her at the cost of my dignity. I thought of Eleanor at home. She'd be waiting for me with her crab pincers, just as her father had.

Alice and I made up, sort of. She apologized. On the way back up the canyon she told me she was thinking of going on a yoga retreat to a place called Feathered Pipe. That she needed to get out of Los Angeles. August in Los Angeles was for the birds, she said, as though I weren't going to be there. Several weeks earlier, we might have been going away together. It wasn't until I was about to get out of the car that I asked her where the retreat was.

She picked up her big cat-eye sunglasses from the dirty console and put them on. She smiled in a way I would never forget.

— Montana, she said. Then she winked

and pulled away before I'd even closed the door.

Killing becomes something that isn't outlandish. When you've seen what I have, a number of awful things become practical.

27

I got Eleanor a job at the café working half my hours so that when she was gone, I was at home and vice versa. She wasn't exactly happy with the arrangement, but at the same time she knew she had to contribute. It'd been over three weeks by that point. I spent my evenings cooking for the two of us, like we were a married couple. I increased her dose of Xanax to a full milligram so that she would fall asleep early. I laid a blanket over her body on the couch. She didn't shower every day so sometimes she smelled of onions and I did a load of laundry nightly while she observed me from the couch or watched mindless television, reruns of old shows about high schoolers. I folded her clothes like I was her mother.

One night we sat on the couch together and watched an old film my mother used to love, *The Major and the Minor*. I took in only art that wouldn't fell me. I watched only romantic comedies and read books only about subjects that didn't mirror anything in my own life.

On the coffee table my phone began to buzz.

Nobody called anymore. I reached for the phone, hoping it might be Alice. Even Big Sky, though that was a ludicrous idea. I prayed to my parents for it to be the man I thought I loved. But before I could pick up the phone, the ringing stopped and a message came through.

Is my daughter there? TELL ME IF SHE IS TELL ME Her name is ELEANOR

I showed the message to Eleanor, who looked utterly nonplussed.

— Don't you think you should call her? I asked.

— She's lucky I don't call the police, she said.

— I understand. But. She's been through a lot.

— It's her fucking fault. All of it. Will you please block her number? I blocked the number and we sat on the couch and drank our tea and took our drugs and Eleanor passed out and I watched the movie straight through to the end.

Once it had reached the one-month mark, I

thought about killing her. It got to the point that there was nobody I *didn't* want to kill. I was finally showing, and even though I tried to cover it up with loose dresses, I could see Eleanor staring at my belly, co-opting it with her eyes. I felt bonded to my child. I didn't need anyone anymore.

I was throwing up every morning. I would do it outside like an animal to avoid Eleanor waking too soon and stealing my morning hours. I wanted to kill everyone.

One day River came by, acting as though we'd never fucked. I opened the door to his knock and shut it quickly behind me so that he wouldn't see Eleanor inside. She was having one of her spells during which she cried and shook on the floor. The same as the ones I'd had. I watched her during these spells. From several feet away I said comforting things. I never touched her, even though I knew how badly she wanted me to.

River stood in a white tee and cargo shorts, his blond hair catching the sunlight. Kurt was with him. The day was bright but not hot. They were going on a hike and River asked if I wanted to come. I pictured us high up on the mountain on one of those dry trails, fucking amid the monkey flower, my back getting scratched by the ragweed. I imagined it would turn him on to know I was pregnant. It turned me on. It also made me feel hopeful that I might pretend the child inside of me was River's and not the man in Marfa's.

I was about to say yes, I was about to say I would just run inside and get my boots, when the door opened. There stood Eleanor, her face a mess.

— Oh, River said, you have company.

— This is Eleanor, I said, about to cry.

— Oh hey, he said, extending his strong arm.

She looked jealous. She lightly took my arm. I felt her pulling me inside. I felt the threat and the pain in her touch.

— Maybe some other time, he said, smiling as though he'd seen something untoward, something a little gross.

I nodded and smiled and told him to have fun and closed the door.

— That's the guy who lives in the circus tent?

— The yurt, I said, feeling faint.

She asked me if we could go for a walk, just the two of us. She was crying. I began to cry, too.

Following our day at the pier, I heard from Alice even more sparingly. Twice a week at most. I considered going to one of her classes, but shame stopped me. I missed her like I hadn't missed anyone since Gosia. I understood I'd become a seedy figure to her, but I couldn't accept that Eleanor's presence was the end of Alice and me.

Then one afternoon, one of those perfect days that can make you feel lonely, I heard the light engine of a car, but it never came up the hill. It parked at the bottom, almost inside the start of the trail, under a tree that would scrape its hood. The car was Alice's Prius. My heart leaped.

Thankfully, Eleanor was at work. I watched out my window and saw Alice's long legs in a pair of tiny spandex yoga shorts, climbing the hill, crossing the big ravine, until she was out of my eyeline. From the window I couldn't see the door of River's yurt. When I found the courage to step outside, I saw no one. She hadn't come for me.

Back inside I waited, trembling, for several hours. I thought to leave the house, but I needed to see her, to confirm where she'd been. At dusk, when I saw her finally descend the hill, I noticed that her previously ponytailed hair was undone.

I left to pick up Eleanor from work. Alice's car was now at the studio. She taught a seven p.m. Ashtanga class.

Over the next two weeks, as my stomach grew and Eleanor's need expanded throughout the house, stifling me more than the heat ever could, I observed Alice come to River's yurt six times in total. There may have been more visits while I was at work. The first time she stayed overnight, I vomited into the toilet of the tiny bathroom, where the smell of Eleanor's menstrual blood filled the air. I'd bought her dog waste bags and told her to triple-bag her large, thick pads but, like the child that she was, she forgot.

I was devastated, jealous on many levels. For one, the fact that they seemed to never go on dates, leave the house, like all each wanted and needed was the other's young and perfect body. I couldn't get it out of my head that it could have been me in there with him had Eleanor not blocked me that time he came to my door. That, even though he was immature, his body and his energy were a great salve. But, more than anything, I was crushed that Alice had left me so cruelly and substituted this boy for me. The feeling of wanting to be her, of wanting to possess her body and her strength — but mostly her past — intensified to a point where I couldn't bear it. I felt again the urge to kill her, to kill myself. I knew I was going to kill *something*.

What had begun to torture me most was the idea that she didn't care that I saw her. Yes, she parked down below, hidden partly by trees. But it was a half-assed gesture.

The fifth week of Eleanor's stay and Alice's withdrawal from my life, I made a decision. I returned home from work and cut Lenny off at the pass as he approached. He asked about Eleanor and I told him she had a bad cold. I told him I was feeling ill, too, and I didn't want to give him something that might lead to pneumonia. He asked me if I hated him. There is no need to tell people you hate them. No need to confront them. I would advise you to lie in wait until you take your revenge.

But he placed his hand on my arm softly. The expression on his face was plaintive.

— Joan, he said, I have been waiting to finish my story.

I noticed he was wearing the watch. I tried not to look at it. I told him to wait a moment, then I went inside to get a carafe of water. I told Eleanor to stay. She hated it when I did that. She hated to feel separate from me.

I returned to Lenny. It served me to know more.

— Thank you, Joan. There isn't anyone else.

It was a role I was used to. Last woman standing. Lenny poured himself some more vodka. I placed my hand over my glass with fanned fingers, as my mother used to do. Lenny placed the vodka down.

— Go on. I remember where you left off.

I was appalled.

— After that day, he continued, I was filled with self-recrimination. The rage had cooled, and in its place an awesome guilt took root. Lenore had grown despondent over the most recent failed conception. I refused to take responsibility. I didn't say a word. Like a child, I sulked. It was the summer, with nothing to do. I reread *Goodbye, Columbus* in the café where you work. I ate anchovy filets from the can. That day at Sandstone I'd been as ugly as I think anyone can be. I'd taken the love of this beautiful woman and just —

He made a crushing motion with both hands.

— Several times I walked onto the beach at night toward the rolling ocean. I never believed in God, but I asked the ocean, the universe, to take me. To swallow me whole. I laid myself down at the shoreline. But it turned out the ocean didn't want me.

— The white man's burden, I said.

— I'm sorry?

— You're a white, wealthy male. Once you were a young, white, wealthy entitled piece of shit. Now you are old and you have the diseases you should have.

He nodded. He appeared suddenly chastened.

— Yes, I know, Joan. I understand. And I'm telling you this terrible thing I did. Not to absolve myself. But to sacrifice the last thing I can.

I nodded, but my rage was so intense at that moment I imagined it issuing from me in a bear-shaped vapor and killing the man. It was the female rage that builds for decades. I thought of the day I watched two skinny teenage boys playing Ping-Pong in the rec room of the hotel where I cleaned. I watched as another cleaning woman, Anna, heavy, with four children and a broken back, vacuumed the floor. The Ping-Pong ball jumped off the table and rolled into the mouth of Anna's industrial vacuum. I saw how she hadn't gone for the ball, but neither did she veer away from it, and the ball was swallowed by the vac and the young boys swore. She turned the vacuum off just in time to hear one boy cry out, Fuck! The fuckin ball! The other said, Give it back!

And Anna sneered. Your little ball is gone, she said. And she turned the vacuum back on, a poltergeist of light and noise. Anna needed that job but she would have lost it that day if she had to.

— The facts, Leonard said obediently. I took Lenore back to Sandstone. To punish myself. It was late August, and there was a party at the ranch. I bought her a dress that was nothing but a swath of purple silk, and she tied it like a toga over one shoulder. She had long thick legs, like a Clydesdale. I wore a tuxedo. Most people were clothed that night; some, of course, were not. There was a band playing on a strange little stage in the main room. Doctor Johnson.

— Oh, I said, and Leonard nodded at me.

— And we watched them and danced. Lenore was easily the most gorgeous woman in the room. The lead singer of the band was eyeing her. He was, effectively, singing *to* her and her alone. Halfway through a dance someone came up to us, a bearded man, oily and tanned, and he handed us both a pill. Back then we called it a mickey. Within thirty minutes Lenore and I were both reeling.

She went to the bathroom and I thought to accompany her, but then some red-haired bimbo came and intercepted me. She had tassels on her tits. I'll never forget the way they swirled. And in my brain the drug was dancing. The red-haired woman sat me down on a couch and sat on my lap, just staring into my eyes and kissing my eyelids every so often. It was a divine feeling. I felt helpless and delicious. Finally I found the strength to get up. I pushed her off of me and went to look for Lenore. The band was not playing and this struck me as ominous. I passed many rooms where people fucked, groups of four and five. One room was just a chain of cunnilingus, woman on woman on woman, and at the head was one man fucking one woman. I stopped and watched several rooms until finally I saw a sight that shot me down. Lenore's purple swath of silk on the floor. This was in the doorway of a large room and the door was open because that was the rule at Sandstone. Open doors, open hearts, whatever nonsense. Lenore was on the bed, naked. Beside her was the lead singer of the band, the man you must have met already, stroking her side, kissing her nipples. Many times I've thought to kill him. But I'm a goddamned coward. He was much younger than me, than both of us, about twenty years. My head was spinning. I had no words. He looked at me, he said, Hello, my friend.

Lenore fluttered her eyes as he entered her. She looked at me and held out her hand and I took it. I was shaking, crying. But she smiled at me as though it were me entering her. It went on for ten minutes, but God knows it felt like a century, with me watching and sobbing like a child, getting all that I deserved. He kept going until he orgasmed. And she came along with him; I'd never seen her climax so hard. Afterward they lay there, the two of them, spent.

— Jesus, I said. I was trembling all over.

— The next morning we both woke with terrible hangovers and started to rework it in our brains that she was raped. Not violently, but that she was taken advantage of while under the influence of a very powerful drug, and I had come to the room too late to stop it. That was our story. In a sense, it was the truth.

He coughed. I looked at the thick blue veins on his wrist, the watch twinkling across them.

— I am sure, Leonard said, you can guess what comes next.

In fact, I had no idea what came next.

— Weeks passed. She took one of the home tests. She already knew because her breasts ached. Her mouth was full of spit. She couldn't hide her happiness. That was the hell.

He began to shake.

— We could have pretended it was mine. No one would have questioned it. It was the happiness in her that I couldn't take. The happiness that someone else had put there. And so we decided and yet we never discussed it out loud. I said, Let Dr. Menta see you. She knew only a bit about Dr. Menta, but it was enough. All right, she said. She said she would drive herself to the appointment. She would get a drink first at the Beverly Hills Hotel and wanted to be alone. I paced the house all that day. I couldn't read or eat. The day was overcast. I pictured her driving through the fog down the canyon. Part of me hoped for a car accident, something absolving. She came back late, past nine.

— Darling, you said, did you do it? You didn't, and that's all right.

— Yes, I said exactly that, I believe, how did you —

— Go on, finish, I said, surprised that men always seemed not to know it when you hated them.

— She didn't do it and I told her it was all right and she cried out in gratitude. She wanted a child at any cost.

— She wanted *that* child, I said, because

she already knew who it was.

— Perhaps, he said, stroking his wattle.

— You did something.

— Yes. I did something terrible.

I shook my head back and forth, vibrating with wrath.

— This canyon is full of the types, you know, their pebbles and sands and crystals. The Bulgarian at the dry cleaner whom I'd known for years. Her breath you could smell from ten feet away. As though she ate bugs and dirt. One morning, along with my pressed shirts, she handed me a little brown sack and inside were two vials, one of black cohosh and one of blue.

— You old sick fuck.

— You know what they do?

I knew. In the hospital once a woman had tried to induce labor with blue cohosh. She'd been ten days past her due date and could no longer tolerate the heartburn. But she was allergic to cohosh. She died during the emergency cesarean. I spent most of the night outside the nursery watching her baby, who had a full head of rich black hair.

— That night I made Lenore her tea, Lenny continued, only it was steeped in triple the recommended dosage of both.

— She had no idea.

— No, I believe she had some idea.

— And she bled.

— She bled so much I was afraid she would die. It started in the middle of the night. The coyotes began to circle and howl, and then the contractions began, and after an hour of screaming and pain, it came out of her. A seahorse shape, blue and red. She held it to her breast, gently, and kissed its alien skull. Even in my fear and guilt, I felt the rage. Another man's seed at Lenore's breast. Within seconds the thing died.

I nodded. I'd made my decision. But I wouldn't give him the slightest of hints. I smiled. I patted the wrist that wasn't wearing the watch.

— There, I said. Do you feel better now?

He nodded. Hideously, he was grateful.

— Thank you, Joan.

— Go home. Take a nap. Somewhere in heaven, Lenore is smiling.

I took his arm roughly, pushed him in the direction of his tiny home, then turned and opened my door.

Of course he made an attempt to follow me, so I quickly shut the door in his face and returned inside, rageful, only to find Eleanor wearing my white slip dress. It was straining at her chest. I couldn't believe it.

— Eleanor, what the fuck.

— What? she asked. She was existentially

frightened of me.

— That's my special dress, I said.

— Oh. I didn't know. Sorry.

— It's my mother's. Please take it off.

She pulled it off. Underneath she wore her cheap underwear and bra.

— I'm really sorry.

I boiled water for tea and she walked to the area on the floor where she kept her things. She dressed in her own clothes and then, with a smile on her face, something I'd never seen, told me that she felt okay that day, for the first time since her brother's passing.

I told her how happy I was to hear that, and truly, I was.

— And I'm grateful to you for getting me the job and for letting me stay here.

I wanted to say that I'd never agreed, that she'd come and never left. Instead I nodded kindly.

— And. I forgive you.

Involuntarily, tears filled my eyes.

— Yeah. And I wanted to tell you. I feel good having you in my life. I know that sounds weird.

— No, I get it.

— Also, I'm really excited about the baby. It's getting closer and maybe that's why. I don't want to be creepy or whatever. But I love him already.

I nearly spilled the hot water on my legs. I turned from her and crushed three Xanax between my fingers and dropped them into her cup.

— Here. I made some tea.

She never refused anything I made her. I thought of all the times I'd cooked for her father, his fawning gratitude. The careful way that he chewed.

She smiled as she took it from me and thirty minutes later she was passed out on the couch. I sprayed down the white slip with Big Sky's cologne to mask Eleanor's sweat and walked to River's door.

For many years my rage was dormant. I'd lived to survive. I could call up the hideous event, but in a far-off way. I could have dictated only the facts. I could not have called up each moment of horror. Back then not a second went by that I didn't feel like something was eating my heart. But in the Canyon the pain turned to rage and the rage was growing around me the way the sun-baked bougainvillea grew around the old swingers' mansion.

I'd never fucked a man to get back at a woman. I'd flirted with the boyfriend of a friend to check my power, though only after the friend had hurt me, had flaunted some faux happiness in my face to make herself feel better. This was new. Alice had not theoretically done anything to hurt me. She'd removed herself from my life but not out of spite. She simply didn't want to be near me. That's the most awful thing someone you love can do.

I knocked on River's door. He opened it, shirtless. I told him my air-conditioning had broken and that I couldn't stand the heat. I asked if he had anything cold in his fridge to drink. I had nothing in mine.

— Yeah, of course, come in, he said.

His bed was unmade and Kurt was lying on top of it.

— Is beer okay?

I nodded and he pushed lime halves into two bottles of Corona with his calloused thumb. He said, Cheers, we clinked the glass, and his thick pink lips covered the whole mouth of the bottle.

— So that girl, is she like a friend?

— She's the little sister of my good friend back in New York. Their dad just died and she came out here to get away.

— That's why I came out here, too.

— Is your mom still in Nebraska?

— Yeah, but she's good. She's seeing this dude. He's a good guy. I'm happy for her.

— That's good.

— Yeah, it's pretty great.

— The last time I was in here, I said, sitting down on his bed and stroking the dog's head.

He laughed nervously. The thing with Alice was apparently becoming serious. I understood that he felt guilty, and that if I referenced our intimacy, he would pull away.

— The last time I was in here, Kurt wasn't.

— Oh, yeah, he said. He was grateful I didn't say anything else. I also knew that would make him want me more. The notion that I might have forgotten the way he made love.

I crossed and uncrossed my legs. The dress made a V shape between my thighs — a gleaming silk triangle. It was impossible for him to avert his eyes. I drank half the bottle. I could feel the heat growing between us.

— I wish there was a pool or something, I said. Do you know the song "Nightswimming"?

— Fuck yeah. That's a great song. I'll play it.

— That'd be great.

He played the song. I lay down on his bed and cuddled with Kurt and swayed my bent legs left and right to the music. The dog was a very good dog. He liked to lie against a warm human body but he wasn't needy. He didn't smell or shed. He was smart and loyal. He never left River's side, even when they were mountain running. I'd never known a dog that good. I thought how lucky Alice was to have a kind and good-looking boyfriend with a perfect dog. The fact she was able to have that was because of the particular love she'd been given by her single mother. I believed that with my whole heart.

By the end of the song River was lying beside me and our legs were interwoven. We kissed like high schoolers for nearly half an hour before I leaned in to his ear and told him to please put it everywhere.

28

— I feel sick, Eleanor said the next day when finally she woke from her drugged slumber. What time is it?

— It's noon. Maybe you have the flu. It's going around.

— I missed work.

— I called in for you. Steve opened. You can go in now. Or I can if you don't feel well.

— I wish you could just stay home.

— One of us has to work.

She nodded and got up. She pulled her hair back and walked groggily to the door.

— You're not going to shower?

— I'll shower later.

She walked out of the door in a way that recalled all the times I'd walked out of Big Sky's door when his wife was at their country house in the Hudson Valley or at the cabin in Montana. I walked out with the fear that he was glad I was leaving. The fear

385

that I might never see him again.

Big Sky and his wife lived at the Montana house most of the time now, and when I found out the location of Alice's retreat, I began to pick at the skin on my deformed thumb. My father had deformed me. I'd had a wart on the finger and my father had picked up my thumb and turned it. He said that warts did not go away with the creams I was using, and he brought out a little laser, like a crème brûlée flare, and burned half of my thumb off. But the wart was also gone.

I went to rip off little pieces of skin that grew over the deformity. I looked at a map of Montana. The retreat was less than a half hour from Bigfork, from their six-bedroom lodge on Flathead Lake, with the kayaks and the water skis tied to a giant oak that grew out of the water. There was a grand main residence with all local woodwork, with stone showers, and with a kitchen that made my chest hurt. And then there was a small but gorgeously appointed cabin on stilts over the water where he sometimes slept alone to hear the lapping of the lake against the pebbles he'd had specially imported from a place in Sandpoint, Idaho. In the beginning he told me he slept in the lake house to think unmolested of me. And I would picture him staring up at the log ceiling, stroking himself and wishing I were there.

I had told Alice where the house was. I'd pulled it up on my phone, the old listing with the photos I'd studied as though there would be a test about my former lover's real life. I'd told her about the grocery store where he bought his big cuts of beef. It's no organic market, he'd said, but they know their ribs. Johnny, the meat guy, he knows his ribs.

It was the next day when River knocked on my door. I'd never seen him look sad.

— What's wrong?

— I told her. I told Alice.

— You told her what?

— About what we did.

— Oh.

— Yeah. It's terrible.

— Why did you tell her?

— Because I couldn't live like that. I pretty much love her.

— Why are you telling me?

— Because you're friends.

— Not really anymore, I said. I felt faint and I didn't think it was from the pregnancy. I heard my burden come to the door.

— May I have a moment? I hissed at Eleanor. It was the first time I'd snapped at

387

her. I went outside and closed the door behind me.

— She's really upset. I think she hates me.

— Well, you cheated on her.

He looked like he was about to cry.

— She's leaving for her retreat in a few
days. She said she'd think about whether
she could forgive me. But either way she
wasn't going to be exclusive with me for a
while.

— Why are you telling me this?

— I don't know, he said. I have no one
else to tell.

— So go tell your dog, I said. I walked
back inside my house and slammed the
door.

I wrote her that day.

I didn't know about the two of you.

Predictably, there was no reply. I felt re-
morse but not really. Mostly I felt fear. I
closed my eyes and saw her at the Whitefish
Farmers' Market, carrying a baguette and a
bouquet of poppies. Big Sky would be coming from the opposite direction with a
brown bag of tomatoes and basil. Then the
pink fucking.

And all I had was this lump of a child on
my couch. I kept checking my phone for a
reply. Alice would know I'd be doing that.

I'd told her all the sad things I did.

I took Eleanor to the place that Alice was supposed to take me — Cold Spring Tavern, a former stagecoach stop, up in San Marcos Pass.

We drove until we found an ivy-covered wooden house on a main road set in the woods. Dark smoke rose from the chimney through the tall trees. You couldn't see the sky. There were old wooden picnic tables and a bearded man flipping big red steaks on a charcoal grill. Motorcycles were parked in diagonal formation as far as the eye could see.

It was so romantic inside the place that I wanted to kill myself. Red-checked tablecloths, oppressive candles, dusty Tiffany lamps, mounted deer busts. The first thought I had was how I wished to be there with Big Sky, how I wished to dance with him in the middle of the afternoon, to fuck in the woods behind the bar or in the charming, slightly scummy inn down the street.

I felt crazy, I have to tell you, the craziest I have ever felt. I had to stifle my laughter. Eleanor would say something serious and I'd laugh and laugh. The kind of laugh where the whole body moves like a rung bell. She looked at me oddly but then she would smile, too. Everybody just wants to be happy.

We sat inside and ordered a couple of lagers and the tri-tip steak sandwiches. When the bartender dropped off the beer, I smelled expensive marijuana on his breath. Eleanor was wearing a t-shirt with a palm tree on it and a pair of khaki shorts that fit too tight around her thighs.

— This is the coolest place I've been, she said. She was given to saying things like that without the corresponding expression of happiness on her face.

I agreed that it was.

— Thank you for bringing me here.

— Well, I think we both were having some cabin fever.

— Do you like that guy who lives in the yurt?

— We had sex a couple of times. He's good in bed.

Those words looked like they'd hurt her.

— Can you do that? she asked.

— What do you mean? I asked, laughing but annoyed.

— Like, when you're pregnant.

Sometimes I would forget I was pregnant, and anyhow I couldn't believe a child would linger in there. I was sure that at any moment my body would dispel it.

I told her of course you can.

— The penis doesn't, like, poke the baby?

— No, Eleanor. Anyway, he didn't put it in that hole.

Predictably, this shocked her. She tried not to show it. She tried to pretend she was mature.

— So you like him?

— Do you like being a virgin?

She shrugged, taking a sip of her beer. The sandwiches arrived, sloppy and beautiful, with apple horseradish on the side. We ate them without speaking. She wiped up steak blood with the crust of the bread. I never finished all my food. My mother told me to always leave a little bit on the plate.

Once we were done, we walked outside with fresh beers and sat on the logs and the motorcycle men stared at me. The kind of staring that never stopped. I had the deplorable thought that I wanted one of them, the largest one, to fuck the baby out of me.

— I'm worried about sex, Eleanor said.

— Honestly it's nothing.

— I mean that I don't know who I am.

— In what way?

Very quietly she told me that sometimes she felt like a girl who liked women and other times she felt like a boy who liked women and still other times she felt like something in between who just wanted to be loved. That it was a painful feeling. That she walked around with it all the time, hanging from her neck.

I asked her if her mother knew and she laughed and I asked her if her father had suspected it; he had mentioned to me once or twice that he was safe for the time being since Eleanor did not seem interested in boys, so he did not need a shotgun for date nights. He was always acting the part of the insanely protective father. Because that was what I missed about mine. I had to confront what protective meant — whether I had, in fact, been protected. Physically protective was one thing. Any father could own a shotgun.

Before she could answer, one of the motorcycle men came over and leaned down between us, his hands on the log table, his arms too close to us both.

— What's cookin, ladies?

I saw the rape in his eyes. I was wearing my white dress and laughed to myself, thinking how anyone would say I kept asking for it. I'd opined often with other women and with men that every man has a degree of rape in him. Women didn't understand what I meant. They were alternately disgusted and confused. They thought I was stupid. But the men didn't. I think they were impressed that I understood.

— Nothing cooking, I said, remembering the impeccable way in which Alice had turned away those Ray-Bans at the farmers' market.

He moved his face frighteningly close to mine. His beard had the stink of meat.

—Yeah? he said.

— We're having a conversation.

He bit his lower lip.

— You want me to get you some more beers so you can continue your conversation?

— No, thank you. We're leaving soon.

He rested his hand on Eleanor's thigh to better balance himself as he squared his leather chest to me.

I used the side of my palm to karate-chop his arm off her leg, and even though he was big, he toppled.

— What the fuck!

He rose quickly, embarrassedly, ragefully.

— Fuckin bitch, he said.

I felt protective of Eleanor, of the secret she'd been telling me, and of the baby inside of me. I grabbed her hand and we began to walk away. He was about to follow, but there were so many men out there, some with their burly women, mullets and studs and dust. Half of them were witnesses. The other half would have egged him on if he'd bent me over and tried to fuck me.

We drove off through the mountains, under the trees that cast a feathered shade on the road.

— That was really . . . You're really strong, Eleanor said.

I said nothing. I could feel her eyes on me as I stared at the road. Big Sky once told me I was the best female driver he'd ever known. I'd taken a dumb pride in that.

— I want to tell you something, I wanted to tell you from the beginning. I wanted to tell you that you shouldn't feel that bad. About all that happened.

— What do you mean?

— You weren't the first person my dad cheated with.

— What?

— I mean, you were the last. And I guess he liked you the most. But there was also another girl. From his last job. She was, like, twenty. I caught them in the house. They were fucking in my parents' bed and Robbie was in the crib. He was, like, two months old. And I was fifteen. And. My dad asked me not to tell my mom. He cried and begged me not to tell my mom. And the

394

fucking worst part of it was that I was attracted to the girl. It was the first time I was attracted to anyone ever. I found them when she was on her back and my dad was, you know, eating her out. And I was attracted to her. Her body was perfect. I guess that's not the worst part. I guess the worst part is that I didn't tell my mom.

Back at my house we drank a bottle and a half of the good wine on which I'd spent an entire day's paycheck. I couldn't get out of my mind the image of Vic's head between a young girl's legs. A twenty-year-old girl with a perfect body. I had never been in his house. No matter how many men I fucked in the time I knew him, and no matter how little I wanted to fuck him and how I stopped fucking him very early into knowing him, I could not believe he'd lied to me. That he'd told me I was the first and the only. That I'd believed him.

But there was Eleanor on my couch, a girl who had lived through a scourge brought upon her by her parents, just as I had. Like the mother I would become, I stopped thinking of myself. I looked at her on the couch. Her bare feet pulled up beneath her legs, the little feet I imagined in her mother's mouth when she was an infant. My mother told me once that she'd put my feet in her mouth when they first passed me to her. Part of her wanted to eat me, she said, and put me back in her tummy.

After the wine hit, Eleanor began to cry. I'd never cried from wine. I didn't understand why people did. She cried about Robbie, about how much she missed him. I took her in my arms. It was the first time we'd touched that way. Heaving, she moved in to my chest. She placed one hand across my belly. I held her tightly and rocked her like a child. She placed her cheek against my breasts, which were fuller with pregnancy. They were so plump and risen that I hadn't worn a bra in weeks.

I let her cheek stay there. I let her brush her lips against my nipple, the most imperceptible of touches, but clear all the same. I knew what it was to miss the breast of a mother.

29

When I was five and misbehaving, my mother would threaten me. I had this toy stroller for a baby doll and it didn't matter to me if there was a doll in there or not, I only needed the stroller and I loved to wheel it around and I wanted to go everywhere with it. The seat was soft nylon with little bunnies holding balloons, plus blocks and bows and baby rattles and pacifiers, all the sweet gumdrop stuff of babyhood. And when I was being bad, when I was refusing to put on the correct shoes or refusing to brush my hair or refusing to eat my Swiss chard, my mother would brandish the stroller, she would raise it high up above her head like she was going to bring it crashing down on my crown, and she would thunder, I'm going to give this thing away! I'm going to give it to Rosanna's daughter! Or she would say she was going to leave it outside on the street for one of the kids who walked down our block with their pit bull to take. The idea was that the baby stroller would go to someone less fortunate, some little girl, unlike me, who was not so lucky to have such a vaunted piece of plastic.

I tried to see the evening that followed my day at the Top of the World without hindsight. I tried for much of my life to isolate it as its own memory, just one night in time, another dinner. But that's proved impossible. It was the last night of my life. Just as breakfast that morning was my last cereal in milk. Just as the trip to Italy the year before was the last good summer I would ever know.

My mother made pastina. Something we had when there was not enough time for a real dinner. But also the thing that was made when I was sick or when I needed something soothing, like a pacifier.

It was evident that their talk had not gone well. The quiet was colossal. Outside the sun beat down on the sticks and the trampled grass. I could see the rock that I liked to sit on at the end of the gravel drive, gleaming with heat. I wanted the sun to go down. I wanted that day to be over and to fall asleep so I could wake up from the events that had transpired. But the truth is I was so connected to my parents that what was severed between them was a larger weight on my mind than what had happened to me in the tall man's cold house. I'd been abused, of course. But you couldn't call it violent. At no point had I been grabbed against my will or shoved into a car. I bore no marks, not even the red marks on a wrist that often showed up when I was younger and my mother yanked me off the floor of a supermarket.

While my mother cooked and washed up, my father sat on a butterfly chair on the patio. He smoked a cigarette with his legs crossed languidly. When my father was on his feet he was always moving, his hands working screwdrivers, doorknobs, polishing the grilles of cars. But when he sat down, he fully sat, his flesh softening into all the ovals of his bones. My mother, on the other hand, barely sat. My memories of dinnertime are of my father and me at the table and my mother rinsing plates before we were even halfway through. I suppose she did sit in restaurants.

That night it was no different. When the pastina was ready, my father and I sat down at the pine dining table. There was a side of chopped spinach with butter. My mother was not good with vegetables. They were always dark and limp. As we ate, she Windexed the shelves of the refrigerator. My father looked at me with a pasted-on smile. He was always smiling at me, even in the wake of misery. Tenderly, he moved some hair off my face. I winced a little, the touch of a man suddenly meaning something other than what it always had. Beyond the screen door the summer evening vibrated with bugs.

We didn't talk at all that night, my father and I. Talking was something I did with my mother. My father listened to me and smiled and ruffled my hair. He was still and resolute in all ways. A steadfast man. Even his veins were powerful.

— My little princess, he said, went to the pool all by herself today. Did she swim or read?

Flashes of hands and the feeling of a tongue went through my mind. It made sense that my father would have no idea what had happened to me that day, but it was unimaginable to me that my mother wouldn't. She'd often told me she was omniscient, a witch, and I believed her. As she bent forward into the mustard-yellow refrigerator, I felt she was trying to trap me with her silence.

— Both, I replied, watching my mother's body for a clue.

— Why don't you bring the dishes to the sink, help your mother clean up.

— I don't need any help, my mother said sharply. Her voice stopped our movements, even our breath. How can I explain her power? It was a magical thing. She was cold but her body was warm; even today, even after everything, I would give both my arms to be held in hers.

After a while my father turned on the television. *The Sound of Music* was playing. To this day I can't watch it. I can't hear the notes of any of the songs without shaking all over. That night we saw the last hour. My father had his arm around my shoulders. Just the day before, his mother had been violently raped, and only a few hours earlier, his daughter had been sexually assaulted. I didn't know what he would do if he learned of the latter, but I knew he'd gone looking for the man who'd raped his mother. I felt it was possible he'd killed him. My father was one of those men with secrets. I thought that all of his secrets were the honorable kind. Revenge killing. Acts of mercy for maimed animals dying by the side of the road.

I didn't understand why my mother was being so cold. I figured it was a combination of horror that my father might have killed someone and disgust over what I had done. I was terrified she would stop loving me and terrified my father might go to jail. Up until the following day I wouldn't have had any of the long conversations with Gosia that would mark the rest of my formative years, but once she had told me that simply going to sleep and seeing the next sun could fix you up. That the new day would be infinitely more survivable. Or at least it would seem to be. So that was what I longed for. I longed for the night to be over. For the new day to dawn. I swore I would never go back to the Top of the World Pool. I would swim exclusively in the pool with the logroll and the tired ducks and the green paddleboats and the mosquitoes. I would be a perfect child.

30

Vic once said to me, What do you have to fear, kid? You've lost so much. What is there left to fear? That was one of his cruelest moments. I'd been with the young boy, Jack, all afternoon. I'd blown off work to go to a Mets game with him. We drank piss-colored beers and cheered and shared a hot dog from opposite ends until our mouths met in the middle. After the game Jack left me to go to Fire Island with his friends; they were off to the gay part of the island, Cherry Grove, where they liked to get drunk as older, mustachioed men hit on them. I called Vic and he came. Out to Queens he came and we ate at a wonderful Thai restaurant with uneven tables and a drop-tile ceiling with water stains.

That night I cried over a bowl of papaya salad and crispy ground catfish. I was crying because of Jack, because I felt stupid. I told Vic it was only fear. The nameless fear that followed me everywhere. But Vic was stung. He had to accept Jack and accept the lie that I was trying to date people my own age or far younger because I needed to feel normal. He brought me into his chest. I was disgusted by the expensive piqué shirt that he doubtless had bought to impress me. He held me but hated me. I could feel it. Pressing my cheek to his chest like he wanted to absorb me. What do you have to fear, kid? he asked as I sobbed. The place was BYOB and he'd gone to the liquor store next door and bought their most expensive bottle of wine, $129.99. He'd left the price on. He laughed, saying, Can you believe that was the most expensive bottle? The wine was spicy and not good; it barely tasted like a twenty-dollar bottle. I hated him for how little he knew about fine things. I hated him for coming all the way to Queens in a black car. For being cruel to me even though I deserved so much worse. What do you have to fear? he said. And I said, You're right, we both have nothing to fear. Nothing to lose. But I have my daughter, he said. I have my daughter to lose. And I wanted to kill him because he was taunting me with fatherhood, with all that it meant. So I pushed away from his chest and said, You have to go get cash. This place is cash only. And I want to leave.

Vic had been right. I'd had nothing to fear. Now that I had a child inside of me, I finally understood what he meant.

On a Sunday the blood came so rapidly and thickly that I felt like I might pass out. And then I did. My sleep was dreamless only when I took pills. There were few times I slept without them, but this was one occasion. And all of my dreams were nightmares about my parents. Even my good dreams were nightmares, as anyone who has lost someone important knows.

After passing out I dreamed of the Atlantic City boardwalk of my youth where my mother liked to play the slot machines and my father and I would pass the time walking the beach, picking shells, digging for sand crabs. On rainy days we would go to the Ocean One Mall, which was shaped like a cruise liner and full of pastel taffy and mosquito-specked skylights. But my favorite place, probably the most magical of my childhood memory, was an indoor midway at one of the casino hotels. I tried many times to remember the name and never could; it lasted only a year or two, shutting its doors around the time I was eight or nine. It was razed to make room for something less gaudy. But right then, like Lenny, I experienced a sudden clarity and remembered the name: Tivoli Pier, in the Tropicana. The name itself was garish, like everything in Atlantic City. There was a Ferris wheel, though I don't think we ever rode it, and bumper cars, pinball machines, and a theater starring animated characters who looked like big-name entertainers, Dolly Parton and Wayne Newton, droopy faces that kids wouldn't know. There was a saloon and a simulated space shuttle ride that was always out of order. There were boardwalk-style rolling chairs that slid you through dark tunnels illuminated with fiber-optic lighting. Along the walls were wax reproductions of Atlantic City's heyday. Women in high-waisted polka-dot bikinis posing on ginger sand, high dives. The part I loved most was a flying-carpet ride. It was a raised dais covered with a Persian rug, and you would sit on the rug and watch a screen in front of you that showed you flying through the night sky. You could choose from a selection of backgrounds. I'd run through them all and my father would watch me and smile.

After several hours and hundreds of tokens we'd meet my mother and go out for a seafood buffet. All-you-could-eat crab legs for $29.99. Coca-Cola with a glistening cherry on top. It was heaven for me. Why, I wondered, wasn't it enough for him?

The rest of the night in the Poconos, the last night of my life, my mother ran a bath. None of her products were expensive. In the years to come I would go to the houses of friends and shower in their parents' master baths and I'd be impressed by the expense or the idiosyncrasy of a particular shampoo. A lotion made of white mallow. A massage oil, the color of gasoline, from the woods of Wisconsin. You can tell a lot about a woman by her bath products, by the range or the minimalism. Sometimes the stingiest lady, seemingly unconcerned about her looks, will own a ferny conditioner from Paris and you will question everything you assumed about her.

My mother's products were mostly mementos from hotels. From our trips to Italy, all of them, from her honeymoon with my father, which was the first time she saw Rome and Venice and even Florence, though she grew up in a town less than a hundred miles away.

She had multiple shower caps, from La Lumiere in Rome and a beach hotel in San Benedetto. She had old yellow lotions from a hot-springs hotel in Castrocaro Terme and conditioner from a little albergo in Como. There was a room fragrance from a cliffside inn in Sorrento, probably the poshest of the hotels she'd ever been to, and from that same place, a satchel of lavender bath salts contained in a small terry pillow. It was this satchel that she dropped into the ugly tub of our Poconos bathroom, and it was the high, bright smell of lavender that brought me away from the She-Ra cartoon I'd been watching and up that carpeted, narrow stairwell to find my mother naked and vacant in the steamy room.

Her breasts were above the water, huge and white, and the rest of her — slim, tan, European — was below.

Many of my boxes now, the ones I have moved around and never opened, the ones that were piled on the ground floor of my Topanga home, are filled with her shower caps, with her lotions and sample sizes of perfumes. They have all gone bad, but I have still saved every single one. None of them, however, contain that bath salt satchel from Sorrento. There was only one of those, and she used it on that last night.

— Mommy, I said. I was wearing my Rainbow Brite pajamas. I don't think my mother ever saw me as a child.

— Please, she said. I knew what she

meant: *Go away, leave me be.*

I began to cry. It was my only recourse. The steam rose around me. How I wanted to be inside that smell, inside her arms in the water, inside her stomach again, where she couldn't push me from her.

On the Formica sides of the sink, which were so small that things were always slipping off, were the two Q-tips I'd used that morning. My father had taken them out of the trash. He was a doctor and he thought nothing of spending money on lobster dinners and trips to the Amalfi coast, but he recycled my Q-tips. He thought I used them too indulgently. My mother didn't care; I don't think she used Q-tips or, for that matter, ever had ear wax or mucus in her nose. I don't remember her having a cold in all of the ten years I knew her.

I heard my father light a cigarette downstairs. I heard the screen door open and then I heard it close.

— Mommy, please, I cried, tell me what's wrong.

She shook her head and looked past me. I knelt down on the humid tiles. The shower curtain was the color of processed cheese.

I fished into the hot water, found her hands, and took them in mine. I brought them to my face. Even after soaking in lav-

409

ender, they still smelled cooked by cigarettes. My whole childhood is contained in
that scent. The mothballs, too. I wanted to
take care of her and I wanted her to take
care of me. She was the only thing in the
world I wanted.

— Mommy! I shrieked, but my voice
didn't seem to reach her. My need was so
primal, so simple, and her interior was so
complex. Like the mantle of the earth, with
layers upon layers of nicotine staining the
cracks.

31

When I woke, I was still bleeding and there was also a remarkable pain. Eleanor was home and she came into my bedroom and asked me if I was okay. I ignored her and walked into the bathroom. I locked the door and stayed inside for a long time. Eventually I told Eleanor to please go out, to take my car and get as many rags as she could.

— Rags? she said. Why?

— Because I'm losing the baby.

I heard her gasp.

— Just go.

Because it had been vital for me to be practical, I decided it was all for the best. I reminded myself of the time I'd seen a picture on Big Sky's wife's Instagram, during one of my morbid nights. I was doing cocaine in my apartment off of a Jimmy Buffett CD. I was scrolling through her feed, which was rarely updated and sparsely populated, but this night there was a new image. It was of a bathroom in what was surely the Montana lake house. Their youngest son, just about a year old at the time, in a Japanese soaking tub. The walls surrounding him were made of smooth knobby stones. It was early evening and there was a fantastic light coming in and you could see the sun out the window firing up the trees, those sensational Ponderosa pines that Big Sky was always saying he hated chopping down. It made him feel like a murderer. So why do you do it? I asked. Because, he said, a family needs a fire.

This child in the bath had no idea how lucky he was. The wife taking the picture had no idea who I was. What child could *I* bring into the world? You would only have had shower curtains with mold on the hems. We could only have stayed in damp motels, eating heather-colored burgers and greasy potato chips as we counted our last dollars on the filthy carpet. I'd eaten too much caviar and I hadn't saved for your future. I'd eaten too much caviar with men who didn't marry me. It was better like this, I thought as the blood rained out. Then a new contraction came, the worst one yet. I screamed so loud the sound might have colored the air, and then this thing, this palpable *thing,* released itself from under me. I caught it in my hand.

It didn't look like an alien but very definitively like a human child. The shape of it and the feeling of it. The eyes nearly sewn shut; I could see the dark balls beneath beautiful, tight lids. It was blue and red with organs and its own pumping blood, close to the surface of its glossy flesh. The nose was the most exquisite I had ever seen.

It fit in my palm and yet it was larger than the length of it; I don't remember, I only kept thinking it was large enough to live, I believed this with my whole being. You will have days when you think God is cruel, or what God is there at all? You may believe there is nothing. I believed and then I did not. Whichever I felt on a given day, the only thing I was certain of was that I must have been wrong. That day I figured it must be a female God to give you gifts like these that cannot or should not be kept. A female God would know who could be trusted with a child. And she would also know who might need a moment's reprieve from the darkness. And then she would take the child back and place it into a real mother's womb and let it grow there.

It had perfect hands and I tell you this not to be sensational but because it was perhaps the only pure feeling my heart had felt in nearly thirty years. One of its hands curled itself around my index finger, wrapped itself nearly all the way around it. My finger was so concretely, so shockingly, held. I'd been held enough by my father in the short time I had him, but I had always pined after my mother's arms, her hands. I always wanted them to make a cap over my skull, to grasp me and suck me into her. But now to have my child, its little fingers, webbed still and yet delicately discrete, to have them press into me, to *hold* me, it was enough love to keep me for another thirty years. It recognized I was meant to care for it as long as it lived. I don't know why I keep saying *it*. Because I knew very well, it was obvious, the child was a boy.

I don't know how long he kept breathing in my hand like that. His ribs, ivory etchings beneath the gel of his skin, moved up and down in elegant puffs. With a finger from my other hand I stroked his forehead. My baby, I said quietly. I felt peace and happiness. I knew it wouldn't last but I allowed myself to feel it for as long as it did.

When it was over, it wasn't sudden or dramatic. The breaths simply stopped. A small chill came over his body. My next emotion was rage. It was more well defined than the happiness because I was better acquainted with rage. At what? Everything. Everyone. I wanted to kill the world. I knew that at the very least I would kill someone. It was more than a premonition. It was a promise I could control. The rage was so great it needed to go somewhere. But for once I did not have rage at myself. For once I didn't hate myself. I loved myself as my child had. I saw myself as something greater than I thought I could be, and though certainly the feeling would fade, it still shone radiantly in that moment.

Then suddenly from outside I heard the familiar screeches. If all the misfortunes of the world could be contained in one sound, it might be the bright hell of the coyote. Then I heard them make a new sound. An angry growl that sounded more like a human imitating an animal than an animal itself. I ran, with my cooling child in hand, to the door. Kurt the dog was being attacked by three slavering gray beasts.

That dog had nothing to prepare him for his horror, staring down the imminence of his own death. He'd been mistreated for the first year of his life and then sent to a kill shelter and had no idea he was set to die until he was saved by a young man with a love of the great outdoors. He'd gone from vicious kicks to steel cages to pure love and heaping bowls of food and scaling mountains and sleeping in a bed with a warm body.

I saw River come running from his yurt. Then I looked down and watched as one of the coyotes' teeth, glistening and white, caught on Kurt's fur. I saw the dog pull back and a strip of his furred skin come away from him. I screamed and one of them came toward me. Everything was going so fast. I didn't think with my human brain and so I suppose that's why I did the only thing that made sense. My hands released my glowing fetus. Everything stopped. The night went clear, a wash of starlight. I felt my knees buckle and the dog ran into my house.

—Where's Kurt! River screamed.

I pointed inside. River, ignorant to what had happened, ran in and came out holding the enormous bloodied dog in his arms.

—Thank you, he said to me, weeping.

— I didn't do anything, I said. Then I went inside and collapsed on the disgusting couch.

When I woke, Lenny was stroking my hand. I noticed he'd somehow turned the air conditioner off. Perhaps with his cane, like a geriatric crusader, hitting the switch on his first jab.

— Joan, he said, thank goodness. I wasn't sure if you fainted or what. My God, those vicious creatures! You're bloodied, dear, did they get you? Did they nip you somewhere? They don't generally go after humans.

I didn't say anything. I was very still. I thought about what those people with their normal lives would think about me now. I knew I would never be able to tell anyone, not even Alice. Nobody wants to hear about great suffering or anarchic decisions. They think it's an offense against their ears, their lives.

— I cleaned up your vomit from earlier. I understand you were embarrassed. Of course, I was, too. I told you a great deal of things about my life that — I won't say I regret it, but I don't feel like you understood. I don't think you understand men on the one hand and love on the other.

I nodded, feeling my hands lit with blood.

— Proust said that hell was the suffering that comes from the inability to love. I weep for your suffering, Joan. I know you have your reasons. I hoped you would tell them to me, as I told you mine, but perhaps your condition is worse, even, than I suspected.

I looked at him, pressed my palm to my empty belly, and cackled like a witch.

He was wearing the watch. He was sure of his mental state in that moment, and that was why he was wearing it. He believed that the drugs were going to save him.

— Joan, are you all right?

— Leonard! I am more than all right! I am absolutely wonderful! Where is my red dress? *Where* is my red dress?

I looked around crazily.

— Joan, please. You're —

— I'm depraved, I said. Isn't it *fun*?

Outside, it was quiet. The coyotes had gone about their evening. Soon Eleanor would be back with the rags and I would use them for the blood. I didn't have a washing machine so I would have to bag them and drive them to the dump. I didn't remember a washing machine in the Poconos. It was possible we didn't have one in that crappy mountain home.

— I've just never seen you like this, Leonard said.

I turned away and walked toward the window. I could see very clearly where the child had fallen. I would have to move out of this horrible house immediately. I could never comprehend how someone could continue to live in a place where a loved one had died.

— Joan!

— Shh, darling. I have a craving for a

chopped egg sandwich. With mayonnaise and some nice cracked pepper. Let me make us a platter. You can't take the pill on an empty stomach.

He nodded agreeably and I moved to the kitchen. My voice just then had come from deep in my lungs, not from the back of my mouth, as a different older man once remarked of me. Speak from here, he told me, jabbing me just below my breasts. You sound unattractive when you speak from the back of your mouth. It's low-class.

It was strange to no longer be in pain after all those hours of it. I boiled the water for the eggs with a drop of vinegar, as my mother had done. Not as she'd taught me but as I'd watched her do. I boiled the water and felt the blood drying in my underwear.

Lenny once said he could understand how a woman like me could turn a man crazy. Not even my looks, he said, which were formidable (*formidable!*) but my presence. I was very *real,* he said.

It didn't take me long to drop Lenny down the rabbit hole. By that point I knew a good amount about Lenore. I knew her favorite colors and music and foods and precisely the shitty way she prepared an egg. Absently I drew my hair into a sloppy chi-

gnon. I'd seen several pictures of Lenore —
in the ocean and in the pool and at formal
events — and I'd noted the way she crossed
her arms and smiled when she was shy. I
imbued my knowledge of her and his love
for her and his betrayal of her into my role.
Had I been going after a part, had playing
Lenore been an audition, I'd have nailed it.

I'd learned that I could keep him in the
hole the longest when I never let the Lenore spell be broken. Mostly that meant being fawning, treating him like he was the
most learned man in the world, the most
gallant and benevolent and brilliant. It was
exhausting.

The eggs were just barely cooked when he
called out to me.

— Lenore, he said.

— Just a moment, darling. I have to get
these eggs off the heat so the yolks don't
overcook. I know how you hate a powdery
yolk.

— Yes, but I also don't like it too wet.

— Of course.

I ran the eggs under cool water and began
to peel them while they were still hot. My
mother could touch the bottom of a boiling
pan. She could hold anything without mitts.
Indeed, her hands were callused, but I always suspected there was something else at

420

work. Witchery.

I mashed the eggs between the tines of a fork. I added a tablespoon of mayonnaise and a teaspoon of horseradish sauce. I added smoked sea salt and freshly cracked black peppercorns.

As I approached Lenny, he finally looked below my waist.

— Lenore, my dear, did you spill something on yourself?

— Not exactly.

— What is that? he asked, pointing to my thighs. Lenore, is that *blood*?

— I lost our baby.

— Oh, dear.

— But it's all right, I said, sitting beside him and taking his hand in mine. We'll try again.

He nodded and looked all around the room. He wrung his hands as old men do.

— Was it painful, my love?

— Not too bad, I said.

— Sometimes it's for the best, you know.

— You're right, darling. You're right about everything.

— Oh, Lenore. That's kind of you. I've studied and read my whole life, my love. I come from a long line of wise men.

— Please, dear, try some of this egg salad.

— My Lenore, he said, not a woman of

421

the kitchen.

— Well, you didn't marry me for my cooking.

He nodded. He licked his lips. He brought his wrinkled hand around to rest on my rear, cool and wet with blood.

— Darling, you're aroused, he said.

— Oh, always when you touch me. You know that. But now is not the time. We wouldn't want to make a mess.

— Wouldn't we, he said, smiling impishly.

— I suppose I could lay down some sheets.

— Go lay down some sheets. I'll eat my lunch and be right behind you.

My legs felt rubbery as I walked up the spiral staircase to the hottest bedroom in the world. I'd taken two Klonopin right before my child was born and the effect was finally at work.

I heard the wretched sounds of him eating, the dentures clacking, the whole mouth working to move the soft food down the throat. That noise was enough of a reason to kill him. My white dress was bright red from the waist down. It was rather lovely. I figured I could dye the whole thing red. I took it off and used it to wipe between my legs. I put on a clean pair of underwear and a green t-shirt that said MONTANA on it. I would love to tell you it belonged to Big

Sky, but it didn't. There was a night he came to my apartment wearing the same t-shirt. After we fucked, as he was putting the t-shirt back on, I was struck with the usual fear. He was about to leave. I never knew when I'd see him again. Every time could be the last time. He was going home to her. She got to have this man in this t-shirt.

I was naked in the bed. Listen, you must always be the first one to dress. This is obligatory. I didn't know to do that. Gosia hadn't lived long enough to impart that wisdom. We lie there naked after the other person rises because we can't bear to leave the space. We can't leave the sweat and the warmth because we love it too much. We love it more, nearly, than we love the asshole rising to put on his t-shirt. Don't be the fucked one. Be the first to rise.

Meekly I asked, Can I hold on to that shirt?

He laughed.

— I mean it. Can I have it?

He continued to laugh and shake his head.

— Please, I said, hating myself.

He left quicker than usual. He usually stayed long enough to come twice. The moment he was out the door, I opened my computer and bought the same shirt off the

423

Internet. Ponderosa pines on a green background.

— Lenore, are you ready? Lenny called from the bottom of the stairs. I looked down and saw the dirty plate on the table. The fork beside it. There were little mounds of egg salad on the table that he must have dropped as he spooned a second serving onto his plate.

My father used to bring all the dishes to the sink. He even asked me to place my dirty clothes neatly in the laundry. If I left something inside out, he considered it disrespectful to my mother. Leonard wasn't the type to pick up his plates. He'd grown up with a live-in housekeeper in some colonial house with a foyer table and fresh flowers every three days.

— Put that fucking dish in the sink, my love.

I could have said anything to him as long as I did it in his sweet Lenore's voice. He stuttered something and dutifully bussed his dishes. Then I heard him make his way up the stairs.

— Remember when we met?

— Of course, I said. You were my boss. I didn't like you at first. You were married and ugly.

— Excuse me?

— You were ugly, Leonard. You *are* ugly. But it's okay.

— I was never ugly.

— That's true. You were never ugly.

He approached the bed and unbuttoned his fine linen shirt. His hands were shaking with his disease. The full extent of his disability was revealing itself to me. The heat was too much for me to bear and I couldn't imagine how he was handling it.

He lay down beside me, shirtless. He wore nice khaki pants and simple black socks. Klonopin is a wonderful thing. Xanax, Ambien. They melt you down to your wolf tone.

— I remember the first night, I read to you from Muldoon. "Incantata." Do you remember? Every stanza is a sentence, I told you, and you, silly thing, you hardly knew what a stanza meant. You wore a lime-green dress. It suited you, but of course a paper bag would have suited you.

He scuttled closer. His touch was odious and yet Vic's had been worse. I could count on one hand the number of times we'd fucked traditionally, the number of times I hadn't simply masturbated in front of him. I couldn't for the life of me call up the sound of Vic coming. Honestly I felt like his love for me — what he thought was love — drowned out his lust.

— Len, I said.

He brought his hand to rest over my belly.

—Yes, my life?

— I'm a whore, my love. A filthy used-up whore. So fuck me. You can feel how wet I am. Only whores are wet like this.

He gasped and began to pinch at me with his old fingers. Roughly and cruelly. How I missed my child. In the mere moments he lived, my child showed me how useless men could be. How boring, how selfish. This old man. This old killer.

I groaned against the invasion of his hand on the place where my child had fallen, but he thought it was rapture. My rage was growing by the second. I felt the tendons in my neck straining like a junkyard dog's against a chain. I closed my eyes. I pulsed my pelvis against his bony hand when I heard the music from that night.

32

My mother didn't know how to use the paltry sound system in the Pocono house — she barely knew how to drive — the only thing she understood was the Vanity Fair circus animals record player that belonged to me, with its fat orange needle in its own little suitcase. And that was the sound I woke up to that night — "The Lion Sleeps Tonight" by the Tokens, turned up as loud as the player could go.

I was waking up all the time back then. Usually between three and four in the morning. I'd look at the clock at my bedside and panic, knowing the earliest I could crawl into bed beside my mother was six. I would have two or more hours of waiting, eyes on the ceiling, haunted by shadows against the window.

But this time I heard the player, which was kept in the spare room between my parents' bedroom and mine. I worried it was my mistake somehow, that I'd left it on, and that one or both of them would yell at me for ruining their sleep. My mother, especially, acted like her sleep was something that could be lost, never to be found again.

I rose and walked to the spare bedroom. The door was open and the record was spinning on its axis. Now I felt with a profound and queasy certainty that my mother knew where I'd gone that day, that she'd seen me in my damp bikini in the cold house of the man who licked me all over.

In any case I felt sure that she was playing my music to lure me out, to wrest the truth from me. She was capable of such a ruse. I thought she could do anything. She was a witch. She was the most beautiful woman in the world. Her breasts were the color of milk, and cold. The rest of her was warm, but her breasts felt refrigerated. I used to love to touch her nipples; several years after I'd stopped suckling from them, I used to reach my small hands down her low-cut blouses, under the tight cheap skin of her bra, and try to hold her nipple between my fingers.

I turned the player off. All that remained was the whirring of the fan in my parents' bedroom. The door was closed, which was unusual. I figured they could be having sex.

I wondered if part of sex was licking someone all over, as the man — Wilt — had done
to me. It bothered me to think of what they
might be doing behind the door. I also
thought it was possible they were discussing
where I'd been in the afternoon. I wouldn't
have expected police to be involved, but I
did think they were discussing whether or
not to send me away to a boarding school.
My mother often threatened this when I was
being bad. She told me they would ship me
off with a small suitcase, to a place up in
the mountains, Castelrotto, where you had
to drink goat's milk every morning and suck
down raw egg yolks. Once she went so far
as to drive me to the train station with my
little She-Ra luggage packed haphazardly
with shirts and socks and my favorite doll,
Marco. I was seven or eight then and didn't
know you couldn't get to Italy by train. I
shivered and sobbed and began to hyper-
ventilate as my mother strode up to the
ticket seller. She took out her huge burgundy wallet and I thought I was going to
die. I began to scream. Even though my father was at work and would have had no
idea of this cruelty, I screamed *DADDY!* so
loud that nearly everyone in the vast hall
turned to look. One of my mother's fears —
the disapproval of Americans. She came

away from the counter, brought my chin up close with her sharp nails, and hissed, You ere me, if you ever touch my jewelry again without asking, I vill come straight ere with you. I von't tell your father and he will think you ran away. You ere me!

I don't think I did anything wrong for the next three years. Nothing of note until that day when I got into the man's car. And now I was expecting the biggest punishment of all. I couldn't wait any longer. I rapped the door lightly. Nothing. I knocked again, this time louder. Still nothing. So I turned the knob ever so gently and pushed open the door.

I can't describe what I saw without going through it all over. I don't mind as much now. It used to be that even thinking about opening the door, cheap cedar-stained mahogany, would send me retching into the nearest toilet.

It was him, my beloved father, on the bed. The sheets were a tweedy brown, so the blood was merely a dark stain. My mother's reading light was on and illuminated the room just enough. Later I would learn that there were slashes in other places, but I only saw the knife in his throat. I knew exactly which knife it was. She used it on bread and meat. In wealthy houses in the future, I'd learn there were knives for bread and knives for meat and knives for fruit. All different kinds of knives. My mother would have considered that spoiled. She used one knife for everything, her *good knife.* She had one good knife in each house, one in New Jersey and one in the Poconos. It had a wooden handle and its blade was smooth and thick. My father's beautiful blue eyes were open, staring.

Daddy! Daddy! Daddy! Daddy!

I used to call his name every night. There was a tradition, a routine. I waited near the window in the formal living room we never used, with the antique furniture and the fireplace maned in stucco. I watched through the drapes for his headlights. If they were nine minutes past six, I thought for sure my life would be over. At the same time, I couldn't conceive of the worst thing in the world — to lose my father. I'd make my way to the garage and begin clapping and calling his name, high-pitched, one clap for *Da,* one for *Dee.* Then he would get out of the car with his briefcase and the smell of hospitals and his eyes would flash at me and he would smile the happiest, kindest smile. He would take me into his arms, no matter what he was already carrying.

What I saw then was impossible. But

that's what happened that night. I learned that the impossible was possible. In a way, there can be nothing more liberating.

I ran to the bed and tried to lift his body. Of course he was too heavy. The knife was in very deep. Do you believe that I pulled it out? I would have done anything for him. I'll never forget that feeling. I believe he came alive for a second when the knife came out. His blood was all over my Rainbow Brite pajamas. I thought my mother would be angry about the mess on me, and that was the first time I thought of her. So I screamed for her. *Mommy! Mommy! Mommy!*

The bathroom door was open and I didn't want to leave my father but I did. I ran with the knife in my hand to the bathroom and there was my mother, in the bathtub, with her wrists slit, but she wasn't dead. She was only almost dead. Her eyes blinked, her mouth moved. And I don't know, I think about this every day, never less than once a day, though sometimes up to a hundred times a day, I think, If I had called for help right away, she might have been saved. But I didn't call right away. It wasn't on purpose. I just didn't think of it yet. My mother was still alive and she was my authority, she was my god. Her nipples and her hair floated above the line of the rosy water. She didn't like to get her hair wet. She only washed it every three days or so. She never went into a pool above her shoulders. The ocean, the lake, forget it.

I knelt beside her face, which was blooming with death, barely seeing, but there was something tender in her eyes, holy Jesus, it made me weep in some sort of gratitude. The weeping was coming from so many places that I can't tell how much of it was gratitude, but yes, I think some of it was. I shrank down below the lip of the tub and took one of her soggy, queenly hands and placed it on the top of my head. And then I rose my head up into the basket of her hand so that it felt like she was grasping me, loving me back; in fact, I'm sure that she was. And I wept and said, *Oh, Mommy, oh, Mommy, oh, Mommy, oh, Mommy,* until eventually she was gone.

It wasn't until an hour after I found them that I dialed 911 from the cream phone on my mother's nightstand. I waited so long, I think, because I could still sense their life forces in the air. As long as I could feel them, I didn't want to call up the external world. My parents and I had been a unit, a capsule; inviting the outside in was forbidden. That was for families who didn't know where their children were after ten p.m. It wasn't until after their deaths that I saw how foolish I was. I had thought I was the one most likely to breach the security of our capsule when in fact the walls were permeable; for years my parents had been waltzing in and out recklessly.

The officers who came thought I did it. For a moment, at least. I was carrying the knife when they showed up. It made me feel closer to my father. They asked me who my next of kin was, who they should call. The sun was rising. Daylight made it real. I didn't have Gosia's number memorized. I didn't know any numbers except my house and my father's office. The only number I had written down was Wilt's, inside *Tropic of Cancer,* so I went and got it because I was ashamed not to have anybody else. I read it aloud to the officer who was not dealing with the bodies. It was six a.m. by that time and I could hear a man's sleepy voice on the other end of the line and the officer introduced himself as Bushkill police and the man said they had the wrong number. I told them I thought it was my uncle, but I guessed it was the wrong number.

Eventually they got ahold of Gosia. She arrived, perfumed and puffy, by ten a.m. That was when it hit me, how alone I was.

Gosia, of course, would become my savior, but that morning there was just a black Mercedes, glinting and foreign in our gravel drive. A tall half-stranger emerged, wearing diamonds, face still rouged from the night before. She smelled like sour flowers. My brown wool life was all gone.

She told me everything right away. She took me out of the house and to the Caesars Pocono Resort. Now it's renamed something seamier, Palace Stream or Lovers' Delight, but it was always one of those honeymoon fuck forts with the champagne glass bathtubs and the fruit salad breakfasts. I've always wondered who is turned on by that, who wants to fuck in heart-shaped tubs. Men with blond beards, women who love baby's breath in their bouquets of red roses. Gosia took me there because it was the first place she saw on the road that was open. My lips were blue and she worried I was dying of shock. The frizzy-haired woman at the front desk said, It's couples only. Gosia pulled what I imagined was an impressive credit card from her wallet and slapped it on the counter. We walked into a purple dining room with gold tables and casino carpets. She ordered herself a tea and me a coffee. She didn't try to make me eat.

She began to tell me everything. It seemed she knew more than anyone in the world.

The night before, when my father had left to see his raped mother, there had been someone else to see. The woman he'd been fucking. The woman had called his doctor's answering service all weekend long. She had him paged several times, up in the mountains. He'd been lamentably ignoring her for days and then his mother was raped. He drove to New Jersey, examined his mother, bandaged and consoled her. Gosia was there with my uncle. She saw the whole thing. My father said he'd be back. Everyone thought he was going to go after the rapist. Just be a crazy man in the streets. But he went to his lover's apartment. An Italian woman living above the restaurant for which she cooked. She was more than the woman he'd been fucking. Gosia told me he loved her. I remember she said this and I felt she was saying it to try to hurt me, to put me in my place. As a second wife herself, she wanted the first wives and first daughters to know they were replaceable. It wasn't until much later that I realized she had a more noble motive.

This other woman was a beauty, *even more beautiful than your mother.* Black hair, blue eyes, blood-red lips, metronome breasts. *And much younger.* He drove to her apartment in the middle of the night. This young beauty had something to tell him. She was pregnant. She said her child would not be a bastard, living above an oven. She commanded him to tell my mother, to tell her that he loved her, that this was going to be his child, too.

She had some kind of a hold over him, Gosia said to me in that purple room. I think how it has affected me that the two most important women of my life were heavily accented. Their voices like church bells resounding in my head.

Your father loved women, he loved them too much.

My father came home that next morning, having not slept at all. I wondered, even that day, I wondered if he had sex with his pregnant lover. With her oils on him, he returned to our mountain home and drove me to the Top of the World Pool, where I met Wilt and got assaulted. That this was not the darkest part of my childhood, can you imagine?

While I was at the pool, my father told my mother about the lover, and of course, she'd already suspected he was fucking someone. Now he told her that not only were her worst fears realized but that there was something else she hadn't even thought to fear. His lover was pregnant, and he would not turn his back on this child.

Gosia told me he was penitent, as much as a man who'd made a grievous mistake could be.

But your mother was dragon, Gosia said. *Dragons cannot stand by.*

She told me that when my father went to pick me up from the pool, my mother called her. She told Gosia everything. Gosia advised her to leave. To pack me up and return to Italy.

Every day I thought about that. What if my mother and I had been the ones to go back to Italy? What if my mother had chosen me the way Alice's mother chose her.

I can count on you, she said to Gosia, *if anything happens. She will be yours.*

Gosia said yes. Of course. *Will be my baby.* And here Gosia cried to me. She took my hands across the gold table and crushed them. *I didn't believe she was going to do it. Some part of me, yes. I almost drove to here. And then I did not.*

My father did not become the bad guy for me. Not yet. That day I hated my mother for killing my father, but also for all the reasons you cannot say. Part of my child brain hated her because she wasn't young enough

438

or even beautiful enough. Because she wasn't strong enough. Or because she was too strong. Because she was so complex where my father was not. I hated my mother, in short, for being a woman.

or even beautiful enough. Because she
wasn't strong enough. Or because she was
too strong. Because she was so complicated
where my father was not. I hated my
mother about for being a woman.

33

In the bed beside me Leonard's penis had
grown rigid alongside my thigh. He was
pressing it against me.

— Mmmmm, he said. Over and over.
Mmmmm.

I was still hearing "The Lion Sleeps Tonight" in my ears. I thought of my father
making a child with someone. The selfish-
ness, especially, to come inside another
woman. All my life, all the men taking what
they wanted and leaving when it was over.
Big Sky. The slug in Marfa, my first bad
man from the Top of the World. The man
who raped my grandmother. What my father did to my mother. What Leonard did
to Lenore. What Vic did to his wife and their
son and his daughter. What my father did to
me. All the men from all the clubs and air-
planes and dockside restaurants. All the fingers inside the waistbands of our underwear.

I heard the door open downstairs.

— Go away! I hissed.

— Please, Eleanor called. She sounded like me, trying to get into my mother's bed.

— Please go away. I need to be alone! The door closed.

— Who was that? Leonard whispered, as though we were teenagers covertly fucking.

— A woman, a friend. Nobody.

— You're so wet, Leonard said as he tried to push himself into me. Those words, coming out of an old man's mouth.

Were women blameless? I didn't care in that moment. I thought of my son — his thin wet bones, the incorruptible gift of him. I felt close to my mother then, to feel her rage in me. I turned to face the old man, swinging one of my legs over his to pin him. I wrapped my hands around his chicken-skin throat. I looked at the magnificent watch around his gaunt wrist. I would come to find out it was worth an inconceivable amount of money. More than Lenny had alluded to, perhaps even more than he was aware. I could feel Eleanor's presence outside the door. I would have invited anyone inside to watch. I knew what I was doing was fine and I knew I could legitimize it, even, to God.

As Lenny was dying, he held my face in

his hands. I thought he was attempting to strangle me back. He was about to speak and I spat in his eye to make him stop. I would not let him have any more last words. I would never again be the basin in which a wretched man would bob about.

Smiling, I closed my eyes and transferred the force of my whole body and history into my hands. Killing a man felt more glorious than I could ever have imagined.

34

In the days that followed, I began to pack up what little I'd unpacked. I told Eleanor I was going to move out and that I didn't know where I would go. She was terrified. I knew the feeling. She sat and watched me as I moved around the place, dropping loose eyeliners into big boxes.

I unblocked her mother's phone number and multiple texts came through, just like that. It was plain that the woman had never stopped, not at all.

Sometimes there were two or so an hour. Half of them asked after her daughter.

Please tell me please is she with you

I showed those to Eleanor. I asked her to please let me tell her mother that she was all right.

The other half I would never show her.

How many times did you fuck my husband did he eat your cunt did he give you orgasms I have never had an orgasm in my life thats

why he went to you. men need to know they
please. tell me how he came did he come in-
side u TELL ME

I believe she thought that her daughter killed me. So that her messages were going into the ether. It must have assuaged her pain. That was the least we could do, Eleanor and I. Not responding was the least we could do.

The next day, one came that made me forcibly send Eleanor home in that moment. I was throwing out all my cheap dishware. I passed the full-length mirror and caught sight of myself. I was wearing my mother's slip dress for what would be the last time. I'd dyed it red with Rit liquid dye in the shower. The shower would be stained forever. Now the color was uniform from top to bottom. I looked like a young girl in the mirror. Perhaps it was a trick of the light. My eyes shone with the absurdity of it all. I felt peace, you see, because I'd embraced the madness. And yet I don't believe it was madness. I use the word as shorthand. The world will call it madness. You can't convince normal people otherwise. There's a simple small line at the mouth of hell. It's not a big deal when you get there. It's just another step is all. If you ever cross it, as I did, you will see that black things become the most honest ones of all.

You must remember that most people don't like to hear when bad things happen. They can tolerate only a little here and there. The bad things must be comestible. If there are too many bad things, they plug their ears and vilify the victim. But a hundred very bad things happened to me. Am I supposed to be quiet? Bear my pain like a good girl? Or shall I be very bad and take it out on the world? Either way I won't be loved.

That was when my phone dinged. My heart jumped. I thought it might be Alice. But it was Mary.

because of you i held my dead boy in my hands. he was blue he turned blue in my arms! do you know what its like to hold your dead baby in your arms!!!

Upon reading it, I threw the phone against the wall. It hit the frog vase with my father inside. The vase cracked into several pieces and all of my father's ashes were lost to the floor, to the grains and crevices of the uncleanable wood. At first I tried to scoop them up. But my hand came back with dust and strands of hair and an uncooked lentil. So I vacuumed the whole area. It was less painful than I would have expected. My mother's ashes remained intact on the mantel.

Eleanor walked in from the deck where she'd taken to sunning herself in the early afternoons.

— I heard a noise. Are you okay?

Since the miscarriage, she'd been attending to me so kindly. She never asked me about Lenny, about the way it happened. Just like her father, she was careful not to ire. She was a quiet, wonderful listener. In an eerie way, the girl and I loved each other. But that didn't take away from the prison of it all.

Now that Lenny was gone, she'd floated the notion that she wouldn't have to leave until his cousin up in San Francisco sold the place. I worried about the cousin coming for the watch, but I never heard a thing.

In fact, the only person who said anything, who made me feel culpable, was Kevin. Several days after Lenny's death, Kevin approached me as I was getting out of my car. We said hello. It was the first time we'd seen each other in a while.

— I wanted to offer my condolences, he said.

—What do you mean?

— Lenny, I mean. Death in your house, Miss Joan.

446

He placed one of his elegant hands on my shoulder and looked at me. I willed my body not to tremble. He knew. I knew that he did.

— Don't beat yourself up about it.

— About what?

— You know, he said. You couldn't have saved him.

Later I would sit with that line. I would wonder which man Kevin was talking about. I could swear I'd seen something in his eyes. A flicker of my history.

— Sorry to know you're going. I wish we could have gotten to know each other.

—We kept very different schedules, I said.

He smiled and regarded me. Since coming to California, I'd known two men — River and Kevin — both of whom looked at me in ways that didn't repel me; that did, in fact, the opposite. They made me feel girlish and small and protected.

— You're pretty, Kevin said. He said it very plainly, like it was an obvious thing but something which needed to be recorded in the atmosphere all the same. I struggled to remember if I had ever been called pretty.

I smiled and thanked him as though it were no big deal and yet it broke my heart in the holiest of ways. That man did more for me in one line than any man had ever done. The word *pretty.* That fucking word.

He nodded and backed away from me slowly, his eyes on me in a hallowed way, until he opened his underground door and disappeared. Three months later a private jet would go down over Musha Cay and I didn't have to read the story to know that he had been on the flight. I felt that it was my fault, because he had shone a light on me.

Back in the house, Eleanor was waiting. Likely she'd been looking out the window. I was more frightened of Eleanor than I was of anyone coming after me for murder or, worse, theft. I worried that if I didn't make a change, she and I would become partners of a sort, which was one of the reasons — besides the death of my child — that I was moving.

— You have to go home to your mother today, I said.

— No, Joan, please.

— Forgive her.

She began to convulse, saying *please* over and over again. I didn't know what to do and so I took the red slip off my body. I stood essentially naked before the girl and took her into my arms, pressing her into my body as she wept. Then I pushed her back and handed my beloved dress to her. She was shocked. The only way I knew how to get people to leave was to give them things that meant something to me. I could afford to give up anything tangible. But I was scared to death to give my time or my heart.

She drove her body back into my arms and I stroked her hair and whispered in her ear, Eleanor. Do you hear me? I'd give the world to have my mother back. And she was a real cunt.

35

I found a rental in the Palisades with a terrific view of the ocean. It was white and modern and almost entirely windowed. It was on stilts, hovering high above the houses beneath it. It wasn't my taste but its clean lines and featureless rooms were blank and I craved blankness. It was preposterously expensive, but once again I had no one for whom to care.

For several weeks I barely left the place. I walked through the high-ceilinged rooms and opened one box every few days. I would unpack only half the box, get tired, and take a pill. I was terrifically lonely, but it was a familiar emotion. I missed Alice so much that I ached when I woke in the morning, imagining her doing sun salutations in her foul yard.

One rainy afternoon — God, how I hated that it never rained in Los Angeles — I rented a pickup and drove up to the Canyon to pick up the Ploum. I'd expected to leave it there, for Kevin or River or the new tenant of the hot house, but I had no furniture. And though I could afford to buy some, I felt the piece would work in my new glassy living room. It was garish and I missed it.

River was playing catch with Kurt when I drove up. He shielded his eyes from the sun and smiled.

— Joan, he said.

His smile was so pretty and his demeanor so light that even just being near him made me feel a modicum of peace.

He helped me load the couch into my truck. It was hotter than ever in the house. Without furniture it looked satanic. It felt like everything that had happened in the house was not real. To see it empty like that, I could talk myself into the idea that I hadn't lost a child and killed a man in the house.

River made a big show of carrying the massive Ploum on his back, like Atlas. In the past I might have effusively complimented his strength. But this time I only looked down at my phone, disengaged. When he came back in, I thanked him and he stood there unsurely. I turned and walked to the kitchen window where I'd spent so much time looking to see if the coyotes were prowling.

Quietly and tentatively, River came up from behind and kissed me on the neck, the way Vic had done in Scotland. But when River did it, it felt cleansing. I didn't turn around and he gently raised my arms and pressed my palms to the wall over my head. He threaded his fingers through mine. We made love; it was a tender and peaceful closure. When it was over, he held my body, both of us still standing. He had such strong arms. It was a good way to leave the house.

He wanted to come with me to see my place. I told him maybe next time. He looked a little wounded and I realized that true power came from not caring about anyone. That was the last time I would sleep with a man. I was through with the gender.

All I wanted was to see Alice, to tell her the way my childhood ended, the way our father met his end. I wanted to tell her why I'd walked through the world in corpse pose. I wanted to know if my mother's intuition was correct. If my father was going to leave us for the woman over the oven and her unborn child.

I'd missed her as much as I hated her. I imagined what she would have said if I'd taken her upstairs and showed her the corpse of the old man. I dreamed of her brushing her hand along his cool chest and saying, Honestly, it's all right. It was your only recourse.

Deplorably, immaturely, I would have felt proud to tell her the way it ended. The way the police came and the ambulance, too, pointlessly. After strangling Lenny, I pushed his body down the spiral staircase. He didn't go all the way down but landed in the middle, arms hanging between the slats and legs dangling, like a tangled marionette. That was where I left him. I told the police that I'd been sleeping off a miscarriage upstairs, and he must have come in, as he'd done a time or two in the past during one of his episodes, and I woke to feel his erection against my rear and I screamed and he jumped; he turned to run but tripped, because he was old and out of it, and this is where he landed, I said, indifferently pointing to the spot. The air in the house was thick with the smell of old blood. The men just wanted to get out of there. They didn't question a thing.

I couldn't stop thinking how I'd been so needy with Alice. I was disgusted that I had always been the one talking. I was disgusted that I'd felt complete with her and that she didn't need me.

36

Months passed and I grew less and less human, but in a wondrous way. At least it was wondrous to me.

My stomach was still sloped. I wasn't eating much and yet I had a considerable gut. It seemed I was holding on to the fat, as I'd heard sometimes happened after a miscarriage. Then again, I had become appallingly sedentary. Days went by that I didn't comb my hair.

I would never have to work again, or at least not for many years. It turned out Leonard's watch was worth not only more than his whole life but more than those of his ancestors as well. I took the watch to an appraiser in the Valley. He was so shocked when I laid it on his velvet tray that I thought he might pass out. I could have taken it elsewhere for a second opinion, but I didn't. He might have ripped me off, but at that price point, it really didn't matter.

I thought about moving back to New York, to Charles Street. I could now, impossibly, afford the type of apartment that Big Sky's friend owned. The one I coveted, with the sauna wood and the thick white towels in the linen closet. But I grew to love my place near the ocean. *Love* is not the right word.

Most days I walked along the water, or sat at its edge with my eyes closed, watching films inside my brain. I never wore shoes. I was a cat lady on the sand. Dogs ran past me.

Eleanor and I texted several times a week. I could manage any relationship over text message. She was back home with her mother, who was on many anti-psychotic drugs. Eleanor told me that Mary watched cartoons all day. Reruns of *Three's Company.*

I wish I didn't love her, she wrote one day.

You can't unlove someone, I wrote. *You can only hate them.*

She's too broken to hate.

I'm sorry, I wrote.

I was thinking maybe of coming out there, to say hi. Maybe we could go to Cold Spring . . .

She would write something like that and I would avoid her for days. She always understood. She pulled back, but it was only a matter of time before she would pitch forward again. I lived in fear of a knock on my new door. I hadn't given anyone my new address. I paid for a post office box in town.

Then one day Eleanor told me she had met someone. A girl *with a good family.* For girls like us, a good family was something to die for. At length she sent me a picture of herself and a woman in her late thirties outside the Freedom Tower. The two of them holding hands and looking at each other. I was so happy for her that I cried.

Naturally and daily I thought of killing myself. Not with pills, as I'd always planned, but to drown in the ocean. I felt I was owed that final beauty. But the instinct for survival is tremendous, which is why I felt my mother was stronger than I ever could have imagined.

One typically cloudless day I was in the Dunkin' Donuts on La Cienega and there was a woman at the counter, a very tall Black woman with beautiful sneakers and calves that sprang.

— I want it sweet, sweet, sweet, she said. I thought her voice was magic. She didn't once look at the man she was ordering from. You hear me? And black. Black like me.

Seated at two separate tables were a Mexican woman and an old white man with paint-stained carpenter pants and a t-shirt spotted with sweat.

— Hello, Billy, the Mexican woman said.

— Hey, Rosita, said the old white man. He never looked at her. You married yet?

— No. I don't wantu.

Billy nodded like he knew she was lying. She had huge breasts with a cavern in between. An old dress with embroidered flowers.

— How 'bout you, Rosita said. You married yet.

— Me? Naw.

— So, Rosita said. See. Why you asking me if I'm married if you ain't?

Billy acted like Rosita hadn't said anything. At the counter the Black lady tested her coffee.

— Ain't sweet enough, she bellowed. I said *sweet*!

It was that very moment that something hurtled into my body and tried to saw me apart from the inside. I thought I might finally die. But the pain subsided and I could once again hear Rosita and Billy talking about how the one good thing about Los Angeles was that your mailboxes didn't get crushed by the snowplow and I clocked myself being surprised that either of them had ever lived somewhere other than this Dunkin' Donuts, and because I needed to be punished for that thought, the pain came again. Something was cracking inside of my rear. Something was whipping me. My body was attacking itself. It got worse quickly until I could no longer stand up.

I called her. I hadn't spoken to her since the Santa Monica Pier, but she was all I had left. She had always been the only thing I had left. I'd felt her beside me in bed when she was old enough to be a straight body. I'd felt her little lips against my neck. Her little legs kicking against mine.

I watched her Prius pull into the parking lot of the worst Dunkin' Donuts in Los Angeles. I was hunched over a table. Nobody in there cared if I was dying.

She emerged from her car in a black bodysuit and saw me through the dirty window. It wasn't her fault that my father had come inside another woman. The next contraction was the worst one yet. The pain started in my rear. If the sound of someone hitting a cymbal could be translated into a physical sensation, that's what it felt like. It shot up through my stomach and out through my head. I buckled. And then Alice was inside, holding me, and I was screaming.

— Too much caffeine, Alice called out to the rubbernecking patrons.

She drove very fast while I stared out the window and occasionally convulsed in pain. I was trying not to look at her. I was trying to be perfect. I was about to have a child and yet I was mostly thinking of not scaring Alice away. She brought one hand to my leg and left it there and I was filled with tremendous gratitude.

At the base of the canyon I asked her if she knew we were sisters.

She told me that, at her mother's funeral, one of her mother's casual ex-lovers had insinuated something. Alice had asked around, but nobody really knew for sure. Her mother was very private.

— Have you always known? she asked me.

— For a long time, yes.

When Gosia died, I didn't hear about it for over a week. Even in her death she was uncomplicated. She'd been skiing in Courchevel with someone who wasn't my uncle. She had a stroke coming down a black. She was rushed to the hospital but gave out in the ambulance. She was sixty-three and well kept. Her platinum hair lush, her neck smooth and mostly unwrinkled. There was no funeral because she hadn't wanted one, and there was no one stronger than her left standing so nobody went against her wishes. In the end she knew nobody wanted to make a fuss about anything. When someone was gone, there was nothing left to do. The carrying on was exhausting. The attending to tradition when you could be drinking wine and grieving in the sun.

In addition to several trust documents and her own jewelry collection, Gosia had left me one other item. A slip of paper in a sealed envelope. It was an airmail envelope, but I don't think that meant anything. The slip of paper was crude, cut off of something larger. It was unlike Gosia, because all of her gifts, all of her gestures, were grand. She didn't skimp or try to save money. The information on the slip was meant for a rainy day of sorts and I think it was the only thing in my life that I went after at just the right time. On the outside of the envelope she'd written, *Wait until you need.*

And inside the fold it had Alice's full name. It didn't say *sister,* but of course I knew. As for Alice, she knew she was conceived illegitimately. She knew her father had an affair with her mother. But at first she didn't know there was another child already. Her mother told her that her lover and his wife were childless, that the wife couldn't have children. But, in addition to the ex-lover's insinuation, Alice found some letters that alluded to a child. She said that the first time I went to her yoga class, she felt a strange tug. It was like magic, and it frightened her.

We looked out the windows as we passed the low buildings, the Home Depot I'd gone to several times looking for new flowers for the rusted bathtub. Looking for a thick board to slide underneath the wobbling chairs on my "patio." Always I left with nothing. I had no money to spend. It was just nice to drive, to waste the gas, to smell the pine in the place.

Another contraction. A bright scream of pain. I clutched my stomach and bit my lips. She pressed down on my thigh until the pain subsided.

— Why did you leave me? I asked.

— I was very upset. You fucked someone to hurt me.

— I mean the first time.

— I don't know.

— I was too needy.

— No, she said.

— But what then?

— I don't know. Something. When the girl came and stayed with you, something

461

changed. I felt something I didn't want to know.

And then it clicked for me. Eleanor's presence had kicked up a scent. Alice smelled the past on me. I'd planned on telling her in a way that wouldn't be off-putting. But when Eleanor arrived, Alice could sense it, the way I was just like the girl. I always knew the right way to deliver information. Everybody else did not.

— I think I know the reason, I said.

— What reason is that?

— I came to California to tell you.

— What? she asked.

— I just want to say. I felt so bad when you left. I loved. I love you.

I worried she wouldn't say it back.

— I would have come back. But then you fucked him.

— That was disgusting of me.

— I thought I loved him, she said.

— But he's very stupid.

We laughed. She took my hand and held it tight. She drove with her right hand on my left knee.

— Joan, I love you, too.

We looked at each other; the car almost went off the road. Another contraction split me down the back. We had so much to talk about that we didn't pay much heed to the fact that I was in labor.

— Do you want to know something crazy? I asked after it passed. She nodded and said of course she did and I started with how Vic had cheated with someone before me. And she laughed for a long time. She said, Now do you see how I was right?

Then I told her I killed Lenny. I asked her please not to leave me again, because of that. I told her how I did it, that it was practically an accident. After the shock wore off, she told me it sounded like a true accident and that I should think of it as such. Then she said, It's all right, Joan. Honestly, sometimes I think it's the only recourse. Killing men in times like these.

She said it destroyed her that she'd never met our father and she wanted me to tell her all about him. Her mother had told her some, they would sit and drink PG Tips and look at the cows in the pasture across the road and talk about his swagger, how he saved lives. Her mother told her how once he'd brought her soup when she was sick with a cold, he'd brought her chicken soup from the drugstore reps, he'd specifically requested they bring the best chicken soup in the world and he arrived at her little place above the oven in a white lab coat and she was delirious with a fever and she felt like she was in heaven and he was God. That's how society makes us look at doctors, I said. But there were also the nights our father kept her waiting. The nights he never showed up, because of his wife. It was strange to think about where we'd been those nights. Had we been at Maggie's Pub?

Another contraction tore through my bowels.

— There was one night, she continued, one night in particular my mother told me about. She'd made this soup, this pistou. She spent the whole day. She used the basil she was growing in a little clay pot against the window. And our father never came. He never called. She smashed the pot of basil against the windowsill. Her whole hand was cut up. She told me she went to bed without cleaning it. When she woke up the next morning, she swore she would never be hurt by him again. She swore she would not pass that pain along to her child.

I laid my head against the cool window. Who knew how Alice's mother might have acted had my father done to her what he did to mine. I'd come to learn, in any case, that it wasn't my mother who was weak. It was my father who was weak to his own trivial needs. It was my father who had driven my mother mad. But once again, *mad* is not right. The world had set me up to believe that it was women who went mad. It was simply women's pain that manifested as madness.

Staring straight ahead at the road, wavy with heat, I spoke very quietly.

— Do you want to know how our father died? I asked.

— What do you mean? she said.

— He didn't die of cancer.

— How did he die, then?

— My mother killed him. She stabbed him many times with a regular kitchen knife. And then she slit her wrists in the bathtub. It looked like every movie you've ever seen and yet it was my mother. And our father was on the bed. He was in the pajamas I gave him for Christmas. They were wool and brown with four-leaf clovers. Nobody in my family was Irish.

— Why!

— Because of your mother and you.

She was shaking and asked me to please God tell her that wasn't true and she was carrying on in a way my mother would have found hyperbolic. Another contraction. Alice became more hysterical. I worried about her ability to drive. But I'd been waiting to get to this point for many months. I'd been waiting to tell her. She was the only person who could make me feel less alone. Along the way I worried it was possible he loved her mother more than he loved mine. But that was not the right thing to wonder. The right thing was, Did my father love me as much as I thought he did?

That was why my mother killed him. Not because he cheated, not because he fathered a child with his mistress, not even because she believed he wanted his second family more. Men love a second chance, Gosia told me. They don't deserve it, not at a woman's expense.

The reason my mother killed my father was because he didn't love her — or me — as much as he claimed to. I remember that time we visited Los Angeles and my father bought me that dress with the Peter Pan collar. I saw it in the store and loved it and my mother said I couldn't have it and then later that night at dinner he passed a shopping bag across the table. The bottom of the bag dipped into the juices of my mother's pollo alla Valdostana. The coveted dress was inside. I cried with love. When he got up to use the bathroom — perhaps to call his lover — my mother said to me, You love your father better, and that is all right. I thought she was being petty, but suddenly I could call up the pain in her eyes. The unfairness that I thought he was the better of the two of them.

My father did not love one family more than the other. It was that he didn't care about either more than he cared about himself. And just like that, I understood why my mother did it.

And here was Alice, my younger sister, who of course knew nothing. I'd imbued her with a sorcerer's wisdom and she was only a child. All she knew was happiness, the gift of a mother's love that had never spoiled. I wanted to give you that. I wanted to be good. I knew at the very least that I would be better.

— Did she plan it?

— No, I said. I don't think so. I also don't think she planned on killing herself. She probably just hated herself as much as someone could hate herself.

Alice was crying so much that she had to pull over. I knew it wasn't good for the labor. But I couldn't stop her. She fell against me and I held her. She cried and clutched me. I said, Shh, shh, and I told her it was all right. Now we had each other. I told her I had always felt her beside me, that it was one of the things that had sustained me. That, starting the week after my parents' deaths, I felt her in my bed snuggling against me. Tugging on my leg as I got up to use the bathroom, smiling while she listened to me pee, trailing me into closets as I dressed. Following me up the stairs and down the stairs. Later, borrowing my jeans, all my old slutty dresses. Reading beside me. Asking me to help her with makeup. Asking about boys. Gosia making *barszcz* with *uszkami,* these terrible dumplings in beet broth, and us pretending to eat them but instead snapping them into the dog's mouth. Our beet-stained hands. Then the two of us under the covers in my bed with a little pink flashlight, talking about our father. And we'd both look up at the canopy of our bedsheets like it was the galaxy and I would tell her fairy tales. The ruby slippers he stayed up all night making. I told her he would have loved her so much. More than *you?* she would ask, because she was only a little girl. Yes, I would say, more than me. I am absolutely sure of it.

intake sheet as my emergency contact. In the car, on the way to the hospital, she'd asked me who the father was this time. I told her the truth. I thought she might turn from me, once more and forever. But she didn't. Look at you, she said. You thought you were barren, but you could barely last a month before you got knocked up again. Slut.

37

I want to tell you about Big Sky's wife, who, one Thanksgiving, right before all their guests arrived, dropped the carving knife on her foot and it went right through the nail of her big toe. Theatrical blood, blooming across the slate. I tried to think of what my mother would have said. She would have said slate was impossible to clean, that it would always be filthy. Big Sky told me the story, how he asked his wife if she thought she definitely needed to go to the hospital. He'd just had his first martini, the nice one before everyone gets there, and this was Montana, where you don't want to leave your house unless it's to go to the river or the mountain. I remember thinking, You are not a good man, thank God. But I only thought it then. It went away when he made love to me and I didn't think of the story again until years later.

In the hospital Alice wrote herself into the

intake sheet as my emergency contact. In the car on the way to the hospital she'd asked me who the father was *this time.* I told her the truth. I thought she might turn from me, once more and forever. But she didn't. Look at you, she said. You thought you were barren, but you could barely last a month before you got knocked up again. Slut.

While we waited, I asked Alice to show me a picture of her mother. She pulled one from her wallet. Her mother — Francesca — had thick caramel hair like Alice's. She was leaning against a stone rail, off the side of a Tuscan motorway, in a green wool sweater and a corduroy skirt. She was not more beautiful than my mother. They were both beautiful.

In triage my stomach felt like it was going to come out of me. Like I was going to give birth to all my organs instead of a child. A male nurse took my blood pressure and it became clear that the awful pain was not just part and parcel of back labor. I knew you were too young, but I never expected it to go badly, not again.

The nurse walked away to get a doctor, but no one came for minutes.

Alice screamed, My sister is sick!

When they finally got me into a room, the

blood was gushing and the contractions were otherworldly. A mustached doctor came in, seemingly unmoved. He talked to me like I was poor. He wore a wedding ring and a college ring. He asked me who the father was. Why does it matter, I asked. He nodded and told me my child was very young, too young, but that was that. It might be okay, he said. But it might not. The contractions came for many hours, but you wouldn't come down and I was too ill to wait. Still, they didn't want to cut you out of me. They said the longer in there, the better. Like you were a piece of under-cooked bread and the heat inside of me, even just a contact warmth, was better than your coming out, exposed to the newsprint colors in the air here.

I have shown you the wreckage of my relationships. I know you won't make the same mistakes. I can feel how strong you are inside of me. I want you to know you were born of a tender union, a short but kind one. It was meaningful in the bedroom if nowhere else. And it was the first time I used a man for something I actually wanted and not for something I thought I needed.

I heard one of the nurses say, It's taking too long, we might lose her. I didn't know if they were talking about me or you. They acted like it was the end of the world, your being so young, but I'd already seen the end of the world and knew better than they did. I knew you would live.

One nurse, a peaceful woman, cleaned my face with alcohol and smiled at me like she loved me. She pressed a cold cloth over my forehead when the contractions came. Hold on, baby, she said. Hold on a little bit longer for me, baby. She had small elfin ears and a pageboy haircut.

When you were ready, you were so small that I barely had to push. I didn't catch you in my hands; the peaceful nurse did, while I was off somewhere in my head. I was thinking about Alice, how she would make a good mother. That she would play the right games with you. Hold your head under the bath spigot so that water didn't get into your eyes. I wasn't delicate like she was. My mother was not delicate, either, only warm-bodied and withholding.

—Your daughter, your daughter, they kept saying. Look at your daughter.

It was a boy, the other one, I won't call him your brother because I don't think he was. I like to think it was you — I have to think of it that way because the alternative

472

is hell — that it was a part of you that you didn't need to bring. And that part of you, like a vestigial organ, was made to disappear. That's what my father once said of a medical bill. That's how he met Alice's mother, by the way. Alice's mother brought in a Mexican friend of hers who worked in the kitchen. The friend had a growth she needed removed from her neck. They had to work quickly and the surgery cost in the tens of thousands. She was an illegal immigrant. I remember my father coming home that night. I was eight years old. He came through the garage and I clapped for him and over a dinner of pizzaiola he told us about how two unfortunate women came in, two cooks in a kitchen, and one of them had a growth and they saved her in the nick of time and he made the bill disappear. And the other one was so grateful, she cried and cried and said, Bless you! They were each other's only friends in the world, my father said. Or America, in any case. My father is such a good man, I thought.

Gosia never told me anything bad about my father. Nor did she really say good things about my mother. And she rarely said anything about herself. I don't think anybody could have done a finer job than she did, given the circumstances. I was ten years old and she was an Austrian pessimist, childless by design. She had lovers in stone cities and her husband — my uncle — was inconsequential. She tried to lead by example. But she also left me alone with what to make of my life. She held me when I screamed, but she didn't tell me how to feel. So that a callus could form over my past. It took meeting Alice to understand the precise ways in which I'd been affected. How the night of the killings informed all that I did with men and all that I didn't do with women. My mother couldn't *keep* my father. Can you imagine that that had once been an actual thought in my head?

Look at your daughter.

There was a long period after they died when I could call them up; I could feel like they were holding me in bed. I was able to do this most easily with sleeping pills. When I went to the drugstore with Gosia, she would let me select some off the rack, valerian and passionflower. Vials with beautiful moonlight blooms. Like a scientist, I would make little concoctions out of them, mixing three or more tinctures in one. I used them at night, but sometimes I would drink them very early in the morning to go back to sleep. When I was fifteen and still waking up screaming in the night, Gosia gave me

Ambien.

The Ambien helped, but then the early evenings became worse. You would think the middle of the night would always be the worst, the witching hours, the hours I'd found them dead, but strangely these became the most peaceful hours for me. In any case, the better the sleep, the worse the morning. If I slept soundly, in the morning came the job of reminding myself: Your parents are dead. Here is how they died. You are all alone.

— She's very sick, they kept saying. As though I had the flu. I didn't feel sick. I felt light. I was hemorrhaging. They ran bags of blood into the room.

Don't ask men how their day was. If they are tired and look unhappy, say, Oh, too bad, at the very most.

I will have these few minutes with you, they said to me, before they have to take me into the white room.

Look at your daughter.

The past was everything to me. For that reason, though not that one alone, I don't want you to have one. Just these words, a small guide. Here is what will happen. I will watch you play soccer on an emerald field at a boarding school that is more splendid

than the one where Big Sky will send his
children. You will be running down that field
and everyone — other parents, younger sib-
lings, the opposing team's coach — will be
transfixed by you, by your long tan legs, by
the winner's gleam in your eye, by your
speed and hair and clavicle. You will be
faster than the rest. Having come from nowhere, you will be more surely heading
somewhere. You will always sleep on freshly
laundered beds. You will eat wedges of
lemon cake on English country estates and
drink iced tea with woolly leaves of mint.
You will vacation in the best places, not just
the good names but places even the very
wealthy barely know about. You will have
enough money for most of your lifetime.
You won't outrun it, as I did.

My mother left me all her jewelry. She left
it for me in her boxes of hair color, which
she hid all over the house. Clairol and Wella
and some old stained boxes of Féria from
Harmon Cosmetics. There were thick gold
chains with crucifixes and emerald rings,
ruby and platinum bracelets, and the famous thirty-two-diamond ring, which we
used to count together, all the diamonds.
Later I learned they were just chips. And
not very clear. There were also, I remembered, the little rosebud earrings that Alice

had, too. I think that was the part that made me feel for my mother the most. That my father bought her and his mistress the same little rosebud earrings. Perhaps they had been on sale. Two for the price of one.

The whole bounty wasn't worth too much, but she used to tell me that she'd come back from the grave and bite my feet if I sold it. I didn't sell it. You may, if you wish. I don't care if you keep it or not, if you wear it around or never do.

My mother was too much for me and she didn't even live past my tenth year. I couldn't stop thinking about all of her *things*. All the books she read at the town pool, wimpled from the wetness of my dripping hands when I went to hug her. Romance novels with tiny print crowding the pages. The times we went to Amazing Savings. Cartons of cheap things in dusty plastic packaging. Tulips, God, how my mother loved her tulips, and her copper pots. I polished them for months after she died, until the house was sold. Gosia would have let me keep them, anything I wanted, but in the end what I wanted was all of it gone.

Look at her. Your daughter.

They wiped you off and brought you to my breast. You felt vaguely amphibian. I didn't want to look at you yet. I wanted to

477

savor the feeling. I wanted to delay the gratification because I knew I would keep living until I got it.

They would need to take you away, put you in an incubator and heat you. They were going to take me away, too. We were going in opposite directions. I want to tell you how bad that was for me. But I can't describe it.

They said, Five minutes, take this time. You should have this time.

Finally I looked at you. And I gasped because I saw that you were her. You were the girl in all of my dreams. You were on the Grecian seaside looking out of portholes, you were in the fast-food parking lot waiting for me to come back. You were two and three and four and five. You were ten. You had been there since the beginning. And since the beginning someone has been trying to take you away.

I told the nurse closest to me that I wanted everybody out of the room. I didn't want Alice to come in, though at that point they would have let her. I'd been waiting for a long time to meet the daughter of my father's mistress. And I didn't hate her. I loved her. But this hard life of mine was not meant to lead me to Alice. I didn't come here for her. I came for you.

I waited until they were all gone and then I took your body in my hands and held you to my chest. I wanted to put you back inside of me. I ran my finger down the perfect slope of your nose and cried out the way I had after that first date with Big Sky. That primal, unlivable ecstasy. But this time the love was real.

I could already see you wouldn't need much from anyone. Your mouth rooted around for seconds before your lips sealed around my nipple. Then your eyes slipped open and you looked at me. Your eyes! You have the teal eyes of a mermaid. Your face is indisputably stunning. Nobody will be able to look away from you. The way that I could not look away from you. Now that I'd seen you, I couldn't bear never having you in front of me.

No matter what, at some point I will not be there. I see you in the parking lot of a fast-food restaurant. You are getting out of the Dodge Stratus and cupping your hands over your eyes. You're looking for me. I know I am here and you are there but still I strain my eyes trying to see inside the store, thinking there is no way I left you in the car. I wouldn't do that. If I were there.

Please go into the store, I think. Go into

the store and ask for me. Tell them I'm your mother. Tell them you can't go to anyone else, even if I'm dead. You can eat some food if they give it to you, but you can't go home with any of them. I go inside your ear and whisper, Not even Alice.

I have told you many things, but I have this other memory, it is the best one I have. I was five or six and sleeping in my parents' bed, on the sheets with the print of the big fat cat. My mother didn't like cats so I don't know why she bought the sheets, probably they were on sale at Marshalls. I was sleeping in a butter-yellow dress with lace trim and I was very tan; we had just come back from Italy where I was outside in the sun all day with the boys and the farmers and the little goats and I suppose the most important part of this story is that I don't have an actual memory of it; all I have is a picture. My mother took the photograph, with her cheap but reliable Minolta. Probably it is the early morning and she thought I looked beautiful. I did, with my dark hair about my face and my pink lips lightly parted and my smooth cheeks. Besides the jewelry and some of her finer dresses, the shower caps and soaps from hotels, and all of the good handbags he bought her, that was the only other item I kept from her things. That *she* kept it, that she took the photograph at all, was the thing that sustained me for so long. The past, you see, was all I had.

As much as I see myself gone, I can just as clearly see us in that fast-food parking lot. It's close enough that I can feel the sunshine on the macadam and inhale the orange smell of the food inside. I look over and there you are. Staring at me, in this way. I can't believe you're really there. You're more real than I dreamed you. And you're looking at me like I'm your mother.

We will enter the drive-through and you'll whisper your order to me. I'll add two chocolate shakes and a box of fries to share. Then we'll park. You'll have my mother's golden waves and my father's astonishing blue eyes. We will drop shredded lettuce into the seams of our seats and laugh and you will tell me to chew with my mouth closed because suddenly I've reverted to one of my mother's peasant habits. We will have money to live well and yet we will eat dirty things in dirty cars. We will never lie to each other. You will always look at me like this.

ABOUT THE AUTHOR

Lisa Taddeo is the author of the instant #1 *New York Times* bestseller *Three Women.* She has contributed to *New York, Esquire, Elle, Glamour,* and many other publications. Her nonfiction has been included in the *Best American Sports Writing* and *Best American Political Writing* anthologies, and her short stories have won two Pushcart Prizes. Lisa lives with her husband and daughter in New England.